The Wrong World

The Wrong World
Selected Stories and Essays

BERTRAM BROOKER

Edited by Gregory Betts

University of Ottawa Press | OTTAWA

LIBRARY AND ARCHIVES CANADA
CATALOGUING IN PUBLICATION

Brooker, Bertram, 1888–1955.
    The wrong world : selected stories
and essays / Bertram Brooker ; edited by
Gregory Betts.

(Canadian literature collection)
Includes bibliographical references.
ISBN 978-0-7766-0696-5

    I. Betts, Gregory Brian, 1975– II. Title.
III. Series: Canadian
literature collection

PS8503.R63W76 2009   C813'.52
C2009-904736-5

The University of Ottawa Press
acknowledges with gratitude the support
extended to its publishing list by Heritage
Canada through its Book Publishing
Industry Development Program, by
the Canada Council for the Arts, by the
Canadian Federation for the Humanities
and Social Sciences through its Aid to
Scholarly Publications Program, by the
Social Sciences and Humanities Research
Council, and by the University of Ottawa.

uOttawa

Contents

This is no idle book. I ask no idlers to trifle with it. It is a stern and terrible book, for behind every word lurks a spectre; and at the end of it, you shall meet God face to face, and no man can face God unafraid.

from "To All the Nations ....!"

We do not write for posterity in the same sense as the older poets—so called finished works of art—not concerned with ending anything—only starting—not personal glory or a great name— names are nothing—but to contribute to the new movement.

from "Free Prose"

Acknowledgements

It was while working as a Research Assistant for Prof. Ray Ellenwood that I first encountered the art of Bertram Brooker. Ray immediately recognized the potential significance of Brooker's underacknowledged contributions to Canadian art (including its letters) and helped direct me toward future projects. I am very grateful for his guidance, insight, and good humour as I navigated Brooker's and my own enthusiasms. This project emerges as a follow-up to my dissertation on Brooker's mysticial writings (that did not address his short fiction) supervised by John Lennox and Steve McCaffery. They both proved invaluable in helping to contextualize Brooker's work within the broader fields of Canadian literature and international avant-gardism, respectively. I am grateful for their support, guidance, and insights. Other scholars that have had significant direct impact on this book through discussions, debates, encouragement, and more, include Dean Irvine, Colin Hill, Christian Bök, John Robert Columbo, Robert Stacey, David Staines, Misao Dean, Sherrill Grace, Glenn Willmott, Brian Trehearne, Scott Duschesne, Neta Gordon, Beatriz Hausner, Nicky Drumbolis, and Elspeth Cameron. I am particularly grateful to John Brooker of the Bertram Brooker estate for generously allowing me access to the family's private collection of documents, for enthusiastically supporting my work on Brooker, and for the conversations and friendship shared over the course of this endeavour. I doubt I will need to convince anybody that I am very grateful for the funding that I have received in direct support of this archival project, including support from the Ontario Graduate Scholarships, the Social Sciences and Humanities Research Council, York University, the University of Manitoba, Brock University, and the Humanities Research Institute at Brock

University. I would like to thank everybody at the University of Ottawa Press for supporting this project and for all the hard work done on its behalf — especially, Marie Clausén, Jessica Clark, and Eric Nelson. Family and friends have kept me grounded and motivated throughout, and been very generous with interest and ideas: especially Diane Betts (who even became a bit of a Brooker advocate in the process!), Peter Wilson, Nathalie Foy, Jan Frith, Chris Trevelyan, and Joe Wilson. None of any of all this would be possible or worthwhile but for Lisa, who gives it all value and helps keep it all in perspective — thank you.

Introduction

I have not sought to chart the boundless. I have been seeking the secret of the bound....

I have failed. The closest I have come to Nature is to approximate to her fecundity. I have spawned millions of words—yes, millions. Few writers, I imagine, have left behind such piles of unpublished manuscript.

from "The World and I: A Voyage of Self-Exploration"

From the turn of the twentieth century to the post–Second World War period, Bertram Brooker's prose documented the dramatic transformation of Canadian society from a primarily agrarian and colonial culture to a modern and industrial post-colonial nation. Brooker sought to use his art and writing to encourage the transformation. Indeed, his vision of the great potential of Canada was dependent on the opening up of its prudish society, including, but not limited to, conservative attitudes that discouraged experimental artists and the arts. Brooker's prose captures his enthusiastic and idealistic response to the rapid and broad social change of the period: "Those of us who are forty or more have passed out of an old civilisation into a new one in half a lifetime—and *that has never happened before!*" ("When We Awake!"). A distinct utopianism exists just below the surface of most of his writing, occasionally bursting forth in prophetic and millennial tones. While his prose fiction tends to demonstrate the need for change on the scale of the individual, his prose non-fiction aims to guide that change to its highest, most spiritual potential. Taken together, Brooker's prose presents one of the richest bodies of writing on the experience, the anxieties, and the hopes of Canadian modernization. If Canada was awakening to its great and future role in the world, Brooker's imagination worked to detail the nature of what we could, and might, become.

Brooker's enthusiasm for social change led to a remarkable willingness to test and try new methods and media. Although from humble beginnings, the diligence of his aesthetic investigations transformed him into Canada's stalwart experimental artist during the interwar period. The recent interest in and scholarly activity surrounding Brooker now convincingly documents his participation in an astonishing array of iconic Canadian cultural phenomena. While it is common knowledge that Brooker was the first to exhibit abstract art in the country (January 1927), and that he was also the winner of the first Governor General's Literary Award (1936), new insights into his multidisciplinary contributions continue to add complexity and nuance to the kind of artist he was, and the place he occupies in the history of art in Canada. Recent work by Anton Wagner and Sherrill Grace documents his role in the formation of the Little Theatre Movement in Canada and pays specific attention to the expression of mysticism in his numerous plays—many of which were successfully staged (Wagner 1989 and 1984; Grace 1985 and 1989). Glenn Willmott produced and introduced a new edition of Brooker's award-winning novel *Think of the Earth* (2000), as well as a complementary study that reads the novel through its interrogation of global industrial capitalism (2002: 66–101). Birk Sproxton edited *Sounds Assembling: The Poetry of Bertram Brooker* (1980), a volume of Brooker's poetry that highlights his engagement with modernist methods, and Dennis Reid produced a catalogue of Brooker's visual art, *Bertram Brooker 1888–1955* (1973), with an astounding introduction that locates Brooker within a community of like-minded artists, notably Lawren Harris and L. L. FitzGerald. Ann Davis explores the mystical aesthetics of Brooker's more than 400 canvases in *The Logic of the Ecstasy: Canadian Mystical Painting, 1920–1940* (1992), while Adam Lauder's master's thesis (2006) has begun to trace the philosophical implications of Brooker's advertising theories as mapped out in his more than 200 articles published on the subject. Elsewhere, I have written about Brooker's radical and experimental poetry, as well as his impact as an editor of two important volumes of Canadian art criticism. Despite this groundbreaking activity, there remain many areas generally left untouched—he was also one of our first filmmakers; one of his abstract sculptures is on permanent display in the National Gallery in Ottawa; he was invited to exhibit art alongside the Group of Seven on more than one occasion; he covered the Winnipeg General Strike as a journalist; he wrote a nationally syndicated general arts column for three years; he produced two unpublished philosophical volumes; and he was an early advocate for national arts subsidies. Outside of the arts, Brooker was also involved in constructing the Grand Trunk Pacific railway and, through his advertising firm, was a designer of the iconic Victory Bonds images. He was potentially even affiliated with the creation of Hockey Night in Canada. His life spanned the period of Canadian industrialization and his art and writing serve as testimony to the optimism the rapid change engendered. As a result of the recent wave of attention that started in 1972 when Dennis Reid began to organize a national tour of Brooker's paintings, a portrait of Brooker as possibly the first English-Canadian avant-gardist, a proto-Futurist with mystical overtures, is emerging. With this collection of Brooker's prose stories and essays, most of which have never been published before, I hope to foster the growing attention to Brooker's writing and to expand the conception of modernist and indeed avant-garde activity in Canada prior to the Second World War.

★ ★ ★

Social transformation, even the most abstract and mystical, occurs most significantly at the level of individual experience; new individual experiences are, in turn, distilled into new art, both of which emerge in response to new culture. Brooker, anticipating the work of Marshall McLuhan by decades, believed that the best of contemporary art always struggled to respond to its environmental and technological context. As he writes in his 1929 essay "When We Awake!", technological advances such as the aeroplane, the automobile and the radio played an increasingly substantial role in shaping and altering individual experience in the modern world—to such a point that modern individuals had become a completely different type of human from their immediate ancestors: "We are, in the strictest sense *primitives*, the first men of a new civilisation whose implications are incalculable." As a result of the explosion of new technologies at the dawn of the twentieth century, modern art was due for a parallel explosion of new techniques: "Books like those of Henry James, George Meredith and Joseph Conrad simply cannot be written by a man who has just breakfasted with an electric toaster at his elbow and whose morning meditation in the garden has been disturbed by ukulele-music trickling out of the sky." Brooker's awareness of the deeply personal impact of technological changes led him to use incidents and settings from his own life and experience as a means to explore the shift he felt happening in the broader culture. Responding to his own demand that artists shift modes of art production with the times, he attempted numerous experimental autobiographies that blend innovative techniques with a modernist attention to epiphanic moments of personal transformation.

The chronological and geographical settings of the stories in this volume correspond to Brooker's emigration from England to Manitoba in 1905 and from Manitoba to Toronto in 1921. In 1910, he returned to England to visit his old home[1]—an experience that emerges in distorted and fictionalized form in *The Wrong World*. The trip to England was transformative in many ways for Brooker. Not only did he first encounter modern theatre on the trip ("Years": 4), he returned from Europe with a passionate drive to engage with, and indeed, enter the contest of modernist cultures. It was after his trip that Brooker began writing 'photoplays' for the cinema (what we now call screenplays), theatre plays, manifestoes, essays, and novels. His manifesto suite "The Spread of Negativism", published here for the first time, was written in Manitoba before the First World War, and responds to the politics and popular aesthetics he found in England. Brooker's prolific turn was no doubt also inspired by the reminder of his family's proximity to poverty. He justified his embrace of commercialism as the best and most immediate means to reverse the debilitating impact of economic hardship.

Though class issues and class-consciousness recur throughout his writing, Brooker's interest was more personal than theoretical, academic or political. He was born into poverty in the slums of Croydon, England, where his father worked as a railway ticket collector at the East Chatford Station (*A Candle in Sunshine:* 5). Brooker left school when he was just twelve years old to work first as a servant and then at the Fuller's Dairy in nearby Upper Ashbridge (167, 262). Despite this mitigating circumstance, he was already a precocious artist and would often scrimp on meals to purchase books and plays. He was already painting at the time—religious scenes, and his first writings, from age eleven, were modelled after *Robinson Crusoe* (178). Growing up in the same borough as Sir Arthur Conan Doyle, whose Sherlock Holmes series had already won Doyle international celebrity, many of Brooker's early works bore the influence of the great author's most famous character. Brooker moved to Canada with his family in 1905 on a doctor's order due to his asthmatic younger brother's health ("Diary" 1905). Once there, the dry, cold air revived his brother, but did little to offset the hard life that greeted the family. The problem was not in finding employment. Brooker, his father and his grandfather all quickly found work on the construction of the Grand Trunk Pacific railway ("Years": 1), then passing through Manitoba en route to the coast, but each of them in turn suffered serious injury and illness from the job in the years that followed (Victor Brooker, 1973). Recognizing the trap of a hard lifestyle, Brooker spent his evenings after each day of gruelling physical labour educating himself through books and music.

By 1910 he had advanced himself well enough to begin selling stories of his own to local newspapers around Manitoba ("Years": 19). By 1912, after returning from his trip to England, he and his brother raised enough money to leave Portage la Prairie, and more importantly, to leave physical labour. They bought and converted an old building into a movie theatre in the small village of Neepawa. The Neepawa Opera House, later renamed The Roxy, as it appears in Margaret Laurence's fictional town of Manawaka,[2] was the town's first moving-picture theatre and one of the first such dedicated-use buildings in the country. Brooker's ambition was fired by the move, and his hunger for ascension accelerated. Already, in that first year off the tracks, he wrote a formal letter of complaint to the Vitagraph Company in New York, highlighting the low quality of the films they were sending him. They invited him, then and therefore, to make his own.

Before the year was out, he sent the company over a dozen scripts for a 'thriller' series focussed on Detective Lambert Chace, a thinly veiled adaptation of Sherlock Holmes (Brooker, "Censorship"). Despite the fact that cinematic historians have thus far overlooked him, Brooker was, in fact, one of Canada's pioneers in film—or, to use his vocabulary, one of our first 'photoplaywrights'. By his own estimation ("To All the Nations ....!"), he was quite successful at the enterprise. All of his scenarios were filmed and screened around North America. Although his 'photoplays' enjoyed a short vogue, he quickly lost his taste for the moving pictures:

> In short, up to a few days ago, I considered myself fairly well established as a successful and swiftly rising photoplaywright. The work fascinated me. All my dreams of literary artistry were forgotten. Style became a thing of the past with me, and my mind was transformed into a seething whirlpool of ghastly plots. (Brooker 1913: 1–2)

After Brooker married Mary Aurilla Porter in 1913, the family moved to Winnipeg, where Bertram worked as a journalist, an advertiser and a playwright. The boost to his reputation from his work in film helped propel his career in journalism in Winnipeg, which was, at the time, the centre of the Dominion for the profession. At the *Manitoba Free Press*, Brooker worked under the mentorship of E. H. Macklin, the best editor in the business, and was surrounded by figures such as F. R. Livesay, soon to be the founder of the Canadian Press, and Martha Ostenso, the acclaimed novelist. In such environs, Brooker developed into a classic white-collar Canadian without having to compromise his "dreams of literary artistry". Journalist and literary editor Thomas Roberton, whom Brooker held in the highest esteem, also worked at the *Free Press*. The two were eventually re-connected in the public eye in 1937 when both received the country's first Governor General's Awards: Brooker for fiction and Roberton for non-fiction. Brooker served in Manitoba during the war (prompting his anti-war polemic "The Price of

Peace"), and as both a journalist and special constable for the local police in Winnipeg's General Strike of 1919. These experiences, particularly the violence of the general strike, soured him to politics and news journalism, in favour of art and business.

A significant portion of Brooker's fiction, though written much later in his life and in a different province, returns to pre-war Manitoba. These stories, including in this collection "The Gilliland House", "A Bad Order", "The Headwaitress", "A Glass of Catawba", and The Wrong World (all but one of which were written in Toronto), document the dramatic social transformations by way of his focus on individual experiences of broader changes in remote communities in the Canadian prairies.

For instance, "The Gilliland House" adeptly makes use of its small-town Manitoban setting to stage a social satire that ridicules suddenly out-of-date aristocratic pretensions. With a name that echoes both Gulliver and Lilliput,[3] the Gilliland house symbolizes the pinnacle of wealth in the hoi polloi community. It sits at the highest point with the best view of Manitoba's Riding Mountain—"[t]here was certainly no view to compare with it in Manitoba." Making paronomasial use of the town's name, Zenith, the highest house in the highest town offers the view of the highest peak in the province and, accordingly, represents the highest status property in the town. The Ontario poet Wilbur Malone, however, seems the only character able to recognize the linguistic instability upon which the hierarchy is built: for it is the "sheerest hyperbole" to describe the view and terrain as mountainous. Similarly, the importance of climbing Zenith's social hierarchy is also greatly exaggerated by Dora McCormick, though she is staunchly unaware of the ridiculousness of her pursued ascent. The house, too, although the best on hand, is notably "only brick-veneered."

The satire finds its focus in Dora's empty appeal to aristocratic values, by which she justifies her scurrilous attempt to finesse a grieving widow of financial compensation, despite the fact that her own wealth and status pretensions are derived entirely through her simple husband Harry's humble petit-bourgeois ethics. As the undesirable Mrs. Banner tells her, "When it comes to lumber [Harry's] the whitest man in the business." The economic structure foretells the tale's final irony: for her elitist ambitions, and unsympathetic indifference to human suffering, the McCormicks lose the palatial residence to working-class "men from the sash-and-door factory and the railroads—men in overalls—men!" Though her downfall is foreshadowed from the outset, with rather overt references to the safety of the balcony upon which the "unforeseen" central tragedy takes place, Brooker establishes a remarkable tension between her descent into ever-increasing monstrosity and her husband's gradual awakening to her (and their) degeneracy. In the end, the widow Speers is not shaken by Dora's indignation, so that the resilient widow who successfully transforms her own victimization into ascension bests both husband and wife. The moral order being thus restored marks the reversal of the economic order. Brooker's pre-modern prairie town rewards integrity and ingenuity over manipulation and pretension.

The next story in this collection, "Bad Order", presents a first-person account from the point-of-view of precisely the kind of worker that moves into the Gilliland House—the rowdy and spirited railway men of Manitoba. The narrator presents his puzzling experiences with Robinson Cuthbert Hicks, an Englishman outsider who joins the North American crew without becoming one of them. Although framed as a mystery, the narrative is more of a straightforward working-class anecdote rendered in colloquial tone. Anticipating Geoff Tavistock, the English protagonist of *Think of the Earth* who also worked as a time-keeper (as did Brooker, "Years": 1), the text presents an ultimately heroic figure negotiating the pitfalls of being a cultural Other in a working class setting. In this story, the Canadian narrator attempts to understand Hicks's unusual non-Canadian behaviour: "Now, who could make a hero of a man like that?" The difference is explained in explicitly cultural terms: his accent offends the other men who spit and curse him; and the character, a modern Crusoe, is said to overtly mirror his native country. Hicks is "an island of his own—silent, isolated, apart from us all." More than class issues, the text highlights the cultural gap between Canada, particularly the Prairie Provinces, and England: "We are not the same, over here."

In "A Glass of Catawba", the third of five explicitly Manitoban texts included in this collection, Brooker oscillates playfully between narrative points-of-view, jumping fluidly between first, second, and third person perspectives, to embody protagonist R. G. Murray's metamorphosis. The experimental mode of narration is well chosen for this subtle story because the plot tension exists entirely in the nervous newspaperman's anxious imagination. As in the other tales, class-consciousness infiltrates the narrative but again through Brooker's unique perspective: poverty is motivating, not debilitating. Murray confronts his miserable existence as the failed heir of an aristocratic line, now relegated to the colonies for having lost the family fortune: "What a difference! Pillars, parlours, horses, maids, gardeners, grounds—all that. And here—hmmmmm—a basement suite." By the time of the story, however, Canada is a *former* colony, and no longer merely extends the cultural and social order of England. As such, the burden of his family's past is not inextricably placed on his sunken shoulders. The "idea" that comes to him in the first line of the text is to embrace the different spirit of the New World, and, thereby, to "wipe out England and his memories." His psychological transformation from exiled Englishman to expectant Canadian is appropriately signified through the different spirits of the place and how they are sold.

He decides to buy a bottle of "native wine" and is recommended port. The story's title comes from the native Ontario grape used for the port he decides to purchase, and presents a significant commercial symbol of the cultural space between here and there. Brooker, in fact, adroitly links the British method of purchasing and valuing port based on vintage years to their colonial enterprise through a childhood memory of his father praising a bottle that "S'been all the way to India and back." In contrast, Canadian liquor is "prescribed" by a doctor, and ranked and priced according to its brand name. As Brooker was well aware from his work in advertising, brand consciousness adds an intangible value even to the glasses in which the port will be served: "Of course, you pay for the name on the wrapping. But it would be fine to get them at Ivey's. There's something about buying a thing there." Brooker uses Murray's acceptance of the commercial allocation of value within Canada to signify his entrance into the culture and his attempt to improve his station within it. The drinks are intended to charm his young colleague Bernard, a "damned clever" and "loyal" Manitoban, drenched in the Canadian spirit, who had "gone ahead" and raised himself to the prominent role of music critic. Bernard's elevation inspires Murray to try again in life, and thereby quite directly provokes the post-colonial turn in his attitude.

The biographical inflections of the juxtaposition are significant. Like Bernard, Brooker himself occasioned as music critic for the *Winnipeg Free Press*. Indeed, the web of allusions in Murray's informed conversations with Bernard attests to Brooker's rich musical background. Moreover, Brooker titled an early experimental autobiography "Diary of Bernard Bradley" and used the pseudonym for various abandoned writing projects.[4] The internal psychological battle of an immigrant Briton becoming Canadian thus stages diverse moments of Brooker's own process of integration—the before and after moments of his settlement—with the loyalty of a Bernard embodying the latter. Brooker was also loyal—later, even after a decade in Toronto, he staunchly referred to himself as a "Winnipegger" (Brooker 1930). An important caveat: this is not to say that the story is autobiographical—the differences are more than profound, as Brooker's family never had a fortune to lose—but inserting his sobriquet into such a tale with obvious biographical inflections adds significance to the protagonist's discovery and embrace of Canadian social and cultural difference through the economic and commercial sphere. At the very least, it exemplifies Brooker's theory of how commercialism contributes to social and, in this case, cultural, change. The lure of brand participation, produced by the power of advertising, pulls Murray out of his cocoon and out of the trap of nostalgia.

In contrast to "A Glass of Catawba", his story "Head Waitress" makes the protagonist's renunciation of her cultural inheritance the result of a more complicated and mitigating swirl of gender, cultural, and economic issues. The story follows Katrin Petursson's life from her Icelandic-Canadian childhood in Manitoba through to her maturity in Toronto. As in "Youth's

Manuscript", the story openly details her reasons and resistance to sexual objectification. More poignantly, she resists Kari Erlingsson's attempts to exoticize and mythologize her beauty as though she were an Icelandic legend who would "inspire a new generation of skalds"—that is, inspire a new generation of Scandinavian poets. She is a second-generation immigrant, an orphan in fact, less between cultures than committed to her new home. As such, she resists Kari's insistence on her connections to her parents' former homeland. She commands him to "stop sneering at everything Canadian—and get a job." After fleeing her lecherous uncle in Lake Rosseau, Katrin becomes a waitress in Toronto—where our first-person narrator first notices her (not to mention noticing her "body that was simply magnificent"). The narrator is less interested in her sexually than in her sexuality—in how and why she maintains her "icy-face" despite attracting a team of middle-aged men "who always came to her tables and enjoyed her shape more than their food." Formally reminiscent of an Icelandic family saga, particularly with its abrupt conclusion, Katrin's story reveals the heroism of her resolve and efforts to overcome the complex obstacles of her life. Commercialism, once again, provides the means for escape from spiritual paralysis and cultural (and personal) stagnation. In this case, Katrin works toward starting her own business in Ontario. Brooker continued to explore the characters of both Katrin and her sister Asta in his novel Mr. Windle, in which they play major roles.

Katrin's intra-provincial emigration and business ambition mirror the choices Brooker made for himself in the years following the First World War. In 1921, Brooker brought his young family of four to Toronto and gradually took over the weekly advertising journal Marketing Magazine, oftentimes penning all of the articles himself (using various pseudonyms). He developed his advertising theories into three books that sold well and were broadly acclaimed and influential: Subconscious Selling: An Application of the Techniques of Auto-Suggestions to Salesmanship (1924), Layout Technique in Advertising (1929), and Copy Technique in Advertising, Including a System of Copy Synthesis, a Classification of Copy Sources, and a Section on Copy Construction (1930). Over his career, he published more than 200 advertising articles in the most prominent journals in Canada and the United States.⁵ He eventually became Vice-President of the MacLaren Advertising Company, working under Jack MacLaren—the famous founder of Canada's first sketch-comedy troupe, The Dumbells. In 1952, Brooker won the prestigious Silver Medal for a lifetime of contributions to advertising by the Association of Canadian Advertisers.

Despite the supposed conservatism of Canada's interwar arts community, Brooker integrated a distinctly revolutionary spirit into his art and writing. Having witnessed and lived through hardship, he never ceased trying to imagine ways to relieve and ultimately end poverty. This desire ran throughout his life and career. In 1913, in Neepawa, he wrote, "Nation must stand shoulder to shoulder with nation, and this people must grasp the hand of this people; and all barriers of national prejudice and jealousy must be broken down until this word 'poverty' be abolished" ("To All the Nations ....!"). Thirty years later, in 1943, in Toronto, he began work on his unfinished play "The Common Man", in which he set out to stage a Canadian communist and an American individualist living in uncomfortably close proximity to one another. In his notes for the play, the wealthy individualist, who "has a real feeling for common men", ends up giving away all his riches, declaring, "Money [is the] root of trouble." Such a leftist sentiment and plot orientation, though seemingly hypocritical for a man who spent most of his adult life working in or alongside the advertising industry, shed light on the complexity of his approach to social justice. For while it is true that leftist sentiment was not uncommon during the interwar period, and was certainly part of the common discourse amongst Christian social-gospel activists, artists, and reform-minded bourgeois, Brooker was by no stretch of the imagination a socialist. He believed in the free market and in capitalism, not because he valued money essentially but for its power to change society rapidly. He argued that this force was useful, indeed essential, to break the conservatism of Canadian society—and especially to break the influence of the church.

His manifesto "Cosmic Patriotism", part of the "Decay of Art" suite, outlines some of the reasons why capitalism and commercialism appealed to his anti-conservatism, including overthrowing aristocracies and preventing war. Furthermore, commercialism "has tightened the cosmic bands that hold this little worldful of people together in peace …. Commercialism is linking art with life, and giving every man an occupation worth living for" ("Decay of Art"). The status quo, he recognized very early in his life, was complacent to the kind of poverty Brooker knew first hand. In his hunger for broad social change, he realized that capitalism, though a "thing without a soul", had the power and the means to change the world. Advertising was rapidly becoming the primary conduit of its expression and development. It was his hope, as he outlines in the other sections of the manifesto, that the spiritually engaged artist would take control of the capitalist machine and ultimately liberate the world to a higher state of consciousness— surpassing capital and degenerate muckraking in the process. Commercialism was but one stage in a teleological progression toward a vaguely defined but passionately defended looming moment of global spiritual integrity. Art had its own special role to play, for it "shall eventually lead them across the psychic bridge to the Next Beyond, where transfigured man shall look back at his last stage of evolution, as he does now, with disgust and contempt. / Man shall some day be surpassed!". As his career advanced, Brooker increasingly soured to the transitional potential of business and advertising, though he consistently theorized advertising's liberating influence in such a deeply conservative and staid country as was Canada at that time.

Concurrent with—though most argue, *despite*—his successful career in business, Brooker pursued his work as artist and author aggressively. While his published literary contributions prior to Toronto amount to little more than pot-boiler popular fiction and a handful of seasonal and occasional poems, Brooker had been reading and following international avant-garde literature since his arrival in Canada ("Years": 2). His previously unpublished Manitoban writings, including manifestoes, poems and stories, attest to his ambitions on the international stage. Brooker attacked Europe's Decadent Movement, argued against patriotic verse, and lambasted artists for paying too much attention to the "muck-racking" world of contemporary politics. He advocated for "Cosmic Patriotism", for an art movement that would provoke, as he later describes it, "the rallying spirit that we require to regenerate the world" ("When We Awake!"). His early writings of this sort, though, were not published in his lifetime, but the ideas continued to circulate in his mind and conversation. In the 1920s, they would resurface in downtown Toronto, over cigars and drinks and Turkish cigarettes at the prestigious Arts and Letters Club, where his spiritually revolutionary ideas resonated with his wealthy new friends Vincent Massey and Lawren Harris. They both encouraged him to explore the ideas further—especially in the visual arts. And so, still under forty, having fully escaped poverty and won a healthy and stable income by his new profession as an advertising critic and theorist, Brooker began to paint.[6]

Just two years after having picked up a brush with serious intent for the first time, in 1927, he caused scandal and made history with the first public display of his paintings: the first exhibition of abstract art in Canada. Between 1925 and 1955, Brooker produced more than 400 canvases, which now hang in all of the important galleries across the country, a substantial portion of which are his distinctive and explosively energetic abstractions. Currently, at the time of this writing, his reputation rests primarily on his innovations in the field of visual art.

His commitment to artistic experimentation inevitably antagonised those less enthusiastic for change, a group that amounted to the vast majority of artists, critics, and appreciators in the country at the time. Thus, Brooker's entrance into the public eye as artist, though historic, was somewhat less than auspicious. In his 1927 diary entry of the event, included in the "Texts" section of the Canadian Literature Collection website, Brooker noted the poor, mystified reception of this first exhibition of abstract painting in Canada. Despite the setback, in 1928, at the behest of Harris and Arthur Lismer, Brooker exhibited his vibrant abstractions alongside the Group of Seven. Though Brooker was invited to exhibit with them again in 1930, at the time, J. E. H. MacDonald publicly criticised Brooker's work to the point that he later, embarrassed, wrote a letter of apology—not for his opinion, which he sustained, but rather for his untactful behaviour (Reid 1985: 17). Apparently, A. Y. Jackson said while surveying Brooker's contributions to the exhibition, "When the day comes that all of the people enjoy these paintings, ours will be forgotten" (Victor Brooker 1982). The isolation had other consequences as well. When in 1931 Ontario police removed Brooker's paintings from the walls of the Art Gallery of Toronto, no one rose in his defence (see "Nudes and Prudes"). From these and other isolating incidents, Brooker was taught by his society to control his revolutionary, and occasionally downright messianic, impulses. Indeed, even his less extreme and anti-social imaginings caused conflict and consternation in a culture that found the Group of Seven's landscape impressionism radical. He saw their work, however, as the beginning of a shift away from realism, and, as he wrote in the *Canadian Forum*, looked forward more to the work that would follow their current fare (Brooker, "Canada's Modern Art Movement"). In a number of lectures around Toronto, and later published in the 1938 *Association of Canadian Bookmen's Library Bulletin*, Brooker encouraged Canadians for the sake of art to explore their own eccentricities and develop their divergent temperaments: "We have a very exciting country, but a very unexcited people. We pay the penalty in a certain humdrummery which pervades our whole life and literature" (1938: 198).

The spirit of optimism and change that followed the end of the First World War led Brooker to conclude that Canada was an ideal location for a parallel aesthetic revolution to the one underway in modernist Europe. Canada's modernism, however, would be less cataclysmic, less infected by the malaise of the collapse of a civilization, and more in tune with the birth of a new one. He praised the country for its youthful openness, for its untouched and unspoilt wilderness. He proclaimed that Canada was a natural host for a grand awakening that would be led by modern artists and that would overthrow the decayed wasteland of the world. Rather than focus on the details of the collapse, or revel in it like the European modernists, Brooker argued passionately for the age that would follow. It is the artist alone, he writes in "When We Awake!", that can sustain the grand sublimity of the ailing religions and yet co-exist with the gritty reality of science. He singled out for praise the artist who was "jogging laggards out of their dose in the bosom of dying orthodoxies, or conversely the narcotic effects of scepticism, so that religion—and hence art—becomes vital and fresh; an hourly response to life's exultations!'". For Brooker, the promise was tantalizing and tantalizingly close: should the revolution of the artist take hold, a new golden age would begin. In 1931 in *Printers' Ink*, the most influential American advertising periodical, Brooker penned an article that looked thirty years into the future to imagine the triumph of art over business:

> My own feeling—and, of course, I don't ask anyone to place too much reliance on 'feelings'—is that the business man of 1961 will be almost completely unlike his counterpart today. In other words, he will not merely be a changed man. He will be an entirely new kind of man. I don't know much about what he will be doing, but I do feel as though I know a little about what he will be like.
>
> As a matter of fact, if I'm right, he won't be a business man in the strict sense. *He will be an artist!* (1931, "Business Man": 44)

While outlining the details of the "new revolution" (49) that lurked just ahead in the future, Brooker assailed the advertising and business industry for its aesthetic, social, and even spiritual shortcomings. A new kind of advertiser, distinctly revolutionary, was emerging to correct the worst offences of commercialism:

> The mechanic and the engineer have had their heyday. Soon the artist will step out from the despised ranks of vagabondage,[7] where for centuries he has kicked his heels, awaiting the 'commands' of patrons. He will be exalted above the people, as were the princes of former times. He will be the merchant-artist-prince of the second half of this century .... And the dynasty of business, at whose door all the sordidness and ugliness of modern life have been laid, will ironically produce successors whose magnificent privilege it will be to beautify the earth beyond all ancient dreams. (52)

While pronouncements of this sort may not be entirely surprising for Brooker or for any avant-garde figure of the era, it is particularly surprising that he tried and was able to publish material with this sort of entrenched millennialism in *Printers' Ink*, an extremely conservative insider's journal written primarily by New York businessmen for their counterparts. If nothing else, it demonstrates the extent to which Brooker used all media outlets available to him to deliver a similar prognosis for the future. It also undermines the often-repeated claim that Brooker's advertising theories contradicted his artistic vision.

In the years following the *Printers' Ink* article, having become one of the continent's leading theorists and advocates of advertising, Brooker also won broad acceptance as an experimental modernist for his visual art. Ironically, while his tentatively Futurist advertising work was being widely praised by the business community, the creative community generally found that Brooker's exploration of similar ideas in his art pushed beyond the boundaries of acceptable discourse and taste. Over his career, as he grew increasingly aware of the limitations of his audience, he began to address and attack the restrictive aesthetics of his contemporaries. At the same time, he fostered links with other Canadian modernists, such as Morley Callaghan, Raymond Knister, Kathleen Munn, Fred Housser, and Herman Voaden. He penned a general arts column for Southam newspapers (syndicated in the *Calgary Daily Herald*, the *Ottawa Evening Citizen*, the *Winnipeg Evening Tribune*, the *Edmonton Journal*, and the *Vancouver Province*) that highlighted, with explanation and praise, cutting-edge activity across the country. The weekly column ran for three years, providing an invaluable multidisciplinary overview of the period. In "Nudes and Prudes", Brooker lambastes Torontonian (and Canadian) prudery for a number of "scandals" such as the removal of nudes by foreign and local artists from gallery walls (he insists his argument did not amount to a vendetta for the removal of his own). He traces the fear of unclothed bodies to the Canadian education system, where art was construed as little more than a craft. He contrasts this philistinism with his own sense of the value of art:

> Beauty, in other words, is the product of a view of things which transcends the personal and glimpses the universal. It is a hint of the wholeness of life—a unity to which the individual, concerned only with purely practical problems of self-preservation, is wholly blind

.... A proper understanding of the real function of art is more necessary today than it has ever been. Now that the orthodox religions
are losing their hold, especially on the imaginations of the younger
generation, art is more significant than ever before as the only unifying experience that remains to us—the only experience that approximates to the religious in its ability to make us feel *at one* with the
universe.

Brooker proceeds to discuss "the tremendous significance of sex" as a
clue to the mystery of universal unity, for which sake we must teach children to consider and appreciate the body "in an atmosphere of candour and
beauty." Art, he suggests, and especially the calm, appreciative nudes specifically referred to in the article, creates just such an atmosphere. His article
is one of the earliest—if not the earliest—to advocate against aesthetic censorship in Canada and reveals both how Brooker differed from the opinions
of his peers, and how he tried to challenge the prudish provincialism that
surrounded him.

His fame as a dynamic and eclectic force in contemporary Canadian art
gained momentum and depth in 1936 with his first novel, *Think of the Earth*,
which won the Lord Tweedsmuir Award (renamed the Governor General's
Award in 1957). The strange, psychological experiment explores a British
émigré's troubled and partly delusional interpretation of his mystical
illumination. Set in a town reminiscent of Portage la Prairie (and named
after a Toronto street near the Group of Seven's art studio),[8] the novel has an
intriguing and nebulous relationship to his own biography, effectively (one
might also say strategically) blurring the lines between realism, non-fiction
and mysticism. The text poignantly revisits his years as a railway labourer in
Manitoba, in a space that Glenn Willmott describes as haunted by "the fateful
structures of immigrant exploitation, aboriginal oppression, imperialist
warfare, and a ruthlessly mobile, capitalist rationalization" (2000: x). Brooker
published two other novels, *The Tangled Miracle* (1936), a psychic thriller and
detective adventure, and *The Robber* (1949), a historical-biblical novel based
on the man freed by Pontius Pilate in Jesus Christ's stead. Hardly bestsellers,

the books were widely reviewed and generally well received. An episode of
The Tangled Miracle, excerpted in the present collection, highlights Brooker's
previous work in film and demonstrates his multidisciplinary approach to
revolutionary mysticism. The segment makes reference to E. A. Abbott's
Flatland (1884), a book popular at the time for demonstrating the limitations
of conventional knowledge and experience. Brooker expands Abbott's satire
to prove the fourth dimension, a presiding fascination of millennial mystics
and avant-garde artists. In fact, all three of Brooker's novels grapple with
occultist concerns such as spurious charlatanism, spiritualism, and the
messianic impulse. Although *The Robber* was reprinted in its first year when
it was selected by an American Christian reading group, only *Think of the
Earth* has been reissued in the half-century since (by Brown Bear Press in
2000). A fourth, previously unpublished novel, *Mr. Windle*, an urban sketch
set in a Toronto rooming-house in the 1930s, will appear in the Canadian
Literature Collection series in the near future. The Brooker collection at
the University of Manitoba archives includes other finished and unfinished
unpublished novels, unpublished essays, two nearly-finished philosophical
tracts, together with more than seventy hitherto unpublished short stories
from which the selections in this edition were made.

More than the mystical or technological revolution that he believed lay in
the near future, Brooker's short fiction highlights the social and economic
implications of the ideological shift in the world during his lifetime. As the
stories are all set within the chronological and geographical parameters of
his own experience inside Canada, we find tales that range from the pre–
First World War prairies to interwar- and Depression-era Ontario cities.
The movement in his own life, from labouring villager to urban artist, exemplifies the dramatic social transition from pre-modern settlement to the
modern urban phase of Canadian history that is documented in these texts.
The success of his own transition, however, poignantly contrasts the difficulty his characters have in achieving the same. In each locus, even in the
urban stories, characters struggle to realize ideals distinctly unsuited to the
modern world—ideals that range from ludditic to hubristic to aristocratic.

Unlike his poetry, paintings and drama that attempt to represent his idealist vision, the stories represent his characters' awkward experience with the uncomfortable necessity to change prompted by the emerging age. His characters are distinctly ill-suited to handle the unique pressures of modernity.

The changing world introduces new pressures and temptations that his characters struggle, often unsuccessfully, to manage. Only a handful of the characters are able to utilize or even recognize the new kinds of demands foisted upon the individual in the period. While characters such as Joe Snell ("Mrs. Hungerford's Milk"), Mr. Wherry ("Like Old Jehovah") and Dora McCormick ("The Gilliland House") fail to adapt, their demise reflects more their personal obstinate, deluded or manipulative nature than the moral implications of the emerging order. Strangely, considering his idealism, Brooker's short stories rarely focus on sympathetic or heroic characters, preferring instead marginal losers who struggle awkwardly with the terms of engagement of a new age. More than anything, his stories present a litany of elegiac characters—a record of rusting soon-to-be relics as they petrify or search for the energy to struggle and re-make themselves.

Joe Snell already knows he is a "stick-in-the-mud" but yet is "powerless" to change. In contrast, Mr. Wherry, the window-dreaming pensioner, and Dora McCormick, the penny aristocrat, fail to understand the absurdity or irrelevancy of their limited social knowledge. Both are lost, regardless of their ignorance of their defeat. Edna Colby ("Youth's Manuscript"), the locked-tight widow, takes too much comfort in her old-world isolation to change, though her defeat grieves her. D. J. McConnell's heart attack forces Edna to open up to her colleagues, yet she insists on remaining 'clammed' in and cut off. She and Joe Snell are each, in their own way, isolated from the cultural current, dead in their tracks, victims of their own passivity. These characters are displaced or realize their displacement from whatever limited power they claim. The texts, which typically include a countervailing and often didactic subtext suggesting how the characters might have prevailed, calmly rationalize the displacement. Brooker was sympathetic to the human cost of dramatic change, but there is no note of nostalgia in these stories reserved for those who shun or back away from transformation.

On the other hand, there are characters that begin in paralysis but do take risks and are rewarded for their efforts. In *The Wrong World*, the story begins with Griffith Proctor Densham, who, like the prairie protagonist in Sinclair Ross's 1941 novel *As for Me and My House*, is locked in a kind of intellectual and spiritual paralysis. Both protagonists fail in their attempts to write or produce significant let alone lucrative art. Unlike Ross's Philip Bentley, however, Densham (after the symbolic death of his wife) escapes his spiritually and artistically stultified life, escapes the prairies, for a taste of European "Ecstasy". Katrin Petursson ("The Headwaitress") hardens herself in response to her litany of difficulties, but maintains her desire for something more. She has every reason to despair, but instead fights her circumstance with "astonishing" resolve. It is not simply a matter of age: elderly R. G. Murray ("A Glass of Catawba") catches and challenges his own penchant for nostalgia by rejecting his ties to the Old World: "In the old days ... No. These are the days .... We're here and we're going to stay here. It's a great country". He realizes, after years of colonial hankering, that he is *here*, in Canada, and that the nostalgic lament of the exile can bring him no comfort. This post-colonial turn, signified through his embrace of new-world drinks and brand names, amounts to a humble but sincere embrace of active living. His triumph in the story, though minute, breaks his indolent lifestyle. These stories, more than half of which deal with the immigrant experience, use the cultural lacuna that lies between the characters and their cultural context to explore the personal implications of social and cultural change. Indeed, the stories attend to the minutiae of life while capturing the broader modernization that was then dramatically transforming Canadian society.

As one expects of Brooker in light of his other experimental writing, the content of his stories is shaped to match his conception of the short-story genre and his overarching modernist aesthetics and ambitions. He believed the medium substantially predetermined the content of the genre. In his longest commentary on short fiction, "Idolators of Brevity" published in the *Seewanee Review*, he laments the form's inherent predilection for smallness, including duration and subject matter. He attributes the trifling tendency of short stories in modern writing to the rising influence of the newspaper.

Anticipating Marshall McLuhan's writings on the impact of the newspaper in the decades that follow, Brooker concludes that the impact of "the article [has] reduced much of our literature to the level of journalese" (1931: 265). He cites market pressures on the short story form, particularly in its manifestation within magazines, but furthermore notes that the influx of daily news has produced a shift in consciousness toward a constantly insisting immediacy that inevitably precludes "massiveness" (266). For Brooker, this change violates the basic function of the artist, in general, and of literature, in particular, as a prophetic, *avant-garde* medium:

> In a word, we may say that literature on the grand scale is never contemporary. It gathers its energies from the heroic exemplars of a past time and leaps forward at such a pace and with such a Herculean stride that it over-shoots the present, and to succeeding futures ever recedes like a will o' the wisp, inevitably ahead of oncoming generations. Its essential grandeur is in this tremendous arch from past to future which swings high over the dwarfed concerns of the 'present' of each generation that catches up to it. (267)

The short story, in contrast, embodies the tendency of contemporary writing to focus exclusively on the problems of this particular historical moment—like the news—in conscious exclusion of source, cause, or deeper implications:

> Contemporary literature in the narrow sense is always *concerned*. The nature of the concern is immaterial. Shaw is concerned about the health, the manners, and the economic situation of his characters; whereas Chesterton is concerned with their fancies, their idiosyncrasies, their morals. Dreiser, O'Neill, and Sherwood Anderson are all concerned, in various ways, with the psychological substratum of the mind. They, and hundreds of other modern writers, are concerned to discover and to chart the 'north-west passage' from the subconscious to the conscious. This 'concern' dominates them in much the same way that the notion of a 'missing link' obsessed the biologists of the decade before last. (267)

Though decidedly sensitive to the superficial tendency of the contemporary short story, his own writing suggests that he sought to blend this trifling nature of the form with his grander cosmology. With his unique blend of cosmic mysticism and economic pragmatism shaping the subtext and defining the parameters of the works in this collection, it is little wonder that the stories he produced are unprecedented in Canadian writing—especially of the time—in form, in content and in experimental ambition.

The third story in this collection, "Like Old Jehovah", uses an experimental form to follow the mind's eye of the aged Mr. Wherry in his daily window-watching routine. The technique is a variant of free-indirect discourse, famously used by James Joyce to change the language of an objective, third-person narrator so that it mirrors the psychological thoughts and experience of characters in his novels. Hugh Kenner refers to this technique as "the Uncle Charles Principle" to describe Joyce's fluctuating narrative point of view (1978: 15–38). Brooker's use of the form is well chosen here for its flexibility in representing both the character's thoughts and subjective experience, while also maintaining an ironic distance that allows for the sudden shift at the end of the story. The story begins with Mr. Wherry waking before dawn to observe the day arrive and go by. Sitting in his small room, he believes he influences, perhaps even controls, the weather. All of the people he witnesses through his window become determinants in his choices about how to orchestrate the day. It is a remarkable fantasy: Wherry uses the weather like a reversed variant of the pathetic fallacy to manifest his emotional reaction to the people he observes. The distracted policeman provokes a snowstorm. The "girl with the skittish walk" who disrobes across the street provokes a solar passion. From his detached vantage, he fancies himself a cosmological causality—like a god or a contemporary version of Plato's Demiurge, the artist/creator of the universe.

After orchestrating the day through to sunset, he walks down to the drugstore for a sandwich and perhaps a soda from a mocking Italian clerk. The clerk laughs at him, "Here comes the Almighty." The parodic mockery of the old man erases the playful hint of magic realism in the text by insisting upon his separation from the real world. Although the spiteful flick seems to undermine the story's kindly investment in the lonely innocence of the old man's imagination, it also functions as an abrupt and direct reminder of artifice, of the sort that Bertolt Brecht made famous in his modernist plays, and must accordingly shift our reading of the piece. The recurring connections between the pathetic Wherry, lost in his own delusions, and Jehovah raise a rather indelicate possibility that the old man with his fantastic powers is Brooker's satiric and allegorical representation of Jehovah in the contemporary world. Surely worse than Nietzsche's proposition, in this reading, Brooker's God has been reduced to a leering isolate distracted from the fact of his fall. In "The Decay of Art," Brooker states, "The Gods are dead" and declares any lingering attachment to such supernaturalism "effete and obsolete." In this story, godliness is indeed associated with exhausted decadence. Wherry, regretting his neighbour getting dressed, laughs that God kicked Eve out of the garden for being jealous that she covered her nakedness. With an unkind parable of the Christian faith combined with overt nudity and voyeurism, it is little wonder the story was not published in prudish Canada in his lifetime.

Of all the stories in this collection, in fact, only "Mrs. Hungerford's Milk" has ever been previously published: in the *Canadian Forum* in 1936 and again in the anthology *Voices of Discord: Canadian Short Stories from the 1930s* in 1979. No doubt, the sheen of social realism in this story appealed to the emerging aesthetic standard then sweeping across the Depression-era country. Brooker's story, however, is no lament for a lost or losing lifestyle or a tale of the disenfranchised underclass. Joe Snell fails because he refuses to see the world as it is becoming—because he refuses to admit the changing ways of the world. The blindness occurs in both the public and private realms and reduces him, through metaphor, to a flailing, disempowered beast. In the public world, his business has fallen behind for his steadfast refusal to upgrade his equipment. Although it is tempting to attribute the hardship to the economic difficulties of the Depression and the transition into industrial capitalism, the only causal explanation provided in the text is Snell's reticence to respond to his own business failings. There are two poignant examples provided: his rejection of his brother's advice to "get a truck and keep up to date" and his dismissal of his wife Hettie's advice to "quit giving estimates" and stabilize his income by charging an hourly rate. Joe resists transforming himself from small business owner to freelance labourer. Instead, he ineffectively claims injustice after a day of underpaid overwork. Since he is the one responsible for the job estimate and contract, his complaints are without merit. Hettie's suggestion provides an obvious short-term solution, whereas his brother—"a fusser" who also owns his own business—offers a long-term strategy for the company. His insistence on horses in the cartage business in the age of the truck demonstrates Joe's distance from sound business decisions. It follows that Joe's unwillingness to change his business mirrors his wilful blindness in the private domain. His daughter Myrtle has grown up without his notice. In order to facilitate Myrtle's emerging social needs, Hettie has developed a few resourceful tricks for managing her domestic chores—such as getting a passing delivery boy to deliver milk on his route. Joe responds to the changes like a displaced monarch, "flapping his arms" ineffectually, ruefully and bitterly acquiescing to the fact of his displacement from power in his own home.

The story was reprinted in *Voices of Discord*, Donna Phillips's leftist anthology of stories from "the radical tradition" (1979: 13). In his introduction to the collection, Kenneth J. Hughes praises such rich realist details as Snell brushing dead flies from the rainwater barrel to get a drink (24). While Hughes eloquently maps the class implications of Joe Snell's displacement, his framing of the text within the radical leftist tradition feels forced and perhaps unmerited. The story lacks any hint of social protest or social prognosis that would attribute full responsibility to anyone but the story's protagonist. Phillips frames the story within the radical literature tradition of depicting the "alienation of industrial workers" (9). Hughes, in contrast, is more sensitive to the fact that Snell is a character of type, a petit-bourgeois, compromised "by the various forces of monopoly capitalism" (27). But Hughes's use of Snell's disempowerment as critique of modern market forces avoids the criticism implicit in Brooker's characterization. As a farmer with cattle and a self-employed small businessman with his cartage business, Snell is content to exploit the unpaid labour of his wife and daughter. He is willing, too, or more appropriately, *too willing* to chastise them for what he deems poor performance of their duties, and for rewarding themselves with a social evening without his approval. In contrast, after an underpaid day as a result of his own calculation errors, on a work day that starts after "the 2:40 train", he treats himself to two beers at the neighbourhood public house and still manages to get home "in the sun" for a dinner made by his wife. This is no exploited labourer, or what Hughes refers to as a victim of "the perilous competitive nature of existence for the petit bourgeois" (26). It is easier to interpret the story not as an example of Marxist disillusionment with capitalism or technology but as a chastisement of a petit-bourgeois; an undisciplined small business owner who refuses to add and incorporate advances in business planning and management. However sympathetic, and the strength of the story lies in Brooker's deft appeal to both sympathy for the protagonist and a logical renunciation of him, Joe Snell is a loser by his own shortcomings, and the story records the cost of the triumph of modernity over him.

Like "A Glass of Catawba" and "Head Waitress", "Youth's Manuscript" also revolves around the workplace, in this case focussed on women working in a Canadian city in "America" after the end of prohibition in 1927. The city, with its network of ravines and corporate headquarters and distinctive neighbourhoods, is most decidedly modelled after Toronto—but it is worth noting, in light of the significance of particularized place in his other stories, that Brooker never identifies the city directly. The lead character is Edna Colby, a fashion artist on "one of the smaller women's publications" in a large firm. D. J. McConnell, not exactly her boss but certainly her superior, manages "one of the largest" magazines in the same company. Prior to the story, McConnell has doggedly proposed marriage to her three times and the text begins with his announcement of his intentions to try once more.

Edna, on the eve of her fortieth birthday, must wade through the insecurities of her age and the comfortable loneliness of her life to make a decision. The narrative spirals up toward an epiphanic turn as the lead character confronts her spiritual paralysis. Unlike Murray's small triumph in the previous story, however, the implications of Edna's awakening are decidedly ambiguous. Through her tears and chocolate soda assuagement, the question remains of how far she will confront and recognize her unhappiness. Strangely, but worth noting, is the fact that like *The Wrong World*, the plot climaxes with a lover's heart attack, and like "Like Old Jehovah", its denouement occurs in an Italian soda shop.

In this story, unlike most of the others, the lead is not characterized as an outsider just arrived in Canada. She is, however, a recent arrival in the city from a "small-town", a fact presented to justify her habitual social reservation. Despite this frame for the story, Brooker's consistent Old World–New World structural paradigm resurfaces through her attachment to Mr. Kolessa, her "distinctly European" music teacher. Brooker reverses his general narrative pattern in surrounding Kolessa with a rowdy crowd of "gabbling people." McConnell, in pointed contrast, plays the insipid and "pretty pompous" North American aristocrat still living with his mother though "well over fifty." His fourth marriage proposition demands Edna choose between diametrically opposed worlds—the cold economic security of the upper class (linked to North America) or the over-sentimental life and vitality of the rabble (linked to Europe). Though she clearly rejects sexual objectification, most memorable in a scene in which she stands nude before a mirror and reflects on the male gaze, the story can be characterized by its, and her, irresolution of the relatively pedestrian problems she faces.

Similar to "Youth's Manuscript", Brooker's expansive mystical romance, the novella *The Wrong World* presents an intriguing reversal of the recurring narrative of Canadian naturalization explored in the other texts. The story follows the life of author and immigrant Griffith Proctor Densham as he struggles to write "a great Canadian epic" documenting the Icelandic communities in northern Manitoba, hoping to produce "a powerful study of their rigorous, half-savage existence." The novel fails, thus prompting Densham to abandon this country and return to England. The return is marked by the remarkable discovery of "ecstasy" in the form of both contemporary experimental art and intergenerational love. In the process, the protagonist quickly forgets about his Canadian dreams and "literary ambitions" and begins writing an extensive commentary on source texts in Shakespeare's plays. Brooker foregrounds the literary reversal as a conscious cultural rejection of the pre-modern Dominion: "This Western country, he decided, was too young, too crude, too obsessed with the mere task of making ends meet. No wonder he had been unable to write. Culture was almost entirely lacking." In his return, and in his discovery of "ecstasy", the protagonist rekindles his connections to his homeland:

> "This is England!" thought Densham. He had not been back long enough to take it all for granted. Every now and then he experienced a curious pungent sensation of the flavour of England,—dwarfed, crowded, damp, insular; and yet—cosy!—even in the pouring rain.

Despite the unabashed nostalgic portrait of goodly Albion, *The Wrong World* was in fact begun in 1926 in Toronto at the encouragement of Group of Seven acolyte and Canadian nationalist Fred Housser.[9] It was Brooker's first attempt to turn his "prairie experiences" into a fictional text, though it deals primarily with the modernist cultural shift in England. The barrenness of Canadian cultural life provides a profound contrast to the explosive emergence of experimental avant-garde activity in Europe.

The Wrong World has never previously been published but the work was re-written and released as the Governor General's Award winning novel *Think of the Earth* in 1936. There remain numerous overt connections to his first published novel, including character names and entire paragraphs shared between the two works. The story is substantially different, however, not just in tone for being less polemical than *Think of the Earth*, and more enthusiastic in its embrace of mysticism, but also in the spiritual implications and orientation of its plot. If *Think of the Earth* was his attempt to write a novel in the style of Dostoevsky (as was claimed on the back cover of the first Canadian edition), then *The Wrong World* might be figured as an attempt to write a tractatus on spiritually transcendent, indeed unearthly, love in the manner of Tolstoy. Whereas Tavistock discovers a profound spiritual integrity through his thoughts of the notably Canadian prairie earth, Densham, the Tavistock figure in *The Wrong World*, attributes his inability to write to the spiritual flatness of the prairies. Densham flees to London where he enters the bohemian world surrounding a highly acclaimed retired Russian vocalist and witnesses the spectacle of modern music and dance.[10] In London, the protagonist encounters such occultist tropes as reincarnation and cosmic consciousness. Such plot turns also appear in *Think of the Earth*, but in accordance with the Toronto zeitgeist during the 1920s and the principles of Brooker's Ultimatist philosophy, any hint of magic is marginalized. *The Wrong World* violates the entrenched nationalism of Cosmic Canadians such as Lawren Harris who argued that the Canadian landscape was the ideal site for mystical awakening (1929: 85–88). Brooker's characters—R. G. Murray and Geoff Tavistock and Brooker himself in "When We Awake!"—seem to embrace this prophetic vision of Canada.

Densham, on the other hand, must return to England before he can discover spiritual ecstasy. The reasons for the transition in Brooker's cultural representation in his stories are difficult to surmise, particularly as the chronology of the production of the other stories has been effectively lost. What remains clear, however, is that Brooker's preoccupation with the liminal experience of a British émigré to Canada, and the ensuing contrast with other immigrant groups, most poignantly the Icelandic community, structures his fictional response to modernity. The paradigmatic personal experience of his characters mirrors the broader cultural shift into modernism, with its tenacious inevitability and its voracious appetite for change.

Bertram Brooker died on 22 March 1955, in Toronto, at the age of sixty-seven. Laudatory eulogies appeared in all the mainstream newspapers of the Dominion, as well as in the business journals. Since his passing, academic debate has too frequently centred on the question of his relationship to modernism, and particularly on how well he fits into European and American models of modernism. The remarkable 1988 multidisciplinary conference on Brooker, for instance, chose for its dominant theme his "Emergent Modernism", rather than focussing on the unique nature of his achievement. Like Baudelaire in his time, Brooker has been accused of deploying outdated forms to house his original ideas (Wagner 1989: 48) and original forms to house outdated ideas (Arnason 1989: 80). Even while his critics debate his merits in relation to *international* modernism, none question the vitality and originality of Brooker's broad contributions to art in Canada. Each of his critics, however, has tended to focus on one particular discipline, such as visual art, literature, drama, or advertising, to the great detriment of a holistic sense of his surprisingly constant and coherent career. Indeed, with an artist as diverse, prolific, and original as Brooker, the commonality of his project to foreign models ought to become secondary to his complex achievement as an early experimental Canadian multidisciplinary artist. Although his celebrity waned from the 1950s through to the 1980s, the 1973 tour of Brooker's paintings organized by Dennis Reid (with the catalogue released in 1978) and the 1980 posthumous publication of Brooker's poetry edited by Birk Sproxton introduced a new era of consideration and attention to his work that continues to accelerate. He is gradually being recognized as a pioneering forerunner to the Canadian avant-garde—a distinctly Canadian breed of Futurist. Ideal art, for Brooker, "over-shoots the present, and to succeeding futures ever seems to recede, inevitably ahead of oncoming generations" ("When We Awake!": 213).

From Futurist fantasies of art on the grand scale, it was Brooker's holistic sense of the impact of all media—including both art and advertising—that led him to conclude that science and technology were changing the relationship between humanity and their experience of the earth. Still, and a key explanation for his attachment and devotion to the trade, it was advertising and not art that spread the news of the emerging era. In an interesting aside in his column, "The Seven Arts" (3 November 1928), he compares his own abstract paintings and fiction to popular detective fiction by noting their similar use of geometrical design of form and content. In the article, he slyly adds that both were rather primitive examples of the same ideas circulating in the surrealist and even "futuristic" aesthetics of modern advertising. In a corresponding 1928 business column entitled "The Modern Bug Will Get You If You Don't Watch Out", Brooker writes:

> Along with music and art and literature and fashions and sky-scrapers and furniture and women's clothes, advertising has 'gone modern'—or is going modern so fast that few can withstand the

magnetic pull of its whirling pace .... Consequently what may be
considered the futuristic spirit has crept into more phases of modern
advertising than backgrounds; headlines have a dash of it; art compositions are often frankly and boldly futuristic, and there are many
advertisers who present the human figure done in terms which get
as far away from realism as possible. The futuristic border, mortise-
scheme and general make-up have found a place in campaigns of
today, and it must be confessed that they do stand out. (286)

In light of this praise of Futurist techniques and styles, it is worth highlighting the fact that he produced a remarkable canvas between 1913 and
1915 entitled A Defence of Futurism that included texts that reads: "I believe."

In 1946, he began notes toward a manifesto called "Bloodless Revolution" that would overthrow institutional religion and capital and "Make
everybody militant for happiness." He reiterates his position outside of the
commonplace discourse of science, religion, and commerce:

the more scientific and hardheaded (commercially) we become, the
more we live in a *fantasia*. Neither satisfies the soul .... World hypnotized for centuries by Christianity which has been opposed to main
instincts of man's nature—largely because hokum based on ancient
beliefs have been accepted, without greatly changing man's conduct
or conscience. (n. pag.)

He was, in the end, a cosmic patriot with little to no faith in the presiding contrivances, answers, or institutions of his time. In one of his many attempts at fictionalized autobiography (written in the third-person), Brooker
notes an anti-intellectual feeling that reverberated throughout his writing:
"Always hated categories, lacked formalized knowledge and schooling.
When he talked and friends pinned labels on his ideas—that's Plato, that's
Plotinus, that's Madame Blavatsky—very impatient, wouldn't be chan-
nelled—preferred Blake and Whitman who followed own bent" (1951: 9).

While scholarly responses to Brooker have shown consistent interest
in the mystical grounding of his writing (with the sole exception being
Kenneth J. Hughes's praise for Brooker's realism in "Mrs. Hungerford's

Milk"), the extent to which Brooker's mystical beliefs informed his writing is only gradually coming into focus. Brooker articulated his aesthetics in terms of a broad-based, indeed global, spiritual regeneration. He was not alone in this millennial and hubristic thinking—there was a substantial group of Canadian modernists heavily involved in the mystical resurgence of the period. It is this core of numinous beliefs that, at first, led scholars to distinguish Brooker from the leading modernists, and increasingly to connect him to the European and American avant-garde; extending this connection to accepted modernists such as E. E. Cummings and W. B. Yeats—and even to those whom Brooker himself characterized as "unintelligibles" ("When We Awake!") such as Wassily Kandinsky and Marcel Duchamp.

Brooker's essays, articles, and lectures are replete with references to the mystical insights of great writers of the past, such as Blake, Keats, Goethe, and Shakespeare, and of the present, such as P. D. Ouspensky, Alfred North Whitehead, and John Middleton Murry, and it was through this mystical tradition that, perhaps with a hint of the quixotic spirit, Brooker believed he found his path into the contemporary international modernist avant-garde. His awareness, reaction, and response to the global initiative began as early as 1911 and continued for the rest of his life. Before the First World War, while living in Manitoba, he mimicked and imitated the paintings and styles of the Russian Futurists, the Italian Futurists, the Vorticists, and the Cubists—those in what Ezra Pound called the "cult of ugliness" (1968: 45)—leading to manifestoes, essays, and inflammatory theatre. He produced paintings and canvases with such titles as *The Next Beyond* (1912–13), *The Cult of Ugliness* (1913–15), *Marinetti, Nijinsky...* (1913–15), *cubist* (1914), *A Defence of Futurism* (1913–15), and *Vortexing upward and outward through vaster births and deaths* (c. 1920s). In 1912, he developed his theory of "the Ultimatists": an elite vanguard of contemporary artist-prophets forging a new vitality in their art. In the notes to an experimental play on the subject of British actor, playwright, and director Gordon Craig's avant-garde theatre, Brooker declared, "the first principle of Ultimatism is that all definitions are impossible" ("The Measure of Gordon Craig": 13). Notwithstanding, Brooker narrowed his sense of the movement to three specific precepts:

"Ultimatism ignores the faeries while it repudiates Christianity, but it insists on spirit" (15). Thus, in deft accordance with the general episteme of both turn-of-the-century mysticism and emerging modern arts aesthetics, Ultimatism proposed (i) a rejection of the supernatural, and (ii) a resistance to preceding dogma. The third postulate, however, distinguishes mystical modernism from other branches of modernist activity: (iii) an effort to sustain a conscious connection to the cosmic context in which humankind participates. As Sherrill Grace explains, Ultimatist philosophy was "mystical, holistic, and quite self-consciously anti-utilitarian and anti-rationalist" (1985: 7). These guiding principles remain constant throughout Brooker's critical and creative writing. They are prominent in his essays and present, if muted, in the short stories included in this collection.

Although he settled into a more resolute career in journalism with all three of Winnipeg's newspapers and in advertising with each paper as well, becoming, on the surface, a more palatable and conventional white-collar Canadian, Brooker's revolutionary fires continued to burn. In the 1920s, in the dynamic space of Toronto's mystical modernist initiative, he crafted exceptional and experimental poems, stories, and plays. Compared to his Manitoba writing, his manifestoes and essays from this era were more explicitly keyed to the Canadian context, articulating for many the confounding influences conspiring to limit innovation and experimentation by Canadian artists. Above all else, it was the challenges to spirituality—including the "encroaching scepticism of a science-ridden age" ("When We Awake!")—that were undermining Canadian art. His criticism during this period exudes a mystical and occultist hermeneutics in that he interprets and evaluates contemporary writing for its spiritual contribution. His 1930 review of Cummings's poetry in The Canadian Forum, for instance, praises the poet but complains that he lacks a certain "fourth-dimensional quality" that would "suggest a more mystical outlook" (68–69). Brooker's mysticism, when combined with his entrenched commercialism, did not set him in opposition to the currents of modernity, technology, and temporal change. In fact, he argues in "When We Awake!" that artists have a responsibility to respond to the contemporary world—and, like it or not, in the contemporary world technology and "mechanization" are creating "a unified and definitely new kind of civilization, all of a piece, that our children are growing up into, half oblivious of its wonder". The cumulative shifts and innovations happening across society need to be reflected in contemporary art if that art is to sustain its temporal relevance. Brooker recognized that liberal attitudes to technology in Canada were disappointingly offset by an entrenched conservatism in aesthetic tastes. He confronted the hypocrisy in Canada's progressivist ideology that decidedly (and illogically) limited the possibilities open to artists:

> But in the arts where form is divorced from mechanics—notably in literature and painting—we permit ourselves to be greatly disturbed by ingenuity, originality, and the invention of new contrivances, new moods, new modes. We can tolerate a machine being new, up-to-date, and ingenious; but the same qualities in a human being are intolerable .... The artist is the last person on earth who is granted the right to originality.

Despite which fact, it is the artist who is most likely to recognize and register the shift, and is the one best suited to responding to the spiritual implications of social change. This spiritual mandate, Brooker writes, the very thing that makes art relevant, has been denied by the conservative and colonial impulse of Canadian critics and artists alike. A mystically oriented and yet unabashedly modernist aesthetic would metaphorically awaken the nation and its citizens to their great potential.

He found hints of this awakening in the painting of the Group of Seven, who

> are seeking something that transcends both reality and romance; something that shines through solidity and carries 'feeling' past mere sentiment to an apprehension of forces which never fully reveal themselves in phenomena unless the mood of the observer is somehow in tune with the source-energy which gives rise to the thing observed (1926, "Canada's Modern Arts Movement": 276)

In short, they were seeking illumination through art, and vice versa. But for Brooker, the world awaited a trigger to set the new era in motion. Whether that trigger would be cataclysmic or intimate was uncertain and subject to open debate in two of his novels, Think of the Earth and The Robber.

In his autobiographies and other writings, he frequently attempts to clarify his own relation to the evolution-based revolution, or what I have taken to calling the spiritual r/evolution: "This is a book about a man who believes that a new kind of life is possible for humanity, a kind of life that has only been dimly conceived hitherto, and never practised. He believes that many now alive may live long enough to see it in effect" (1951, "Opening": n. pag.). In "When We Awake!" he defines the artist in a way suggestive of the role the artist-type might play in provoking the r/evolution: the artist is "*a person whose experiences crystallise into unified wholes that can be embodied in some medium, as contrasted with persons whose experiences seem fragmentary, unrelated and chaotic*" (author's italics). The artist breaks from conventional apprehension and, to borrow from Alfred North Whitehead's vocabulary, *prehends* a larger synthesis between their particularity and that which lies beyond. The uncovered synthesis, or the feeling of the synthesis, is translated, embedded, or created in the artwork. Notably, the artist's particular expression is codified in the shifting idiom of the cultural context.

Interestingly, Brooker recognized that while the artist passively responds to their cultural milieu as "a sensitive receiving-station" ("When We Awake!", genuine art can yet fundamentally and actively change the context into which it emerges—enacting and enabling a revolution led by avant-garde art. This idea of an ideological vanguard forging ahead through art is notably similar to statements by the stalwart avant-gardist Guillaume Apollinaire, who argued in "The New Painting" that "the function of the artist is to modify the illusions of the public .... the humanity of the future will form its image of the humanity of today on the basis of the representations that the most vital, that is, the newest, artists will have left of it." (121) In harmony with Brooker's appreciation of the religious potential of art, Apollinaire concludes that "today's art, although it does not emanate directly from specific religious beliefs, nevertheless possess several of the characteristics of great art, that is to say, of religious Art". For Brooker, likewise, the experience of making genuine contemporary art "is obviously akin to the experiences which in the past have always been called religious" ("When We Awake!"). His essay "Nudes and Prudes" includes various quotations from Walt Whitman that stress and support the religious significance of art.

Brooker embraced the idea of an ever-increasing society of artists and mystics leading a r/evolutionary charge of humanity's moral and spiritual consciousness. Such teleological thinking was not uncommon in the modernist avant-garde—as in the rampant idealism in Surrealist André Breton's foundational statement: "I believe in the future resolution of these two states, dream and reality, which are seemingly so contradictory, into a kind of absolute reality, a surreality, if one may so speak" (Breton 1924: 14). Or included in Futurist F. T. Marinetti's ecstatic ejaculation: "We stand on the last promontory of the centuries! .... Why should we look back, when what we want is to break down the mysterious doors of the Impossible? Time and Space died yesterday. We already live in the absolute, because we have created eternal, omnipresent speed" (Marinetti 1909: 47). Even amongst the Dadaists, who wrote *against* more than *for* anything, one could recall Hugo Ball's sacerdotal experience while reading his *verse ohne worte* "like a magical bishop" (Ball 1974: 67) or Tristan Tzara's proclamation: "Here is a tottering world fleeing, future spouse of the bells of the infernal scale, and here on the other side: new men" (Tzara 1918: 297). These are not presented as equivalents with Brooker's line of thought, but as examples of a similar irrational and/or idealistic euphoria by figures of the canonized avant-garde.

"Prophets Wanted" contains Brooker's surest articulation of the place he sought to attain in the spectrum of competing modernisms and avant-garde schools and movements. Following the national success of his *Yearbook of the Arts 1928–1929*, and with Canadian art having "swung violently to the Left" after the onset of the Great Depression ("Art and Society": xxi), Brooker turned his attention to international currents of mystical modernism. In the article, though Canada disappears as a potential site for the spiritual revolution, his faith in the possibility of an awakening consciousness has not waned. The primary focus of his attack is Irving Babbitt and his advocacy for a "new" Humanism that rejected all religious dogma including Romantic nature worship, and that preferred ethics over aesthetics for evaluating literary merit. Brooker dismisses this philosophy as teleological for relying upon a conviction that humanity had reached the end of its evolutionary development; when, in fact, "there are, indeed, no ends." He describes the philosophy as uninformed and mechanistic, strategically using the vocabulary of the English avant-gardist Wyndham Lewis, whom he connects to Babbit as yet "another crier in the wilderness of pessimism."

Brooker was familiar with the Canadian-born Lewis, and praised him in 1927 in a lecture on William Blake. Borrowing from Lewis, Brooker introduced his talk by arguing against the "splitting up of artistic tendencies into schools and groups, each with their blasts and manifestoes" ("Blake": 1). As Brooker's spiritual revolution was predicated on a grand cosmic unity, he therefore resisted the partisanship of groups, schools, and movements. He turned to one of Lewis's most mystical utterances to contradict the modernist artistic disunity: he quotes Lewis in The Enemy writing: "If you say that creative art is a spell, a talisman, an incantation – that it is magic, in short; there, too, I believe you would be correctly describing it. That the artist uses and manipulates a supernatural power seems very likely." Brooker interprets Lewis' supernaturalism through the Weltanschauung of mystical modernism: "He means more — he means that to be at all, in any real sense, is to become one with the world of imagination, to give up the self, literally, to god, who is, so to speak, the sum of human imagination" (11). It was by this act of surrender — reminiscent of Pullman's earnest prayers and ascension at the end of The Human Age — that Brooker reasoned artists could evolve into cosmic consciousness. In his essays on Canadian modernism throughout the 1920s, Brooker frequently borrows Lewis's particular criticisms of Joyce, Eliot, Pound, and Gertrude Stein and their distortion of time. During this same period, Brooker's flirtation with Lewis and his avant-garde school of Vorticism led him to produce one drawing called "Vortexing upward and outward through vaster births and deaths." By "Prophets Wanted" however, Brooker had registered that their shared resistance to the aesthetics of High Modernism and the occasional use of mystical language did not mean that they were in complete accord. Brooker dismisses Lewis, in the end, as "cloistered and unadventurous", unwilling to accept that "soon" the human race will be "utterly changed." Lewis, he realized, despite having a revolutionary imagination, was not actively working to support a specific revolution (let alone cosmic consciousness) and was therefore not revolutionary enough. Lewis, he concludes, is afraid "to die into life." The article was published in John Middleton Murry's journal *The Adelphi*, demonstrating his increasing affinity with the so-called philosophers of flux. Brooker was not directly influenced by Henri Bergson, as some critics have suggested, but was certainly sympathetic to Bergson's followers such as Alfred North Whitehead and Murry. This article connects Brooker to the mystical modernist and vitalist camps that Bergson inspired.

It is perhaps indicative of Canadian modesty that Brooker's interest in the mystical possibilities of the artist in light of contemporary scientific discoveries is most often used to distinguish him from these and even less experimental international arts movements of his day. David Arnason, for instance, dismisses the idealist impulse in Brooker's poetics as essentially a "Coleridgean romanticism" (1989: 80), despite the fact that Brooker found even Joseph Conrad already out-of-date. In point of fact, Brooker's mystical indulgences do more to connect him to the European avant-garde than to F. R. Scott's anti-bourgeois satires or A. J. M. Smith's experiments with surrealism (Trehearne 2005: 119–138). Brooker, like his radical continental counterparts, was actually trying to lead society forward into a new ideological space. His writing bears the hallmark of this combative, deeply ambitious, literally avant-garde subtext. The essays that accompany the stories in this collection theorize the changes underfoot and demonstrate Brooker's earnest attempt to shape the direction of the progression. For indeed, despite living through two wars, the Depression, and the collapse of the mystical movement that he was so heavily invested in, all evidence suggests that Brooker sustained his belief in revolutionary progress and in Canada's special role in the world. In this way, in combining the essays with the stories, this collection presents a great artist's thorough engagement with the subtleties and complexities of the modernist milieu in Canada—all shaped by the hand of an activist hoping to guide and lead the world forward to "the Next Beyond."

NOTES TO THE INTRODUCTION

1 Victor Brooker dates this trip in 1909 in his list of corrections for Dennis Reid's catalogue (11 October 1972), whereas Brooker himself dates it in 1910, see "Years": 4.

2 See Laurence 1970: 31.

3 One of Brooker's early feature columns for the *Manitoba Free Press* was titled "Gulliver's Adventures in Winnipeg".

4 Notably "Shorts About Bernard", "Interior", and "Bernard". In Brooker's fictional autobiography *A Candle in Sunshine*, he gives the character Bernard Richard Bradley his own birth date (1).

5 This figure reflects only confirmed publications—there are a number of journals he wrote for regularly outside this sum. He was, for instance, a regular contributor to *Advertising Age*, which does not run bylines. The bibliography in "The Destroyer: Modernism and Mystical Revolution in Bertram Brooker" provides further details, see Betts 2005: 325–336.

6 According to a letter from Victor Brooker to Dennis Reid (11 October 1972), Brooker's first oil paintings were produced in 1922. However, these were rough sketches of ideas rather than fully developed canvases.

7 Vagabonds: homeless wanderers. This may be a subtle allusion to the most popular and prominent Canadian poets of the time, including Bliss Carman and Wilson MacDonald who occasionally self-identified as "vagabonds".

8 The afterword to "Around the Ward" offers more details on Brooker's use of the street name and of his relationship to Harris, see Harris 2008: 85–88.

9 See Brooker's "The Bread of Carefulness" diary entry, 16 April 1926.

10 Documented in the Kalinova poems collected in Brooker's posthumous collection *Sounds Assembling*—and available in the "Texts" section on the Canadian Literature Collection website.

SHORT FICTION

:

Like Old Jehovah

The old man who lived over the corner drugstore turned restlessly in his bed. His eyes were old, but in the blue square of night framed by his window he could detect the pallor of morning. Crooking his elbow under his head, he turned to the east, and lay waiting for the day. He had spied on the coming of dawn many times, as a younger man might spy on a woman. He knew many strange and secret things about the way a day is born and dies.

The day never starts in the city. It starts in the country near the edge of the world. It is a little timid at first, the way it comes tip-toeing over the fields. But once the cocks start crowing it feels like hurrying. With light steps it runs here and there, flicking whatever it passes with a gentle tap, to make sure that everything is awake in the country before it goes on to the shacks at the fringe of the town.

By that time the day is bolder. It gives up worrying about whether the sun will be late. The big laggard has washed his beaming face and is already peeping over the world.

The day starts to cry out, "Wake up! Wake up!" as it leaps over the railroad tracks and comes to the first dishevelled streets, still sprawling in sleep. It has to shout, now, because of the clanking and whistling of the switch engines and the rumble of early trucks. It would really like to steal quietly into the city and rap very softly on the windows, so as not to startle anyone.

How much better it would be if people opened their eyes and were glad that night had crept away, ashamed of all it had been doing in the darkness. How splendid it would be if people jumped up, when light came down the street, and went to their windows joyfully, nodding to it and calling out, "Good morning!"

The day would be able to go on then, encouraged, brightening over the squalid tenements and grim factories, popping into little hole-in-the-corner stores, tickling the eyelids of the tramps on the benches.

But the day is easily put out by the way city people act, as though they wish it had never come. By the time it reaches the down-town corners it has given up caring very much whether it becomes a nice day or not.

The old man who knows why the days sometimes don't behave very well is already at his window, over the drugstore. It is nearly nine o'clock. Trolleys and automobiles get in each other's way, clanging and honking. Crowds of office people and clerks and early shoppers wriggle rudely against one another when the traffic lights change. Everybody is in a hurry. Nobody pays any attention to the day.

Even the policeman on the opposite corner is too busy to notice, because he is talking to the bank messenger and the caretaker who is squatting down awkwardly to polish the brass plate outside the bank. The three of them keep on talking. Every now and again the stooped old caretaker shakes his rag in the messenger's face, and then the policeman screws his neck around in his collar, and fingers his belt portentously. No one notices the sunshine glinting on the bright edges of the letters the caretaker has polished.

Before long the day starts blustering a bit, so that the heedless crowd will become aware of it. By noon the wind is plunging down between the buildings like an angry bird, swooping off hats, flapping overcoats open and jerking at women's skirts as they cross the corner from the bank to the cigar store.

And in the afternoon, growing angrier and more and more jealous of the attention the crowds are paying to their own little scurrying affairs, the day begins to pelt them with icy sleet.

The old man who knows better then anybody the way a day feels, watches from his window with a crooked smile.

"Sort of jealous, like old Jehovah," he says to himself very quietly, so that nobody will hear.

The sleet keeps falling. The flakes get bigger and whiter, clinging like fluff to cheeks and noses. On the little flat hats the women are wearing, the soft snow lies like icing on a moving multitude of cakes. The big raucous youth on the cigar store corner, who bellows and slaps newspapers under people's arms all day, is so plastered from head to foot that he looks like a snowman stamping to and fro.

The day has seen so much ill-humour in hundreds of passing faces that it seems to have caught the infection of petty spitefulness. Only the hoarse-voiced newsboy keeps smiling as he hops about, stamping and shouting. He jokes boisterously with his sullen customers, and because of this one cheerful voice, the day relents, and decides to redeem itself.

The snow dwindles to tiny flakes, and ceases altogether. In the west the clouds roll back out of the way somewhere, and the sun suddenly gleams through the haze. In no time at all it is flashing on the long procession of windshields and getting in people's eyes. For half an hour before it sinks the unexpected glory of it blazes like a warm glow of hope and promise in the sky.

The old man, who has a lot to do with managing the sun, blinks and draws back a little from his window. To himself, very secretly, he nods and whispers: "Just the way old Jehovah hung the rainbow up in the sky once. I know!"

The day lingers to watch the last light on the hurrying faces, and the old eyes at the window twitch expectantly as the girl with the skittish walk comes round the corner, stepping lightly as though she can hardly keep from dancing. Every night she disappears through the door between the bank and the jeweller's store, and in a moment or two a light appears over the jeweller's, and she comes close to the window, taking off her hat.

There are flimsy curtains over the window, but when she is undressed and stands in the light near the dressing table, doing her exercises, it is easy to see her.

After so many spiteful, stingy, cringing faces and fat, slumping bodies, the day delights in the slender figure of a youthful woman, bending and swaying and touching her toes. But when she begins to dress again, the day darkens quickly, feeling guilty at having stayed so long.

The old man chuckles quietly, as he thinks of the garden of Eden, and says to himself: "Old Jehovah got sore when Eve started covering herself up with fig leaves. You bet he did. Sure, he kicked her and Adam out of there."

The light goes off behind the flimsy curtains, and the old man pushes back his chair and gropes for his hat in the dark.

Downstairs in the drugstore, the thick-lipped Italian soda clerk says to the cashier: "Here comes the Almighty."

The girl smiles at old Mr. Wherry as he goes past to his usual place at the end of the fountain. "Don't tease him now," she says severely to the clerk, but he moves away with a silly swaying motion of his hips and plumps his hands down with a smack on the counter.

"Been a queer kind o' day," he leans ever and bawls in the old man's ear.

"Kind of," says Mr. Wherry, screwing up his eyes secretively. He isn't going to tell young Tony how much he's had to do with it. He isn't going to tell people all he knows.

While he waits for his sandwich he wonders what kind of a day he will figure out for tomorrow.

The Gilliland House

I

When it was first noised around in Zenith that Mrs. Hugh Gilliland was going to stay in the East, and that the house was to be put up for sale, there were few who took the story seriously. But when an item appeared in the *Argus*, and a sign, bearing the familiar legend—"For Sale: Robt. Bonnick"—was stuck in the lawn facing High Street, there was gossip at once. The families in the town who might conceivably buy it were few. Bob Fleming had the number reduced to six, and would stand straddle-legged at the door of his implement establishment ticking them off on his fingers to anyone who would listen.

"I'll bet four bits that whoever buys it will be somewhere in them there six that I've named," he would declare oracularly, stowing his hands away again in his pockets.

The McCormicks were mentioned more frequently than anyone else, for it was well known that the lumber business had been good the last few years, and besides, Dora McCormick had often been heard to say that she hankered after just such a place—an oldish place, with shutters on the windows—even though it were only brick-veneered. It was the shutters—and the view, of course—that attracted Dora, for the house faced out of the town on the west slope of the hill, overlooking the "flats," and on a clear day you could see the low ridge of the Riding Mountains from the verandah.

Harry would have preferred to build a new place, as soon as they could afford it—a good substantial frame house, something like Dennings', but with the best lumber. For one thing it would be a good advertisement. It would show what could be done if you spent a little extra on really good stuff. And then their own place was pretty well falling to pieces. They had been trying to sell it rather than put the money into it that would be necessary to make it really liveable. The East End was no place to live now, in any case, since the roundhouse was built and railroad men had scattered cottages over the bit of prairie between the English church and the tracks. It was just a matter of deciding where to go. They had been looking at a good many lots, especially in the West End, for Dora insisted on that—she really couldn't think of living anywhere else. She simply must have a bedroom facing west on the edge of the town, so that she could get up in the morning and see the mountains, the very first thing, while she was dressing. It seemed so silly to be living in a town with a view like that—like the view you got from the Gilliland house, for instance—and not be in a position to enjoy it. She was so anxious to get there—somewhere on the west slope—that she had reconciled herself to the idea of a frame house, provided it had shutters and was painted a dark greenish-grey, something like Ogletree's, but even darker, if anything.

All this, of course, had been talked about, and when the "For Sale" sign went up a good many people thought of her and said: "Dora McCormick will get her wish now."

The only question was whether Harry would move quickly enough. He was very deliberate, and had spent several months mulling over plans for the new house, holding off the purchase of a lot until he was certain just what he wanted to do. For once Dora had to admit that the delay was really a godsend. If they had gone ahead in the spring, which is what she had urged, they would have been tied up in the deal by now, and the Gilliland house would have been an impossibility. She could see that it was a blessing, after all, that Harry was slow to move; and had even said to Audrey—"you see what comes of looking before one leaps."

But if he had been slow about building, it was a different thing to delay snapping up this. There were the Pratts to consider, if no one else. Everyone knew what Ailsa Pratt was like when she got an idea in her head. Harry must certainly look into the thing at once. And then, as to the "present place." It must be sold, of course, but should it be fixed up a bit to sell? It would be silly to decorate, even though the dining-room and the two back bedrooms did look awful; but the roof would have to be fixed, at least.

"Suppose someone should come in to look at it when it was raining some day," she exclaimed, in the tone she employed to make people realize how practical she could be when she chose. "And the back balcony. The floor-boards are all warped and sticking up. And the railing will have to be repaired, or renewed altogether, perhaps. It really isn't safe. You couldn't take anyone out there; and yet the view is quite nice, you know, from up there—looking toward the church—especially just now, when the gardens are so lovely. And then there's the plumbing, of course. We really should have done something about it months ago. Don't you think you'd better get Speers to come right away, dear?"

She talked Harry into feeling they could easily manage it, even though Mrs. Gilliland had put a higher price on the property than most people had expected, and Harry at once got an option on it, moving quickly for once under Dora's urging. So that within a few days, leaving Audrey at home—for Speers was in the house working—Dora set out for a walk to the "new place," as she called it already, carrying her purple parasol even a little more daintily than usual, her long well-kept fingers arched delicately on the slender handle.

It was a hot afternoon, but a shower in the morning had laid the sandy dust on the avenue running directly west from their old house to Dufferin Street, which curved with the contour of the hill just before it sloped down to the "flats."

"We've bought the Gilliland place," she said to Mrs. Denning, who was on her way down town in the dog-cart with the children. Mrs. Denning had seen her coming, walking with slow smooth step under the trees, and looking her best in the long plum-coloured dress. Pulling Tony in near the sidewalk to wait for her at the street-crossing, Mrs. Denning called out: "How ambitious you are, Dora, going walking on a day like this."

Coming up to the trap with her dimples showing already a few paces off, Dora broke the news to Mrs. Denning. "We have the keys now, so I thought

I'd go down and look it all over, my dear. There'll be so much to be done, and I'm so anxious to get in. You know how I've always doted on the place."

The Rev. Mr. Stone, who was coming out of the rectory as she passed, was delighted to hear of their luck, rubbing his hands over each other and smiling into the shadow under the parasol where her eyes, brilliantly violet in such a light—"dangerous eyes," he sometimes thought—sparkled with anticipation as she spoke lightly, but possessively, of the new place.

And finally, as she came in sight of the highest gable of the house, rising above the trees that surrounded Langdon's long bungalow, Mrs. Govey came bouncing along with a bulging satchel in one hand and a bouquet of flowers, wrapped in newspaper, held stiffly out in the other.

"I just know somebody is sick whenever I see you, Mrs. Govey," Dora exclaimed, holding her sunshade so that the dear old lady could not get too close.

"It's the little Munroe girl—you know?—the little fair-haired girl who was the snow-queen in the Christmas entertainment."

And after listening to the recent history of the Munroe household, Dora managed to get in a word or two about the new house, extracting what pleasure she could from Mrs. Govey's frequent ejaculations of "how splendid"—"how perfectly splendid."

II

Through the gate she went at last and up the stone walk to the house, the shutters tightly closed and the whole place looking the least bit sinister, but that was simply because it had been unoccupied nearly a year, or perhaps because her last visit had been to old Mr. Gilliland's funeral. Nevertheless she shivered a little as she swung the door inwards and stepped into the hall. The glare behind her made the rooms look dark and cavernous, the niggardly light filtering through the slats of the shutters adding to the feeling she had that it was all underground.

The staircase winding up in front of her led into deeper darkness, and there was a passage-way under the stairs to the back of the house, the door standing open and revealing a shadowy depth beyond that almost frightened her, although she knew it must be simply the way to the kitchen.

The hollow sound her heels made on the pine floor-boards as she advanced a step or two, bringing her opposite the parlour door, caused a little flutter in her breast. The grey marble of the fireplace, dim in the gloom, looked sepulchral, now that the big picture was gone from above it and the whole room denuded of the fine old furniture that once had made it all so dignified and comfortable.

There was a musty, rotting smell that distressed her, too, and she decided not to explore further until the shutters and windows had been opened and the place swept out. It could all be fixed up in no time, and once the sunlight and air were let in the whole character of the place would change. Apart from the location and the garden and the view, it would really just suit them. She knew how many bedrooms there were, and there were two rooms, at least, in the attic. It was really just ideal.

She went out, locked the door, and wandered down the garden, which sloped deeply over the brow of the hill to a rustic summer-house half-hidden in the trees and overgrown with creeper. Roses were in bloom and climbing nasturtiums, and along the high board fence hollyhocks in full colour. She would have pansies here, she thought, in a bed that had been scratched over by the neighbouring dogs; and there some asters, perhaps. Her mind was filled with plans as she strolled about, and finally, having reserved this deliberately to the last, she moved to the precise spot where the best view was to be obtained—she remembered it was close to a spreading rose-bush, for she had stood a long time there with Wilbur Malone at a garden party last summer, listening to him rhapsodizing about the view, comparing it with Ontario and saying it justified him in staying in the town—he, a poet, who knew Canada from end to end and loved every bit of it, but none better than the ridge on which he had been born, "a good many years ago now," he had said, thinking how close it was to half a century, "and long before people came along to build a town here and foolishly call it Zenith."

It was a clear day and the hills—for it was the "sheerest hyperbole," as Wilbur had said, to speak of them as "mountains"—lay blue in the distance, with the bush surrounding Afton dark below them, and then the lighter green of the ridge as it curves around by Keshawa, with the chimneys of the Indian school just showing—glittering, sometimes, when the sun struck them at a certain time of day—and below the ridge the bush rising up from Hark Valley—the gleaming end of Shallow Lake projecting into the clearing—and then rolling farm land, yellow now with ripening wheat, or black in summer fallow, the fences slanting down to the "flats," dotted with shacks here and there—and closer still the White Mud River—no more than a brook as it meanders through Zenith—almost completely hidden in the trees at the foot of the hill.

There was certainly no view to compare with it in Manitoba, Dora thought, watching a binder already at work in the fields this side of the valley, and feeling her bosom lift heavily with a slow-drawn breath of yearning toward the peaceful beauty of the scene.

Coming out of the garden and turning up High Street to go the other way home—through the town—she saw Mrs. Joe Banner standing at her gate, gossiping, Dora knew, with a neighbour. The neighbour went on before she could pass and Mrs. Banner, poking unruly strands of grey hair behind her ears, accosted her.

"They say you've bought the Gilliland house, Mrs. McCormick," she said, wrinkling her nose in the glare as she looked up under Dora's sunshade.

"Well, we have an option on it," admitted Mrs. McCormick, civilly, pausing in the middle of a stride.

"I'm glad to see you people get it," chirped Mrs. Banner, "for I was sayin' to Joe only last night—'I hope we don't have them Pratts down here,' I said, "alongside us, you might say."

Dora was looking beyond Mrs. Banner at the little church she had turned into a boarding house. It was screened, fortunately, from the Gilliland house, by an old grove of pines that had been planted when Dufferin Street was the drive into Procter's farm. Without the slender, arched windows the building would pass as a high-roofed one-storey cottage, with lean-to additions on one side and at the back, for the tiny bell-tower had blown down years before the Banners moved in, and there was now a decidedly domestic air about the place—chickens strutting in the garden on one side, behind rusted netting, and on the other a fine crop of potatoes as far as the fence.

Dora scarcely listened to Mrs. Banner's grudge at the Pratts, breaking in as soon as she could with a comment on the Gilliland house that was meant to end the conversation; but the old lady, leaning over the gate to hinder her passing on the narrow sidewalk, exclaimed in a confidential tone: "Joe aint been doin' much contractin' lately—his back's so bad—but when he does he never goes nowhere else for his lumber—that's honest. 'I never deals with anybody but Harry McCormick,' he says, 'when it comes to lumber. He's the whitest man in the business,' he says, 'between here and Brandon.' So we'll be mighty proud to have you livin' around the corner from us, you might say."

The afternoon had been curiously disappointing, Dora felt, as she went on, ascending High Street hill and passing the shops. It was the house, of course, looking so gloomy with the shutters closed in the middle of the day. And then she wished it were not so close to High Street. However, there was the Presbyterian parsonage on the corner, and Mrs. Banner wouldn't always be at her gate when she passed to come into the town.

Unless they were able to get a good payment on their own house it would not be so easy to finance, for it was only these last four years that the business had prospered, and there had been many debts to pay off. But Harry could manage it, somehow, she felt sure, unless something quite unforeseen happened. The children were healthy, thank goodness, and now that Freddie was getting along so well in Fawcett Parker's office it looked as though they could settle comfortably into middle age—there was no use blinking it—she had passed her fortieth birthday.

What was Audrey doing in front of the house, looking up and down the street, she wondered anxiously as she turned the corner?

And there was Harry joining her. What was *he* doing home? Something must be wrong. They were waving to her and Audrey was coming at a run. It couldn't be a fire surely. Speers was there, and surely he could have handled a little blaze if it had started. But what would start it?

"Mr. Speers!" Audrey cried to her, running up and seizing her arm and clinging to it while she recovered her breath.

"What has happened, darling?" Dora demanded, impatiently.

There were boys coming out now from the side of their house, and she noticed that there were heads out of windows on both sides of the street.

"What about Mr. Speers?"

"Oh, mother!" the girl sobbed, trying to check her tears. "Mr. Speers went out on the balcony—and the railing gave way. He fell over—and—oh, mother!"

"Has he hurt himself badly?"

"His head was all twisted underneath him—oh!—and the doctor said—his neck—his neck's broken."

"Oh, Audrey! Surely—surely not."

"Yes, mother, they've taken ——"

But by this time Harry had reached them. With agonized eyes she peered into his face. "Surely he isn't dead, Harry?"

He took her other arm and held it tightly. "Yes," he said.

"My! My, my!" Dora sighed. "But how, Harry? How could he—falling that little distance?"

"The railing gave way—he fell backwards and landed—never mind. I mean, never mind asking. But he's dead."

They went into the house and she sank, half-swooning, into a deep chair.

III

Harry looked very dismal when he came home from the funeral a few days later. "How old he looks," Dora thought as she watched him through the window coming up the walk. He was treading slowly, scratching the side of his face, a sure sign, she knew, that he was getting something into words in his mind so that he could start at the beginning of it as soon as he got into the house.

The funeral had been especially tragic. It was known already that Speers had no insurance, his savings amounted to nothing at all, and the widow, left with her four children, was living in a rented house.

Dora's finely-chiselled nostrils drew up quickly in a long, agonized breath as she listened to the woman's plight. "It's just terrible, Harry," she murmured through bent knuckles pressed tightly against her mouth.
"I'm glad you're on the council, dear," she added, a moment later, swinging her feet off the chesterfield and sitting up. "You will be able to see that they're looked after properly."

"Yes," Harry said, opening his mouth very wide and rubbing the hollow in his cheek. "Yes. That's true."

It was clear that he hadn't thought of it. "I was wondering ——" he began, absentmindedly, but got no further.

"What were you wondering, dear?"

"Well, I thought ... I was thinking coming home ... it's a deuced sad mess, you know ... I was wondering if, perhaps, we should do something. I don't know. The thing happened here—and—well, you know how you feel. She was there, you know—and the youngsters. Pretty sad, Dora. Pretty terrible."

Dora looked at him carefully, at the top of his greying head and his shoulders, for he had bent forward, bringing out his thoughts painfully, his eyes fixed on the floor.

"Do you think it would be wise?" asked Dora, sagely.

"What do you mean—wise?"

"Wouldn't it look as though we felt some responsibility for the accident—felt liable in some way. And wouldn't that, perhaps, encourage the woman to—I don't know what sort of woman she is, of course—but mightn't it suggest——?"

Harry lifted his head and looked over her shoulder through the window. "She'll have a lawyer who'll suggest that to her quick enough—if you can recover damages—I don't know whether you can—for an accident of this sort."

"Oh, it can't be possible, Harry. It isn't even as though he had been working when it happened. He had no business to be out there, if it comes to that. He was really just killing time—gazing around. It was his own time—not ours—when it happened."

"But it was on our property."

Dora folded her arms behind her and leaned back against them. "But, really, Harry, don't think I'm hard about it—I'm just trying to think of how it will look to a judge. The man really had no business to be out there. You couldn't call it trespassing, of course, but—you see what I mean—I can't see how we can be held responsible."

"Perhaps not. Although ——" He brought his heels together, and then his toes. "The railing being defective ——"

"Surely that's our business, dear." Dora suddenly sat up very straight. "Our own household knew it wasn't safe. If there had been any necessity for him to go out there we would have warned him—even Audrey would have warned him, if she'd known."

"I understand all that," Harry admitted. "But—for one thing—the door was open—wide open. Audrey says so."

"Certainly. It was a hot day, you remember. Surely we can have some ventilation."

"Oh yes."

"What amount had you in mind?" Dora asked abruptly, but he was still a long way from deciding on that. He had simply been wondering. If it had happened at another time—last year, say—they would have felt freer. He wouldn't have hesitated. But with this obligation on their home—the Gilliland property—they would be badly tied up. Dora agreed, emphatically, her thoughts reaching eagerly into the immediate future—to the occupancy of the new house. She insisted that the plight of the Speers was a matter for the council. "A thoroughly logical case for town relief," she declared. "Much more deserving than a good many who get it."

But the council, when it met a few days later, was in a mood to grant only temporary relief, for a lawyer had already advised Mrs. Speers that she could claim compensation from the McCormicks. The law was quite clear. A suit, indeed, had been entered, and the council postponed any further consideration of the case until it could come to court. The suit was for fifteen thousand dollars.

When she heard of it, Dora hardened her eyes, and refused to listen to Harry's suggestion that he should see Mrs. Speers and try to settle the thing out of court for a reasonable sum.

"My dear," she exclaimed, eyeing him coldly, "if you did you would immediately convey the impression that we feel responsible, and I must insist, dear, that we do not feel responsible. Everybody knows that we are greatly distressed—and if the action couldn't be misconstrued we would have done something—we discussed it—right after the funeral. But now— we must fight it—even if it is distasteful. We must bring a lawyer in from Winnipeg, if necessary. I don't blame the poor woman. Some lawyer has put her up to it—Gower, I suppose—it sounds just like him. Goodness! Fifteen thousand dollars! Why, it's ridiculous! It would break us."

"Very nearly," admitted Harry, ruefully.

"It would put us back five years—at the very least."

"Yes. Just about."

IV

Dora simply could not believe her ears. She came out of the court-room in a daze, gripping Harry's arm for support, but holding herself erect and looking past the faces that crowded the steps with the saddened, sympathetic expression that she had managed to maintain throughout the trial.

Ten thousand dollars! It was simply incredible. They might just as well have given judgment for the fifteen. It couldn't be paid. It would mean mortgaging everything all over again. It would be like those three years running when the crops were bad.

She looked at Harry and found she could hardly see his pale face, set in a grim expression—was it a sort of smile?—could he suddenly be cynical, after all these years?—but she could not see him clearly—there was a film over her eyes. He was looking straight ahead.

"Can you believe it, Harry?" she bent near him to whisper.

He did not flutter an eyelid, but a tiny muscle jumped in a quick tremor along his jaw.

Somebody spoke to her, but it was like a voice heard in a dream, and she moved along at Harry's side, as though floating.

Neither of them spoke again until they reached home. She had thought to ask him if it would be possible to appeal, but she could see herself it was useless. The law was perfectly clear—precedent after precedent had been read out.

She stopped in the hall, waited for him to close the door, and stood facing him, eyeing him, pouring her bitterness at him, standing there together, silent, in the house she had come to hate.

He dropped his eyes and would have moved past her into the parlour, but she put both hands to her hat, feeling for the heads of the hat-pins, and her bent elbows barred the way.

"Well—well," he spoke at last, for her whole manner demanded it. "It's no use. I haven't hoped for anything else. Foss told me weeks ago it was useless." He fidgeted with his tie and tightened it with a jerk. "There it is."

She smiled cruelly at him and brought her hands down with the hat in them, her fingers gripping the brim like talons. He went past her into the parlour and kicked a stool nearer the fireplace. "What the devil!" he said, under his breath.

She came in, swinging the hat as though it were a sharp disc that could cut things in two. Dropping into a chair she looked hard at the cuffs of his trousers.

"The option," she said, suddenly, flicking a knife-like glance across his face.

"It expired yesterday," he barked at her from a dry throat.

V

It was fall before she could bring herself to go past the place. She had been along High Street, shopping, and coming out of Blair's she looked that way, down the hill. The pine grove was just visible over the roof of the livery barn.

She thought she would walk around that way home. It was cool. She would look at the place again, now that she had given it up and put it out of her mind.

Walking briskly past the store-fronts, her purse wedged under her elbow, she sent her glance travelling ahead.

"How unlucky," she said to herself, for when she had passed the stable, there was Mrs. Banner coming towards her with her daughter, Ethel, the two of them dressed in their best things, their heads held high on their way across town to a Methodist tea.

"Well, well, Mrs. McCormick," the old lady said, as they came alongside. "Aint it funny you should come along, and me thinking about you so hard only an hour ago."

Dora gave a quick, surprised acknowledgement that Mrs. Banner was there.

"Well, come to think of it, it was more than an hour since the first load come," she heard indistinctly, for a wagon was rattling past in the ruts. "You knew, I s'pose."

What on earth was the woman talking about, Dora thought, looking at the cheap brooch aslant on Mrs. Banner's bosom.

A hand, suddenly, released from Ethel's arm, was flung back in the direction of the house around the corner. "Didn't you know it was sold?"

Dora shook her head gravely.

"You didn't!" Mrs. Banner almost shouted. "You didn't know it was— d'you mean to say, Mrs. McCormick, you don't know who bought it?"

"I haven't the faintest idea."

"Gracious, Mrs. McCormick," the woman exclaimed, her eyes swerving into their corners at her daughter, while her mouth remained open in amazement.

Dora could only look dumbly at her.

"Mrs. Speers!" The words made a hissing sound in the air between them.

"Mrs. Speers!" Dora heard herself echoing.

"An' you didn't know! Why, she's movin' in. She's settin' up in opposition to us, just around the corner. She's bought it to run as a boarding house. There you are, look. There's another van comin', now, Ethel. Why, she's cleaned out old Middleton of all the second-hand furniture he's got. Gracious! An' you didn't know."

"No," said Dora, moving forward again a step, and looking sympathetically back. "But it's hardly surprising, is it? I hope it won't affect your—your business, Mrs. Banner."

Turning the corner she saw the van drawn up at the gate. Two men were unloading beds. She couldn't bring herself to look closely until she had passed by on the opposite side. Slowly she cast an oblique glance over her shoulder, and saw immediately a wooden sign fastened under one of the shuttered windows—it had been hidden by the van before—which read: "The Gilliland House—Board and Rooms."

She dragged her glance away, thinking of the garden, the sloping hill, the distant view—thinking of the men who would soon be lodging there—men from the sash-and-door factory and the railroads—men in overalls—men!

It was still incredible. It was more incredible than ever.

Her eyes closed tightly, and she said to herself, almost aloud, drawing her lips back from her teeth: "The Gilliland House!"

Bad Order

There's men and men; an' you'll never find two
That's made o' similar stuff.

   –Song of the Rail

Things happened thick and fast up there, as they have a habit of doing when a few hundred men of the rough, tough sort get together to trail steel over new country. And this is only one of a hundred stories I could tell you of the things that occurred on the M.M.B. We were building a branch from Moose Mirror to Edmonton, through brand new country. The only town of any size we struck the whole way through was Jasper. There's a girl in Jasper—but I'll tell you about her again. She doesn't come into this story.

Railroad men as a rule dont believe in Fate; chiefly because they never think about it, I suppose. But this is a yarn of how Fate intervened in the affairs of Staggard; and Staggard, and one or two more of us, have had a sneaking sort of suspicion that there may be something to Fate, after all; since it happened.

Staggard was the General Foreman—second in command to O.W. Now O.W.—Otis Wells, the Track Engineer—was a mere youngster. He couldnt have been more than three and thirty, and he didnt look that. None of us knew where he got his pull: all we knew was that he came up from the U.P. We knew this because he couldnt talk about anything else but the U.P. He was terribly fond of his own voice, and when once he started relating his adventures down there he never knew when to stop. We forgave him for that. What we never forgave him was his habit of firing men right and left on the slightest trumped-up provocation, and wiring for men on the U.P.—old chums of his—to take their jobs. We bawled him out once, when he fired Craddock—but that doesnt come into this story either.

Staggard was scared of his job. That was the only thing that kept him straight the best part of that summer. He was a big, ugly, freckled, red-haired brute, with an unprecedented thirst, and an unrivalled vocabulary of the vilest epithets that ever a man soiled his mouth with. But he could handle men. He handled them with his tongue for the most part; and his tongue seldom failed him.

As I was saying, he kept away from the booze for the best part of that summer; and we began to think that O.W. had discovered a very subtle method of making his underlings toe the mark. Most of us resented the importation of men off the U.P., and accordingly we were extremely careful of our behaviour. O.W's system—if it was a system: we were never quite sure whether he had deliberately evolved it, or whether it was the natural outcome of his desire to have his old employees under him again—at any rate, it appealed to our pride, and it worked. For several months we behaved like a Sunday School class at a picnic.

Then Crusoe came. His real name was Robinson Cuthbert Hicks; but somebody labelled him Robinson Crusoe as soon as we heard it, and Crusoe stuck to him to the end. He was tall, straight, solid, handsome, and English to his finger-tips, which were decidedly not the tapering, effeminate sort. There was nothing womanish about Crusoe except that he brushed his hair a little too often. That was the only flaw we could find in him, at first, though goodness knows we tried hard enough to discover others. He was the latest importation from the U.P., and we hated him at first sight. Moreover, we mistook him for a prig because he kept his mouth shut. Men are just as hasty as women at jumping to conclusions, I think. At any rate we thoroughly misjudged Crusoe. Thinking back to that time I cant quite understand our attitude. Crusoe wasnt a baby, a sop, or a fop. He had knocked about the world a lot; and for hardness and coolness could have given many of us pointers. In fact, he did, as you'll see.

Fate is strictly inexplicable, providing it exists. I, for one, cannot rid myself of the idea that Crusoe was destined to play the part he did in Staggard's life from the very beginning of things. It looked, at first, as if it were going to be an adverse fate. Staggard's aversion for the Englishman developed into a sort of mania. He couldnt stand the sight of him, ignored him, kept out of his way as much as he could; but we, looking on, felt certain that some sort of crisis was developing. Crusoe was put at time-keeping at the start, although we were all certain that O.W. hadnt brought him up from the south merely for that—a paltry sixty a month. A good deal of his accent stuck to him, and when he came round twice a day, taking the men's numbers, calling them out in his British twang, I have seen Staggard turn swiftly on his heel and spit violently on the ground, as though the very sound of Crusoe's voice nauseated him.

At that time we were camped in tents two miles north of Jasper, and the whole gang were at work unloading material. The yard there was steadily growing, and by the time the new tracklaying machine was finished we had several hundred tons of steel, and a million and a half of ties piled between the tracks. Tracklaying Gang No. I. was formed as soon as the machine was ready for service. Staggard was sent out in charge, and Crusoe, promoted to sub-foreman, went along too. As soon as Staggard heard of Crusoe's appointment he was sure that the Englishman was nothing but a spotter for O.W. He told us so in very picturesque language, and he also told us of at least half a dozen things that would happen to Crusoe before Tracklaying Gang No. I. reached Siding 33.

But nothing happened—to Crusoe. Gang No. I. laid eighteen miles of track and the reports came in, and as far as we could tell everything was going smoothly. Then—they had been out about three weeks—Gill told us that Staggard was drinking. Gill was a P. & H. man. P. and H.—otherwise, Patterson and Hutt—were the boarding contractors; and Gill was their travelling commissary agent. He went to the front on the material train twice a week. Gill was a likable chap, chummy with everybody, and he told us just how things stood at the end of steel.

"There's nothing the matter with that Englishman," he said, "And Staggard's making a d----d fool of himself. He's got it into his nut that

Crusoe's a spotter, and nothing can get it out. He worries himself sick, and now he's taken to sly drinking in his car at nights. If Crusoe is a spotter it's the worst thing Staggard can do; but I dont believe he is a spotter. I cant see what you fellows have got against him."

"He's a b----- U.P. man. That's enough to put us against him," muttered Turretson, who was always unreasonable.

"That's baby talk," said Gill, who was always candid. "You're all sore on the U.P. men, and Staggard's let his soreness develop into a mania. And the mania is going to lose him his job if he isnt careful. It's nothing but flat lunacy to hate a man the way Staggard hates Crusoe."

The next time Gill came back from the Front, he had worse news for us. "I guess it's all up," said he. Staggard it seems had been drinking himself into a temper, deliberately; and when he had got himself into a sufficiently hostile frame of mind, he walked casually up to the Englishman and told him to get his C.G. from the timekeeper, and hike for a warmer climate. Crusoe turned on his heel and went on giving signals to his men, who were lining, as though Staggard didnt exist. That's the trouble with Englishmen. They're so everlastingly cool. "Did you hear what I said?" shouted Staggard, boiling mad. "Yes," answered Crusoe, without turning his head, "but I dont take orders from a drunk." And then he did turn, met Staggard's rush with a neat upper-cut, and followed up with a stunning blow which sent Staggard spinning down the dump. He called his men up then, and had them carry Staggard back to his car.

Gill had been talking to Crusoe two days after the scrap. Staggard hadnt stirred out of his car, and was drinking himself silly. Gregg had been doing his best to straighten him up; but it seemed useless; and an attack of the "snakes" was all but inevitable. "That chap's a Bad Order," Crusoe had said to Gill and Gregg. "He's due to be chalked B.O. like any ramshackle old box-car on the system. He's strictly N.G. from the company's point of view, and he's a rotten example to the men. And the sooner O.W. gets wise to him the better for all concerned."

You see, an Englishman is different. They seem to breed a sort of patriotism in the Old Country that extends even to the firms they work for. A thoroughly honest employee over there considers it his duty to peach on a fellow-employee if he is injuring the firm in any way; and he does it without a scruple. But we are not the same, over here. We never had a good word for the company. We wouldnt have cared if the company had gone broke the next day. We were boomers, and there was plenty of track to be laid those days. Our code of honour, if we had any, was to stick to a fellow to the last ditch, and then put round the hat to buy him transportation to the nearest construction camp on another road. Gill and Gregg tried to impress this on Crusoe; but you know what Englishmen are. You cant move them an inch. The only thing they could do was to impress Crusoe with the fact that if he peached on Staggard, life on the M.M.B. would be made unbearable for him.

That was the way things stood when O.W's new track-motor arrived. It was a heavy, cumbersome thing, with a roof to it, and a triangular derailing apparatus, that was no good, of course, except at a crossing. O.W. was like a kid with a new toy. He had it set up the day it arrived, and got Cohun to take him for a trial trip to Siding 29 that evening. A bunch of us were standing round the pumphouse when he came back.

"Great," cried O.W. leaping off at the switch into the main lead. He was smiling, and showing his splendid teeth a little more than usual. That was what got on your nerves. He was perpetually smiling. I never saw such an irritating optimist. Marching over to where we stood, he button-holed Hesselwood, the B. & B. Master. "What do you say to a trip to the Front tomorrow, Hesselwood? Just to try her out." And before Hesselwood could answer he was calling out to Cohun. "Have her ready for a trip to the Front at seven in the morning, Cohun."

Somebody nudged me, and two or three of us who knew how things were at the end of steel almost groaned aloud. We decided to wait up for the material train, and find out from Shorty Walker, the conductor, how Staggard was. The material train left Jasper every morning at eleven, and returning, got in at eleven-thirty at night. We waited, and Shorty Walker confirmed our worst fears. Staggard was roped in his bunk, with a Galician as strong as a horse to look after him. Shorty said he had never seen such a touch of the snakes in his life. We turned in, feeling pretty blue. Somehow or other we liked Staggard, and somehow or other we heartily disliked the Englishman. We were more than usually sore at him, because we felt that it was his fault. If he hadnt got on Staggy's nerves ... How babyish it all sounds now. Some idiot even suggested putting the new motor out of business, to delay the trip. We had sense enough to laugh at that.

O.W. was away at 7.15 next morning. We watched him cross the big bridge, and then we went over to Templeton's car. The B. & B. men were fixing it up. Templeton was to take out the first Ballast Gang in a day or two. We hadnt been talking more than twenty minutes or so—Templeton was proud of his car, and was telling us about the furniture he meant to get—when we heard the rumble of an engine going by at full speed. We knew it couldnt be the switch-engine, for she was down town on the transfer, getting a load of barrels. Templeton sprang to the window. "It's the 201," he cried, and we all made for the door. The 201 and a caboose were thundering past the main switch, hitting for town at top speed.

"That settles it," we cried in chorus, for the 201 was the tracklaying engine. Evidently they were bringing Staggard down to hospital. The pumpman came running over with a butterfly someone had dropped off the 201. Templeton unfolded it, and read aloud—"Send Hesselwood's motor to Pine Creek Bridge, and pick up O.W. and the others. We are taking Staggard and Crusoe into hospital. They didnt see us in time, and we smashed into the new car. Nobody hurt. Gregg."

"Staggard AND Crusoe," somebody jerked out. And—"Surely there hasn't been any shooting," said somebody else. We didnt think about O.W. for the time; but we cooled down after a while, and sent a man north with Hesselwood's little motor. Then we waited for news from the hospital.

Gregg came out on the switch engine in about an hour. He looked like a man that had just wakened from a nightmare. We took him over to Templeton's car, and gave him some brandy.

"John, the big Galician, woke us in the night, yelling Fire," he began, shuddering. "We scrambled up, and ran, just as we were. All except Crusoe."

We collectively cursed Crusoe. But we were wrong, as usual. It seems that he was the only one in the bunch who kept his head. He hurriedly but calmly flung on his boots and clothes, while the others ran through the cars in their shirts. Staggard was tied down in his bunk, kicking and shrieking in the midst of the flames; and they cursed the knots they had tied so securely. Their shirts caught fire while they tried to untie him, and Gregg pulled his shirt over his head and ran stark naked back, yelling for a knife. He met Crusoe, half-dressed, running between the bunks, tying a handkerchief over his mouth as he ran. He was unclasping a big knife when he dashed into the smoke and flames that were rolling out of the end door. The others snatched clothes from the nearest bunks, jumped down the steps and hurtled round to the further end of the burning car where Staggard lay. Just as they got there the door, all ablaze, fell outward, and Crusoe backed out, dragging Staggard along the floor, almost naked save for flaming ribbons of his nightshirt which still clung to his scorching flesh. Crusoe's shirt, the handkerchief about his mouth, and his hair were all afire. When he had got Staggard out on the end platform, he fell against the brake-wheel, spun round, pitched headlong off the steps, and rolled insensible down the dump. His shirt and the handkerchief were still blazing when they picked him up.

O.W. never knew just what happened. Gregg fixed him with some semi-probable story; and Staggard came back, having vowed a vow that he would never touch liquor again. He kept it too, as long as we knew him.

There was a peculiar scene the first day he walked out to the camp. Crusoe, who had been out of hospital about a week, kept his mouth shut as tight as ever; and when the two met, Staggard went up to him, and offered his hand. He didnt say anything. He couldn't. "I have no particular reason for shaking hands with you," said Crusoe, coldly, and walked away.

Now, who could make a hero of a man like that? We couldn't. We let him alone. And we began to think that the fellow who christened him Crusoe must have been inspired; for he seemed to live on an island of his own—silent, isolated, apart from us all. Of course, all Englishmen arent like that. Take Packer for instance—but that's another story.

Mrs. Hungerford's Milk

Joe Snell drove his dray into the yard and unhitched the team. The yard was muddy and the hooves of the horses made a sucking sound as they plodded side by side into the stable. Joe followed them in and dipped some oats out of the bin with a rusty basin. After a long day in the sun, the darkness of the stable and the cool smell of wet straw and manure were like a soothing hand passed down over the back of his head. He slapped the shining rump of the roan mare as he went beside her with the oats. On the way home he had tried to cool his parched throat with two glasses of beer. His throat was still dry, but his head was better. He felt like whistling. His head swung lightly on his shoulders as he bent to come out of the stable door.

It was near sundown. The house made a great patch of shadow which fell across the slanting roof of the cow-shed. Long, spindly shadows from the haphazard rails of the fence lay across the straw and mire.

It was nice in the yard with the sun going down and a bit of breeze springing up. The twisted, scrub oaks along by the fence were beginning to sway with it. He took off his hat with a sort of swoop and pitched it, like a quoit, aiming for the stoop outside the kitchen door, but it fell just short and rolled in a puddle. "To hell with it," he said.

It looked good around the yard. Some folks would be all for painting the house; but he liked the grey, old blistered sheathing. He liked the marks of weather over everything, the stains of wear and time, the bleached boards, the sinking steps. It was all right. Ramshackle, his brother called it. But that was just him. He was a baker in the East end. He was a fusser, his brother was. He'd even got the women up on their ear about things. Said he ought to get a truck and keep up to date. But, what the hell, his brother was spending every nickle he made—keeping up to date!

He went to the rain-water barrel and dipped himself a basin of water. With one swoop of the basin he skimmed the dead insects aside and plunged it down deep, bringing it up quickly to keep the dead flies out of it. There was a bench by the kitchen window. While he was bending down washing he could hear Hettie clattering with pans around the stove. When she was quiet he could hear Myrtle humming upstairs.

He dried himself and picked up his hat from the puddle and brushed the mud off it on the bench. He was a heavy, solid man, nearing fifty. He had put on weight these last eight years or so. His huge middle bulged out of his trousers. His jowls and neck had thickened. The strain of dragging heavy loads on and off his dray for years had driven a crooked wrinkle down between his brows, like a cleft in the trunk of an old tree. His flattened upper lip was drawn tightly across his teeth in a fixed expression, like a clown's smile, forced and permanent.

He went through the woodshed and poked his head into the kitchen, resting his enormous, rough hands on the doorposts. Hettie was at the stove, stirring potatoes in a fry-pan with a long iron fork.

"Hullo, old woman," he said. She was nearly ten years younger than himself, and he liked to tease her. She had kept a young woman's figure in spite of hard work and three babies, two of which they had lost. She managed to look smart with very few clothes because she was always making over her dresses, and was now able to pass them on to Myrtle, who had turned eighteen.

She turned from the stove and sighed when she saw his strained, worn face. "Pretty tired—eh?" she said.

"Yup," said Joe. "I been on that blasted job of Rutter's all afternoon, since the 2:40 train. Took me three trips."

"I thought you figured two," said Hettie. "I thought you said last week it would be a five-dollar job."

Joe stepped to a broken bit of mirror by the window and began combing his matted hair. "That's what I figured. He asked me for an estimate—and that's what I told him. It's only a couple of blocks to where he's moved to, and he didn't look to have much stuff there in them little offices. But that's just him. He'd got more stuff squeezed into that bit of a shack than most guys would have on a couple o' floors. He's a squeezer—that's what he is."

"A squeezer!" said Hettie laughing. "That's good, Joe."

"They weren't ready—either," Joe grumbled. "That girl he's got—Cassie Williams—a proper fusser she is. Fussing with this and frigging with that—"

"She's not such—"

"Well, anyway," said Joe, raising his voice and beating the air with the comb, "*anyway*—I'll bet it took me a solid hour putting on that last load, with *her* chasing in and out with dribs and drabs of stuff. And when it was all on he came out himself, the little runt, and pulled a five spot out of his pocket. Had it folded up in his vest pocket all ready. You're durn right—*he* knew it was a bargain. 'It's taken longer than I figured,' I says, 'it ain't like stuff you can just throw on. And, anyway, it's made three loads, so that'll be seven and a half,' I says."

"Did he come through?"

Joe put the comb down with a whack. "No! *That* guy!" He picked up the comb again and gave it another whack on the shelf. "No *chance*! Said I'd asked him five bucks and five bucks was all I'd get. Looking at me all the time like I was trying to rook him."

"He's a tightwad," Hettie said. "Always was."

Joe squatted his thick body in a chair. "Yup!" he said, with a loose, downward fling of his hand. He had got it off his mind. It didn't matter. He moistened his lips with a loud smack. "Yup!" he said again, with a wry smile. He sat staring at the floor boards, tapping one foot to a tune that was running in his head. He had forgotten what he was waiting for.

Hettie stood with her back to the stove, looking at him. "You'd better quit giving estimates, Joe," she said, in a tone you use to a child. "Tell 'em it's by the hour. That's the only way you'll ever make anything."

A smell of burning recalled her to the stove. Joe stood up and shook himself like a dog coming out of water. "How's the supper?" he said, striding about and flapping his heavy arms.

"Here it is," said Hettie. She was loading up a large plate from two or three pans she had been warming. "We've had ours. It got pretty late—and Myrtle's going to that dance."

Joe stood waiting. His eyes, still gritty from the dust that had been blowing all afternoon, roved about the kitchen. The cleft in his brow suddenly shifted in a crooked, angry line over one eye which had opened wider than the other in a furious stare.

"What's this here?" he said, pointing at a covered milk-pail on the table by the window. "That ain't Mrs. Hungerford's milk—is it?"

Hettie had the plate in her hands, facing him, ready to go into the front room where the table was set. "It'll be going over in a minute or two," she said quietly.

"Why ain't it delivered?" Joe demanded. He suddenly felt very angry and strong. The weariness of the long day's work seemed to have left him. Throbbing anger and strength surged through him.

Hettie looked at him in surprise, but kept her voice even. "We was kind of late with the milking," she said, "and Myrtle's been getting ready for the dance."

"But it ain't even dark yet," said Joe.

"It's quite a drive out there," Hettie said. "Must be all of twenty-two miles out to Ormrod's—and after that rain there'll be—"

Joe spread his legs widely apart and stared at her. "Yeah, but it don't take her all night to get dressed, does it?"

Hettie held out the plate so that the steam would float under his nose. "Come on in and get started, Joe," she said. "This'll all be cold."

He flapped his arms angrily against his sides. "She's getting too high and mighty—is she?—to run over there of a night?"

"No, no," Hettie said quickly. "Don't start that again, Joe. We had to fix up her dress a bit. The poor kid hasn't a thing to wear. She hates going anywhere in the things she's got."

"Sure!" Joe shouted. "That's what I'm a-saying. She's getting too durn high and mighty—chasing around with that Lambert fellow."

"She just wants to look nice—that's all."

"Well, she won't look nice if she don't deliver that milk at the right time—I'm tellin' you. If she can't do a little job like that—"

"You don't need to worry about it," said Hettie. "It'll go over any minute. The paper boy takes it, once in a while, on a Saturday. He goes right to the house to collect on Saturdays"

"That's not good enough!" growled Joe. He started across the floor toward the stairs which went up in the wall just inside the parlour door.

"Here!" cried Hettie, running after him and putting the plate down as she passed the table. "Don't say nothin' to her. Don't spoil her evenin' for her."

Joe swung around and glared into her anxious eyes. His head was throbbing. The deep cleft in his brow was twisted in an ugly knot over one eyebrow. "I'm goin' to spoil somebody's evenin' if that milk ain't delivered this minute," he bellowed at her.

"They ain't wantin' it," she said, her chin quivering.

"Who gives a hoot whether they're wantin' it or not. That's their business. It's our business to get it over there right smart after milkin'. He turned away from her and walked over to the bottom of the stairs. "Ho! Myrtle!" he called out.

"Yes, dad," cried a young voice from the room above.

"Don't say nothin' to her, Joe," said Hettie, plucking at his shirtsleeves. "You'll get her bawlin' and get her eyes all red and spoil her evenin'. I'll take it over myself, if the boy don't come right away. I'll take it myself, as soon as I've got your supper."

His big, watery eyes were pale with anger as he listened to her. His anger made him feel strong—invincible! His voice, coming out of his great chest, roared in his ears like a torrent. "I ain't goin' to have them Hungerfords kept waitin' for their milk," he shouted. "You talk to me about runnin' my business, but where would I be if Dave Hungerford quit gettin' me to do his haulin' for him. He's a durn good customer o' mine, ain't he? And if we're late night after night with the milk, maybe—"

"But we're not late *night after night*."

Joe thrust a square, horny nail under her nose. "A good many nights lately it's been. I told her off only last—last Wednesday, was it?" He turned to the stairs again. "Myrtle!" he shouted. "Come down here. Come on down here!"

"Leave her alone, Joe," said Hettie, getting in front of him and taking hold of his elbows.

He paid no attention to her. He was listening for Myrtle's step on the stairs. He was going to get the two of them together and tell them off. They acted like he was a back number lately. When his brother came around they always sided with him. "Just trying to buck you up a bit, Joe," his brother said. Well, all right, he'd buck up for once and tell them where they got off at.

Myrtle was coming down. He heard her heels, the same as a woman's, on the stairs. She and Hettie were like a couple of sisters, doing everything together, and siding with each other all the time. They'd left him alone a lot lately. "They act like I was just a lodger around the place," he said to himself. He thought of the many nights this summer when he had come home tired and gone to bed early, hardly saying a word to them. They were always working at something or other, and there didn't seem to be anything to talk about, so he'd go to bed. They'd got now so they just went ahead and did things and left him alone.

He wasn't young anymore, and he got tired easier, but he still had a lot of strength. He felt his strength in his head for once, somehow. His head was throbbing with noise. It was full of heavy words that he could throw at them like stones. The words were rattling about in his head and he felt the weight and strength of them and their hard, sharp edges.

Myrtle reached the bottom of the stairs, looked at him, and stood still. She was flushed and panting. She had on the dress they had been fixing up, and Joe hardly knew her. They'd done her hair up different. He had heard them talking about what she ought to do with her hair. She had lost all the little girl look.

The sight of her shook him. He caught his breath and looked around quickly at Hettie. Her eyes were suddenly alight with love and admiration, and he suddenly saw that they *were* alike, after all. When Hettie's eyes sparkled like that she *did* look like Myrtle. Everybody said she did, but he hadn't been able to see it. Myrtle looked older and she looked younger.

They stood there, waiting for him to speak, but the words like boulders in his head seemed to be rumbling away out of hearing. He felt his strength slipping away.

"You look mighty cute, Myrtle," he said. "Don't she, Hettie?"

"Yes, it's a cute dress," Hettie said. "It's that old grey one of mine—dyed and fixed up."

"Mighty cute," said Joe. He leaned against the wall and kicked his heels back lightly against the wainscotting.

"Better eat your supper, Joe," said Hettie. "It'll be cold."

The mention of the supper brought the throbbing back. "Listen, Myrtle," he said, quickly, before the noise in his head should subside again. "I was just talking to your mother about Hungerford's milk."

"I heard you, dad."

"Well, all right. I don't want any monkey business about it. I don't say much around here any more—but I'm not going to lose a good customer. It's bad enough—these times. You and your mother got the notion I'm a back number, just because things—"

"Now, Joe," said Hettie, "you're just—"

"Listen to me for once, will you," bellowed Joe. He wanted to get back the strength he had felt a few minutes before. He had felt able to hurt them, then, and he wanted to hurt them. He wanted to fill the house again when he came home, the way he used to, instead of sort of sneaking off to bed to be out of their way. He tried to take hold of himself inside, the way he would take hold of a heavy trunk and up-end it. He wanted that feeling of weight in his hands—to threaten them with its fall. But it wouldn't come. Between the two of them they had softened him—what with the dress, and the hair done different, and the way they looked at each other, and their soft voices.

The noise in his head was gone, but he could make it in his lungs and throat. It would be a shout without strength in it, but he wasn't going to sit down and eat his supper and let them go ahead fixing things to suit themselves.

"Listen to me," he roared. "You think I'm getting to be a stick-in-the-mud, don't you? Eh?"

"No, we don't, dad," said Myrtle, softly.

"You're going to spoil her evening, Joe," pleaded Hettie.

"To hell with her evening. What about *my* evening? What about *me*? Ain't I got nothing coming to me after a hard day's work? What do I get out of it? You ain't got nothing to say to me any more—neither of you—you're all wrapped up in your own doings. You can't even run over with Hungerford's milk. A little job like that! You talk about *me* letting things go to rack and ruin, but—"

"We don't, Joe," said Hettie, her eyes burning into his. "We just—"

Joe raised his arm and flung it downward with enormous force. "This is *my* say! You keep still. I'm sick of this kind of life. This is no life for a man. I won't stand for it—do you hear? I'm going to change it. I'm going to have a wife and daughter that has some respect for the old man—or—or—I'll walk out on you. I'll—I'll—"

But he couldn't go on. It was just shouting. It didn't come from any feeling of power inside him. The words poured out of his lungs from nowhere. He wasn't making them up. Nobody was making them up. They just came out of his throat and he let them go. But his throat was dry now. His eyes were smarting. So that they shouldn't see the tears in his eyes he went to the table and scowled down at the plate of food Hettie had put at his usual place. There was a dull ache at the back of his head. He flapped his arms once; violently, to let them know that he was through, and sat down to his supper.

A Glass Of Catawba

The idea came to him the last thing one night as he stood looking out of the window just before going to bed. Vangie was sitting there reading as usual. Eternally reading. In the same chair, squeezed in between the piano and the hallway arch. Saying nothing for hours on end. Just quietly turning the leaves. Her large, shortsighted eyes perceptibly moving from left to right and from right to left across the page. There. Slowly to the right. Quickly to the left. Right. Left. Right. Left. Jove!

He went to the window.

Every night when they were home together like this he would go to the window and look out, just before he said—"Well, Vangie, what do you think?"

It seemed to finish the evening, always a little sadly, but it finished it. Why it should make him a little melancholy to part the curtains and look out on the deserted street, he didn't quite know. It wasn't deserted tonight. There were people trudging through the snow, half-turned against the wind. A street-car had just stopped at the corner. He had heard the wheels scrape a minute ago as it came round the bend.

He watched them out of sight. Perhaps a dozen people. Most of them carrying parcels. Not many days to Christmas now. The Ramsays were coming over. That would help. Bernard always helped. He always seemed to make his visits an occasion. You remembered that he had been there. You looked back on it and recalled things he had said.

But somehow Christmas was never quite Christmas out here. He had been here twelve years now, and yet Canada was still somehow foreign. He liked it. He wouldn't want to go back. Not the way things were. But there was still something foreign about it.

Couldn't they do something this Christmas that would make it more like home. Not like home in the sense ... not like his old home. Hmmmmm! What a difference! Pillars, parlours, horses, maids, gardeners, grounds—all that. And here—hmmmmm—a basement suite. A basement suite. With the pipes showing.

No, not like that. Not to recapture here anything of England. No. Quite the reverse. Something that would help to wipe out England and his memories. Something that would make this feel like home. Make him satisfied with it, and stop this fool hankering.

What was there to hanker for, anyway? Two fortunes frittered away. Not such a lot, but still, for most people—fortunes! Gone! If he'd kept out of that Edmonton real estate deal. If he hadn't bought that fool business. Well, it would have gone somehow. No use kidding himself. He couldn't hang on to money. He was like his father. That great house—a castle—Murray's folly—yes, they had rightly named it—sold up, sold up when he was a boy. And his uncle, too. Look what was left of that mess. A few thousands each. True. But nothing compared with ...

A girl with her back to the wind, loaded with parcels, down there. Snow's getting deeper. Two inches more today. At least. Yes. Christmas.

Well, what about it? A chicken. Just imagine turkeys fifty-five cents a pound! A chicken. Some muscatels and almonds. A glass of port.

Eh? A glass of port! That would help.

No. A dollar and a half for a prescription. The port itself wouldn't cost more than that. Three dollars for a bottle of wine! Ridiculous! And he'd only spent two and a half on Vangie. Another book. Always books. "Honestly, Rod, there's nothing gives me more pleasure." But what about the library? Can't you get ... "But it's nice to own a few, Rod. They feel better in your hand. You know. You can cuddle them."

Hmmmm. Another book. Maurice Hewlett. That's her latest crush. The Forest Lovers. Two and a half.

And then three dollars for a bottle of wine! But it would make a nice touch after the dinner. "Bernard, old chap, will you have a glass of port?" Yes, it would help. It would make a bit of an occasion. Bernard would open his eyes a little. He would feel flattered, somehow. He was always feeling flattered. Things happened every day that flattered him. And no wonder. There is something about him. A damned clever chap. And yet loyal. No difference now from the way he was out in Souris. And yet, since he came to Winnipeg, look how he's gone ahead.

Nice to sit down with Bernard over a glass of wine and hear him tell about things at The Herald. Critical, of course; but not cynical. Now they'd made him music critic ... well, it was natural he should feel a cut above the other reporters. But never cynical. Outspoken, yes. Courage of his convictions. Fine chap.

Three dollars. Well, of course, he could manage it. But was it right? There were so many things, and after all ... a few minute's enjoyment! Besides, no glasses. You couldn't serve it ...

No.

There's Logan going home. Jove, it's coming down.

"Well, Vangie, what do you think?"

"I'm ready, dear. I can finish this chapter in bed."

"Gee, your eyes look bad."

"They're allright. Ready?"

"I guess so."

* * *

At the bank next morning he approached Wallis. Yes, Wallis would be the chap. At the bank, after all, he had a certain standing, a certain background. They knew he had been manager for the Ottawa in Souris before he bought that fool business and lost his seniority. And though he was only on the temporary staff at the Commerce they treated him somehow ... well, they knew ... he had let out a little ...

"At Flores, in the Azores, Sir Richard Grenville lay, and a pinnace like a fluutered bird ..."

He would quote it lightly, attitudinizing. But somehow he would get it in that the Murrays and the Grenvilles were all mixed up ... at the time of the Armada.

And of course it got around. About his father, too, Murray's Folly, and all that sort of thing. Oh, they knew. And, of course, they didn't know about the basement suite. And the pipes. Wallis certainly didn't. Wallis would be the chap. "I say, Wallis, how does a chap go about getting something to drink for Christmas, eh? I mean wine. What about native wine? Do you have to have a prescription for native wine, old dear?"

Didn't the chap ever smile? That's so? Port. Yes, port, that's what he wanted. You'd have to have one, eh? Hmmmm. Yes, ridiculous. A good graft for the doctors. Yes, thanks Wallis.

A dollar and a half, then, for that. He could stand it. He would stand it. And the glasses? Well, it seemed ridiculous to buy glasses just for one occasion. Couldn't he laugh off the glasses? Do you suppose Bernard would notice the tumblers? Rose certainly would. And anyway the whole enjoyment would be in doing it right, doing it lightly. "Will you have a glass of port, old chap." Just like that, rather carelessly, as though it didn't matter. What do they cost—glasses?

★　★　★

He had never liked the doctor. What didn't they have somebody else? Well, Vangie ... Of course, that kind of chap always makes a hit with the women.

"Ah, Mr. Murray. And what's the trouble today?"

No, old man, I'm not a woman. You can take your damned smile off. There it goes. The crowsfeet smoothing out around his eyes. The nose-pincher and the black silk cord going up. How do you ask for a prescription, anyway?

"You do look a bit seedy. Take a chair. Overworking?"

Seedy be damned. Seedy! Prescription. Christmas. Will you have a glass of port, old chap?

"I was wondering. Not just up to the mark, you know. And Christmas coming. Thought I'd like a little port. Can you ...? No, no. Just a bottle. A quart, I suppose, eh?"

What's he talking about? A half case. Ah yes, costs no more for a script for a quantity. Does he think I'm an infant. What, held down to thirty a month now? Thirty a month. Ridiculous. A bottle's plenty. Just a mouthful after dinner. Christmas comes but once a year, eh? Rarely touch it.

Well, he's going to have it.

"Yes. R.G. Murray, doctor."

And if Vangie says anything. But she won't. She's a good sport. What? Two dollars? "I thought it was ..."

"Two dollars, now we're cut down to thirty a month. Sorry. I'd like to give it you with my compliments, but you've no idea of the demand. Really. Oh yes. Yes, I ... Thanks ... Oh yes. Well, Merry Christmas."

Two dollars! Where's that hat? Oh yes. Merry Christmas. Two dollars. Ridiculous! Robbery!

★   ★   ★

Do a great business, these little drugstores. Bright looking shop for away out at this end of town. Rance is pretty keen. How do. Waiting for Mr. Rance thanks. Guess the booze is all behind there. What brands of port are there, anyway?

It wasn't brands in the old days. It was years. Somebody talking to his father: "What is this, General?" "This is some of the rare old '72. S'been all the way to India and back."

General Murray. Moustaches going grey, even then. And his shoulder blades. He could always remember his shoulder blades. Well, a glass of port, dad. Just for old time's ... No, damn it. To blot all that out. Blot it out. What's the use? It'll never be like that. Not within miles. Just the bank. Perhaps a manager's job again one of these days. Away out on the prairies. Farmers talking about crops, crops, crops, crops, crops. Vangie in the choir and the Ladies' Aid. And the kids. What'll Vincent do? Some funny little lawyer's office, perhaps. And Marjorie? And perhaps there'll be more. You can't tell. But back there ... the rhododendrons, the pond, people touching their hats, the vicar ... yes, the red cushions and red hassocks in the old pew ... and that girl ... what was her name? ... no, that was later ... that was Lord Axford's daughter ... no, this one was a Miss ... Hmmmm ... Gwen ... Gwen, that was it. Jove! Eh? That day his mother came back from Exeter and caught up to them in the lane and took them into the carriage with her and asked them about the berries over at Lovell's ... mother ... how long, now? ... twenty three, twenty four ... yes, twenty four years ... eh?

"Oh yes. Hello, Rance. Port. Have you got any port? Just a mouthful you know, at Christmas time, eh? Oh, I don't know. What's good? Eh? Yes. Is that allright? Well, honestly, I don't know a thing about this stuff out ... That's good, is it? Ymmmm. How much is that? Is it? Well, I don't know. I thought ... Yes, about that. A dollar seventy five, eh? Catawba? It's allright, is it?"

Two dollars. A dollar seventy five. It's the freight, I guess. Three seventy five.

"Yes, it looks allright. Allright. Fine. Yes. You know. Little wine, women and song. Fine. Allright. Thanks. Goodnight, old man."

Well, he has it, against his ribs. Vangie, old dear, here it is. It is an extravagance. Absolutely. I know. But this is different. This is just once. In the old days ... No. These are the days. We'll have a glass of wine. A glass of Catawba. We'll do things right. We're here and we're going to stay here. It's a great country. Look at young Vin. Look at the opportunities. Look at Bernard. Great country this, Bernard. Bernard, old chap, will you have a glass of Catawba?

★ ★ ★

No, the glasses shouldn't be expensive. Four of them. That's enough. Probably Vangie won't take any. She might. But Rose won't. Still, he ought to have four. You know. You can't tell. What would they charge you at Ivey's, do you suppose? Of course, you pay for the name on the wrapping. But it would be fine to get them at Ivey's. There's something about buying a thing there. Even the cheapest they have. What would they be? Fifty cents apiece? Two dollars. Six dollars before he's through.

Dash it, they certainly get their windows up in great style, eh? Look at that floor walker. That's right, that's where I've seen him. St. Stephens. Must be a warden there. Always thought the fellow ...

"Glasses. Wine glasses. Thanks."

Wine glasses. By Jove, this is going to be a real Christmas. I believe Vangie will like this idea. You know. After all, she's full of luxurious notions. Reads those books all the time. Bound to. And Bernard. You'll see. Flattered. Oh yes, I think ...

"Wine glasses."

Nice looking girl. Yes, look at those now. Beautiful stems. That brings back the ...

"No. Just wanted four. Thirty a dozen? Thirty dollars a dozen? Hmmmm. Well, I thought ... Twenty? That would be ... each? Ymmmm. Well, that's more than I ... Nothing at all? Well, I thought about a dollar apiece, you know. Ymmmm. Well, thanks. No, I guess not. Thanks."

Ivey, The Jeweller. Jove!

Of course, there's Rutherfords down there on Main Street. Pretty cheap place. But why won't the tumblers do. Couldn't he laugh off the tumblers? He'd better. Six or eight dollars for glasses. Ridiculous.

But his feet move. People pass. Corner of Portage and Main. Traffic cop. Cars. Crowds. Past the bank. City hall. Fifty cents apiece. Not a cent more. Two dollars. Five seventy five. That's the limit. Enough, too, for one drink of wine. "I say, old chap, will you have a glass of Catawba." Well, he had the damned Catawba, anyway.

Rutherford's Credit Jewellery. Credit, eh? Not worth it. Fifty cents apiece. Or the tumblers. He goes in. Girl all made up. Scratchy voice. Wine glasses. About what price? About fifty cents, or have they anything cheaper. He has to be cheap. Who's going to know, anyway? Seven fifty a dozen?

Nothing lower than that. Too much money. Why hadn't he gone to Eatons?

He stands thinking. Girl scratching her head with a pencil. A thoroughly scratchy person. Well, allright. Clink, clink, clink, clink. Four of them. Box. Paper. String. Check. Scratchy looking writing. Thanks. Two fifty. Jove! Six and a quarter. Six dollars for a drink of wine after dinner. Ridiculous!

Out. People. Parcels. Christmas. Oh well. Once. Just once. "Not bad stuff, Bernard, is it?"

⋆   ⋆   ⋆

"Can't we open the old country parcel, daddy?"

"This is only Christmas Eve, my boy."

"But we'll have so much to open tomorrow. Can't we have something to play with today?"

No, no. Ridiculous. What? Now, Vangie. Keep 'em quiet? I'll keep 'em quiet, I'll keep 'em quiet, I'll keep 'em quiet!

Round the table. Into the living room. I'll keep 'em quiet. Now, now. No cushions. Here, where's the girl's ribs? Goodness, mother, the girl has no ribs. Eh? No ribs. The ribless wonder! Walk up, ladies and ... What, *you're* asking for it? *You're* asking for it, eh? *You've* got ribs, have you. Bang! Too bad, Vin. Now! Be a man, Vin. Vin! Hit his head on the stool, dear. There, there, that's allright. Now, Vin. I'll tell you, we'll open Aunt May's parcel, eh? Look at that. The boy's not hurt. Bump? What bump? Where is it? That's your supper, man. Ha, ha, ha, ha! That's that great big potato. Ha, ha, ha, ha! Allright. Where is it, Vangie?

Paper crackling. String snapping. Vin's turn to have the stamp. Now. Stand back, ladies and gentlemen. Jove! Another doll, Marge. Guess we'll have to send it back. Too many, now. What? Allright. What'll you call it? What's this? An aeroplane, Vin. Look, it *goes*. You wind up this elastic band. Careful. Come in here. See. Wheeeeew! Eh? Isn't that great? Careful, now. Don't grab at it, Vin. Let it come down. Look out, look out, LOOK OUT!

Crash ! Jove! I knew he'd do it. Quick! A bowl or something. Dear, dear, dear! It's the wine. Knocked it off the buffet. Well, thank God it was only the neck. You're a bad boy, Vin. Half of it, anyway. Jove! Huhhhhh! Well! What'll we put it in? Diddddd, diddddd, diddddd!

* * *

Picken's Auction Rooms.

Junk. Dust. Musty books. China. Glass.

"A decanter. Have you got a small decanter?"

Dash that boy, anyway. Can't serve it in a medicine bottle. All the way downtown again for this darned thing. Haven't got one? What? You sure, now?

Voice from the back. With what stuff? Oh, over here. Sure. There you are, you see. These fellows! How much?

Voice from the back. A dollar, he says. No, you can bargain with these fellows. No, I'll give you seventy-five cents for it. No.

Voice from the back. Says to give it you. It's dirt cheap. Seventy-five cents from a dollar. Quarter. Thanks.

Six and a quarter and seventy-five. Seven. Seven dollars for half a bottle of wine. Still, this will be better. Better still. Polish it up. Little tray—decanter— four glasses. Paper caps. Pass the nuts. Rise. Go to buffet. Lift tray. "What do you say to a glass of wine?"

* * *

"Well, it certainly was a lovely pudding, Vangie."

Nice girl, Rose. That cap suits her. Bernard ought to take his off. There, now. There's telepathy for you. Much better without it. What, the nuts? Rose, how about you? Stop that, Vin. Stop it. Vangie looking at him. Half smile. Half glance at the buffet. This is the time. Right now. This is what he's been waiting for. Tray. Decanter. Four glasses. I say, old chap ...

Vin's music lessons. No, doesn't know Miss Cooper. Who doesn't? Oh, of course, Bernard. No, he wouldn't. Leonard Crane. Chopin. Nobody in town ... tone ... town ... tone ... Leonard ... marvellous technique ... technique ... town ... tone ... push the chair back ... rise ... tray ... I say, old chap ...

"Sorry, Bernard, thought you had some. Pass the crackers, Vin."

He doesn't want nuts. He wants to talk about Leonard Crane ... studio the other day ... no, never been inside his studio ... suppose so ... Steinway ... Chopin ... little thing of Ravel's ... Raveldebussycyrilscottplayedherelastyear ... listen ... never mind ... he'll stop in a moment ... there's plenty of time ... bestcriticsscottmoderncriticsdiscords ... ymmmmm ... yes, beautiful.

Now. Actually. The moment. The exact pause. If he can keep Vangie from breaking in. Chair back. What's the matter with his throat? Tray. Everything allright. Faces looking up. Smiles. Vim's grin. Say it, man. Just a moment more. That's it, lift the tray. What the devil! Trembling! Say it. Yes, by Jove, it was worth it, it was worth it.

"Bernard, old chap, will you have a glass of Catawba?"

Head Waitress

E very now and again you see a man or a woman (with me it is more often a woman), who somehow strikes you. The man may not look particularly distinguished, perhaps not even very intelligent, and the woman may not be exactly beautiful—but they have a quality that makes them interesting, and for no reason at all you start wondering about them. Of a woman, perhaps, you say to yourself, "I'd like to know where that girl came from and what has happened to her to make her *like that*."

There was a head waitress in a restaurant in Toronto who made me feel that way. She may be there yet for all I know. Of course she *was* a striking looking girl. She had a body that was simply magnificent. But that wasn't it. That alone wouldn't make you wonder where a girl came from and what her history had been. This girl looked a little foreign and she was very austere. She wore a manner like armour. I was going to say "invisible armour," but it wasn't invisible. You just know at a glance that a woman of that sort knows how to handle men. And *she* did.

Anyway, she started me wondering. I made up my mind to find out about her. And what follows is her story. To my sorrow I don't come into it. It is just the story of how she came to be the way she is.

Her name was Katrin Petursson (pronounced Pee-ay-toor-soon) which is Icelandic. She was twenty eight years old. Her youth had been spent on the rough, rocky land in the neighbourhood of Lake Rosseau where the Icelanders had built a scattered settlement, naming it Hekla after their famous volcano. Her father had been the village schoolteacher, whose wife, dying in childbirth, had left him with Katrin, a baby of three, her sister Asta who was two years older, and a brother Arni who was then eleven.

It was a strange childhood for the Petursson children, growing up in a house where an already ageing man was both father and mother, and who, when they went to school, often walked with them to the door and then left them to mount the platform and become their teacher. He was a lanky, thoughtful man, a great lover of Iceland, and at nights in the little cabin, when the curtains had been drawn across the bunks where the children slept, they would peep out and watch him bending close to the lamp, writing very slowly, or sitting back with the end of the pen in his teeth, staring into space. He was translating the *Heimskringla*, the Icelandic "Book of Kings," into English. The scratching of his pen was the only lullaby Katrin could remember.

Her brother Arni went to the war when Katrin was ten years old and never came back. About two years later her father was drowned under circumstances which gave rise to talk of murder or suicide. When he failed to return one night from a trip to Port Carling a search party went out and at dawn his rowboat was found capsized and adrift in the lake. There were no signs of struggle, his body was never found, and his death remained a mystery.

The two girls went to live with Aunt Hulda, their mother's sister, who late in life had married Captain Jon Tomasson, one of the head men of the village. He held a master mariner's certificate and was away all summer on a freight boat; but in winter he sat around the stove drinking enormous quantities of beer and "mola kaffi," chewing snuff, and telling outlandish stories which Asta and Katrin thought were much better than the ones they read in their few books.

Aunt Hulda was delicate and the Petursson girls, who had been used to looking after themselves at home, ran the house. Asta had left school and did dressmaking for several of the women in the settlement. When Aunt Hulda died, just at the time when Katrin was finishing school, Asta became mistress of the little household. She was eighteen, fair-haired, mature in build, and possessed a flashing smile which made her the talk of the village. Katrin was taller, bigger, and at an awkward age. She watched and worshipped Asta, copying everything her older sister did and aching for the time when she would be as old, and able to put her hair up and go to dances.

All this time the Petursson girls had been befriended in many ways by Gudmund Eggertson, the Lutheran minister, who had greatly admired their father and was carrying on the unfinished translation of the *Heimskringla* which he had left. Pastor Eggertson had little respect for Captain Tomasson and felt that the atmosphere of the house in the long winters when the old man sat around the stove entertaining his cronies, was not good for the girls. The pastor knew something of Captain Jon's youthful reputation, and when Asta blossomed suddenly into womanhood, he grew more and more anxious that the girls should go to Toronto where he had a cousin who would keep a motherly eye on them and help them find congenial work. He whispered what he feared to his wife and was not reassured when she told him, after a talk with Asta, that the girl not only knew the facts of life but was aware of the danger and had even repulsed the captain two or three times when he had shown signs of drunken amorousness.

"There's nothing to worry about," his wife had said. "Asta is a strong, capable girl with plenty of character, and she's old enough to take care of herself. She wasn't a bit confused when I talked to her—said it only happens when the captain drinks a little more than usual, and he's quite easy to handle—"

"But, my dear!" exclaimed the minister.

"I know—I know what you're going to say," answered Mrs. Eggertson. "It's not a nice atmosphere for the girls. I told Asta that, and she admits it, in a way; but she says—and I must say it is the Christian attitude, after all—that the captain is really a good old soul when he's sober, and that if the girls left him he'd probably be drunk all the time and have no one to look after him."

Katrin knew nothing about these anxieties until later, but one night while Asta was at a barn dance in the adjoining village and was not expected home until the small hours, the captain got rid of his cronies a little earlier than usual and went to bed. Katrin was wakened by the hearty farewells and by the freezing air which swept past her door while the men stood on the verandah slapping each other's backs. She was surprised to hear her uncle

go to bed without "banking down" the stove as usual. She called to him and
he reeled into her room.

"Aren't you going to fix the stove for the night, uncle?" she said, sitting
up in the bed in the dark.

He dropped heavily on the bed and groped for her, pretending to be very
gruff. "Wha' are you doing awake 't this time o' night?" he growled, and
started tickling her the way he had often done when she was a little girl. She
laughed and pushed him away.

"Kiss your ol' uncle goo'night," he muttered, groping for her again and
digging his fingers into her back while she quickly kissed his beard.

He went out then and rattled about the stove, and presently she heard
him throwing his trousers over a chair in his room and heard the springs
of his bed creak. She had dropped off to sleep again when he called and
wakened her. "Katrin, come here—come here," he was calling. She put on
her slippers and felt her way to his door. It was a cold night and the house
was chilly. "Komdu hingad, Katrin," the captain called again. Moonlight
reflected from the snow filled his room with a pale light. He was in bed with
the covers drawn up to his neck.

"What's the matter?" said Katrin, going over to him. "I'm terrible cold,"
he said, grasping her hands and making her sit on the bed beside him.
"I'm an ol' man, Katrin. I get terrible cold of a night, sleeping alone." He
was running his hands up and down her body. "But you're warm—warm 's
toast," he said, "Eh? Aren't you?" He threw the covers back and tried to pull
her down beside him. "Get in wi' me for a minute an' warm me up—eh?
There's a girl."

"But why didn't you fix the fire?" she said, struggling away from him.
"I'll give you Asta's comforter. By the time she gets home the house'll be
warm."

"Come on, Katrin—get in here wi' me," he pleaded, thickly. "Not afraid
o' your ol' uncle, are you? Jus' want t' get warm."

She wasn't frightened, but his breath reeked of beer and he was rough
and scratchy. "I'll get you Asta's comforter," she said. But when she came
back with it he grabbed her again and pulled her into the bed beside him.

She was a big girl—bigger than Asta—and could have prevented him, but she didn't want to struggle with him when he was drunk. His hands were so big and coarse and his beard was horribly rough. "Just for a minute, then," she said, thinking he would start snoring almost at once. But when his hands slid over her and touched her breasts she fought him off with clenched fists and ran out of the room.

His muttering soon sank into drawn-out snores, but Katrin did not close her eyes. She propped her head high on the pillow and drew up her knees under the bedclothes, holding herself stiffly. Every few minutes the floorboards would crack with a noise like distant pistol-shots as the frost increased outside. To keep herself awake Katrin counted the sounds and had reached a hundred and twenty three when she heard sleighbells in the distance. It was a cold, calm night and the sound travelled distinctly a long way, but in a few minutes she heard the snorts of the horses and Asta's low, laughing voice.

Katrin ran on tiptoe to the front window, made a hole in the frost with her breath, and watched her sister unbundle herself and get down from the cutter. In a moment she was in the house and while she warmed her knees at the stove Katrin whispered what had happened. "That settles it," said Asta. They were crouched in the dark, but in the glow from the little ventilator holes in the door of the stove Katrin could see her sister's eyes gleam with a cold anger she had never seen before. "Did he ever get *you* in bed with him?" asked Katrin. She was shivering, although her nightgown was almost scorched by the heat from the stove. "*Me!*" whispered Asta, pulling her dress down over her knees and jumping up. "Don't talk about it. We'll go over to Eggertson's tomorrow—and they'll send us to Toronto, to that cousin of theirs—what's her name?—Valdheidur something—it's an English name. She married an Englishman. She's a niece of Bishop Ragnar in Iceland."

The two girls slept that night in Katrin's narrow bed, but long after Asta was asleep Katrin lay awake thinking about Toronto and all she had heard about it, wondering what their life would be like in a big city, and what Mrs. Valdheidur something-or-other would be like, and what the shops would be like ... and ...

Mrs. Valdheidur Digby was married to a connection of the famous seed people in England, an old Quaker family, but her husband, who was a manufacturer's agent, handling Irish linens and laces, was not a Quaker. He was very fleshy and red in the face, and looked as though he might have a stroke any minute. "My God," he said, when he saw the Petursson girls, "I don't know why they don't get some of these Icelandic girls in the movies, I'm damned if I do." His wife, who was thin and intellectual-looking, smiled impatiently and said to Asta, "That's all he thinks about——"

"You'd like to know what I think about," said Mr. Digby cryptically, looking at Asta's legs. It was the period of very short dresses and her crossed knees would have attracted attention anywhere.

The girls did not like Mr. Digby, and even Aunt Val, as she insisted on being called, was too intellectual and citified to make them feel at home. A few months later, when they had settled down in a boarding house on Breadalbane Street and Asta had a job in Seaton's dress department, where she earned enough to send Katrin to high school, they began to appreciate Aunt Val's good qualities. She introduced them to her friends, gave Katrin piano lessons, and invited them up to Jackson's Point for their holidays. Because of time missed at Hekla, Katrin was eighteen when she got through high school, and during the summer following, while she was at Digby's cottage, a young man came out from Iceland with a letter to Aunt Val from her uncle the bishop.

Kari Erlingsson was a tall, squarely-built youngster who had come over with the hope of earning his living as a musician. "At home in Iceland," he said, "they think you can pick up gold on the ground in this country."

He was very proud and excessively temperamental, and every second sentence he uttered began with—"At home in Iceland." He flew into a temper whenever Aunt Val talked English to him and told him he would have to learn it if he intended to stay. Kari accused her of caring nothing for her racial traditions, and made himself generally obnoxious, except in the lake where he flashed powerfully through the water, or at the piano with Katrin in the evenings when he sang the old songs of his homeland, pouring into her eyes all the passion of their plundering Viking forefathers. He called her

Katrin Arnadottir, after her father's name, in Icelandic fashion, and said she should be painted as one of the heroines of the old sagas—the great Gudrun Osvifisdottir, who made her husband kill her lover—or Bergthora, wife of Njall.

Katrin had blossomed like her sister, except that her features were larger and more austere and the dazzling smile flamed less frequently on her lips. She was bigger, heavier, more serious. Her body was proportioned on a heroic scale. The thrust of her limbs and the firm vigorous curves of her bosom and hips gave to her figure a majesty that made one think immediately of sculpture. Kari swore there wasn't a girl in Iceland like her. One day when she stood on the dock in her bathing suit, about to dive, he called from the water, "Ah, if only Einar Jonsson could see you. Old as he is it would kindle something." They sat on a rock together, Kari telling her that she should be sent back to Iceland to "inspire a new generation of *skalds*." Katrin looked with level eyes across the lake, feeling his passionate gaze fastened on her body and holding herself so that she felt like rigid steel. "He doesn't love me," she kept saying to herself. "It's just my looks. He stares at me the way the boys at Hekla used to look at Asta. That's not love."

One night when they had walked out to an isolated, sandy point, screened from the main shoreline by gnarled old willows, and lay in the moonlight close to the lapping water, Kari rolled nearer and kissed the side of her cheek. She grasped his throat, pressed his head down into the sand and knelt over him.

"*Thvi kyssir thu mig?*" she said through her teeth, with a queer savage playfulness. "Because you are beautiful, Katrin Arnadottir," he said. She shook his head from side to side and banged it down again in the sand. "Why do you kiss me?" she said again. "I've told you," he choked. "No you haven't told me," she retorted. "Do you kiss people unless you love them?"

"Let go of me and I'll tell you," struggled Kari. He flung his arms around her, exerted all his strength and rolled over so that she lay under him, her stubborn hands still clinging to his throat. "Let go of me," he cried, trying to tear her hands away. "Let me tell you something."

"Why do you kiss me if you don't love me?" she panted.

"What makes you think I don't love you—you goose! I'm mad about you. I've told you there's no girl in Iceland like you."

"Get off me, Kari!"

"I won't get off you. You want to know if I love you, don't you?"

She flung him off and battered his head in the sand harder than ever. "Not like that!" she cried. "No one's ever going to love me like that unless—until —"

She gave his head a final bump, leapt to her feet, smoothed down her dress and walked away. Kari was on fire. He ran after her, tried to embrace her, pleaded, argued, almost wept. But she kept pushing him away and when he became calmer and walked gloomily beside her, she said, "A year from now—if you've learned English—and make up your mind to stay—and stop sneering at everything Canadian—and get a job—I'll know by then whether you love me."

He sulked for days and Katrin suffered, for she knew now that she was in love. But she doubted him. Everything he had said to her—all his admiration—it all came from his love for Iceland—Iceland—always Iceland: "There's no girl in Iceland like you." Yes—Iceland! "If only Einar Jonsson could see you." Yes—Iceland. Something about "inspiring a new generation of skalds." Yes—Iceland—always Iceland! And yet that was what she loved—his faith, his passion, his mania for Iceland—her land, which she had never seen. He had brought her a breath of it. Its cold sea was in his eyes. Its winds were in his hair. When she looked at the sharp angles of his forehead she could imagine the rocky, barren shore. Treeless, tragic, glorious Iceland!

She was afraid he would go back—she couldn't blame him—why should he stay? He would go back—and forget all about her.

But Kari had begun to like the comforts of Canadian life and before many days had passed he was getting her to teach him English. Aunt Val helped, too, and in the fall, in town, he went at it seriously.

It was an exciting fall for Katrin. Asta was getting married in October to the assistant manager of Seaton's photographic department. His name was William Arthur Cole. He was tall, talked very rapidly and was always brushing his hair back from his high forehead. One of his photographs had won a prize in an exhibition at Chicago. He had been secretary of the Toronto Camera Club for years.

They found a nice little semi-detached house in the Danforth district, which had built up very quickly with small houses as soon as the viaduct over the Don was opened, and by Christmas they were well settled. Katrin had a pleasant, homey place to spend her evenings. In the meantime she had found herself a job in a broker's office, and was beginning to soften in her attitude toward Kari. He was changing very quickly, and although he had no position he was making money. It was the year 1928 and the stock market was booming. Kari interested his relatives and friends in Iceland and soon had a substantial fund to play with. Katrin, who knew from the inside how risky a game it was, became fearful, feeling that the market couldn't last. But it lasted right through until fall and was still going up. They became engaged and began looking for an apartment. In the evenings they frequently walked up and down Yonge Street looking at furniture in the store windows. For Christmas presents that year they gave each other articles of furniture for the apartment. They were both making money.

At a New Year's party at Digby's they met an Icelandic girl from Winnipeg—Helga Palsson—who had eyes for no one but Kari. She was a sleek, dashing, sophisticated sort of girl, and towards morning became more tipsy than the rest. When she saw Kari in the hall with his overcoat on, ready to take Katrin home, she made a scene, trying to drag his coat off and make him stay. It was very embarrassing for everybody, and on the way home Kari insisted that he hadn't flirted with her and never wanted to see her again. But it soon became clear to Katrin that he was seeing Helga almost every day, and was completely captivated by her. One night, on the porch of her rooming house, she took off the ring he had given her and without a word pressed it into his hand.

"What does this mean, Katrin Arnadottir?" he said, humbly.

"You're in love with Helga Palsson."

"Katrin—!"

"Don't fool yourself, Kari—and don't try to fool me. I know when a man's in love with me and when he's not."

"Katrin," he burst out, "I don't know what's happened to me—really, I don't. I loved you more than I thought I could ever love anybody, and then she came along—and it's—it's intoxication—it's like madness. But I'll stop seeing her. I'm engaged to you, and I'll go through with it. I'll go through with it. Don't look at me like that, darling. I can't help it. She is—she —"

"I don't want to hear about her," said Katrin wearily.

"I know—but she's done something to me. It's a sort of slavery —"

"I'm going in. Goodbye, Kari. Go and tell her—you're free."

She saw him only twice after that until the market crash in the following fall. She had expected all summer to hear from Aunt Val that they were married, but when Aunt Val did speak of them it was to say that Kari had been sold out and had lost everything, and that Helga Palsson had gone back to Winnipeg. For a moment tears welled into Katrin's eyes and she clutched at Aunt Val's shoulder. She could still grieve for him, and for their shattered future, but when he came one night and tried to tell her that the intoxication was all over and that he had been mad to forsake her, the light went out of her eyes, leaving them stone-grey and lifeless as ashes. He broke down and sobbed, but she was like ice. "It's gone—on both sides, Kari," she frowned. A deep wrinkle he had never seen stood like a sign in her forehead. "It's dead."

That winter the brokerage firm she worked for was closed up, and three of her employers went to jail. Her savings had gone, thanks to Kari's advice to buy on margin, and she went to live for a while with Asta who was expecting a baby and was glad of her help. Asta had a miscarriage and nearly died, like their mother. The premature baby lived only a few hours.

William Arthur was now manager of Seaton's photographic department, and even when Asta was quite recovered he wouldn't hear of Katrin leaving them, or attempting to pay them anything for board. She wanted to go out and get any sort of job, but William Arthur was optimistic and felt there would be a quick upturn very soon. Their evenings together were quiet and tranquil, Katrin played the piano a good deal and Asta would sometimes sit beside her and sing the old folk songs they had learned as children. She sang them tenderly in a soft, untrained voice which suited their primitiveness.

Sometimes a tear would drop on the keys, but Asta would pretend not to notice it. Some of the songs, she knew, reminded Katrin of her summer at the lake with Kari Erlingsson.

When fall came and Asta was stronger Katrin began to look at the "want ads," and made a few trips downtown alone to apply for jobs. She needed something to do, something to occupy her mind. But times were bad and she found thirty or forty girls ahead of her wherever she went. She gave up the idea of office work. It was overcrowded. One day she saw the Tabarin advertising for an experienced waitress. She went down, told them she hadn't any actual restaurant experience, but—and they hired her mainly for her appearance.

The Coles were shocked when she told them. William Arthur, talking very quickly as usual, insisted there was no hurry—she should wait—any number of things would turn up. But she took the job, moved to a rooming house, because she knew her hours must be disturbing to Asta, and began to live a secluded life, reading a good deal and making her own clothes. At heart she felt like a widow.

Although William Arthur was "looking around" for her, nothing else turned up, and she stayed at the Tabarin. She was a strong, upstanding girl, and she could look very austere. The cooks and the orchestra players learned to leave her alone. Once she was used to it she liked the work, and before long she had regular customers, mostly middle-aged men, who always came to her tables and enjoyed her shape more than their food.

In two years Katrin became head waitress of the lunch room downstairs. She was just the build for it, and her austerity was a great advantage to her in managing "the girls." They played no tricks on her, and although they called her "icy-face," and thought her severe, they got along well with her and really liked her.

After a year downstairs she was moved up as head waitress of the dining room on the second floor where there was an orchestra and dancing every night. She liked the new work better than ever, but still she was not busy enough. She never looked twice at a man, except in sheer friendliness, and her "early evenings off" began to drag. With the notion of starting a tea

room of her own some day (she was a great one to save), she had begun
to study Interior Decorating and Domestic Science at the Tech. Like most
Icelanders she was an excellent student, astonishing Asta with her progress
in cooking when she sometimes spent a Sunday with the Coles. An interest
in art developed from her other course, and she began to read books about it
and attend the picture exhibitions at the Grange.

She never thought of Kari, but she was often aware of the effort she had
to make to keep his name and his blue Icelandic eyes out of her mind if she
felt the least bit dreamy.

Youth's Manuscript

After the swarming Sunday evening traffic on the highway the city seemed deserted. Scarcely a soul was to be seen in Kendal Park as D.J. McConnell drew his luxurious new car quietly to the curb under the chestnut trees.

Edna always asked him to stop there, in the crescent opposite her boarding house, so that she would not be seen arriving "in state," as one of the roomers had remarked a few months back.

"Your obedient servant, Mrs. Colby," said D.J. with heavy playfulness, seeking her hand and fondling it.

A loud whack on the roof of the car startled them.

"What? Kids throwing stones?" D.J. demanded, glaring around with his stern Sunday School Superintendent's manner.

"It's the chestnuts," laughed Edna. "They make quite a racket outside my window at night."

She pointed at the prickly green burrs strewn all over the grass under the trees. It was the time of year she loved best. The maples on the other side of the little block-long park had turned to a deep russet colour. In the flower beds tall red blossoms, whose name she could never remember, stood up like banners, with little purple foliage plants in curlycued borders around them.

The day in the country had been wonderful. They had been out to see Mr. Kimber's chrysanthemums. He was the president of their firm and it was an event for Edna to go out there with D.J. He had wanted to stay all evening, but she wanted to be home in time for Mr. Kolessa's party.

If the girls at the office knew she had come home to her boarding house crowd instead of staying out there with wealthy people like the Kimbers and their friends, they would have thought her crazy. But she never told the girls anything. In the office they called her "the clam."

She had told D.J. almost nothing about herself. He knew she had been a widow for some time, but no one knew how long. She never told anyone. At the office she never mentioned her birthdays; but that afternoon, on the way to the lake, she had let it out that tomorrow was her birthday. It had slipped out because she wanted D.J. to see how important it was for her to get back early.

"Mr. Kolessa's birthday is today," she had said, "and it's his party until midnight. Then it's my party from midnight on."

He had pounced on it at once, and all the way home he had been pressing her to have dinner with him tomorrow night at Gleneagle Inn, promising her a birthday present she could wear for the rest of her life.

She knew what it would be. He had proposed to her three different times at the Gleneagle, sitting on the rocks in the dusk with the dark water flowing past. She knew by his tone that if she went out there tomorrow he would expect her to accept his ring.

Some of the girls, perhaps, would think she ought to feel flattered that D.J. McConnell should want her. He was manager of one of the largest of Kimber's magazines, whereas she was a fashion artist on one of the smaller women's publications. He knew nothing about her work. His office was two floors up from the art department, and if it had not been for a pouring rainstorm one night at quitting time he might have passed her for years without speaking. On the elevators he nodded only to a few old-timers. Everyone thought he was pretty pompous. He had a large important-looking head and large eyes that were always too wide open. She had wondered whether it was thyroid trouble, or perhaps his heart. He was well over fifty. Toward the end of the summer he told her that his doctor had advised him to give up golf. Perhaps some of his gloominess was due to worrying about his health.

"Sit here a minute," said D.J., leaning toward her.

"No, I must go! I must go! They'll be waiting for me," she said, astonished at the panic she felt suddenly throbbing through her.

"You'll be up to all hours, drinking, I suppose," said D.J., severely.

"Once a year, on my birthday, I have a glass of sherry with Mr. Kolessa."

"Well, Edna," said D.J., his wide-open eyes fastening on her solemnly, "this will be your last birthday as a single woman."

"Tomorrow I shall be forty." She brought it out challengingly, and watched his surprise.

Scarcely anyone ever guessed her age. There was no sign of grey in her blonde short-cropped hair. Such large blue eyes in so small and pointed a face gave her an elf-like air. There was an unworldliness and a deceptive meekness in her manner. She was, in fact, a small-town woman who had never warmed to the ways of the city. Except among a few intimates at the boarding house she seemed elusive and reserved.

"Forty!" D.J. repeated, with a note of grave finality in his voice.

"It's an awful birthday to reach," she said. "But don't build too much on it—tomorrow night. I like my freedom too much. I may disappoint you again."

She opened the door quickly and jumped out. Bending to wave to him, with an unpromising smile, she called out: "Goodbye, David Jonathan."

Her teasing use of his two Christian names brought a vexed frown to his face.

While the glistening car swung around the crescent, she allowed her mind to imagine for a moment the luxury she would live in if she married him. He was eager to get away from the huge house where he had lived with his mother and sister since boyhood. To be ordered about and fussed over at his age had grown unbearable.

Once he had taken her through a half-finished house of the type he wanted to build for himself and her. Then he had shown her a wooded lot he intended to buy, overlooking a beautiful ravine at the north end of the city. Only the other day he had pointed out to her the little English car he intended to buy for her own use.

"It's sheer bribery," she thought.

For a moment more she stood still, making a wry face, as though she had taken a bite of a bitter apple, saying to herself, first under her breath, and then out loud, listening to its sound: "Mrs. D.J. McConnell! Mrs. D.J. McConnell!"

Then she turned and faced the little park and the place she called home.

Two men were leaving as she reached the steps. George Copp, with a glass of whiskey in his hand, came out on the verandah to see them off. One of the men, red-faced and paunchy, shook his head gravely. "This will be his last, George," he said.

"Never see another," said the taller of the two, who was staggering a little.

"Nonsense!" George burst out, boisterously. "He'll be going strong when the three of us are under the sod."

Catching sight of Edna he moved aside from the doorway to let her pass.

The odour of beer and whisky completely obliterated the stale smell of cooking and furniture polish which usually met her in the hall. Unused to liquor all her life, the fumes in the air were almost stifling as she squeezed her way between knots of people toward the fireplace. They were mostly students or teachers at the Academy of Music, and many of them shook her hand or nodded as she passed.

At last she reached a little space that was being kept clear around Mr. Kolessa, who sat, as she expected, in the big blue chair with his feet up on a hassock. One frail hand, lifted to catch the warmth of the fire, glowed with uncanny transparency.

Bending quickly, she kissed him on the cheek, her lips barely touching the cold dry skin. "Many happy returns, Mr. Kolessa," she murmured, her breast suddenly heaving with unexpected breathlessness.

"Not many, Edna. Not many, my dear," wheezed the old man, patting the upholstered arm of the big chair for her to sit beside him. "Eighty eight. Eighty eight today. Ten years more. That's the best I can look for."

He had come to America with a famous Ukrainian choir, and stayed, as singer and teacher, and later as music critic, all these years. Only the slightest accent remained in his voice, but there was an unmistakable foreign graciousness in his manner and gestures, and his high rounded head, now bare of any vestige of hair, was distinctly European. Edna had never seen him look paler. The yellow skin, stretched tautly over the prominent bones of his nose and cheeks, had often made her think of parchment, and now she thought of an old manuscript. The book of his life could be read, she thought, in the wrinkles which seared his face from chin to brow. How little room there was left for time to inscribe any more lines between the crisscross furrows!

Looking around at her friends and thinking of how they were all ageing, she choked back the nostalgic remembrance of herself, at sixteen, entering Mr. Kolessa's studio for the first time.

"Alas that youth's sweet-scented manuscript should close," she breathed to herself, almost in tears at the thought of the little Rubaiyat bound in heliotrope suede that a boy named Ronnie had given her. She had forgotten his last name. It was so long ago.

Penny, the maid, stood in front of her with a plate of hot little sausages.

As she took one, Mr. Kolessa's voice sounded behind her. "Give Mrs. Colby a glass of sherry, Penelope," he called out. "You don't want this beer they're drinking, do you, Edna?"

"A glass of sherry," she said, nodding. "Just to drink your health."

Edna fingered the stem of the glass awkwardly when Penny handed it to her.

"Hold it just a minute," said George Copp, lifting his own glass, and stepping up on the long stool in front of the fire.

Every year he did the same thing. First he called for attention and waited with a patient smile and a few tipsy winks while everybody turned to face him. Then in his resonant baritone voice which quickly silenced the mutterers in corners, he launched into his annual speech, referring at first with deliberate vagueness to a man they all honoured, a man of amazing musical knowledge and aptitude, a man whose zeal for the finest music had never slackened, a man whose counsel and advice and fatherly eagerness for everyone's welfare, a man who—could he say it?—yes, he would say it—a man who had drawn from all of them through the years the deepest affection—he might as well out with it —

But by this time tears stood in his eyes, and with a gulp he swung around and lifted his glass. In a snuffling voice that was meant to be loud and firm, but could scarcely be heard, he burst out: "We love you, Daddy Kolessa!"

Then, while those near him clapped George on the back and shoulders, there was a chorus of hushing. The old man was trying to get up. On either side somebody was lifting under his arms. He flung back his head, as though tossing a mane of hair from his brow. For a moment his mouth opened, but only a hoarse cry of mingled pride and grief came from his crumpling lips. Then he sank down in the chair, dabbed at his wet cheeks, and began nodding and smiling with the pleased air of a child who has said his piece.

"Where's my drink, George?" he fussed, blinking tears from his eyes.

"Here it is."

They clinked glasses and drank, and then the old man asked: "Where's Virginia?"

"Here I am," said a round-shouldered woman, her eyes shaded by a freakish feathered hat, who had been standing near.

"Do you feel like playing, Virginia?"

"What would you like me to play?"

"On my birthday, always the same—Liebestraum," said Mr. Kolessa, his voice quite firm. Now he was the music master again. "Everybody very quiet," he said, watching Virginia settle herself at the piano. He lifted his long frail fingers to his temples and closed his eyes.

"All right, Virginia. Dream of love."

Sitting on the long stool with her back to the fire, Edna clasped her hands in her lap, and when the piece was finished she returned from dreams of her first music lessons and joined in the applause.

Mr. Kolessa sat hushed until his silence spread through the room. Many who were near watched his closed eyes, a few wondering anxiously if they would ever open again. But with a great sigh he stretched out one hand behind him like a blind man, groping for Virginia. She came close and without opening his eyes he took her two hands and pressed them for a moment to his lips. It was not the stooped grey woman beside him who stood in his thoughts, but little Virginia, the tiny child who called him Daddy from the first because she had never known a father.

In the hall and in the corners of the room the chattering started again, and now it was Edna's turn. George had found the music of their duet, and stepping unsteadily, he escorted her and Virginia to the piano. Virginia sat down and turned up the corners of the pages while George pulled at the ends of his bow-tie and Edna cupped her hands, one in the other, holding them out from herself in a gesture of offering, the way singers do. She had sung in a country church choir as a girl, and after years of lessons with Daddy Kolessa she had become soprano soloist in a downtown church in a poor part of the city.

Virginia looked up for a signal. George looked at Edna. Edna inclined her head. George Copp's nod to Virginia was almost a bow.

It was an old-fashioned duet in canon, the two voices following one another as in a "round" song. They sang it every year at Mr. Kolessa's parties.

"Go pretty rose, go to my fair, go tell her all I fain would dare."

George was hoarse and Edna was nervous, fearing he would get confused when their leads were reversed, but they began prompting each other with little smiling nods and at the close George made a sort of race of it, so that the listeners burst into laughter and applause when the two singers finished together, bowing their congratulations to each other like old-fashioned performers in vaudeville.

There were no cries for an encore. It was getting late. People were leaving. There was much handshaking and saying of goodbyes. Somewhere at the back of the house a few students were harmonizing songs such as "Down by the old mill stream."

"Where's Louis? He hasn't played tonight," Mr. Kolessa called out.

Someone went out to the kitchen to find the young violinist who lived in the house, but he could not be persuaded to play. He simply shrugged and jerked his head in the direction of the raucous singers who were repeating "Moonlight and Roses" for the third time.

"Ask the boys to come in and hear Louis," said Mr. Kolessa.

"No, no," said Louis. "They're having a good time."

Dropping on the floor and hunching up his knees, he joined the little group left around the fire, where a remark about violinists launched Mr. Kolessa into a succession of anecdotes about Kubelik and Ysaye. His memory was phenomenal, and the others sat with leaning heads anxious not to miss a word. They were so engrossed that no one noticed the clock in the hall chiming midnight, but before the last stroke sounded George Copp and the boys from the kitchen came lurching into the parlour. George went over and lifted Edna from the low stool. When she stood up, smiling shyly, he threw up his hand and the six or seven voices broke into "Happy Birthday to You."

They were in a mood to repeat it, but Mr. Kolessa hushed them with a raised finger, and lifted his glass: "To you, Edna," he said with quiet tenderness.

Among the few that were left she heard "Edna, Edna, Edna," murmured around the room. She blushed a little, and being unfamiliar with toasts, she held up her half-emptied sherry glass and drank with them all.

Reaching her room at last, Edna switched on the rose-shaded light over her pillow and sank down on the bed, exhausted and troubled, although her face felt flushed by the mouthful or two of wine.

Now that the party was over she could not escape thinking of what she should say to D.J. tomorrow. No, today! This is my birthday, she reminded herself.

Too many things were circling like chattering birds in her mind. She had enjoyed the party, but toward the end old Mr. Kolessa had been quite pathetic, and George Copp so noisy that quiet conversation was impossible. It disturbed her that they all drank so much, and she almost shuddered to think of what D.J. would have thought of her friends if he had come in about midnight.

The best part of the evening had been when a few of them sat around Mr.

Kolessa, listening to his talk of the violinists who were famous when he was young. Recalling the rapt earnest expression on the faces of the musicians who remained, and how she had experienced a kinship with them and a sense of homage and reverence for masters of the past, a sharp feeling shot through her, like a barrier suddenly raising itself between her and all thought of D.J.

If she married D.J. it would mean that she would scarcely ever see Mr. Kolessa and the others again. Unless she came secretly. But she could see that it would be impossible to keep secrets from D.J. He was possessive, jealous and suspicious already, and after marriage—

"I can't marry him," she burst out, almost aloud, jumping up from the bed and starting to undress. She attacked her clothes with a sort of fury, as though violent action would somehow give force and finality to the decision she had reached. Besides, to disrobe in her room as usual made her feel that she was still herself, and would remain herself. She could dismiss the anxiety which had sometimes disturbed her when she had thought ahead to undressing before D.J.

Her face felt hot and she peered into the mirror to see if her cheeks were flushed. With a start of astonishment she found she was naked. Usually she brought her nightgown from the closet and flung it on the bed before she undressed, ready to slip on. But tonight her thoughts were in a turmoil.

For a moment she stared at herself, not dreamily as she sometimes did, but with an intense conscious curiosity, trying to estimate what her body would look like to somebody else. Forty! But she was slender, her breasts were firm, and her skin was still white.

She looked at herself steadily, thinking: "This is my body. This is my privacy. I won't surrender it."

She turned to the closet door, but with a sudden shiver she stood still. She was afraid to open it. It was nonsense, but she felt that if she opened it D.J.'s wide round eyes would be there, staring at her. It was absurd, but it made her think that if she married D.J. there would be this to bear—this staring!

With her husband there had been no staring. She was so shy that on the first night, and for many nights, she had turned out the light and they undressed in the dark. They had been young then, whereas D.J. was old, and she thought of things she had heard about elderly men marrying young wives. Not that she was young, but perhaps he would feel bound to prove his virility, and she began wondering fearfully—he was often short of breath—thinking of what would happen if he had a heart attack. What would she ever do? Would there be anyone to call? What could she do for him alone if he fell down groaning?

She was shivering so much that she flung open the closet door and snatched her nightgown from the hook, shutting the door again without looking. Covering herself quickly, she slid into bed and turned out the light.

Tomorrow she must tell him. Today!

She tried to think of her birthday, but all that came into her mind was a panicky repetition: "I cannot! I won't!"

The chestnuts falling on the roof of Cooper's garage kept her awake a long time, but now she was happier, because she felt that nothing could make her weaken.

All day long Edna's heart had been thumping. Every now and then she drew in a deep breath and crushed her hands together. They were cold. Sometimes she felt a little faint. These queer sensations drove everything from her head. All her thoughts were buried deep under a vague feeling of impotence which she had experienced in dreams just before waking.

"If I am like this, what must D.J. be feeling?" she wondered.

Somewhere in her mind throbbed the urgent need to decide. It was useless to remind herself that last night she had come to a firm resolve. Her intention was no longer clear. Her numbed will seemed powerless to choose.

If she had run across D.J. that day in the corridors or on the elevators, the sight of his too-wide-open eyes might have restored her confidence in what she was determined to say to him. But she rarely saw him in the building, and today she had scarcely moved from her drawing board.

In the afternoon she went down to the cafeteria for her relief with Janet Hobbs, hoping that coffee and a little talk would disperse the stupor that had been hanging over her since morning. But Janet was obviously puzzled by her mood, and after a few searching questions which Edna evaded, her friend lapsed into a shrugged-up silence.

They took the elevator, standing close together without a word. As they stepped off, the noise of a screaming siren came from the open window at the end of the hall.

"Fire reels?" said Edna.

"More like an ambulance," guessed Janet.

Eyeing each other nervously, they ran the few steps to the window. An ambulance swung around the corner on screeching tires and jolted to a stop outside the main entrance. Two uniformed men leapt out and ran back to open the doors, but the doorman called out to them as he hobbled down the steps, pointing to the side of the building.

"They'll have to take it up in the freight elevator," said Janet, as the men got back into their seats.

"An accident, d'you suppose?" Edna said.

Together they hurried to the door of the art department and almost ran along the passage that led to the big studio. The door was open and most of the artists were leaning out of the high casement windows. Red-headed Stella had jumped up on one of the men's backs, and he was jiggling her up and down.

"Who's hurt?" said Janet, crossing the floor with three of her masculine strides.

"They're taking McConnell to the hospital," said someone.

"What happened?" asked Janet, looking over her shoulder quickly at Edna.

"Heart attack," said the new French boy.

Edna could gasp out only two words: "Is he——?"

"Collapsed beside his desk," said Paul.

Edna sank down on a chair and nearly slipped off onto the floor. Janet and Paul jumped to help her, but she waved them off as though she needed air. Gripping the seat of the chair with both hands, she shook her head several times and then her chin sank forward until it touched the amethyst brooch she wore at the opening of her blouse. D.J. had given it to her at Christmas. As soon as her chin touched the cold stone she began to shiver.

"Get her a glass of water, Paul," said Janet.

"I'll be all right," muttered Edna, brushing tears from her cheeks.

Two or three of the artists had turned from the window and were staring at Edna curiously. Janet strode toward them and said in a lowered voice: "See if Tommy has a bottle in his desk."

The youngest of the apprentices scurried out after the French boy.

"You'd be better off lying down," Janet said, her flat voice sounding surprisingly soft. "Kate Lawson is out of town this week. You could stretch out on her chesterfield."

"What goes?" cried out one of the boys to the old janitor who passed the open door slowly, with a plodding step, shaking his head.

"They've taken him to St. Mike's."

Tommy appeared with a half-filled bottle of rye. Paul came behind him with a glass of water from the cooler.

"Give her a good shot," said Janet.

"No, no," murmured Edna, piteously. "Never drink."

"Fix you up," said Tommy, unscrewing the cap of the bottle.

"Never drink," repeated Edna, trying to rise.

"Give her the water, Paul," said Janet.

Grasping the glass tremblingly in both hands, Edna sipped several times, then held the glass out blindly, her eyes closed to squeeze back her tears. Somebody took the glass from her and she felt arms around her shoulders, lifting her up.

"Come on in to Kate's room," Janet was saying.

She allowed herself to be led.

"Shut the door, Jane," she said, when she found herself on Mrs. Lawson's couch. Without opening her eyes, she said to Janet, whose strong step came close on the carpet beside her: "Did they give me whisky?"

"You wouldn't take it."

Edna opened her eyes, and a single tear rolled out of sight across her temple into her hair.

Janet had a cigarette in her mouth and her silver lighter lifted to it.

"You don't mind if I smoke?" Janet said.

"No, no, no," murmured Edna.

The lighter clicked and Janet inhaled deeply. "Do you feel better?" she said, the smoke issuing from her mouth in jerks with each syllable.

"Yes, I do."

Janet moved over to sit on the edge of the chesterfield beside Edna's feet.

"Were you going to marry him?" she asked quietly.

Edna shook her head.

"I thought you were."

"He told me you were."

"He—he told you?" faltered Edna.

"When?"

"Last week. I was out with him, and he said he guessed it would be the last time. He said you didn't quite know it yet, but he felt sure you'd marry him."

"I didn't know you went out with him, Jane."

Staring at Kate Lawson's framed diploma on the wall, Janet shrugged her shoulders. "You're such a clam," she said, screwing up her eyes as though studying the small print.

It was true, Edna thought. She never talked to the girls about her affairs or encouraged them to talk about theirs. It hadn't occurred to her all day to mention to anyone that this was her birthday.

She dragged herself upward on the slippery leather chesterfield and propped herself on her elbows.

Staring at Janet's masculine face with the fringe of black hairs like a man's sideburns growing down beside her ears, she leaned forward and whispered: "Did D.J. ever ask you to marry him, Jane?"

"Oh, yes."

The two words sliding out at her in so casual a tone gave Edna a queer little shock.

"He tried several of the girls. Didn't you know?" asked Janet, incredulously.

"Tried?" Edna groped in a puzzled whisper.

"Oh, he wasn't a wolf," Janet answered promptly. "He never made passes at any of the girls. So they say. He was just crazy to get married. Surely to God you know why, Edna."

"Why?"

"Did he never tell you?"

"Tell me what?"

"That his mother and sister were driving him nuts. He had to get away from them. Do you mean to say he never—?"

"He told me he was sick to death of a fourteen-room house. He wanted to build a house of his own, with a terraced garden. There was going to be a pool—not a swimming pool—just a small round one with a fountain in the middle. One night he showed me the lot."

"I guess we've all seen the lot," said Janet. "On the Parkdale ravine."

Edna clasped her hands behind her head and looked at the ceiling. Her shivering had ceased. The tremours had gone from her heart. "I guess I must have been the last one he 'tried,'" she thought to herself, with a hurt feeling of repugnance.

"He had an attack a few months ago, you know," said Jane.

"He didn't tell me."

"He wouldn't. It was Kate who told me."

Janet crushed her cigarette out in Mrs. Lawson's spotless ashtray. "Let's go out and get high," she said. "You'll take a drink tonight, surely."

"I never drink, Janet. I have one glass of sherry once a year on my birthday.

"You can get drunk on sherry," said Janet.

"I had my glass this morning, just after midnight."

"Is this your birthday?"

"Yes."

"You're the limit," said Janet, getting up and brushing down her hips. People were scurrying by outside the closed door. It was quitting time.

"Let's go out to a bar," Janet said. "You can sit and sip coke if you want to."

"I don't feel like it. I guess I'll go home."

But seeing her reddened eyes in the washroom mirror she hated to face people in a crowded bus. When she reached the street the low sun was flashing on westbound windshields as the stampede of evening traffic swept past. Turning her back on the blinding sunset and the noise of the intersection, she started homeward through a shabby district of short shady streets. Dirty children were playing in the gutters. But she neither saw nor heard. Her senses waned until all she could feel was a strange eager expectation of freedom stirring in her. She expected very little. Only to go her way alone, to become again the quiet isolated person she had been before she had met D.J.

"At my age some women would feel lonely," she thought.

Tears welled into her eyes, but they seemed to be tears of relief, of happiness, as her heart swelled, welcoming back the one deep silent person who never disturbed her—herself!

She had dreaded her fortieth birthday, feeling that fear of the future might drive her into a marriage she knew would be stifling. But now, even if D.J. should live, she would see no more of him.

It was a struggle to thrust him out of her mind, to forget that tonight he would have proposed to her for the fourth time. Perhaps she should have gone with Janet to celebrate her birthday. A glass of sherry with Janet! It might have loosened the tight reins she held on her heart.

Her steps were unsteady as she stared ahead unseeingly, trying to banish D.J. and the luxury he would have lavished on her—trying not to think forward—

At last her thoughts veered to childhood memories of happy country faces, birthday cakes, candles, kisses!

"Alas, that youth's sweet-scented manuscript should close," echoed in her mind.

She should have gone with Janet. Where could she go? What did she want? It was only a little gnawing want. A yearning for the treats of bygone birthdays.

At the corner she saw a sign over a storefront. Dreamily she went in and sat down at a table in a cubby-hole. It was an Italian place. A radio was going. A plump dark waitress came out from behind the counter.

"What'll you have?" she said.

"Give me a chocolate soda," said Edna.

She caught the girl bending to stare at her downturned face, and it was only then that she knew she had been crying all along the street.

(from) The Tangled Miracle

"Not a bit like a detective story—is it?"
from *The Tangled Miracle* (143)

Coffee was served on a long, stone-flagged veranda overlooking the wide lawns at the back of the house. Behind the guests, as they sat facing the Sound, were the open windows of the morning-room, and Rhoda thought she heard a muffled noise inside as they settled down in a semi-circle.

"It's been arranged this way," she thought, turning her chair a little in the hope of observing the windows, "so that somebody inside can hear what Hood is going to say. Is it Mrs. Leckie Smith they're keeping out of sight?"

But her speculations were halted by a sudden hush in the chatter around her. They were listening to Hood, who was sitting next to Rivers, and had drifted into conversation with him on the topic which had been the reason for the gathering. "Go right on—go right on," Garth whispered to him.

"Well, I was just asking Mr. Rivers," Hood began in a louder tone, "if he remembered the old trick movies—twenty years ago. There was one in particular—a comedy—in which a man was being chased all over the place. You remember they nearly always had some sort of a chase in the comedies in those days—well, and in the more serious pictures too. The chase," he digressed, with a hint of deeper significance in his manner, "possesses universal appeal. To hunt—to capture—*to find something that has been lost*—it's the great lure! However, I was going to say—the man in this comedy escaped his pursuers by all sorts of clever stunts, done with trick photography. He got on a roof, I remember, and when the crowd was within reaching distance, he jumped over—but instead of landing in a heap, he broke up into cubes as he went down. The cubes were strewn over the sidewalk like kiddies' blocks, but they were suddenly jerked together, and there was the man again—alive—and he darted off in a fresh sprint. And then he ran through a lot of rooms and passages—flinging doors open—and when he came to one that was locked he reduced himself to the thinness of a piece of paper and slid under the door—the way you'd slide a letter through. I've often wished I had that picture. It would make an excellent introduction to a lecture on the fourth dimension. Audiences find it hard to *get in* to the subject. What I usually do is this."

He took a letter from one pocket and a pencil from another. He unfolded the letter and spread it flat.

"This paper has only two dimensions—length and breadth. It has a little thickness, of course, but let us pretend, for the moment, that it hasn't. And let's pretend that it is a sheet of paper thousands of miles in extent—a flat world. On this world you could draw a picture of a man—like the one who slipped under the door—a man of only two dimensions—a flat man. Suppose that this man is you, Mr. Rivers. If you were really flat—living in a two-dimensional world—you would have no experience of thickness or height. Let me show you what I mean."

He pulled a table toward him and rapidly drew something on the paper. Holding it up, he displayed a crude, childish picture of a man's figure and a square.

"In a flat world there could be no such thing as a room—with walls, I mean. There would be no height. A square would be the equivalent of a room—and the four lines that enclose it *would be sufficient to keep the man out.* The lines are merely the thickness of a pencil mark on paper—but that is also the thickness of the man. To him the lines are as thick as himself. He can't get over them or under them. In a perfectly flat world the words 'under' and 'over' would have no meaning."

Hood paused and smiled. "Don't get this mixed up with the old notion that the earth is flat. The world I'm talking about is utterly fictitious—merely to provide an analogy. Here it is. If a three-dimensional object—like this pencil—which has length, breadth, and thickness—were to enter this flat world—you see what would happen."

As he spoke he punctured the paper with the point of the pencil and pushed it through.

"It's impossible for you to look at this the way a flat person would. You see the pencil sticking out above the surface of the paper and below it. But the flat person—only able to see *flatness*—or, in other words, *lines*—would see only the tiny portion of the pencil which *goes through* his world. He would see it as a line. Is this clear, so far?"

There was a murmur which indicated that one or two of Hood's listeners had not been able to follow.

"Look," cried the scientist. "In your mind's eye—cut off the pencil above and below the paper—cut it off so that all you have left is the part that *goes through* the paper—which is the thickness of the paper—which is the thickness of a line. *That* is all the flat person would see—not a pencil at all—but a strange line which has suddenly appeared in his world, apparently out of nowhere—not made with hands, so to speak. In other words—a miracle!"

There was a stir of new interest as Hood used the word which had been in all their minds so frequently in the last few days. Rivers leaned forward and fixed his glance on the pencil as though hypnotized by it.

"Now," went on Hood, "let's carry the idea a step farther. Suppose this pencil were blue from the point to the centre, and red from the centre to the rubber at the other end—half blue—half red. If I were to push the blue end through the flat world—the flatlanders would see a blue line, wouldn't they? If I kept on pushing until the red portion went through—they would see a red line. In other words, they would think that the blue line *had become* red, without anybody touching it. It would never occur to them that anything had *gone through* their world. They would say that the line had *appeared* in their world—*out of another*. And if I were to withdraw the pencil—like this—they would say that the line had *disappeared*—into another world, which they would not be able to grasp or understand. Either the appearance or the disappearance would be a mystery—a miracle."

Rivers and Ogiltree nodded as Hood paused again. They were following his argument with concentrated attention. Garth and Spence looked blank. Garth was nearly asleep.

"You may have heard," Hood went on, "that in some quarters time is regarded as the fourth dimension. If we go back to our red and blue lines, you will see how such an idea arises. When the red part of the pencil follows the blue portion through Flatland—the change from blue to red would not seem to occur in space. In other words, there would not be an appearance of two lines succeeding one another—one above the other. There would be no *above*. The pencil would be the thickness of a line—and the line would change from blue to red *in time*—it would *become red* the way a sunset changes colour while you sit and look at it. In other words, the flatlanders would say that the blue was in the past—and the red in the present. It would be inconceivable to them that the blue and the red could exist *at the same time—outside of their world*. And yet, you see, that *is* the explanation. The blue half of the pencil and the red half *exist together* in our world—*and they don't get in each other's way*. We can see the two halves as one pencil—*as one body*."

"As one body," repeated Rivers in a reverential whisper.

"Yes," said Hood. "The analogy is really very clear. We are hazy about what the fourth dimension *is*—it's *direction*—so to speak. But if there is a fourth dimension—the bodies in it would *go through* our world the way this pencil goes through this piece of paper. But we wouldn't say they had *gone through*. We can't understand how a person could step through a brick wall, for instance. If any one did, we would say it was a miracle."

"It *is* a miracle," cried Rivers, flashing a look of triumph around at the others. "It *is* a miracle. It *has happened to us*."

Rhoda felt satisfied, as she glanced at the faces of the four directors, that Mortimer Hood had made a deep impression on them. Rivers had evidently grasped more of the scientist's discourse than any of the others, and his enthusiastic acceptance of Hood's theory—although it was only half sketched—made them feel that they could accept it too, without properly understanding it.

There was a sudden flurry of talk—very hazy and disjointed—but one thing emerged very clearly. The attitude of hostility toward Hood had completely disappeared. He was regarded as their ally, and a powerful one, able to convince the world—by scientific demonstration—that their leader's physical assumption could have taken place.

But, if they were satisfied, Hood was not. Once having started on his favourite subject, he was not going to let them off so easily. He managed to stem the flow of talk and launched into another phase of his explanation, quoting such writers as Fechner, Zollner, Morosoff, Ouspensky, Hinton, Bragdon, and others. As soon as he dropped the analogy of Flatland, and attempted to hint at the possibilities of existence in four dimensions, his hearers found it difficult to follow him. Finally, after excursions into alchemy, theosophy, spiritualism, and metaphysics, he made an effort to sum up in simple language.

"It looks very much as though the normal, three dimensional world that we see and know so well," he continued gravely, "is only a partial, distorted reflection or mirage of reality—falling as short of reality as man's conception of this world would be if he could see nothing but shadows— like the man in Plato's cave. We all have our different ideas of eternity—but let me suggest this. If there is such a thing as eternity it must be a world where there is *less matter*—and *more time*. I wonder if I can make that clear. Our ideas about matter have changed a great deal in recent years. To-day scientists are leaning to the view that there is no such thing as 'dead' matter—or what we used to call 'substance.' Instead of thinking that force acts on matter—moving it or changing it—it is now generally recognized that the matter and the force are the same thing. It is all force. The only thing in the universe that isn't force, so to speak, is time. Motion in time is what produces—for us—the illusion of matter. In this table, for example, the illusion of solidity is caused by the motion of millions of molecules, whirling around like miniature solar systems, but very close together. When they are so close that their movements interlock, we say that they make up a 'substance' which is hard—solid. When their motion is freer—when we can see more force at work—more motion—we are not so conscious of what we call hardness—and we call such substances fluids. When the motion is still freer—the illusion of matter disappears entirely—and we have what we call a gas—invisible to the naked eye ..."

THE WRONG WORLD

:

Chapter One

The two men had barely exchanged the usual greetings which occur after long separations when Gawthorpe's visitor experienced a queer sensation. A moment before he had been conscious of a gap between them; but, in a moment, the parenthesis of all those dissociated years was swept away.

"What do you smoke?" Gawthorpe had asked.

But it was far from a casual question. In the tone of his voice and the lift of his eyebrows the older man betrayed a half-mocking expectancy which amounted almost to a challenge, as though an answer which lacked a degree of fine discrimination would constitute an affront to his own admirably mannered elegance.

"They tell me that everybody smokes Turkish in America," Gawthorpe went on, rapidly, with an air of avoiding the issue of his challenge. "But I hope you don't; because I can't offer you any. I detest them. Perhaps you'd like these. I get them—through some friends of mine—the Milónoffs— direct from Russia. You might say they are my only extravagance."

The nicety of diction, the delicacy with which the little shallow green box was opened, the implied assumption that a person of his tastes could not be denied these little prodigalities, the whole meticulous solemnity enveloping a matter so trivial as cigarettes—all this, although occupying only a few seconds, served as well as a two-hour talk to bridge the years and convince the trans-Atlantic visitor that his former choirmaster had lost nothing of that exaggerated polish, that preciosity of manner and bearing which, as a boy, he had mimicked and admired.

A match flared between them and through the first whiff of smoke

Densham mentally sized up his host: the same sloping shoulders, long pendent nose, dark brown eyes reposing in narrow sockets, the same sallow skin and high forehead, the same ascetic, oriental appearance, and that something about him which suggested the hangout—even the laziness—of the East.

"It's a long time since I smoked Russians," Densham remarked. "These are corking.''

He walked across the room and dropped the blackened match in an ash-tray on the mantel. "Funny that you should mention that name, though. I've been trying to think of it all day."

"Milónoff, you mean?"

"Yes. I saw Madame Milónoff this morning. That queer withered old giant was wheeling her in the little park beside the churchyard. George Pethick used to call him "Malachi," do you remember? He looked so much like a prophet. They were the first people I recognized; but for the life of me I couldn't think of her name. She never got better—eh?"

Gawthorpe dropped into a chair and motioned Densham to the lounge.

"No. I suppose you don't remember her before her accident—before she was married?"

"O yes. She sang the solos at one of the Philharmonic concerts."

"Of course. 'The Martyr of Antioch.' Yes, yes. What a beautiful voice! An exquisite personality! Born to a career, you know—to conquests of an unusual sort. All the qualities of a great artist! As the Lord liveth, a splendid women! What a tragedy!"

Densham leaned forward.

"She has never walked—since?"

"Only a step or two. She is not lame, you know. It's her heart. A terrific shock to her whole system. She has been ill a great deal. It has aged her, of course. She can't be more than ... How long have you been away?"

"Close to fifteen years."

"Well then, she is not much over forty. Getting about in a chair makes her look older, too, of course. She was never what you would call beautiful, you know; except her eyes. But she was always—well, you remember, probably—upright, vital, rather—rather splendid. One doesn't use the word 'superb' much, but she was really that. And even now; yes,—now, perhaps, more so—like a deposed queen!"

Gawthorpe became thoughtful, sank back in his chair and drew at his cigarette.

Across the room Griffith Proctor Densham, his old chorister, also smoked silently. His appearance was youthful, in spite of his thirty-four years. He had not grown up. There was still a singular questing eagerness in his greenish eyes. His parted lips and the quick distension of his delicate nostrils bespoke a spirit which the world and the flesh had never completely yoked.

He had left Croydon at the age of nineteen to go to South Africa. His parents had died there during his schooling in England, and he went back to make his home with an uncle in Cape Town. For two years, until he came of age, he endured the routine of his uncle's office. Being one of a family of seven his inheritance was not large; but on attaining his majority he sailed for Canada. The idea of a fruit-farm in the shadow of the Rockies had fired his imagination. From an early age he had been tantalized by literary ambitions. It seemed to him that "out there" he would have little to do; he could live a hermit-like existence and write without hindrance.

Almost eighteen months passed before he realized the folly of this headlong plunge into unfamiliar surroundings and an occupation for which he was entirely unfitted. He sold the farm for a wretched price and hastened to Winnipeg, where a great deal of money was being made in Western real estate. For a while his literary pursuits were entirely abandoned. The excitement of the "boom" enslaved him. He was even persuaded to make a profitless trip into the Peace River country. On his return he determined to "unload" his holdings, put the money into bonds, and definitely set himself to write a great Canadian epic.

The scope of the proposed novel was soon narrowed. During a cruise on Lake Winnipeg he became intensely interested in the life of the Icelanders who fish in those waters. They usurped his broader scheme, and through the following winter he roughed it in the northern country, gathering atmosphere for a powerful study of their rigorous, half-savage existence.

But in the early summer, at Minaki, where Densham had ensconced himself on a diminutive island with the intention of labouring faithfully at his fiction, a new experience lured him from his work. Sentimental by nature, his affairs of the heart had ever been tempestuous and temporary; but a suddenly conceived fancy for a young Calgary girl, who had been forced to land on his island during a storm, soon developed into a serious and lasting infatuation.

She was not of the type which usually attracted him. She was quiet, calm, downright. At first he had suspected an unusual elusiveness behind her level gaze. Later he discovered that it was the honest reflection of a practical, even-tempered personality. The glamour of the affair ebbed. In its place arose the thought that she would make him—the writer of books—an admirable wife.

There was nothing temperamental about her. She was younger than he, and a bit awed by what she smilingly—but not jokingly—called his "genius." She believed in him. He knew that he could reckon on having pretty much his own way. And, of course, when his things began to be published, she would be inordinately proud of him. Besides, she was possessed of a quiet, contagious good-humour that would act as an antidote in his frequent fits of depression. They became excellent comrades; a relationship which, as it stood, loving patience with the fruits of success—fame, wealth, travel, the homage of superior people! All this made her feel necessary to him, and recognizing in him a sort of genius, she endured what actually amounted to something like martyrdom. She lived with him thus for five years, keeping out of his way as much as possible, and finally, after a brief illness, got out of his way for ever.

Her death was not so much of a shock as he had believed it would be. For, in his inmost heart, he had more than once contemplated the possibility of her death. It had seemed to him at times that he could get on better without her—without anyone. His aunt had "spoiled" him; and since marriage his wife had pampered him. "These women have ruined me," he sometimes thought; and pictured himself thrown upon the world at an early age, to shift for himself, to starve in a garret, like Chatterton. He tortured himself with the half-belief that under some such circumstances he might have written a masterpiece.

His thirty-first birthday arrived a few weeks after his wife's death. It did not occur to him what day it was until he was preparing for bed. The night was warm and he was leaning out of the window, gazing blankly at the stars, giving no conscious guidance to his thoughts. Suddenly the day of the month occurred to him; and he said, out loud—"Thirty-one; and nothing done!"

A frenzy overtook him. "This must not go on," he said to himself, and immediately began to put his clothes on again, without any clear idea of what he was going to do. Presently he found himself in the street. It was past midnight; but he strode feverishly on for more than two hours, filling his lungs with deep draughts of the night air, and pumping into his soul a stern and inexorable determination to *finish* something.

He took up again his Icelandic novel, and worked at it intermittently until the beginning of summer. In July, in order to steep himself afresh in the atmosphere of the story, he planned to spend a few weeks at a quiet resort on Lake Winnipeg, near which, in his previous rambles, he had discovered a tiny Icelandic settlement.

It pleased him to take a pad and write in the open. One day he drove his canoe through a screen of high reeds into a creek that ran back into a marsh. Beyond the marsh was a sort of lagoon, enclosed on three sides by wild cherry and cranberry trees. "Like a natural amphitheatre," he thought, "floored with crystal." But the water, really, was not very clear; and he regretted that there were not water-lilies afloat on it.

However, the spot was almost ideal. Densham visited it often. Lying face downward in the sand he wrote slowly, pausing often, chin in hand, seeking the 'right' word. Occasionally he would stand up, throw back his shoulders, and, in conscious imitation of Flaubert, declaim his sentences out loud, at the top of his voice; attempting to detect flaws in his phrases by the constriction of his breath at certain points in their bellowed utterance.

One day, when he was doing this, a man appeared through the bush on the opposite side of the lagoon, visibly astounded at the sight of Densham standing with his feet planted wide apart, shouting strange sentences at the sky.

"What the devil?" he cried. "I thought someone was drowning. Is this a new game of hide-and-seek, or something?"

Densham went round to him, rather red in the face, and explained that he was a writer; rather expecting that this news would not only account for his eccentricity, but would occasion a certain amount of awe in the attitude of the other, who was roughly attired and wore a week's growth of beard. To his surprise, however, the announcement rather amused the newcomer, who turned out to be a lawyer named Potter, a bachelor, and something of a hermit, who lived in a shooting-lodge on the edge of the marsh, just behind the strip of bush through which he had lately struggled.

They began to talk of literature and it ended in Densham staying for a meal at the lawyer's shack. Potter announced that he spent his summers in almost utter seclusion, fishing and reading. "Mostly the same books, too," he declared, "over and over again. I rarely pick up new ones; but this year I'm reading Henry Adams."

Densham had barely heard of Adams, which meant that the conversation drifted into late afternoon, carried over another hastily prepared meal, and lasted far into the night. After that Densham spent most of his days with his new acquaintance, while at night, in spite of the mosquitoes, he burned his lamp and devoured Adams's Works, which Potter lent him in rotation.

He discovered in Adams a justification for his lack of will. One phrase from the "Degradation" he repeated to himself many times—"Thought then appears in nature as an arrested,—in other words, as a degraded,—physical action."

"I have been living a lop-sided life," Densham said to himself. "Like everybody else I have glorified my brain, my reason; I have preferred to think—rather than feel. All this time I have been trying to write with my intellect—a lower energy than instinct! It has never occurred to me that I lack emotional experience. I must throw myself into the stream of life."

The thought had a strange and delicious thrill for him. He endeavoured to picture himself as a man of action, holding the attention of crowds, or perhaps on some lonely adventure, with a few loyal followers, questing, conquering! But he found it difficult to thrust himself into this unwonted role.

"No," he thought, "this new slant Adams has given me must be translated somehow into terms of writing."

He began thinking over, in turn, the great masterpieces of literature.

"It is the wealth of feeling, not the subtlety of thought, that makes them masterpieces," he told himself, and began thrashing about in his mind for the memory of a book he had once read which had applied some such test to the works of great authors.

He did not think of it until his holiday was over and he had got back to Winnipeg. Then, of a sudden, in the jostle of Portage Avenue, late one afternoon, it came to him. He experienced an overwhelming desire to run about—like Archimedes—shouting his discovery to the thronging stream of people making their way homeward.

"Ecstasy! Ecstasy! That's it!" he bellowed, inwardly. "By a chap named Machen. What's the name of that book? But, never mind. I've got it, now. That's the supreme test of literature. It must have ecstasy in it."

As he looked about him at the dull faces swarming past he felt that perhaps it was a test, too, of the *worthiness* of life. What was life worth without it? And yet how few of these groundlings possessed it!

"Nine out of ten of them," he said to himself, "have scarcely ever pronounced the word. It has become altogether remote from common life."

That being so he must seek it in places apart from the seething and swarming of cities. And before he knew it the idea of returning to England had seeped into his mind.

The more he mulled the matter over the more it appealed to him. This Western country, he decided, was too young, too crude, too obsessed with the mere task of making ends meet. No wonder he had been unable to write. Culture was almost entirely lacking. Ecstasy was unknown. In England he felt sure he would find vestiges of it. It was to be a high quest, pursued with fanatical fervour. His heart leaped.

Before he could get away his thirty-second birthday came round. "Thirty-two," he said to himself, "and still nothing done. But I am about to start life all over again."

To his friends Densham indicated that it was only a trip he was taking; but he sold up most of his belongings, put a few half-precious things in storage, packed his books, and told himself that he would not come back.

The first glimpse of English fields—seen from the boat-train to London—confirmed him in this belief. He found it difficult to understand how he could have stayed away so long.

And now, in Gawthorpe's study, with Gawthorpe's familiar sallow face opposite him, he wanted to dismiss the hiatus, those wasted, vacillating, purposeless years. He could not bring himself to confess his failure. When it became necessary, at Gawthorpe's prompting, to speak at length of his experience, he deleted any reference to his literary ambitions. Instead, he talked a great deal about his dead wife. He had thought of her very little for some months; but as he talked it began to appear wonderful to him that she had been able to give so much when he had been prepared to give so little. Her mere kindness—to put it only at that—in the face of his neglect, his selfishness, his lack of sympathy with her type of mind, became transfigured in his memory, and made him humble. He extolled her. He complained that he had never been worthy of her. He was in a mood to flagellate himself.

It soon passed. A photograph of George Pethick, his chief crony in the old days, attracted his attention on the wall above Gawthorpe's head.

"Where is George?" asked Densham. "Has he kept in touch with you at all?"

"He's on the halls," remarked Gawthorpe, a bit drily. "Doing rather well, I'm told. Imitations, barnyard noises, and that sort of thing."

"George! Barnyard noises! Are you serious?"

"Quite. I haven't seen him for some time; but I understand he appears quite often at the Hippodrome or the Tivoli, I don't know which. Perhaps both."

Densham threw himself back in his chair and laughed heartily. "Life will be the death of me yet," he cried; "I was only just then about to tell you of the solemn ambitions George and I entertained as boys. He was going to be a great actor. I was to be a great writer. We used to go on the most terrific hikes and discuss our respective futures. How confident we were! It didn't seem easy, mind. We were determined to work very hard. We pictured ourselves starving, even. We were prepared to sacrifice everything that everybody else seemed to prize. We were convinced, of course, that neither of us would ever marry. Life—at least, the sort we mapped out for ourselves—was pretty austere, pretty bleak. That was in the bargain. We felt superior to the sort of people who took life easily. I remember that we often talked of you. We admired you so much, you see; and until these ambitions formed themselves we were modeling ourselves after your—your graceful pattern."

Densham looked up and met the other's glance. Gawthorpe nodded knowingly. He was hugely amused.

"Then we began to feel that you were too easily contented. We would have admired you more if—instead of your lessons, the choir, concert engagements, and all that—you had starved yourself and written stupendous compositions. These compositions, of course, would have been frightfully neglected. Nobody would recognize your genius—except us—and perhaps a handful of others. And then you would have died. We should have liked to have attended your funeral."

They both laughed aloud simultaneously.

"Yes, out of our meagre earnings, we would have got a wreath for your grave. And then, of course, almost at once, your works would become famous. And we would go about, appropriately melancholy, telling people— 'Yes, we knew Gawthorpe. He was a wonderful artist—a great genius.'"

Gawthorpe was half-reclining, both hands clasped behind his head, and his eyes fixed on the ceiling. "I'm inclined to think, Griffith," he remarked, in a sober voice, and without changing his position or the direction of his glance, "that this last—this idea of me—was more of your conception that George's. Eh?"

"Perhaps," said Griffith. "I have never wanted to take things easily for myself, and yet things have never really been hard for me. If I had been thrown on my own resources I might have got somewhere. Even out there—if things had not prospered with me quite so well—I might have accomplished something."

Gawthorpe sat forward and looked at him searchingly. "Got somewhere? Accomplished something? You seem to be accusing yourself."

"Well, I am. You see, the ambition stuck. It's still there. But that's all. George did get behind the footlights, at least; if only to make barnyard noises. I have not even clucked in print."

"You mean to say that it still torments you—this aspiration?" In Gawthorpe's voice the younger man detected a strong element of curiosity, amounting almost to anxiety—to a desire for the fullest confidence.

"Yes," Griffith answered. "Nothing else seems to satisfy me. There will be no peace for me until—well, until I have created something. I sometimes wonder if other people experience quite the same urge—to create—to ..." But he did not finish. Something in Gawthorpe's aspect arrested his groping thought. The musician was bent forward. He had become suddenly older. At the same time there was an expression on his face and a flare in his eyes which Griffith had never seen before, and never dreamed of seeing. It was as though Gawthorpe had removed a mask that had been there for years. He seemed uncomfortable, too, almost bashful, as one might be who shows his true features for the first time to an old friend.

He did not speak at once, and when he did it was not in the familiar, languid, carefully-articulated tone. His voice was hollow. It seemed to come from some deep place within him, long disused. "In the image of God—eh?"

"What?" cried Griffith. The ejaculated word seemed to explode and slap against all four walls of the room. Not only Gawthorpe's phrase, nor his unaccustomed tone, but the dead silence in the room, in the house—a vibrating stillness which impinged upon the senses—had startled him. His own voice, uttering that single word, had crashed in his ears. Immediately afterward the silence came rushing back, enveloping them, a more unearthly stillness than before, like darkness after a flash of lightning.

Gawthorpe was the first to speak. The recital of that boyish estimate of him had penetrated to the secret core of his thoughts. It stripped him of his elegance, his poise. It recalled those early aspirations so relentlessly sacrificed to a mode of life, a mere attitude. The dead bones of those old ambitions clattered into life and thrust accusing fingers at him. He had to acknowledge their grinning presence.

"Perhaps we all have in us the impulse of the Creator!"

Their eyes were boring into each other. They were no longer two men. Their lives, their temperaments, their very names dropped from them. For a thrilled moment they became creatures—naked souls—abreast in a dark tide, aghast at the mysteriousness, the cluelessness of the sweeping enigma of life.

"Do you believe in a Creator?" asked Densham, in a hushed whisper.

"Yes."

The unhesitating and passionate affirmative rang across the room. It seemed to Griffith that it was uttered too readily, too violently; but he had no opportunity to probe the other's faith. The question had unleashed a flood of words.

"Yes, we are all creators in miniature. Even the lowest forms of life are born with that instinct—to reproduce themselves—create a new generation. Think of it. Millions of creatures plunged into passionate existence out of dead clay. They have their ecstatic hour and are gone, as the grass withers. But the race is re-created over and over again. Man arrives. His first act is to create a weapon. We do not know him as man until he does that. Then he gets up on his hind legs, develops a brain, becomes lord of the mud-heap!"

The glowing end of Gawthorpe's cigarette described a wide arc in the air. "And what happens? This brain of his is a new thing, an entity in itself, able to detach itself, contemplate itself, calculate, invent. It generates a passion of its own. What shall we call it? The frenzy of genius, if you like. But look; to what end does this passion burn. The same end, my dear fellow; always the same ... Creation! Beethoven creates a symphony; Wren a cathedral; Shakespeare a tragedy ... and the verger at the church—you remember old

Hawkins—well, you should see his garden. It's a creation too. Yes, we have in us the impulse of the Creator!"

Two deep parallel lines suddenly engraved themselves across Densham's forehead.

"And we squander it!" he cried, as though the words were wrung out of him.

"Yes," Gawthorpe admitted, "the older will of the senses is too much for it. That ancient impulse of pagan Nature thwarts the uprushing inspiration. As yet our blood is too hot and our minds too cold."

That phrase from Adams which had changed Densham's whole outlook on life now stole across the younger man's consciousness. He uttered it aloud, quietly:

"Thought is an arrested, a degraded physical action!"

"What do you say?" questioned Gawthorpe, looking sharply up.

"Our minds are cold precisely because we divorce them from what we feel. We think too much and feel too little. That 'impulse of pagan Nature,' as you call it, is Life itself. All the bright, virile things in Nature are unconscious. They do not contemplate themselves. They *are*! They content themselves with *being*! Only this little, doubting, rebellious, festering spot that we call our brain, this last arrived and degraded scrap of once passionate matter, this alone, in all the immense garden of existence, distils poison—the poison of doubt! That snake in the Eden story is a splendid bit of allegory. It prefigures the coiling, venomous brain of Eve, mother of this whole sceptical race, the first creature who believed it more blessed to *know* than to *be*."

His greenish eyes paled with the vehemence of his mood, until they appeared almost yellow. The little red flecks that stained his pupils were more than usually prominent.

"That queer, puzzling old Tree of Knowledge, too—eh? What a miracle of inspiration! Here we have been at it, generation after generation, biting deeper and deeper into the apple, and never getting any nearer the core. It isn't possible for us to know *anything*—in its essence. But we can *feel*! And if we'd let them alone—our senses, I mean—there would come flooding in to us all the infinite glamour of life, the inexplicable joy in merely being alive

... Heavens! What is there to know that can surpass that? What is there to doubt?"

His upflung hands crushed themselves against his temples. He spoke again, but in a low tone, as though to himself;

"Only the flaming rebelliousness of our own minds keeps us out of Paradise."

Gawthorpe, who had been aroused from his usual lethargic acceptance of things by Densham's vehemence, felt himself out of his natural element. He had been surprised into an unexpected, impassioned avowal, devastating to his peace of mind. His eyes narrowed and with a slow nestling movement against the cushions of his chair he relapsed into his accustomed languor. "You are more orthodox than when you went away, Griffith, aren't you?" he observed, with a touch of cynicism.

"Because I speak of Paradise?" asked Densham, getting up and striding to the fireplace. "No. I'm far from orthodox; but I am changing. I'm beginning to believe again in some sort of Paradise—not a place that we are going to, so much, as a place we have become estranged from. There's a passage in Pascal that I often think about. He says that the wretchedness of man is proof of his former high estate. What man is wretched, he says, because he has not three eyes? But who, having had two, is not inconsolable at the loss of one. I forget just how he puts it; but the idea is that man is wretched because he has lost something—some former glory. No one regrets that he is not a king, he says, except a deposed king."

Densham stopped. The quotation from Pascal suddenly reminded him of the words Gawthorpe had used in describing Madame Milónoff.

"A deposed queen! Born to unusual conquests!"

For some moments he was lost in thought.

"I was thinking of what you said about Madame Milónoff, 'A deposed queen.' You know, for years I have seen nothing regal—except mountains. And today, even at a distance, there was—as you say—an air about her. The chair might have been a throne."

Gawthorpe stretched himself with feline gravity and pointed to a photograph hanging above the lounge. "There is a photograph of her, before she was married. She presented me with it the night we did 'The Martyr.'"

Densham went over and examined it intently.

"Yes. I recall her now. What wonderful eyes! I don't remember *them!*"

Gawthorpe rose, crossed the room and threw his arm about Densham's shoulder. "If you care," he said, with an air of mockery, "I might secure an audience for you."

"Oh," cried Densham, a trifle abashed. "I never knew her, you know."

"But wouldn't you like to? She has quite a court. I often drop in on Sunday nights—after church. Usually there are a few people there. Will you come along some time?"

'Yes, I'd like to," said Densham. His quest for Ecstasy came into his mind.

"Her eyes," he thought, "look as though they have glimpsed it."

Chapter Two

O n the following Sunday night Densham sat in his old place in the choir. Before the service he had been surrounded by what remained of his former cronies, and it seemed strange to him that he did not feel more elation at rejoining them. All that had happened to him in the few crowded days since his talk with Gawthorpe had been vaguely disappointing. He was seeking a new experience, and all these people he had met, all the places he had revisited, were of the past.

He was getting no nearer to his conception of Ecstasy. More than once during the past two or three days he had been haunted by the eyes of Madame Milónoff; and at last he was to see her. The youthful and challenging glance depicted in that photograph had disturbed him.

During the sermon he endeavoured to picture her. It was with a sense of regret that he realized she would be much older—an invalid! He did not promise himself too much. And yet!

"Like a deposed Queen!"

He recalled Gawthorpe's phrase, and there immediately sprang into his mind a glimpse he had once had of the Empress Eugénie. He and George Pethick were cycling to Aldershot, and they had caught sight of her, in an open landau, turning into the drive of her estate at Farnborough. But the Empress had meant very little to him. He was born too late.

There was a rustle of starched surplices around him. They were getting up. The sermon was over.

After the service Densham had to wait while Gawthorpe had his customary two-minute chat with the vicar. That, too, came to an end. They left the vestry, bound for the Milónoffs.

It was a gloomy two-storey stone house, enclosed in spacious and well-kept grounds, within a few minutes' walk of the church. The clank of the lofty iron gate, as Gawthorpe swung it open, rang in Densham's ears like a bell, presaging something unusual, unexpected—he knew not what.

The door was opened by a diminutive maid whom Gawthorpe addressed familiarly as Polinska, bidding her "good evening" in very bad Russian. Whereat she smiled, blushed and curtseyed, all in the same moment.

They passed down the hall and entered the drawing-room. Erect, in a wheel-chair, just inside the door, sat Madame Milónoff. Densham's gaze immediately encountered her glowing eyes. The enigma of that elate tenderness, shining through her curved lashes, belonged to an infinitely receding, mysterious and scented past. In that instant, while her eyes smiled into his, it seemed to Densham that he plunged through limitless time into an age of glamour, ancient gallantries and resounding wars.

She withdrew her glance and Densham realized that he had not yet really looked at her. It seemed impossible that he had been there only a moment.

Madame Milónoff was leaning forward, extending her hand to somebody beside him. It was Gawthorpe. Densham had completely forgotten him.

Their voices, exchanging the usual greetings, came to him indistinctly. He felt Gawthorpe's fingers closing upon his knuckles. He was drawn forward. Madame Milónoff lifted her liquid eyes.

"I have taken the liberty of bringing an old friend," murmured Gawthorpe.

"Old?" she reproved him, making a perfect circle of her thin lips as she prolonged the vowel.

"An old chorister, I should say," explained Gawthorpe. "Mr. Densham. He has recently come back from Canada. I haven't seen him for fifteen years. We were speaking of you the other evening. He remembers you singing the solos in 'The Martyr of Antioch'."

"How dreadful!"

"Dreadful?" echoed Griffith. It was the first word he had uttered.

"Can't you imagine how old it makes me feel?" she laughed, arching her eyebrows, and assuming a pained expression. Then, with a startling suddenness, she dropped the pose, gave him a friendly smile, and warmly thrust forward her slender hand. "No, it was lovely of you to remember. And so nice of you to want to come."

At that moment somebody across the room attracted her attention. She nodded, and her lips—such thin, sensitive lips—framed the word—"Yes."

"Myron Balakirev is going to play," she said to Gawthorpe, and with a fleeting smile at Griffith turned to watch the young pianist settle himself awkwardly at the instrument.

Griffith glanced about him for the first time. There were perhaps a score of people present, mostly of foreign extraction, he decided. There were more men than women. A tall man, with a conspicuous short square beard, and a pile of waving black hair surmounting his massive head, was talking to a beautiful young woman who was reclining against the cushions of a low divan, near the French windows. When Balakirev struck the first chord he drew himself up, and leaning against the door, which opened into the garden, fastened his gaze on the girl's foot, elegantly stretched out to display her embroidered slipper.

Out of the corner of his eye Griffith could see that Gawthorpe also was regarding the pair with interest. "That's Milónoff," the musician whispered, without turning his head. "And the woman with him is Kalinova—do you know?—with the Russian ballet?"

Griffith did not speak. At last he was in an atmosphere that did not smack of the past,—his past. The faded beauty of the room, the elegant and almost romantic appearance of many of its occupants—strange to him because of their distinctly foreign air—the curious depth and distance he had seen in Madame Milónoff's eyes and the effect of the wheel-chair, which elevated her fragile body as though she were enthroned,—all this, and perhaps the silence and the rapt demeanour of all these people,—impressed Griffith as like a tableau of some old historic salon, presided over by this frail, grey-haired woman, whose extended hand had prompted in him the entirely strange inclination—a few moments ago—to drop on one knee and press his lips to her bejewelled fingers.

Almost stealthily he glanced at her now and was again amazed at the tenderness of her gaze, fastened abstractly above the piano. Her face was faintly lined, as though by some secret and indefinable sorrow. This air of immitigable melancholy was not tragic; it did not appear to have been evoked by any sudden or calamitous shock of intense suffering. It was rather the visible measure of a concealed yearning, a treasured aspiration, perpetually thwarted and frustrated and leaving her less and less hope, as the years passed, of its felicitous fulfillment.

Her brow, rather broad, but delicately moulded at the temples, was obscured by a drooping mass of black hair in which threads of silver gleamed abundantly. Shining dark-brown eyes, a straight sensitive nose, unusually thin lips, a piquantly pointed chin and high rounded throat,—these features, poised in a listening attitude, impressed themselves vividly upon Griffith's mind at one glance.

"No," Griffith thought, noting the sadness of her mouth, "not deposed! Her empire has never been anything but a promised land. She has viewed it only through the haze of her dreams. What was it Gawthorpe said— 'born to unusual conquests?' Of what sort? What strange hope lay in the trembling expectancy of her eyes? What might have been her frustrating destiny?"

The music ceased. Gawthorpe was introducing him to a large flabby man who seemed wrapped in unutterable ennui. The talk was of the most perfunctory sort. Densham glanced almost wretchedly over his shoulder and caught Madame Milónoff's gaze gently fixed upon him. Her eyes widened, and with a quick, smiling gesture she placed her hand upon a chair that was vacant beside her.

"Strangers are such a treat for me," she said, when he had seated himself. "You can imagine how—secluded—my life must be."

There was the merest trace of a foreign accent in her low vibrant tones. "Her voice and her eyes are still young," he thought; and aloud, leaning toward her, he said: "Yes. As I recall you at the Philharmonic you were so ..."

He stopped and looked at her, helplessly; a deep melting sympathy mingled with rebelliousness at her fate burning wholly undisguised in his glance. She felt it, looked sideways at him, and accepted his emotion with a perceptible enlargement of her humid eyes.

"So young—so all that I'm not now? Is that what you were going to say?"

His lashes did not even flutter. "No," he said, simply. "You did not seem young to me, then. I was little more than a boy, you see. But there was about you—a fire, an impetuousness—something dauntless. I remember I used to watch you breathe, when you were singing—with a queer sort of curiosity—almost as though you were not of the same clay as—as ourselves—the chorus, I mean. We used to regard all the soloists in that way, to some extent. But, you see, you were Russian—foreign. I think I saw you only three times ..."

"And have I changed so very much?" she asked.

He turned to meet her questing glance, her lifted lashes, her parted mouth; and he found it impossible to lie, to dissemble, to say anything polite.

"Yes," he said, and his tone and the burning truthfulness of his gaze sent a faint flush to her cheeks. "But not as I had expected. When I heard of how your career had been cut short so suddenly I felt a wave of bitterness—rebelliousness—come over me. There is little enough of the artist in me, but enough, at any rate, to enable me to realize—not fully, perhaps, what this has meant to you. And then, there seems such a tiny pinch of artistry scattered about the world—and even though it be only a condiment, something added, almost like an afterthought, to a few, a very few natures—for me it is quite the most outstanding thing, the only truly replaceless thing in life. And so...."

"I see," she said, gravely, when it was obvious that he did not intend to go on. "But, to feel like that, one must be very much of an artist ... indeed, indeed."

"I fear not," he almost groaned.

She was startled by his bitterness. "You sound as though life had not been very kind to you," she ventured.

"No, that's not it. I think I could have borne that. But to misuse the kindness that *does* come, to waste one's gifts, to beat the air! Is anything worse than that? To feel in oneself the heat of inspiration—and then to let it boil away—mere vapour—steam—air—nothing!"

He flung his head upward in a gesture of despair.

Madame Milónoff was amazed at his vehemence. "You have tried... ?" she began.

"For more than twenty years—I can hardly believe it—since I was ten—I have been trying. And I get nowhere."

He absentmindedly ran his fingers through his hair.

"But we were talking of you," he murmured, in a quiet tone. "It's just like this beastly ego of mine to obtrude itself. It isn't well trained, you see. Every now and again I cry—'To heel, Densham!!'—but it doesn't mind. Here it is again, you see, running about and getting in everybody's way. Do talk. It's the only way to keep me quiet."

"But I don't want you to keep quiet," she smiled at him; but he was not looking at her. He was gazing stolidly at the floor. "What a queer boy," she thought, and glanced for a moment across the room. It was a signal.

"Miss Landsberger is going to sing," she told him. "Some Russian songs, I think—but in English. Do you feel like Russian music? Or perhaps music doesn't appeal to you."

He began to tell her something of his musical likes and dislikes, but was interrupted by the commencement of a song;—that beautiful lament of Rachmaninoff's

> "How often at midnight in days long since fled,
> Dear children, I've watched with deep joy by your bed,
> How often your brows have I sign'd with the cross,
> And pray'd there: 'God keep us from sorrow and loss
> The love of the father protect you.'"

It was sung with an exquisite appreciation of the simplicity and solemnity of the music, and towards the end, where the voice rises and drones on a high monotone at the words:

> "My heart aches—the children are children no more!—

What anguish to lose them forever!"

Griffith felt his heart contract, and a sensation of pervading melancholy stole through his veins.

The ever-present consciousness of his unfulfilled dreams dissolved into a calm sadness, induced by the nearness of this woman who retained so much tenderness in spite of her frustrated destiny, and by the sweetness of resignation portrayed in that song, so characteristic of the genius of her country.

"Do you never sing now?" he asked, when the buzz of talk recommenced; but before she could answer two girls, accompanied by a slim youth, approached her with the urgent request—relayed, it seemed, from a majestic woman of unwieldy proportions, who kept up a constant succession of nods across the room while they were talking—that she, Madame Milónoff, should sing for them—"*at least one little song.*"

She instantly demurred; but Gawthorpe, seeing what was afoot, joined the group and made the specific request for Borodine's "The Fair Garden," saying he would accompany her himself, and that, as she knew it by heart, she need not move.

Still she objected. Densham, who had suddenly been seized by an unaccountable fit of trembling, added his mite to their entreaties—"Just the tiniest little song; to please an old admirer who has not heard you sing for—for ages!"

"Well, if you will have it," she murmured, dazzling him with the humid brilliance of the glance she turned upon him, "'The Fair Garden,' then. Would you like me to sing it in Russian, or in English?"

The question was put to Griffith.

"In English, I think, please. I don't know it, you see. Perhaps you will sing something else in Russian. Or, maybe, some other time ... I don't know: somehow—yes, I'd like to know what it's about."

"Very well," she said, brightly, and to Gawthorpe, who was about to go to the piano,—"You remember my key?"

He bowed and took himself to the bench. The accompaniment, like the faint quivering of leafage in early spring, commenced *pianissimo*, and then her voice, faint too, and as though floating in a tranquil and scent-laden twilight, —

> "Garden fair, shaded park,
> And poetical castle,
> Full worthy ye of kings,
> Enchanting paradise;
> Whose garden walks and e'erchanging pathways
> Lead thro' deep, sweet-smelling thickets and bow'rs
> To slim reeds filled with nests.
>
> Oh happy, happy ye,
> Having for sov'reign dear
> A lady fair, in spirit kind,
> Whose famous coat of arms
> Over the palace portal is blazon'd on high."

The final note, sustained over the still quivering accompaniment, diminished until it was a mere breath, and the song ended with a liquid, wave-like *arpeggio*.

The next day, and for many days thereafter, Densham heard in his ears the ringing ecstasy of her tones as she sang, with sublimity of feeling—"Oh, happy, happy ye, having for sov'reign dear a lady fair, in spirit kind ..."

No further opportunity to converse with her had presented itself that night until he took his leave. Others were crowding about her. He bent over her hand, and she, inclining herself toward him and raising her eyes, said in an intimate and low tone: "Will you come again? To tea some afternoon. There is so much I want to ask you. Wednesday?"

He began to stammer something; but her glance and a slight pressure of her fingers told him there was no need.

"I shall expect you," she said.

On the way home with Gawthorpe he was unusually silent. He walked with raised head; his gaze fixed on the stars.

Chapter Three

When George Pethick entered his dressing room at the Hippodrome on Monday night he found a note from Densham.

Dear George:

It may surprise you to find that I am back in England. Being unable to locate you today I got a couple of aisle seats for this evening. One of them is enclosed, and I hope you will be able to join me as soon as your turn is over. Till then, au revoir —Griff.

In the stalls Densham was glancing over the programme. He experienced a queer sensation on turning over a leaf and finding the Russian Ballet billed in large letters. When he looked over the Amusement column of The Times that morning, before running up to London, it had been merely Pethick's name he was seeking, and once finding it under the heading of the Hippodrome, his eye had not roved further.

Now, he eagerly scanned the page before him. There was Kalinova's name, separately displayed, as *premier danseuse*. He had not been presented to her the night before. Several minutes before anyone had started to leave he had glanced in the direction of the divan—one of a score of glances he had turned in that direction—and found that it had been vacated. Milónoff had gone, too. Through the French windows he could see into the garden, which was black and shadowy. As he looked two figures passed out of sight down the path, faintly outlined by the glow of the stars. One of them was certainly, Kalinova. Neither she, nor Milónoff, had appeared again before he took his leave.

"Tonight," he thought, "I am to see her in her 'war-paint'."

He wondered if Milónoff would be there, and began to search discreetly in the stalls and boxes; but there was no sign of the handsome, bearded Russian.

The orchestra had started by this time, and soon the curtain rose. The tumblers, who came first, amused him intensely. They were followed by a brazen slip of a girl, who sang a number of American song-hits; changing her costume between each, with the aid of a chic little dresser in white apron and cap, in full view of the audience.

While this was in progress Griffith saw—out of the corner of his eye—someone entering the lower box on his left. He glanced around and beheld Milónoff, his piled and waving hair looking as though it had just been pomaded, his short beard squarer than ever—not unlike, Densham thought, the beards of Assyrian warriors carved on ancient tablets in the British Museum.

The Russian settled himself comfortably in the front of the box, within a few feet of the stage, and turned upon the audience a callous and contemptuous glance of amused disapproval. Those thick brows, almost meeting; those black eyes, too small and too close together; the pallor of his brow and cheeks; the thick lips and even teeth; the whole man, in every feature, in every attitude, enraged Densham unaccountably whenever he looked at him.

Nevertheless, throughout the third turn, which interested Densham very little, he continually glanced in Milónoff's direction, and on one occasion believed he had surprised the other in the act of bestowing on him a look of coldly interested recognition.

Almost immediately afterward the asbestos curtain was rung down, an electric letter "E" glowed beside the stage, and the orchestra commenced a sobbing, barbaric chant—the prelude to the Ballet.

The first number, a Cossack dance, was brilliantly executed by a double sextette whose high, polished boots clattered to an accompaniment of extravagant dissonances, ending in a mad tattoo by the tympani.

The stage darkened. Curtains could be seen ascending and descending vaguely in the inky gloom. A stately air given out by the oboes and horns floated into every corner of the crowded, silent theatre. At last a faint glow illumined the stage, and there could be dimly discerned a background of tall poplars rising from behind a semicircular balustrade of gleaming marble. The light slowly increased. There was a rustle of programmes in every part of the house. Whispers were heard on all sides—"Kalinova!" A thin voice behind Densham murmured: "The Death of a Peacock".

Presently the *premier danseuse* appeared in a gorgeous head-dress of osprey feathers and an immense fan-like train, dotted with heart-shaped eyes of shimmering silver. She was behind the balustrade, moving majestically forward, her head thrown back, the long curve of her throat silhouetting its ravishing whiteness against the green of the plume-shaped poplars.

At the head of the steps, leading down from the wide terrace, she swept her train behind her and imperiously faced the audience. In an instant the house thundered with applause. The costume was calculated to strike one breathless. Her hips and breasts were tightly sheathed in two bands, sparkling with sequins, and joined only by silver cords stretched taut across her flesh when she stood—as she did at that moment—with her chin in the air, leaning arrogantly forward. Her arms were swathed behind her and concealed in a silken cape which terminated in the train. Loose silver cords, hanging from the band about her hips and attached to her sandals, enclosed the slender beauty of her limbs.

A soaring, rapturous melody played by the solo violin accompanied her slow descent of the staircase, melting into a movement for all the strings which rose in a swelling tide of sound as Kalinova raised and spread out behind her the glittering train.

Applause rang out again. The *danseuse* lowered her head, inclined her body forward, and with precise, bird-like steps advanced to the footlights. The great fan slowly drooped. A new, lilting rhythm was announced by the wind instruments. Kalinova swiftly threw up her head in an incomparable gesture and began the dance. It was at once stately and joyous, a light, parading, strutting step, taking her in wide sweeping circles.

Densham watched every moment with entranced attention. Presently, at a moment when her back was to the audience, he noticed a stir in the cape, as though she were extricating her arm. When she again faced the house a golden-shafted arrow had been ingeniously fastened to her costume—as though it had entered her breast.

She reeled, and from her knees upward drooped slowly back—back, until her prone body seemed almost to be lying on the air. Then, with a wounded jerk, she twisted to one side, lurched forlornly across the stage, dropped to her knees, and collapsed in a pitiful heap—within a few feet of where Milónoff was sitting, hunched forward, his eyes fixed in a glassy stare.

The descending curtain intervened. Densham saw Milónoff dart a swift glance sideways at the audience and then sit back with closed eyes as though feasting his intoxicated soul upon the memory of Kalinova's prostrate loveliness.

Densham himself was thrilled in every fibre by her exquisite allure. The number that followed irritated him. He glanced at his programme. Kalinova was to appear again in the finale which bore the title—"Mêlée Fantasque." He awaited it impatiently.

Finally the curtain rose upon a scene of indescribable confusion. Riotous colours literally attacked the eye. Inconceivable pillars towered out of sight. Unearthly trees, of the strangest hues—blue, pink and purple—flung their writhing branches against a sky of burning copper. In the centre of the stage, around a sculptured fountain, there was already surging—when the curtain went up—a crowd of prancing figures in the scantiest and most bizarre attire. In their wildly gesticulating hands they held long wide scarves of every known colour. These were flung into the air, flicked into each other's faces, rolled and unrolled round their bodies. Meanwhile the orchestra was creating a deafening and toneless din, devoid of any semblance to music to save in its bacchanalian beat; and so fast that the feet of the dancers, in keeping time to it, seemed hardly to touch the ground.

Minutes elapsed. The dance was utterly patternless, except that every now and then the entire group, one after another, in the wildest disorder, approached the fountain, flung their scarves upward and scampered backwards away from it in attitudes of ecstatic obeisance.

After a time a more or less concerted movement took place. The dancers gathered close about the fountain, which continued to spray thin jets of water into the wide bowl.

The orchestral din slackened it precipitant tempo. The scarves were thrown high into the air, across the spraying water; uplifted hands grasped their floating ends; and for a moment a sort of dome was formed of these fluttering, multi-coloured ribbands. Through this silken lattice there suddenly shot a pair of snowy arms. Immediately the ends of the ribbands were loosened; swiftly they were snatched aside, and there—poised on the fountain's broad lip, with the water streaming over her—stood Kalinova!

On her head was a silver helmet with a raised vizor, over which two serpents were coiled. Two silver medallions covered her breasts, and from her waist to her thighs she was enveloped in chain mail, also of silver, through which her skin gleamed.

For a moment she remained there. Then she leaped into the arms of the revellers crouched before the bowl of the fountain. They caught her, carried her with high, tramping tread about the stage, flinging about her their rainbow-hued scarves.

Presently she dropped to her feet and whirled about the stage, her arms extended, her head thrown back; every motion depicting the wildest abandon. In the midst of this a man, clothed in a leopard's skin, dashed from the wings and grasped her about the waist. It was Stepinine, her partner.

The revellers darted between them, Stepinine leaping over their scarves every now and again, to reach Kalinova's side.

Finally, when the pace and the noise had reached a point of almost unendurable frenzy, Kalinova was caught up by her partner and carried high above his head—still writhing and gesticulating—off the stage. The curtain came down amidst an ear-splitting blare of trumpets.

Densham did not wait for the encores. He made his way to the bar and stood there, abstractly sipping his drink, with the jabber of other drinkers in his ears, puzzled and irritated by the scene he had just witnessed.

A grim smile curled his lip.

"Very well, my boy," he said to himself, almost aloud, "there's Ecstasy for you, with a capital 'E.' I hope you like it."

His whole being revolted at the thought. He recalled the engrossed, fascinated gaze of Milónoff, leaning half out of his box, his cheeks white with uncontrolled desire.

This, then, was the logical conclusion of an abandoned plunge into the stream of life. This was the apotheosis of *feeling*, as opposed to thought.

"*Hic Jacet!*" he murmured. "Here lie the remains of pursued Ecstasy! What then? Is there nothing that does not crumble in the grasp?"

He left the question hanging in his mind and went back to his seat. As he passed down the aisle the audience burst into a sharp guffaw. He looked at the stage. In front of the "street drop" stood a single figure, motionless, waiting for the rippling laughter to subside. It was George Pethick.

He had grown stout. His face—thin almost to emaciation in his youth—had filled out; but his small hands and feet, his hair parted slickly in the centre, and those huge, round, mischievous eyes were unmistakable. He had developed a grimace which accentuated the tilt of his upturned nose. His impudent goblin-like appearance was unspeakably comic to Densham. It was like looking at a devilishly clever animated caricature of his boyhood chum.

Later, when Pethick squeezed into the seat beside him, minus his make-up, he looked worn and aged. Not a glint of lustre was left in his protruding eyes; his mouth was drawn; his cheeks flabby.

"Well, Griff," he whispered, as their hands met in the semi-darkness, "back from the wild and woolly—what?"

The two men gave each other a searching look and felt at once that they were precisely that—boys no longer; but men—and so long parted that their boyhood together was no longer a tie; so many years, events, divergences of thought, occupation and condition had slashed across it in the meanwhile.

Outside, they began in a half-hearted way to tell each other something of what had happened to them in the interval. In a few minutes they were seated at a table in Stolling's, a tiny restaurant frequented by professional people. They conversed merrily, endeavouring to hide from each other their mutual lack of interest.

Later on the talk reverted to the performance, and Densham remarked:

"By the way, George, I saw Kalinova at Milónoff's on Sunday night in Croydon."

Pethick's goblin-like eyes grew rounder than ever. "He even takes her to his home, does he? I see him about with her a lot in town. He was there tonight, in a box."

"Yes. I saw him."

"He's there three or four performances a week. Of course, he's notorious. I don't suppose you remember Cissie Hulatt? No. She flared up and went out very suddenly. But this is quite the maddest crush—even for him."

"Is she married? Kalinova?"

"No. But there's a Bohemian bounder—a real Bohemian, I mean, from Bohemia—an arch-duke or a prince; yes, Prince Bienjonetti, they call him, who is supposed to have followed her here from Europe. He's furious, of course. It's rumoured that they fought a duel down at Epping; but it isn't generally believed."

"Do you suppose Madame Milónoff knows of it?"

Pethick glanced quickly at his friend with a mocking, elfish expression, as though he hardly credited such ingenuousness.

"Oh, absolutely. Why, Milónoff is more than notorious; he's famous. Of course, she's an invalid; never gets to town; probably doesn't hear much. But she must know something."

"What's his business?"

"Importer. Rolling in money. She's wealthy, too. That house in Croydon belonged to her mother, I believe. I wonder she didn't divorce him—years ago."

"I don't," said Densham. "She isn't ..."

But instead of finishing his sentence he changed the subject.

Chapter Four

Two lean greyhounds came bounding toward him down the drive when Densham entered Madame Milónoff's gate on the Wednesday afternoon. He paused and fondled the long, damp noses snuffing at his legs.

"Princely creatures," he thought, as he dallied there, talking to them caressingly, while they leaped about him.

They were part of the scene, vivid because of its strangeness, and drenched in an atmosphere of damp, mouldering, ancient calm, into which he found himself strolling with grave thoughtfulness. It was indicative of his mood that he could spend precious moments, just inside the gate, teasing the dogs with the curved end of his stick, while he glanced leisurely about at all the tall rhododendrons, whose dusty leaves hung motionless in the afternoon sun, at the brown earth of newly-raked flower beds, at the low, grey walls of the old-fashioned house, the upper windows of which, with their leaded, diamond-shaped panes, seemed to be shrinking from observation, so thickly overhung were they with ivy.

As he approached the steps an agitated exultation seized him, magnifying and surrounding with brightness the tiniest objects and the minutest sounds. From the back of the house there came the faint "clip ... clip" of a gardener's shears, and he could hear through an open, up-stairs window the low humming of a maidservant rustling quietly about her tasks.

He was astonished to find himself trembling, ever so slightly, as he raised the heavy bronze knocker, fashioned in the form of a tragic mask. The vacant eye-sockets and drooping mouth seemed to regard him with grim

foreknowledge of his ordained destiny, while he stood waiting for the door
to open.

Anton, the old footman, came at last. He opened wide the door, and
Densham's vision was immediately dazzled with the glory of the down-
going sun pouring through the high, stained-glass window above the
turn of the stairs. It flooded the spacious hall, and with this halo behind
his venerable head the palsied old servitor looked more than ever like some
Biblical prophet, whose arms might at any minute be lifted in lamentation.

Instead he lifted his thick brows and gave Griffith a steady, appraising
glance. "M'sieur Densham?" Griffith inclined his head.

"Your honour is expected."

The hall looked larger with the sunlight streaming along the polished
floor and striking the mirrors of the antlered clothes-rack with scintillating
bursts of light. The great canvases, too, looked heavier and gloomier; the
slender bronze figure on the stair-post seemed more remote.

The rumble of Anton's voice interrupted Densham's observation of these
half-strange surroundings. The old footman was preceding him down the
hall. At an open doorway near the foot of the stairs he paused, and ushered
Densham into Madame Milónoff's presence.

She was seated in her wheel-chair, facing the door, in a small, cosy
room, into which the dying blaze of the sun did not penetrate. Twilight was
already settling about her, and as he moved forward Densham experienced
a delicate pang of melancholy. Grey, erect, immobile—there was about
her figure the pathetic poise of one who has waited a very long time, with
resolute expectancy, for some revelation, some miracle, some perfect and
sufficient fulfillment of an inexpressible hope.

He bent over her hand, and she said—"It's so good of you to come. I
didn't ask you on Sunday night how long you intend staying in England;
but I suppose you must have a hundred places to go, and not half enough
time."

He took a low seat beside her and leaned forward, clasping his hands.

"I think I am going to stay here," he said, and paused. A sudden impotence attacked him, draining his mind of words. He felt incapable of murmuring anything but "yes" and "no." The sensation was akin to that enchantment, experienced sometimes in dreams, which holds one breathless, unable to stir or utter a sound, while the peopled vision passes within arm's reach.

"Then you have no ties to speak of in Canada?" she was saying.

"No."

His brain refused to set itself to the task of conversing with her; it was concerned only with the strange heaviness which numbed his power of speech. "What has come over me?" he kept repeating to himself, and in answer, out of the confused web of his thoughts, there floated a phrase of De Quincey's—"the weight of twenty Atlantics was upon me."

Instead of ignoring it the current of his consciousness swept him on to fresh questioning—"What made me think of that? What is that from?" His errant mind tracked it down, placing it in the context which he had once fondly memorized.

All this flashed through his brain instantaneously. She was speaking again.

"And do you find your friends much scattered after so long an absence?"

"Not as much as I had expected." He spoke mechanically, without real volition.

"I suppose we don't move about much in England. Although I am indoors so much that everyone else seems so active and restless in comparison."

She was looking at him and he at her as though both of them were aware of some long enduring but interrupted familiarity which gave to these trite remarks an air of polite mockery. It puzzled them both; and yet was cogent enough to establish between them an understanding that the usual pretences and pettinesses of casual conversation might be dispensed with from that moment onward.

It was she who lifted their talk into this new plane.

"You were so frank with me on Sunday that I feel I have known you a very long time."

It was said aloud, and yet hardly addressed to him. It was an uttered thought, a justification, a reason for this odd feeling that they had known each other intimately in some half-forgotten past.

"You must have been astonished at my vehemence," Densham remarked. "I thought about it a great deal—afterward; and wondered what could have caused me to pour out my feelings as I did. It seemed to me that you must have drawn me out,—and yet I can't remember anything you said that might have given me an excuse."

She leaned forward. "You are not going to apologize," she protested, with a soft rebuke in her glance.

"Not for that," he went on. "It was just because you did not seem like a stranger to me, I suppose, that I could do it. But just now, when I first sat down, I didn't want to talk at all. Just the reverse, you see. And yet it springs from the same thing. One doesn't remain silent in the presence of strangers."

He stopped and regarded her with a look that demanded her understanding, and she accepted what he had said with that slow enlargement of her eyes which seemed to invite him to look and find there the complete accord and sympathy with his bared emotion which his glance craved.

"I have thought about it, too," she said, very quietly, "and I think it must be that you sense in me something of the disappointment, the tragedy of lost opportunities, which you seem to have experienced yourself. You shouldn't, you know. I mean you shouldn't give way to disappointment, to disillusionment. You have the best of your life before you. You are still young—without handicaps ..."

"Except one," he interrupted, almost fiercely. "Myself! 'The fault is not in our stars, but in ourselves, that we are underlings.' Externally, perhaps, I am not confronted with handicaps; but inside—inside I am chained!"

He paused, frowned, looked at her as though wondering whether to go on, and decided to do so.

"Do you know, I spent a lot of time, once, digging into the source-plots of 'Hamlet.' I was consumed with curiosity to know how much of Hamlet's vacillating character was attributable to Shakespeare's invention, and how much to the original story, if there was one. I found that there was not merely one, but many, and that they extended back through a host of quaint variants of an old tradition which had its roots in the myths of most ancient peoples. But right up to the lost drama of Thomas Kyd, on which Shakespeare is supposed to have based his tragedy, the story was always one of external difficulties placed in the path of Hamlet's revenge. Shakespeare removed them all. One almost fancies him taking Kyd's melodramatic manuscript and saying to himself—'Suppose we take all the knots out of it, all the stage tricks that hold up the action, all the creaking machinery—and place the whole burden of the delayed vengeance on the protagonist.' That's precisely what he did. Hamlet's only handicap is himself. And it's well to remember that the story springs from a myth about some primeval dragon-slayer, so ancient that there are literally scores of versions of it in every language and literature—even in the Bible. The dragon-slaying element had been eliminated from the actual Hamlet story long before it came to Shakespeare; but 'the native hue of resolution'—that was there—the valour becoming to a prince, the intrepidity fitting to a stage hero—it was there until Shakespeare, wearied of swashbuckling gallants, 'sicklied it o'er with the pale cast of thought'."

His eyes underwent a change of colour as they often did with the mercurial flashes of his humour. They darkened perceptibly and a bluish glow replaced the gleam that mostly haunted them. "How I talk," he cried.

Madame Milónoff had been listening with a deep interest which was not confined to his subject alone. She was absorbed, at the same time, in wondering what had led him to such studies. And, more than that, she had been watching with carefully veiled curiosity his way of telling her all this, the confidence with which he gave it out, the flash of his eyes, the tense lines about his mouth, the abruptness of his occasional gestures.

"How do you pull yourself up like that?" she asked. "It must have been a most intriguing quest. Cannot you believe that I'm interested?"

He shrugged his shoulders.

"But, you see," he murmured, humbly, "I came with the vowed intention of not talking about myself. I wanted ..."

"But you haven't been talking about yourself—it's been about Shakespeare."

"Yes—about Shakespeare; about Hamlet. But why do I tell you all that? Why did I plunge into all that research? Because it throws some light on this queer puzzle ..." He clasped his temples. "This restless, inconstant, wayward intellect."

"Why should I concern myself so much about it? Why am I not content to live, as other people seem to?"

He looked up at her and smiled ruefully.

"But above all," he blurted out, in a helpless tone, "why should I burden you with my troubles?"

He folded his arms tightly, with an air of taking hold of himself. "I wanted you to talk today."

"But that would simply be reversing the roles," she said. "Must it be so one-sided?"

Anton appeared with the tea-things before he could answer. There was a pause while the tray was arranged before her. Then, as she busied herself with serving him, he asked—"Do you get out very much? I suppose you ..."

"In a bath chair," she replied, simply. "Oh yes. Anton takes me out—every morning when it is fine. And often quite late at night, when people are not here. Sometimes even after they have gone. I love the stars—I love the stars—they make up for so much, and they help me to feel humble. They cool my soul."

She had betrayed the fire that was burning in her. It flared in her eyes, flushed her cheek, and agitated her white hands. He repeated that phrase to himself—"They cool my soul." What was this hope, this expectancy, that flamed within her? Whence sprang this need to humble herself? His sympathy—it was almost pity—surged through him again.

"I wonder if you would let me come some time and wheel you," he said, over his tea-cup. "Somehow I feel we could talk better in the open air. And there is so much that I want to tell you, to ask you. Why should *that* be? I come back from Canada, expecting to talk for hours on end with old friends—not so much about old times—but to find out how they have changed. Seeking always, you see, for something that will explain the change that has taken place in me. But they haven't changed. And we talk about trivialities. None of them have probed their own souls. They don't like the word 'soul'. No doubt they are much happier—just because they are able to forget that they possess such a thing. But I—I—well, I flung myself into life with immense resolution. I felt there were tremendous tasks ahead—dragons to be slain! I began to equip myself for the ordeal. Presently I sallied forth to achieve, conquer, make a noise in the world. I can't remember when I wasn't writing something—and always, always, with a purpose. No knight ever believed his lance more potent than I my pen. My enthusiasm was almost blasphemous. I felt myself to be a man sent from God. I hardly suppose you can understand. Well, I should like to be able to tell you what happened, but I cannot. I don't know myself; unless it was that there were too many dragons. I began to ponder which I should attack first. It took some time to come to a decision, but after a while I began. I fought with all the zeal I was capable of; and it was a lot. I have never lacked zest. But before I could finish, the particular dragon I was fighting seemed to lose importance. Another began roaring in another part of the field. I made off in that direction and started all over again. I have been starting ever since, eternally starting, never finishing. Not one of the dragons is dead. I have nothing to show for all my wounds and weariness. Nothing!"

He put down his tea cup and abruptly rose. She did not deter him with a sound or a gesture, but sat with widened eyes, as though his misery were no new thing to her, as though she wholly comprehended it and had shared it from the beginning of the world.

He had stalked nervously to the window, but coming back and standing over her, he looked into her face with an intensity that amounted almost to fierceness.

"See what you have let yourself in for," he said, with a hard, squeezed tone, "by the mere appearance of taking an interest in me."

With a motion that was so sudden as to seem entirely involuntary she extended her hand to him over the side of her wheel-chair. He clasped it in both his, dropped upon a low foot-rest at her side, and kept her soft fingers imprisoned in his own.

"My dear boy," she said, "it isn't 'mere appearance'. I shouldn't have asked you to come today if—if I hadn't wanted to let myself in for something, as you say. I hoped for this—just this—that you would tell me more about this torment that exasperates you. You said enough on Sunday to make me curious. You see, I too have my moments of torture. I, too, have sometimes believed myself to be *sent* ... Perhaps life was too kind to me at the start, holding out glowing promises of a high destiny, conquests, triumphs—ah, you know what I mean, so well. Is it any wonder that we felt some sort of kinship—so soon?"

She gently withdrew her hand. He allowed it to slip lingeringly through his fingers.

"I like you to come to me, as you would to a father-confessor—I am old enough, you see ..."

He leaned forward to interrupt her vehemently. Age had dropped from her in his eyes. She was as old as Time, and yet as youthful as a flower. Time, space, circumstance—nothing earthy, it seemed, could impinge upon this proximity of their two souls—so near, familiar and exalted by mutually experienced suffering.

She bestowed on him a glance that possessed the significance of an accolade. So it seemed to him, obsessed as he was with her queenliness.

"I should like to help," she murmured. "I don't know how, of course; but you are still so young, so full of—well, let's use your words—'valour' and 'intrepidity'—Oh, yes, yes."

But he was already crying out—"No, no, no!"—and groping blindly for her hand, unable to withdraw his eyes from hers, so full were they of hope for him.

She let him have her hand and for a space they sat silent, feeling no necessity for speech. Suddenly his clasp tightened and he raised her fingers impetuously to his lips.

Her eyes deepened and were swept by strange gleams as though some long forgotten memory were striving to exhume itself from her past. In a stifled, anguished voice she cried:

"It's unbelievable that we haven't met before. Tell me. Who *are* you?"

He felt himself dropping out of the existing moment into an immemorial retrospect. He experienced an impossible sensation of having become suddenly fleshless.

"Somewhere—some time," he murmured, in a hushed, hoarse voice, "a long, long time ago—before the earth and the sea were made—we must have been—together! That's all I know. I don't know even that. I've never believed in such things. But—what else? And you—you feel it, too?"

It was a whisper that came to him, a breath, tenuous as air, and yet her whole being floated out of her with it and united with his.

"Yes."

Chapter Five

That night in his room, after sitting for an hour with bowed head, gazing fixedly before him, Densham suddenly jumped up and went to the tiny secretaire which he had scarcely used since taking up his lodging there.

With characteristic impulsiveness he drew a sheet of paper towards him, removed the stopper of the ink-well, and selected a pen. The corners of his mouth were drawn down in that accustomed grimace which accentuated the stern line of his upper lip. Deep lines appeared in his forehead. His glance roved over the wall above the writing desk.

How would he address her?

She came vividly before his mind, a solitary figure, surrounded by grey shadows, her white hands like drifted snow in her lap. He recalled that last look she had sent him as he retreated from the room.

As so often happened, a phrase of grandiose prose from a much-beloved book soared upward to express his thought.

"When the waters of sad knowledge ..."

How did it go? He got up and went to the bookcase where some of his favourite volumes had been hurriedly installed. His own pencilled index on the fly-leaf of one of them guided him quickly to the passage he sought;

"I sit now, alone and melancholy, with that melancholy which comes to all of us when the waters of sad knowledge have left their ineffaceable delta in the soul."

He dropped the book on the window-sill, thrust his hands deeply into his thick hair and strained his head back against the nest of his clasped fingers.

Sad knowledge!

Yes, he thought, that ancient tree must indeed have been forbidden. To generation after generation it brings nothing but sadness.

That deep and unutterable sense of the continuity of existence, which had come to him in that twilight-filled room, emphasized more than ever his impatience, his distrust, his quarrel with the fleshly world.

He had glimpsed in her eyes the radiance of imperishable youth. He felt that he could come near to her only by shaking off the flesh. They could reunite in that companionship of which they had both experienced a mysterious augury only by destroying and leaving behind the whole conception of an earthly condition.

Across the black gulf of his habitual scepticism this thought fell like a ray of intoxicating light. He suddenly felt his heart elated by an unusual happiness. His need to write to her returned.

He sat down again at the table, dipped his pen, and began:

Dear Madame Milónoff:

I have not yet told you why I came to England. A single phrase from a great book impelled me to uproot myself. It was this: 'Thought appears in Nature as an arrested, a degraded physical action.'

I began to suspect that the secrets of life, if they can be fathomed at all, are unapproachable through the intellect. After doubting everything else I began to doubt the efficacy of my mind, my own faculty of doubting.

It occurred to me that all our sadness, our impatience, our scepticism, springs from the attempt to get outside of Life and see it whole. I determined that Life was not to be seen, not to be known; but only *experienced*. I believed that the happiest and most beautiful creatures do not contemplate themselves. They are content with *being*. In this, I thought, might lie the richest ecstasy. I made up my mind to pursue it. I tried to crush back my thoughts, my reason.

'We think too much and feel too little,' I told myself. I came back to England because I thought that in this tranquil landscape, on sunny downs and beside the lapping sea, I might give the quietus to my eternally questing mind. Here, I believed, ecstasy might be found, in surrendering oneself to the glamour, the beauty, the blessedness of Nature.

How we deceive ourselves! It is so palpably wrong to think of brute nature as content with being. There is no content. All Nature is restless. The blood of every tiniest creature throbs with the impulse of this blind, inexplicable quest—for what? For something new? For 'perfect adaptation'? For 'the peak of fitness'?

Just since this afternoon I am coming to believe that the biologists are all wrong. It seems to me that all of us—all Nature—is seeking something old; not something new. Something older than the universe, older than Time, which has been experienced before, and toward which—finding it lacking—all Life yearns. I am left to the thought that matter itself—dead though we have been apt to deem it—is itself impregnated, in its minutest particles, with this urge to seek a state from which it has been exiled.

Why do I tell you all this? Because it is what I really meant this afternoon. 'Before the heavens were brought forth, or the earth or sea were made', we lived a life other than this; and deep in us, deeper than our thoughts, closer to the heart of our being than our blood, there is the unconscious, but vitalizing memory of that lovelier existence. And for millions of years—which, perhaps, is but an hour of that other life—every particle of matter has been groping, straining forward in the dark, blindly seeking the Paradise from which it has strayed.

Both of us seemed to sense something of all this, this afternoon. With a suddenness passing comprehension we both recognized in each other—like exiles meeting in a strange land—the familiar spark of that other youth, which seems never to grow old nor wearied of seeking its lost dwelling place.

Even my first glimpse of you on Sunday night gave me some premonition of all this. I marvelled then at the depth of expression in your eyes. I asked myself then—'What is it in her glance which speaks of an infinitely receding and mysterious past?'

But to-day I felt sure. You will not readily realize what that means to me, to feel sure of *anything*! You have given me hope, where there was nothing before but the blankest scepticism. You contain in yourself the sweet evidence, the very spark of that something divine in us 'that was before the elements and owes no homage unto the Sun.'

Do you remember that wonderful passage of Sir Thomas Browne's?

And Francis Thompson, too. He sensed it. 'O Titan Nature! a petty race may find you too vast, may shrink from you into its earths; but though you be a very large thing, and my heart a very little thing, yet Titan as you are, my heart is too great for you.'

I am afraid you will be amazed at all this. I couldn't help but write you, though. For over an hour I have been sitting here thinking. When may I see you again? There is so much that I want to say to you.

Griffith Densham

The following day he spent in London, securing an interview with a publisher.

He had lain awake most of the night, disturbed by the most vivid recollection of what had transpired between him and Madame Milónoff during the afternoon. His unposted letter to her, lying sealed and stamped on the flap of the secretaire, troubled his thoughts. Half a dozen times he all but got out of bed with the intention of re-writing it. He luxuriated in the novel sensation of believing in something. Invariably his imagination was most active during the early hours of the morning. His fantastic theory—in the dark, and with the radiance of Madame Milónoff's eyes still a potent memory—seemed to him sound, sane and worthy of the most exhaustive elaboration.

After a while he did get up, turned on the light and smoked a cigarette in an easy-chair by the open window.

Life had taken on a different hue. He looked up at the distant stars and a thrill of happiness shot through him as he realized that in a day the mighty, whirling universe had been transfigured for him. The vast swing of these glowing, hurrying spheres through the profound ether possessed for the first time a recognizable significance, a purpose.

These stars were homing to the Paradise they had strayed from. Instinctively, from the earliest times, mankind had reached the astounding conclusion that this life was not all, that something lay beyond it. Perhaps they were right, after all. He shaped his thought paradoxically—"Men have been constantly concerned with a Heaven to which they are going, instead of one from which they have come."

He left his cigarette-end smoking in the ash-tray and went back to bed; but it was a long time before he slept.

In the morning he awoke with a sense of being in a strange universe. It was not that the room seemed unfamiliar. Indeed, that was in itself the essence of the new sensation—the feeling that these solid, physical things about him were no longer of any importance, their very existence only a delusion. A singular clairvoyance edged his thought so that it cut through the thickness of mere appearance to the heart of some palpitating actuality which he had never before suspected.

Slowly he recalled the extravagant imaginings of the night that had just passed.

"Homing Stars! An exiled universe! Paradise Lost!"

He sat up and rumpled his hair with both hands. A musing sceptical smile drew down the corners of his mouth. He was trying to laugh at himself, at the folly of false hopes, at the entirely unusual sensation of waking into a world that meant something, that was vital, possessed of an aim and a goal.

He got up and looked at himself in the mirror; but as he gazed at the reflection of his mocking greenly-glinting eyes, the cynical laughter died out of them. A new and austere determination could be read in the set of his jaw. Within him he felt the lift and buoyancy of a strange, invigorating power.

At breakfast he decided to go up to London, interview a publisher to whom he could gain access, through a mutual friend, and set himself to some definite task. Even the distasteful prospect of sheer hack-work had no terrors for him.

As the train sped toward Victoria he analysed the causes underlying this hasty determination to fling himself into some sort of occupation. Madame Milónoff was more than indirectly responsible for it. It was she, certainly who had inspired this sudden, but profound consciousness of an unsuspected potency, behind the mask of the material. But there was, too, another, a more practical influence. He could not continue to visit her in the role of a sluggard. The ache to achieve was awakened in his heart.

On looking up his friend he was surprised to learn that the publisher whose interest he wished to arouse was a permanent guest at the Suffolk Hotel, where he always put up when staying overnight in the city. The three met at dinner that night, and Densham was more than ever amused to find that the editor of one of the oldest and most dignified English reviews turned out to be precisely the figure he had most often noticed in the smoking-room of the hotel, during his previous stops there.

This shabby, dishevelled, Micawber-like person, whose insolently truculent air had more than once attracted Densham's attention, proved himself to be the gentlest of creatures, when properly introduced.

In the lounge, after dinner, the talk drifted toward the specific nature of Densham's capabilities. His Shakespearian research-work immediately established a point of contact, and late that evening the men separated, Densham glowing with the prospect of putting to practical use his months of study in a series of articles on the source-plots of 'Hamlet'.

In the morning he took an early train for Croydon, and found a note from Madame Milónoff awaiting him at his room. For several moments he stood gazing at the unfamiliar writing which he nevertheless knew—at a glance—to be hers. His pulses quickened as he tore open the envelope and read:

Dear Mr Densham:

Tomorrow night I am entertaining at dinner—people you
would not find interesting. But if you can come in about ten o'clock
Anton will show you to the library where I will find you as soon as
they leave.

Till then —
Natálya Milónoff

Perhaps you shall wheel me under the stars as you wished.

The letter had been posted the previous evening. It meant that tonight he
would see her again. The day passed slowly.

When he approached the house, excited by the unusual hour of the
appointment, and eager to tell her of the commission he had secured in
London, a hum of voices reached his ears. Her guests were leaving. He
walked past and loitered until they were gone. Then, with a recurrence of
the trembling which had affected him two days before, he lifted the tragic
mask—more sinister than ever in the dim light of the porch at night—and
knocked.

Anton came. In a few moments Madame Milónoff appeared with a filmy
blue wrap about her shoulders, wheeling herself down the hall.

He and Anton assisted her down the steps and into the bath-chair.
Densham was surprised to discover that she could walk at all.

"If it were not for my heart I could hobble about with a stick or a crutch,"
she told him. "But I have to be so careful. The slightest strain or over-
excitement makes me quite ill. But let's forget about all that. Tell me what
you have been doing."

They were at the gate by this time, which Anton had come down to
open.

"Which way shall we go?" asked Griffith.

She signified that it did not matter, and settled herself sideways in the
chair so that she could look up at him as he walked behind.

He told her of his interview with the publisher and his chance to make
use of the reams of notes he had made at the time he was studying 'Hamlet'.

She expressed an eager curiosity to learn how he was going to handle it. He began enthusiastically, but when it occurred to him that their hour was slipping away he was filled with impatience.

Not until they were close to the house again, the hour nearly up, did he feel emboldened enough to bend nearer to her and engage her eyes in a deep glance.

"Somehow we seem like quite ordinary people tonight, don't you think?" he murmured, with a perceptible trace of disappointment in his voice.

"Surely not," said she, rather soberly.

"I mean that we have not talked as I had expected—hoped. We have been too human for my liking. On Wednesday we seemed to get—to get behind the material; on a different plane. You know what I mean—don't you?"

They were at the gate. He opened it, placed his foot against it, and guided in the chair. Then he bent over for an answer.

"Yes," she said, "It has been there—the other—underneath our talk. It has not been a bit strange, this outing with you. I still feel—as I did on Wednesday—that I have known you a very long time."

"But not in the same way," he demurred, in her ear. "Not as intensely."

He brought the chair to a standstill opposite the steps and moved to one side so that he could look directly into her face. It seemed to him that she was deliberately keeping her feelings in check.

"You live so intensely yourself," she cried, almost as though she envied him. "But you mustn't expect all of us poor mortals to keep up with you. After you had gone on Wednesday I felt quite exhausted."

He bent closer. "Did you? Did you?" he exclaimed. It seemed to give him a sort of savage pleasure that he could stir the depths of her.

She saw his impassioned look and held up her hand, palm outwards, as though protecting herself from the fierceness of a flame.

"And have you thought of it since?" he demanded, hoarsely.

"A great deal. Too much. It is so strange! I can't! I mustn't! Please ring for Anton."

"Can't we manage together?" he asked, coming to the front of the chair.

She sat forward. He put his arm about her and lifted her up. She stepped to the ground, leaning heavily on his arm.

"Let me carry you," he whispered.

"No, no. I can manage this way."

She stood still for a moment, looking up at the thickly strewn stars. With one arm about her and the other supporting her wrist he stood gazing down at her, his heart aching. Slowly her eyes turned to his, and without another word they laboriously ascended the steps.

"Will you come Sunday night?" she asked, while Anton helped her into the house-chair.

He murmured a polite affirmative and went away, raging inwardly.

Chapter Six

During the next few weeks Densham spent a great deal of time at the British Museum, delving among old folios and volume after volume of Shakespeariana of every sort. His evenings he spent in his room at the Suffolk, arranging the mass of material he had gathered during the day.

At week-ends and on occasional odd evenings he ran down to Croydon, becoming a constant visitor at the Milónoffs and the Gawthorpes.

Milónoff, who was rarely to be found at home, nevertheless ran into him at times, greeting him with effusive cordiality and displaying an apparently deliberate anxiety that he should feel entirely welcome and at home in his house whenever it suited him to come.

One evening when Densham was there alone, Madame Milónoff left the large drawing-room where they had been talking to speak to a caller of some sort in the hall.

Densham, in the interval, dropped onto the piano bench and struck a few chords. His glance wandered through the open French windows into the starlit garden, while his fingers slid quietly over the keys. Presently he began a soft accompaniment, and in an untrained but pleasant voice, commenced singing, almost under his breath—

"One little hour for love and life,
And then we say 'Goodbye.'
One little hour for patient strife,
For you, sweetheart, and I."

Then, with a quick *accelerando* and a raised tone which sprang from him unconsciously as the music surged under his fingers, he finished the little song —

"One little hour goes laughing by,
And one in which to play.
And then, sweetheart, for you and I,
One little hour to pray."

From behind him, as the last chord died away, a low sibilant voice that he knew and detested, spoke with insinuating softness:

"I did not know you sang, Mr. Densham. That was very pretty."

Griffith swung around on the bench to confront the unwelcome host he so rarely saw. Milónoff sank into a chair as though desiring a chat, pressing his fingers lightly against his piled up hair with an effeminate gesture which displayed a curiously fashioned ring on his little finger, as tapered and tiny as a woman's.

"I don't really sing," murmured Densham, doubly embarrassed by the Russian's unexpected appearance and the accident of his arrival at that particular moment. "I have sung in choirs in various places, and that little song was written by the organist of a choir in Winnipeg which ..."

He paused. Madame Milónoff was wheeling herself swiftly into the room. Her husband bared his teeth at her.

"Our young friend sings very well, Natálya Feódorovna. Could you hear, out there?"

"Yes, I heard," she answered, in a low voice. "What was it?"

Milónoff crossed his legs with a graceful swing. "Mr. Densham was just telling me."

His short beard rose and fell as he uttered these words, with an exaggerated suavity and an air of appropriation of her guest which caused Griffith to bite his lip.

"I was saying," he went on, "that it was written by a former friend of mine, organist of the church in Winnipeg where I used to sing—a chap named Dichmont."

"Won't you sing it again?" asked Natálya Feódorovna. Her hands took wing and fluttered toward him.

Milónoff stirred. "No, sing something else. Do you know any more American songs?"

Densham got up and moved away from the piano. "Oh, I'm not a singer at all," he muttered, with an air of apology for having centred attention upon himself.

Milónoff rose, too, and after asking him a few questions about his life in Canada, carried himself out of the drawing room with impeccable deportment.

On another occasion, just as he was leaving the house—it was near midnight—he ran into Milónoff swinging jauntily up the drive, his coat open, the bosom of his dress shirt-front startlingly white under the gleam of a high moon. His narrow bloodless face, in that light, and with that expression of swaggering satiety lurking in the hollows of his bony cheeks, was more distasteful to Griffith than ever; but when he stopped, shook hands, and insisted on the younger man stepping back in to swallow a night-cap with him, Griffith felt it impossible to refuse.

It puzzled him to discover in this man an obvious intent to make friends with him. There was no mistaking it. Over the whisky and cigars Milónoff attempted to draw him out, intimated that his wife had told him something about the 'Hamlet' articles, and frankly—almost insolently—indicated that he was glad she had discovered such an interesting *confidant*.

"Really, *mon cher philosophe*, it is a pleasure for me to see her happy. She admires you. I don't wonder. You must come often, *sans cérémonie*. And here, too,"—he made a sweeping motion that included the decanter, the cigar box, his books, the whole luxuriously appointed room,—"at any time."

Outside, breathing hard, and violently gripping his stick, Griffith wondered how he had managed to keep himself from striking with all his force at that row of shining teeth between the waxed moustaches and the crisp curling beard.

On that particular night he had left the house with an unusual happiness elating his step. That white shirt bosom coming up the drive had broken in upon a mood which he had hoped to sustain until sleep closed his eyes.

It came back now, marred by the intervention of Milónoff's blenched physiognomy, and sullied by the sting of the whisky in his veins; but still potent, unmatchable, never to be forgotten.

For the first time he had called her, that night,—in a firm voice, and without avoiding her eyes—by her name and patronymic, "Natálya Feódorovna!"

There had always been an odd attraction for him in this quaint Russian fashion of addressing people, and more than once—to himself—since he had heard Milónoff so address her, he had lingeringly mouthed the flowing syllables of what seemed to him the most beautiful name in the world.

He loved her. Only a few days had passed since he had completely confessed it to himself; but already it was a very long time. And there was no longer any doubt in his mind that they had belonged to each other—he phrased it exactly thus—in some long forgotten time and place. He did not believe in reincarnation, and his fanciful theory of exiled matter or energy was by no means conclusive or demonstrable, even to himself. But, nevertheless, his recognition of something fadeless and familiar in her was proof against frequent gusts of scepticism.

It persisted; and this vitality, the validity of the impression itself, bearing down all opposition and mastering his faithlessness, was sufficient to make it stand, unsupported by any concomitant idea, entirely isolated and upright amid the wreck of his dreams, his hopes, his theories,—like a bright column rising from the abysmal foundation of Verity itself.

That she had made this possible for him—this certainty of *something* eternal and unvitiated by the maddening cycle of matter—gave to his love a property of adoration. It was precisely *that* mood which he had wanted to carry away.

After a long evening together she has sung to him that glamorous fragment of Borodine's which had been in his mind since the first Sunday night. It ends:

"Oh happy, happy ye,
Having for sov'reign dear
A lady fair, in spirit kind,

Whose famous coat of arms
Over the palace portal is
    blazon'd on high."

The bench had been moved away, and she was sitting at the piano in her wheel-chair.

The last note reverberated like a breath into the furthest corners of the long drawing-room, lighted only by the rose-shaded piano-lamp, and fanned by a gentle and scented breeze from the garden.

Madame Milónoff lifted her hands from the keys and turned her chair toward Densham who was seated close at hand, his head bowed forward, his fingers thrust deep into his black hair. He did not stir, until the faint noise of wheels told him she was coming near to him. He half-rose, clutched the two sides of her chair, and dropped on his knees at her feet. Her unfurled fingers floated to her lip.

It was then that he had looked up and uttered in a firm, ringing, but low tone, those words—magically lovely to him—"Natálya Feódorovna!"

They gazed at each other with an ecstasy which seemed heightened by the long retarded avowal of their love. Neither of them moved. The moment was unsurpassable. There was nothing in the wide universe that either of them desired. Aeons of time swept noiselessly over their heads.

"Sov'reign dear!" Griffith cried, at last, and watched two tears form and tremble, upheld by her silken lashes for a moment, before they coursed down her cheeks.

She caressed his hair with her fingers.

"Is it true?" he murmured, drawing himself nearer.

Her raised hand drooped like a flag suddenly bereft of wind. She sat very still. Only the pulse agitating her white throat told him that she was alive.

Presently, in a whisper that seemed to rise through sunken tears, she spoke:

"Yes, dear. It is true. Everything is true."

A pale hand, like an opening flower, unfolded, touched his shoulder tenderly and sank again into her lap. The gesture seemed to leave a faint cadence lingering in the air.

"It is all true. All my dreams. They have all been one."

She pressed her clenched hand into her palm, as though it were a seal. "How strange it is!" she whispered. "How like a dream—and yet I never ever dreamed that love would be like this."

Densham covered her hands with his.

"I haven't even said, 'I love you'. There are no words," he heard his own voice saying. "It is like ... no ... it is not like anything. It seems impossible that there should be ... such peace."

She leaned over him and pressed her lips to his hair. Her eyes were abstractly fixed on the shadow that enveloped them. She saw nothing. She did not think. Her capacity for thought seemed to be numbed, her senses stilled, by a subliminal experience, mounting like a flame into new and incredible horizons of being.

After a while he stirred, rose, and unable to look at her, walked slowly across to the fireplace, flung his arms down on the mantel and let his head droop forward on his crossed wrists.

She watched him go with unutterable tenderness in her glance. Minutes passed. Her eyes regained that regal and commanding gleam which matched the serenity of her brow and the nobility of her poised head.

"Griffith," she whispered, at last. "Say 'goodnight' to me."

He lifted his head and looked at himself in the mirror of the mantel-top, as though to assure himself that he could let her see his anguished face. Pale and swaying he went to her, dropped at her feet and kissed both her hands.

"Don't go like that," she murmured, looking anxiously into his glooming eyes. "Smile at me."

"O, I can't!" he cried, struggling to his feet.

She held both his hands. "Why do you let yourself suffer so?"

"I can't help it," he groaned. "I should like to die—here—in your arms. I have found peace—but it is not mine to have. We have found each other too late—and in the wrong world!"

Chapter Seven

Madame Milónoff awoke two mornings later to find her maid already in the room, drawing the blinds. It was chilly. Rain was beating against the windows. A fire, started an hour before, was cracking gaily in the tiled chimney-piece, on the mantel of which an old-fashioned glass-enclosed clock, with a swinging shepherd boy for pendulum, told her that it was past her usual breakfast hour.

The accustomed "tick ... tick ... tick," faint and familiar, beat its delicate rhythm into her awakening ears—the pulse of a new day.

"It is a grey morning, little mother," said the maid, in Russian, coming from the window to arrange the breakfast tray.

"Not in here, Polinka." She leaned back against the pillows and deliberately sent her gaze roving about the room to alight and flutter away from the beloved companions of her invalid condition—her dressing table, from which came a gleam of ivory and silver; the azalea blooming in a jardinière of beaten copper near the window; the little carved walnut table by the fireplace strewn with books; the two statuettes on the chest-of-drawers—one drooped in a deep curtsey, the other inclined in a courtly bow; the wicker work-table, from which peeped a loop of cherry-coloured ribbon; the carnations—two vases of them, one at the foot of her bed and another near the closed and curtained door; the pictures, mostly tiny things in frames which closely hugged their precious contents; except for a large pastel of a woman with a saintly face, whose benign and sorrowful gaze rested with an air of blessing upon the reclining occupant of the room.

After bestowing her usual glance of greeting on these intimate objects Madame Milónoff turned her attention to the tray. First she picked up the letters lying in a little heap beside her plate. Among them was a bulky envelope addressed in a hand which caused her shoulders to rise with a quick inhalation of her breath. She tucked it under the coverlet and began her breakfast, while Polinka, sitting on a low stool beside the bed, read out the items of interest in that morning's 'Times.'

They were unusually brief, for Polinka had noticed the envelope. She knew whose writing it was, and her timid heart fluttered for her mistress. At first she had wished that Densham might have been handsomer; but as the weeks passed she began to think of him with a sort of idolatry, because she could see that he had taken captive the kind heart in whose service she delighted.

"The news is very little this morning, madam," she said, and went quietly out with the tray.

Madam Milónoff tore open the envelope and began to read:

Dearest —

You are here—so near to me that I can feel your arms about me, as they were last night—and yet something impels me to sit down and write. It is only that I want to talk to you—no, after all, it is not even that—but just that I want to be with you, now, ever, always!

When I left you I walked slowly home, murmuring—over and over again—your name—over and over again—'Natálya Feódorovna!'— as though it were a charm to keep you near me, the very fragrance of you and the deep look in your eyes, the memory of your caressing fingers, the light touch of your lips on my hair. So long as I kept repeating it, over and over again 'Natálya Feódorovna!!'—so long, I felt, you would never leave me.

And the stars leaned out of heaven to listen. Their little white glances were never before so pale. How dimmed they seemed— those immense luminaries—by the radiance of our love! Even the world seemed to shrink under my feet into a tiny ball. But it didn't matter. I needed no earth to tread!

How you will laugh at me! ... leaving you so dejected and returning to you in such a transport of joy.

Laugh then, dearest one; but let me hear you. I am jealous enough that I could wish you never to laugh nor speak again, nor stir from where I left you, until I return to your side.

'We have found each other too late,' I said last night. I didn't mean it. But I was obsessed by the thought that we have been cheated of half our lives.

But, today, you seem so near, and the future seems boundless. The years stretch out before me like a bright landscape, sunned by the sweet light of your eyes. O Natálya Feódorovna—say that you will be kind, that you will let me stay beside you, even in this queer *wrong* old world.

It doesn't seem half so wrong today. Right and wrong; what has seemed bright and what has seemed dark, no longer possess either gleam or shadow. All I know is that I love you. There is room in my heart for nothing else—no other thought—and yet it is not a thought. Nothing could be less finite—less bound.

If only I could make you see what it means to me. When I met you I had left behind my youth. Foolish as it may sound to you. I was resigning myself to the thought of age. The bleakness of the second half of life chilled me. It was not that I had lost hope of loving or being loved again. I did not think of love, did not wish for it or expect it. At best it seemed to me an exasperating and a transient thing ... torture ... an hour of ecstasy ... dregs! No, it was not that I expected ever again to love. It was that I felt my dreams falling shattered all about me. Never to soar, never to create, never to accomplish—conquer—achieve! Nothing but a life eked out in common ways; a pittance of comfort, perhaps; a little ease; and then ... the guttering of the brief candle. Cannot you imagine the barrenness, the bitterness ...?

But how all is changed, dearest alchemist!

Out of the mire of my irresolution you have rescued my birthright—the right to strive, to climb,—the right, above all, to make the ideal real!

O dearest when I started I meant to say so much; but "words are such feeble things." Do you know that little song:

"I have no words to tell you how I love you;
Words are such feeble things!
But I have thoughts, sweet tender thought about you—
And thoughts have wings."

Imagine! It must be eleven or twelve years since I sang that; but you have brought the words back to me. That is one of the thousand wonderful things about you—that you call up all the beautiful things I have ever heard, or experienced.

All that is beautiful in life, all my faith, my love, the craving of my heart, is centred in and about you. You have renewed my youth, my enthusiasm, my pride in myself, my desire to *do*! O, keep your wings under me, dear angel.

I am all—all—wholly yours. Do with me as you will.

It is dark. I yearn for your soft voice above me, whispering that "it is true". I lean into the night and kiss you—deep into your soul.

Griffith.

Madame Milónoff pressed the letter to her bosom, and sank back against the pillows. Her wildly beating heart—too weak to sustain the emotion his words evoked—seemed to be stifling her. For a long time she lay very white and still.

That night Densham left London by an early train after dinner. It had not been dark when he reached the house. Few lights were burning. His heart rose.

Polinka came to the door.

"Madame is out," she said. "Anton has taken her for a walk."

"Has she been well today?"

His many visits had accustomed Polinka to Densham's place in her mistress's heart. It was she who had softened Anton's stern regard for the frequent caller. The old footman, always possessing the air of being about to break out in lamentation, had often lifted his prophet-like arms, below stairs, and predicted calamity for Madame if she allowed herself to love "the gloomy Englishman"

"But if it is comfort to her," Polinka had protested.

Anton shook his beard in her face.

"Eckh! such a goose you are. What a little pigeon! Know you not that her heart cannot stand it—goose!—the *grande passion*? Comfort! Psssh! Who but a little pigeon gets comfort out of love?"

She was reminded of what Anton had said by Densham's question. She came a step forward and pressed her little red hands together as though she were going to pray.

"No, your honour, not as usual. The letter, your letter. Ah!" Her blue eyes rolled upward as she prolonged the low exclamation.

"What? Tell me, Polinka!"

"I went in—after. The letter—it was there—in her hand. I think she— what do you say?—faint?"

Densham grasped the girl's arm. "But she is better—allright now?"

"Yes, your honour," Polinka replied, soberly, with a tiny curtsey.

"I'll look for her. Probably they are not far."

"No, your honour. They are not long gone."

He found them in the little recreation ground by the church, where he had seen her that first time. There was no moon; but the stars were brilliant, and he could see the oval of her face against the dark background of the chair, coming towards him.

The night was so still that he could hear her recognize him with a whispered cry,— "Griffith!"—when he was still some paces away.

Anton halted the chair.

"You startled me," she murmured, faintly; both her hands pressed to her heart.

"Ah madame," he answered, in a low voice. "How thoughtless of me."

"You may go, Anton. Mr. Densham will bring me home."

Without a sound the old footman glided away into the darkness.

Griffith went round to the back of the chair and pushed it toward a bench under a laburnum tree which hung over an old wall. They did not speak until he had faced her about and had seated himself so that he could take her hands.

"You must not write to me like that," she said, after a while. "I wish you could. It seems so hard that when you *do* come—after all these years—to fulfill my dreams, I must shut my heart to you..."

"O no, no."

"I must, dear, if I am to live ... and I can't die, now that I've found you. But I swooned, after reading your letter today. O Griffith! It is you who must be kind to me. Learn to love me ... quietly."

She drew his hands toward her and laid them against her throat.

"I knew of no sweeter death," she went on, and stopped suddenly with a gesture of her hand to her temple, as startling and alarming as a trumpet call.

"No, no! what am I saying? I have never wanted so much to live."

He freed his hands and thrust them wildly into his hair. "O, Natálya! Live! live! Dearest. I didn't know. I am so selfish!"

"No, no."

"I didn't think. I didn't know. O, black heaven! O Natálya!"

He began to sob.

"Griffith," she breathed above him, for he had fallen on his knees in the grass, and his face was buried in the folds of her dress.

He looked up through his tears and was shocked into quietness by the dry-eyed anguish of her face.

"Have pity," she said. "Take me home."

He sprang to his feet. "Home!"

He was about to say, "There is no home for us, neither for you nor me, no happiness, nothing but bitterest rue on this side of the grave." The words framed themselves in his distracted mind; but he did not utter them.

He went to the back of the chair and leaned over her. Their faces were so close that even in the deep shadow they could see the slightest play of expression in each other's eyes. His were dull with the effort of repression. Hers were questing, seeking some sign of calm.

"Will you be good to me, Griffith?"

He flung one open hand above his head as though to hold back the wrath that seemed to be pouring upon them out of the black night.

"Through a thousand lives and deaths!"

Chapter Eight

Towards the end of that week, at a late hour one evening, Kalinova and Prince Bienjonetti entered a fashionable restaurant within a stone's throw of the theatre district. They were merry. The *danseuse* clung to her stately, middle-aged companion with an abandon of manner which made the pair unmistakably conspicuous as they moved toward the table that had been reserved for them.

Not far away sat George Pethick, Mr. and Mrs. Gawthorpe and Densham. It was Pethick's birthday and he had celebrated it by asking the Gawthorpes up to the city for the performance at the Hippodrome, with a little supper afterwards at the sort of place where Mrs. Gawthorpe—who rarely came to London—could see a little of what is falsely known as "high life."

She was a silent, rather timid, melancholy woman, whose role in life kept her constantly in the background. Pethick, more than anyone, had the ability to amuse her. She was fond of him, and constantly remarked that an hour of his fun was more refreshing than a week at the seaside. "George is better than a dozen bottles of tonic." These, and similar pronouncements were made the more often because she suspected her husband of secretly despising Pethick's avocation.

The four of them were vivaciously engaged in calling up memories of old choirboy pranks when the entrance of Kalinova caused a perceptible stir that for a moment interrupted the conversation.

Densham was immediately interested in the newcomers. He leaned across Gawthorpe—whose demeanour was more languorous than usual, on account of the champagne—and asked: "Is that the Prince you spoke about, George?"

"T'is he; the 'sweet prince,' Griff," observed Pethick, with a professional grimace.

Mrs. Gawthorpe laid a sobering hand on his arm. "Now, George, not a 'really' prince."

"Certainly!" Pethick ejaculated, in a low tone. "A real Bohemian from Bohemia, with five Christian names, and the most sumptuous flat in Mayfair. By the way, Griff, your friend Milónoff seems to be getting the cold shoulder lately."

Gawthorpe bestirred himself, caught Pethick's eye and shot a meaning glance at his wife.

"What do you mean about Milónoff?" asked Mrs. Gawthorpe, immediately on the alert.

Pethick dabbed his lips on his serviette. "Griff and I were talking about Milónoff the other night," he observed, airily, and was about to launch into some lengthy circumlocution when his glance—averted from Mrs. Gawthorpe—fastened with an expression of surprise on somebody or something over Densham's shoulder.

"Speak of the archangels!" he muttered, under his breath, with a motion toward Gawthorpe. "Here's Milónoff now!"

The Russian, paler than ever, and with an indescribable dullness of expression in his deep-set eyes, was already level with the table at which Kalinova and Bienjonetti were seated. Kalinova glanced up and looked him squarely in the face without a sign of recognition. Her wine-glass was half way to her lips. Without turning her eyes away from Milónoff she thrust her arm toward the Prince in an invitation to clink glasses. Bienjonetti was quick to respond. Her eyes veered round to his as their fingers came together, and Milónoff, with an incredibly swift and involuntary clenching of his fists, passed on and sat down, some distance away.

Pethick did his best to minimize the significance of this incident, quieting Mrs. Gawthorpe's suspicions as best he could. But the conversation did not again drift into easy or humorous channels. Fortunately there was little time left to get to the station for the last train to Croydon, and Pethick's party soon broke up.

The next morning Densham had hardly commenced his breakfast, with the Times propped against the cruet, when the other occupants of the Suffolk dining room were startled by the sharp crash of falling china. Densham had upset his tea-cup; but quite unconscious of the hot liquid dripping on to his knees, his whole attention was grippingly concentrated on a brief item in the paper.

A waiter came hurrying to his side. Only then did he realize that something embarrassing had happened.

"My God!" he muttered, with the merest glance at the spilled tea and broken cup. "I'm sorry." And then, again, more vehemently than before—"My God!"

Some sixth sense—for his glance had immediately leaped back to the paper—seemed to tell him that people were staring. Thrusting the paper under his arm he jumped up, almost upset the bending waiter, and hurried out.

Darting upstairs, two steps at a time, he kept repeating, under his breath, over and over again—"Milónoff murdered! Dead! Milónoff! Dead!"

He got to his room and slammed the door behind him. Catching sight of himself suddenly in the mirror he started back, flung the paper on the bed, and grasping his temples in both hands tried to calm himself. But from between his clenched teeth the words still issued:

"Dead! Dead! Dead!"

The news item was very brief. The shooting had occurred in the early hours of the morning at Bienjonetti's flat. The Prince was being held on a charge of murder. He had told the police that Milónoff threatened him and he was forced to shoot in self defence. Kalinova's name was not mentioned.

"Dead! Dead! Dead!"

While his lips moved slowly and mechanically Densham's brain was racing. Presently he jumped up, flung some things into a handbag, and with an indescribable last look about the room strode heavily down the corridor, down the stairs, and out of the hotel.

In less than half an hour he was in a train bound for Croydon. The compartment was empty. He gave full rein to his whirling thoughts.

As soon as the train started to move Densham seemed able to leave the dead Milónoff behind. He counted for nothing. He had never really been between them.

Densham closed his eyes and whispered:

"Sov'reign dear!"

Slowly he withdrew and clinging thoughts from the sweet image of her, passionately remembered, with parted lips and widened eyes, close to him—intoxicatingly close! Lovely as were his memories of her, he wanted now to thrust forward into the future. He raised his hand and pressed a kiss into his palm.

"Goodbye, dear, for a tiny minute, while I think," he murmured, as though she were actually there, opposite him, regarding him with those tender humid eyes.

But his mind would not fling out for him a projection of what was to come. Strive as he might only *she* came; she—radiant, joyous, with fluttered breath and all her soul poured into her gaze. He felt himself yearning toward her. His eyes closed again and he gave himself up to the contemplation of her exquisiteness. His lips trembled apart.

"Natálya Feódorovna!"

It was a whisper; but it seemed to ring and re-echo in his ears. He could do nothing but murmur her name and call up ecstatic memories of her.

Once in a while he would lean forward in the seat and put a question to himself, fiercely demanding an answer.

"Is it possible that she won't marry me?"

But there was no answer; only her smile, her fingers thrusting through his hair, her cool lips touching his.

"Will she say, 'I am too old. I'm an invalid. You would tire of me.' Surely she won't say that."

As before: only her frank gaze bent tenderly upon him, her hands stretched out to him, her breath quickened with pleasure at his coming.

He felt her near him. His soul seemed filled with her presence, leaving no room for thoughts, doubts, fears, longings. Her being flooded into his, answering every question, satisfying every desire.

He struggled no longer. She was with him. She had not waited for him to come. She had joined him. Already they were one.

He did not look forward, as he had done earlier, to the thrill of running up the steps, going to her, taking her in his arms. He no longer tried to picture what room she would be in when he arrived, what they would say, how the day would pass.

They were together, now! He was more conscious of it than he was of the movement of the train. Many times before he had experienced this sensation; but never so vividly, so intensely. Some emanation of her tenderness seemed to envelop him.

The present was overwhelmingly satisfying. They could never now be parted. Distance, time, flesh, life, death—all these figments of the brain were dissolved in pure ecstasy. Their exile in the wrong world was at an end. They belonged to each other. They were together. She had come to him.

He looked out of the carriage window and noticed that the train was passing through Penge. It was raining. Spattered drops streaked the glass. He watched the steady downpour, the people moving about in the soaked streets under glistening umbrellas, the dejected cab-horses splashing through the mud.

"This is England!" thought Densham. He had not been back long enough to take it all for granted. Every now and then he experienced a curious pungent sensation of the flavour of England,—dwarfed, crowded, damp, insular; and yet—cosy!—even in the pouring rain.

In a few minutes he would reach Croydon, take a cab, and ... it suddenly struck him with more force than usual that the house he was going to, Natálya herself, Anton, Polinka—were not a part of this England he sensed so keenly every little while.

He began to think of her foreignness—that something in her eyes, her bearing, her gestures, the unconstrained flow of her feelings expressed spontaneously by the facile motion of her quick fingers, the pouting of her lips or the contraction of her dark brows. There were moments when her challenging eyes, her serene brow, the composed curve of her lips, and the thrust of her deep throat, gave her a majestic and sovereign air. So he recalled her now.

A rush of excited anticipation, restlessness, passionate expectancy, swept through his soul.

The train was slowing down. Familiar sights flashed past the window— the coal-yards, Addiscombe Bridge, the row of larches along Lansdowne Road, the end of the long platform, ... noise, steam, porters darting about, the guard's whistle, a slight jerk ... Before he knew it he was hurrying up the slope. Outside it was still pouring with rain.

He gave Madame Milónoff's address in a parched tone to a waiting cab-driver. "I'm in a hurry," he added, glancing sharply into the man's haggard face. He sprang in and was driven off at a good pace.

Only then, as the four-wheeler rolled noisily down George Street, did Densham realize that there would be the opposite of rejoicing at the house he was approaching. He began to wonder how the news had been communicated to her. It would come as a shock; but she would not grieve. Milónoff had made that impossible. She had long ago ceased to love him, even think of him, except as an occasional intruder in her house. No, she would not grieve.

Nevertheless, when he at last ran up the steps, he felt a weight dragging at his heart. They were a long time coming to the door. He took off his hat and flicked the gathered raindrops from its brim. Finally Polinka appeared. At sight of him she covered her scared face with her little hands and began rocking herself to and fro, moaning in a low, liquid voice.

Densham stepped across the threshold, closed the door behind him, dropped his handbag, and grasped the girl's elbows.

"Tell me," he whispered fiercely, thrusting his face close to her fingers, through which tears were streaming, "tell me, how is madame?"

Responding to his pressure Polinka withdrew her hands. She darted one wild glance at him and flung herself upon the floor, clasping his knees, and crying out in a stifled voice—"O Holy Mother! O dear little sacred heart of Mary. Have mercy on us!"

Densham bent over her and tried to raise the tear-soaked face; but she fell back in a sitting posture, swaying from side to side, and muttering through her clasped fingers—now pressed violently against her mouth, as though to hold back her bursting heart—"Dear little mother of Jesus! Ah! Your honour, your honour!"

At that moment Anton appeared, coming out of a door at the end of a gloomy hall. As soon as he caught sight of Densham he hurried forward, with a downcast head. His hair was wildly tossed over his huge brow. One hand opened and closed convulsively in his thick beard. The other swung clenched and rigid at his side.

Densham waited for Anton to speak. His own tongue seemed fastened to the roof of his mouth, and he was trembling from head to foot.

"Your honour has seen the newspapers?" asked the old footman, stopping short in front of Densham, without looking at him.

"Yes, Anton."

There was a pause. The two men stood stock still. Densham was gazing into the worn, withered old face in mute interrogation. Anton fixed his glance on the cowering Polinka, sobbing incessantly in a little heap on the floor.

"It is terrible," said Anton, with low distinctness. "Murder is a sudden thing. Such a shock. Your honour will understand. Go upstairs, Polinka! Go away! You are not wanted, Polinka! Your honour will pardon Polinka, sir. She has the heart of a little mouse. Polinka!"

He went to her and bent his giant form over her, but she shrank from him, thrust him away, and broke into a more violent paroxysm of sobbing.

"Please come into the library, your honour," Anton requested, when he saw it was no use attempting to calm her.

The guarded, subdued tone of the old servitor had a quieting effect on Densham's nerves. He strode into the library. Anton pulled across the heavy curtain which hung over the door and faced the lover of his mistress, this time with a level gaze.

"Madame?" Densham whispered, his hands writhing behind him. "How is madame?"

With an effort to control his voice which showed in every seam of his gnarled face, Anton spoke at last in a hollow tone.

"Madame's heart," he said, and raised his hands as though about to fling them upward in a gesture of abandoned lamentation. Instead he twice beat his breast.

Densham groped forward.

"Yes ... yes?"

The silence was full of dread. It fell about him like darkness, like a black pall.

Above him the deep voice spoke again:

"Polinka took in the newspaper with Madame's breakfast. It is usual. Every morning she do that. Polinka began to read."

Over Anton's shoulder Densham saw the curtain flung back from the door. In another moment Polinka had dropped to her knees at his feet.

"I am the wicked one," she sobbed. "I saw it in the paper. I shake very much. Madame ask me, 'What is it, Polinka?' I shake more. I speak nothing. Madame snatch the paper. I scream, 'No, no, no, no!' I fight—I—what you say? I struggle with madame. But she see. She see it. Ah! Holy Mother!"

The distracted girl smote the carpet with her forehead and a torrent of sobs convulsed her afresh.

Densham poured upon her a look of amazed and recoiling horror. She did not raise her head; but he saw—as in a dream—her hand creeping across the carpet until it found the toe of his shoe. He felt her patting his foot.

He looked away. Suddenly he thrust both hands deeply through his hair. The gleam of an unexpected and mysterious recognition flamed in his eyes. She—radiant, joyous, with fluttered breath and all her soul in her gaze—as she had come to him an hour before, flooded his sight and senses again with her presence. She had not waited for him to come. She had joined him.

In a strangely calm voice he presently spoke:

"Tell me, Anton."

With half-averted head he stood, listening.

The old man took his hand from his beard. His eyes were suddenly glazed over with a stony look. His voice was like ice in the air:

"Madame Milónoff is dead!"

ESSAYS AND POLEMICS

:

To All the Nations ....!

I am not as conceited as Bernard Shaw. I hesitate to call myself "an exceedingly clever man"; but I am at least, a moderately clever man. I have made a comparative success of various occupations calling for considerable education, foresight, intelligence and ingenuity, and I am at present deriving an income sufficient to keep me alive from the sale of scenarios to Moving Pictures concerns. I commenced to write when I was eight years old, a week after I had devoured "Robinson Crusoe," and I have been writing ever since—and reading ten times as much as I have written. And now—tonight—as I sat smoking in my old, dilapidated armchair, a terrible thought came to me; a thought that I have crushed and smothered a thousand times during the past few months; a thought that wrecks what little peace still lingers in my soul; a thought that threatens to mar my whole future existence;—the thought that I am wasting my life.

Try as I could that thought would not be smothered into silence tonight. The hurried ideas, summoned at random, and crammed into the theatre of my brain were not virile enough to crowd out that terrible thought. It was as though some frightful spectre that had been knocking at the door of my consciousness for centuries had at last gained admittance, and stood confronting me, a decisive grin of defiance distorting its horrible features. For hours I sat facing it, staring at it, and all the while my soul wrestled. Now that it is over I can think of no parallel for that awful struggle, save the story that is told of Jacob wrestling with the angel until the daybreak.

It is dawn, now. And I am wondering—even as I pen these words—wondering whether it was an angel that I wrestled with last night. Do you believe in angels any longer?

153

You have heard men speak of having wasted their lives, and so have I; and heard them speak lightly of it; but I cannot think lightly of it. Like Carlyle life is a grim and earnest thing for me. With the first overwhelming flood of realization I remembered a tremendous line in one of James Lane Allen's novels—"One chance," cries the hero of that book, towards its close, "One chance in all of eternity to be an honest man—and to have lost it." And I feel that I have had one chance to be a man—not a particularly honest man—but a man; and that I have lost it. I can see now that I have been a mere drifting log in the wide stream of existence, a mere mote in the broad beam of life that lies athwart the world. I can see now that I have been a coward—a shiftless, worthless coward. I can see now that I have done always what other men have been doing. I can see now that I have lost the one chance I had in all eternity of being a real man; and lying as I am in the pit of despair, I am raising my voice now that they may hear who pass by, and hearing may understand, and understanding may change the mould of their lives. Like Dives in Hades I would that all men might be warned of this awful state wherein I lie.

I have waited in silence many years. Over and over again I have said to myself—the time is not yet. I have deluded myself. I have said to my soul—this book that you are to write must roar like the sea. It must contain vast thunderings. There must be something of the lightning in it. Every word must sting. Every sentence must crack like a whip. Every paragraph must be saturated with poison. Every page must end with a dagger-thrust. I have diligently studied the great writers of the past. I have written reams, only to throw them aside. I have been merciless with the scratchings of my pen. All that this book might sink to the hilt, like a keen sword, in Humanity's side. And in the silence and solitude deeper and deeper channels of hate have been carved in me.

But I have changed, now. I labour no more after style. I am no longer concerned with dramatic forms of speech. The volcano that smoulders within me shall burst forth out upon you unhindered.

What are words? What is a sentence? Has a paragraph an identity? Can a page of a book speak? It is not words I am concerned with now. I know now that words cannot express anything. Yet must I write with words. But it is not the words that shall smite your souls—not the words; but my soul behind them. For though this book never be printed, though not one word of all this reaches any living eye in the world, yet, in writing it, the angry sparks of my consciousness shall blaze through the ether and beat against the souls of men for evermore. There is so much heat in my heart, that Humanity cannot escape being scorched, no man shall escape the heat of my heart. Even the unborn are destined to be smitten to the heart's core by the residue of my passion, even though they remain unborn for a thousand centuries. I am the overflowing scourge whom God has sent down to chasten the earth.

Rough-hewn, this book shall be hurled in the midst of scrambling humanity. Misshapen, crude, ugly—like some fiery rock wrenched from the heart of the world; I hurl it back at the world. This is no idle book. I ask no idlers to trifle with it. It is a stern and terrible book, for behind every word lurks a spectre; and at the end of it, you shall meet God face to face, and no man can face God unafraid.

I

Listen.

What is that low vast terrible murmuring?—those sighs issuing from thousands of thousands of throats?—that calamitous moaning that never abates, never ceases for a second?—that tumultuous torrent of tears?—those sobs?—those frenzied fists beating at breasts?—those cries in the dead of night?—that chaotic chorus of wailing?

Whose voices are these?

Whose bodies are these, rocking to and fro, racked in torment? Whose eyes are these so red and wet and swollen with tears? What is this on the ground here? Is it blood? Whose blood? Who are these people walking in blood?

The Underfolk!

II

I am the Champion of the Underfolk.

I am a mountain pouring forth the frightful lava of a soul on fire. This is not a book. It is an eruption. Beware of it, and me, and that awful Urge—I know not what it is—behind us both.

For I am not alone. Pervading my solitude there is a terrible presence.

The Spread of Negativism

I. THOU SHALT NOT!

Today we are in the midst of an age of analytical criticism. Today all thought is destructive. We have become a race of iconoclasts.

When Greece ejected its Gods and entered its age of Agnosticism, it created the finest examples of sculpture the world has ever seen. When Europe ejected a host of out-worn dogmas and became Protestant, it gave birth to the Renaissance in Architecture, Letters, and Art. And with the inundation of iconoclastic tendencies in the realm of thought, which we today are witnessing, has come this much-despised but worthy thing Commercialism. And Commercialism stands for construction. It seems therefore that a period of destructive thought is always accompanied by a period of constructive arts.

Today we are destroying creeds while we are building airships. We erect sky-scrapers while the metaphysical gates of Heaven are tumbling about our ears. We construct Dreadnoughts while the pamphleteers are smashing every scheme of polity. And while a certain sect who regard ill-health as a myth are flourishing, the sale of patent medicines is increasing, and the hoardings are covered with advertisements for pills and ointments.

The battle-cry of our modern civilization is—Progress! In the name of progress we are hewing down all ancient barriers. In the name of progress we are casting to the winds all ancient dogmas and doctrines. The folly of such a course is pointed out with admirable clearness by Mr. G.K. Chesterton, in the following extract from "Heretics": -

"Nobody can be progressive without being doctrinal; I might say that nobody can be progressive without being infallible—at any rate, without believing in some infallibility. For progress by its very name indicates a direction; and the moment we are in the least doubtful, we become in the same degree doubtful about the progress ... But it is precisely about the direction that we disagree. Whether the future excellence lies in more or less law, in more liberty or less liberty; whether property will be finally concentrated or finally cut up; whether sexual passion will reach its sanest in an almost virgin intellectualism or in a full animal freedom; whether we should love everybody with Tolstoy, or spare nobody with Nietsche;—these are the things about which we are actually fighting most."

And Nietsche himself, in more flamboyant manner, states the same truth, in "Thus Spake Zarathustra".

"A thousand goals have existed hitherto, for a thousand peoples existed. But the fetter of the thousand neck is lacking, the one goal is lacking. Humanity hath no goal yet."

Not only are there a thousand goals, but a thousand different paths to every one of the thousand goals—a thousand sign-posts, a thousand self-appointed guides. The pulpit, the lecturer's platform, the stage, the columns of the newspapers;—all those are the means to a thousand ends; but the only one end which all seem to be driving at, is the slandering of everyone else.

In thought and literature we are all critics. In action we are all constructionalists. It is imperative that we must construct something, although the result will inevitably be destructive. We must all be making something, even though it be a catapult to break windows or kill birds. We must all invent something, even though it be a new rifle or a new bullet for the destruction of future generations. We must all construct something, although it be a speech or an article of a destructive tendency.

What are we coming to, when the Queen of England issues a mandate that pads and rats and hobble skirts must not be worn at her coronation. What are we coming to, when the professors tell us not to wash too often. What are we coming to when Miss Cicely Hamilton turns Antichrist, tells us that we must not become as little children, and that it is better to recognise the infant "for what in truth it is—a small barbarian."

"Everybody's Weekly" recently published under the heading of the "Trend of Thought," a succinct paragraph on the intellectual confusion of our day, concluding with the words—"What the world waits for is a thinker with a grand constructive genius."

But the world has had many thinkers with constructive genius. Christ's commandment "Thou shalt love thy neighbour as thyself," is the most positive thing ever uttered. And surely the writer of the "Trend of Thought" remembers that Huxley, whom he puts down as one of the originators of our modern confusion of thought, was contemporary with the greatest constructive and synthetic philosopher that ever lived—Herbert Spencer.

It is not a man that the world waits for—it is a policy. It is not a genius of constructive thought that is wanted—it is a system of constructive thought. And, moreover, it is not a system such as Comte's "Positivism" that is wanted. Positivism has merely taken a place among the negativistic "isms" of the hour. What the world wants is a system of thought that applies to every-day life; not a system that can be followed only in the church or the study, for all such systems have failed; not a system that deals with the direction of progress, for all such systems have failed; but a system which deals with the ways and means of getting at some common direction.

2. THE MUCK RAKE

We are all inoculated with the poison of Negativism. We are not only a race of iconoclasts—we are a race of muck-rakers.

It started in America, of course, where all these things are carried to the limit and a little beyond; but the seed of it came from Europe. "The Jungle" was written after Zola had given "The Downfall" and "The Dram-Shop" to the world. Tom Lawson's "Frenzied Finance" was a sort of echo of the Liberator and Whitaker Wright frauds, heard through the megaphone of American vituperation and bombast.

In short, there being no more gods to cast down, the revolutionists have commenced to cast calumny in the faces of men. Nietsche, with thunderous, semi-biblical verbosity has accused us of everything—everything under the sun; calling us "Back-Worlds-Men"—"Despisers of Body"—"Tarantulae" and "The Much-too-many."

Shaw with much paradoxical paraphernalia has muck-racked our Imperialism, our Militarism, our Marriages, our Parliaments, and above all—our Shakespeare. Chesterton, with more paradox and less malice, perhaps, has not only done a considerable quantity of muck-racking in his time, but has achieved still more notoriety by muck-racking the muck-rakers, in his inimitable portrait-gallery of "Heretics."

Ibsen is also of the galaxy, and Maxim Gorky. In fact, Russia is full of them. And then there are Mr. Galsworthy and Mr. Maurice Hewlett. Mr. Blatchford and Mr. Bart Kennedy also, along a different line.

Not one of our honoured institutions is spared. We wake up in the morning to find that some eminent muck-raker has discovered another one at which to cast the mud of his persiflage. Today it is the War-Office. Tomorrow it is the Post-Office. Yesterday it was Capital. The day before it was Labour. Last week it was the Salvation Army. This week the House of Lords. Next week—Heaven knows what.

In England, one of our most popular papers—"John Bull" is almost entirely devoted to this sort of thing. It pays. It pays to muck-rake. It pays to publish sensational articles on Canada and Crippen, on Mormonism and the White Slave traffic. In Canada there is a newspaper, sold in secret practically, called "The Eye-Opener," which does little else than publish the most disgusting details of the lives of politicians, eminent and otherwise. In England again, the periodical—"Truth"—is practically devoted to error. The journalist's pocket-book is the register of dishonoured reputations, and the author's stock-in-trade, a host of degraded institutions.

And when we come to the critics of the critics, we find the same principle prevailing amongst them also. "John Bull" for instance, is not satisfied with criticizing every man, woman and child that comes to its notice, but criticizes everybody else's criticisms of every other man, woman and child, awarding imaginary biscuits each week to other critical editors, and thus making the nauseating circle of the criticism complete.

With the art critics and the literary critics it is the same. They fasten on some insignificant defect in the painting or drawing or writing or acting of some eminent person, and, with the assistance of half-a-dozen dictionaries, a vivid imagination, a dyspeptic stomach, and a dampened towel, they make a mountain of a mole-hill, and of swans—geese.

They talk much of Post-Impressionism, of Pre-Raphaelitism, of the Renaissance, of Realism, and they stand in front of a picture at the galleries, and say to their diminutive souls or diminutive neighbours—"Methinks yon eyebrow is bad." They are obsessed with adverbial phraseology, and haggle over split infinitives. They are looking for what is wrong and not for what is right, for what is bad and not for what is good, for what is blameworthy and not for what is praiseworthy, for it has become fashionable to blame. It is supposed that anyone can see the good points in a work of art, but that only a very clever person can see the bad ones. It is supposed to be a sign of strength to pull everyone else to pieces, and a sign of weakness to praise.

If the plot of a novel is good they will criticize the dialogue. If the plot and dialogue are good, they will criticize the atmosphere. They love to prate about atmosphere. If the plot and the dialogue and the atmosphere are all good, they will complain that the characters are not true to life. If the plot and the dialogue and the atmosphere and the characters are all perfectly done, they will say it is too long. If it is not too long, they will say it is too short. If it is neither, they will complain about the title. If they can find absolutely nothing in it to criticize, they will say that it is a studied imitation of Dickens or Scott or Thomas a Kempis or the author of "Black-eyed Susan." If it is immoral, they will say it is not. If it is not immoral, they will say it is. If it is dramatic, they will say it is sensational. If it is not dramatic, they will say it is dull.

To such a pass has our civilisation come.

In a recent number of "Everybody's Weekly," there appeared an article by John Foster Fraser, entitled "Let us Praise Britain!" It is the first article of the kind that I have seen for some time. Why cannot we have more of them? "After all," says Mr. Fraser, "we have done something in the world, we are doing something, and we will do more." He says—"There ought to be established a "Society for the Praising of Britain". Most certainly there should. Here's my hand on it, Mr. Fraser. And there should also be established a "Society for the Praising of Everything". But, who is there to be a President of it? Who will be the members?

4. THE SUPERMEN

The chain of negation is complete.

For years the anarchists have been crying—No Rulers! For years the revolutionists have been shrieking—No Rules! The Socialists have been crying—No Capitalists! and the Protestants—No Popery! And now, the clarion voices of the Futurists right round the world—No more man! We are human, all too human! Make way for the Superman!

At first sight this idea of a Superman appears to be a constructive idea. Many have hailed it as the last hope of a degraded civilisation. And Mr. Chesterton in a splendid page or two about ideals, although he ridicules it, still admits it to be an ideal.

But is the Superman an ideal?

Mr. Shaw had accepted it as such, and written a play about it, as usual. And yet, Nietsche's "Beyond-Man," is no more an ideal than is Shelley's "Prometheus," or Emerson's "Over-Soul,"—not anything like such an ideal as Wagner's "Siegfried," or Wells' "New Republican," that Mr. Shaw ridicules in the same play that he presents us with his Superman ideal.

The "Beyond-Man" as Nietsche conceives him, and the "Superman" as Shaw conceives him, is nothing but Man minus the Animal, and minus almost everything that distinguishes him from the Animal. In short, the Superman is the last possible negation. The Negativists have personified every destructive tendency that ever existed, and have named him the effigy they have made—The Superman!

Nietsche is the high-priest of the Destructionists. His own words shall convince you—

"What is great in man is that he is a bridge and not a goal; what can be loved in man is that he is a TRANSITION and a DESTRUCTION.

I love him who liveth to perceive, and who is longing for perception in order that some day beyond-man may live. And thus he willeth his own destruction.

I love him who worketh and inventeth to build a house for beyond-man and make ready for him earth, animal, and plant; for thus he willeth his own destruction.

I love him whose soul is over-full so that he forgetteth himself and all things are within him: thus all things become his destruction.

I love him who is of a free spirit and of a free heart: thus his head is merely the intestine of his heart, but his heart driveth him to destruction."

This is the doctrine of the destruction of man, in order that beyond-man can rise phoenix-like out of his ashes. But what does Nietsche know; what does anyone know of that which lies beyond and above man? Who knows to what end evolution is striving? Nietsche himself says—"Humanity hath no goal yet." But still he urges us to destroy ourselves, to make room for beyond-man. Still he urges us to sacrifice ourselves for a dream.

Maeterlinck, in "Wisdom and Destiny" raises his voice against such suicidal folly, saying —

"In this world there are thousands of weak, noble creatures who fancy that sacrifice always must be the last word of duty; thousands of beautiful souls that know not what should be done, and seek only to yield up their life, holding that to be virtue supreme. They are wrong; supreme virtue consists in the knowledge of what should be done, in the power to decide for ourselves whereto we should offer our life."

It is precisely this however, that Nietsche is ignorant of, that everyone is ignorant of. No one seems to know what should be done, and as Mr. Holbrook Jackson says—"it is as impossible for man to visualise Superman as it was for ape to visualise man."

Prof. Max Muller in his book on the "Science of Thought," defines thinking as simple addition and subtraction. Let us therefore, for a moment, examine this idea of a Superman, in the light of this theory of addition and subtraction.

In the first place, the conception of Man that we all possess is simply an accumulation, an addition of varied perceptions of what men have been in the past, and what we perceive of them in the present. Now, the essence of the Superman idea is that we must subtract, distinctly a negative proceeding, several of the intrinsic characteristics of man. We must subtract all bestial instincts. We must subtract the values of good and evil that men have created. We must subtract pity, for the Superman, they say, will have no pity. We must subtract culture, for culture was created by the past, and the Superman shall have broken with the past. We must subtract the idea of God, the idea of Heaven, the idea of Hell—and above all, the idea of hope, for the Superman has no hope. The Superman will be sufficient unto himself.

And now, what is there that we must add. Strength? The beasts have strength, and so had Samson and Goliath of old. Moral strength? The martyrs possessed it—the martyrs both of religion and of science—Socrates and Christ. The Will to Power? All men possess it. Who has not heard of Alexander, of Napoleon, of Rockefeller? The will to live alone? The hermits and the monks have existed for centuries, despised by the very men that now hail the approaching birth of the Superman.

What is there to add?

The philosophers know nothing can be conceived that is beyond or above experience. The Superman is possible, but he is not conceivable, simply because the future is unknown. We can find nothing to add to man that shall make him a Superman, except the things that all men in some degree have possessed. And as soon as we begin to agree as to what we actually do possess, as soon as we cast out Negativism and begin to have a few positive ideas about the most fundamental realities of life, we shall begin to achieve what is now a dream in the minds of a few philosophers—we shall become men instead of preachers, heroes instead of muck-rakers, and after all, from a hen-pecked race may rise the scions of the Superman.

5. COSMIC PATRIOTISM

We have seen how the Negativists have arrived at the last possible negation—namely, the Superman. There is nothing left in the universe that has not been denied, that has not been execrated, that has not been destroyed, at least in theory. A counter-revolution is therefore due. It is possible that before long there will be nothing left to praise, as soon as the cult of praising is commenced. History so far, has been a chronicle of revolutions.

Here is what Mr. Shaw has to say about the matter, in "The Perfect Wagnerite."

> "Ecclesiasticism and Constitutionalism send us one way, Protestantism and Anarchism the other; Order rescues us from Confusion and lands us in Tyranny; Liberty then saves the situation and is presently found to be as great a nuisance as Despotism ... And so for the present we must be content to proceed by reactions, hoping that each will establish some permanently practical and beneficial reform or moral habit that will survive the correction of its excesses by the next reaction."

This is precisely what we must not do, however. We must not be content to proceed by reactions. In short, we must not be content with anything until it is perfect. We must all be artists thus far. We must all be pessimists in so far that we can see what is wrong, but not so far as to talk and write and preach about it for ever, without setting it right. We must all be optimists enough to love everything that is worth while loving, but not enough to bellow jingoistic eulogies from morn till night.

Mr. Chesterton has caught the right spirit in "Orthodoxy," from which I have borrowed the sub-title of this article. He writes —

> "My acceptance of the universe is not optimism, it is more like patriotism. It is a matter of primary loyalty. The world is not a lodging-house at Brighton, which we are to leave because it is miserable. It is the fortress of our family, with the flag flying on the turret, and the

more miserable it is the less we should leave it. The point is not that this world is too sad to love or too glad not to love; the point is that when you do love a thing, its gladness is a reason for loving it, and its sadness a reason for loving it more."

The cure of Negativism is to be found in Cosmic-Patriotism, and not in Positivism. Positivism is as much wrong as Negativism, simply because it is extreme. It is neither negations nor assertions that are required. It is the spirit of patriotism—the spirit that shall maintain that this world is "somehow good," that it is worth living for, fighting for, dying for. But above all, it is the rallying spirit that we require to regenerate the world.

It would be ridiculous to turn round now and say that there is a God, that there is a Heaven, that there is a Hell, that man is perfect, and the whole wide world an El Dorado. It would be absurd to revolt from Negativism now, and praise everything that the Negativists have blamed. It would be suicidal to state that everything is right, and nothing wrong. What we have to do is to construct, to build, to create.

The time is ripe.

Commercialism is here, and Commercialism stands for construction. Already it has cast down all artificial aristocracies, and is building up a democracy that will some day be the patriots of the world. Already it has done more than Christianity ever did to prevent war between nation and nation, and thus, this thing without a soul, this sordid thing, as it is so often called, has tightened the cosmic bands that hold this little worldful of people together in peace.

Commercialism has proved that honesty is the best policy. Commercialism is developing the minds of thousands who were once serfs, and creating a new race, such as Mr. H.G. Wells anticipates, will be the strength and stay of the New Republic. Commercialism is linking art with life, and giving every man an occupation worth living for.

Religion was chiefly concerned with death and not life—death as a means to a larger life after death. Feudalism was chiefly concerned with death and not life—death as a means to more power, and honour, and glory, and worship. But Commercialism is concerned with life, here and now—life as a means to larger life here, and for our children. I do not say that the founders or the maintainers of Commercialism share this broad view of their activities, probably they do not, but whether consciously or not, they are working to this end.

And here and there this idea is leaking into our philosophy. Maeterlinck says, in "The Treasure of the Humble" —

> "We know that the dead do not die. We know now that it is not in our churches that they are to be found, but in the houses, the habits of us all. That there is not a gesture, a thought, a sin, a tear, an atom of acquired consciousness that is lost in the depths of the earth; and that at the most insignificant of our acts our ancestors arise, not in their tombs where they move not, but in ourselves, where they always live ..."

Yesterday the world was concerned with destruction. Today the world is concerned with every kind of construction, except in the realm of thought. If only our thoughts could be linked more closely with our lives, the destiny of man might be changed in one short, ever-to-be-remembered epoch, whose unsurpassed achievement should stand like an imperishable monument to the greatness of man, unto the end of time ...

The Decay of Art

The death-knell of Art is sounding!

Boom! Doom!—Boom! Doom!

With Botticelli or Brangyn, with Pre-Raphaelitism or Post-Impressionalism, with Symbolism or Realism, we here have no concern.

Art is not entirely a thing of colours and academies. It lies far-flung athwart the world. It is born of the womb of Imagination. It is the child of ecstatic moments, half-remembered, half-immortalized in form or colour, in rhythm or in tone. And Art is dying.

Why?

Art was inspired by the idea of God. The Gods are dead. Art was inspired by the greatness of Kings. Today we have only Republics; or else—Popinjays! Art was inspired by the romance of War. Today we have Peace; or else—Murder! Art was inspired by the ecstasy of Love. Today, love is dragged in ignominy through Divorce-Courts, or lies stagnant, loathsome in the Brothel.

Pop goes the Past!

Our civilisation is empty of Gods and Kings and Wars—empty of ecstasy. Our supreme moments are not now experienced in temples, or in king's palaces, or on corpse-strewn battle-fields. We find our ecstasy in the theatres, the moving-picture shows, the music-halls. A few of us, perhaps, have had supreme moments elsewhere—at prize-fights, at Cup-Finals, at Lord's. And the ecstasy-providers are almost always professional.

How then can we have any Art, when ecstasy is only to be got at second-hand, through the medium of money-grabbers?

Moreover, Art is dependent upon concentration. And Life has become so strenuous, so complex, that few can concentrate. Our lives are filled with duties, to ourselves, to our families, to the nation, to society, and to our particular political party. We are partizans all. We must have some sort of conviction about every topic of the hour. The sin of society is to remain neutral.

We must either be Socialists or Individualists. We must be Whigs or Tories; Republicans or Monarchists; Orthodox or Agnostic. And to support parties we must read, write, argue, spout. We must attend meetings and lectures and soirees and banquets and conferences. In short, we must waste nine hours in reading and listening and feasting and applauding other people, for every one hour of actual work we do ourselves for the cause in question. Art is not a matter of parties, political or otherwise. It is in no way connected with tea-drinking or with mock-turtle-soup.

Life is short and Art is long. We are all too busy.

Art is dying!

But there is still a weightier reason. We are too clever.

Instead of artists we produce cleverists. In the absence of ecstatic inspiration, amid the roar and rush of our narrow partisan lives, the soul of man is decaying—the mind of man is developing.

We are drifting away from Emotionalism, away from Sentimentalism. We have discovered a strange Mind—Ecstacy. We have made wondrous expeditions into the newly explored realm of Cleverdom.

Competition, Commercialism, the Struggle for Existence have sharpened our brains and deadened our souls. In our endeavours to be clever we have forgotten how to be great. We have sold a glorious birthright for a mess of pottage.

We are a race of Gradgrinds.

Art is degenerating into an accessory of all sorts of propaganda. We are obsessed with LEITMOTIFS.

Bernard Shaw is a propagandist of the most pronounced type. "Man and Superman" is nothing but a philosophical dissertation shopped up, and labelled—"Tanner"—"The Statue"—"The Devil"—and so on.

Wagner was not less guilty, although the issue was perhaps, more thickly veiled, in his "Nibelungenlied." And what of Ibsen?—of Tolstoy?—and Hassal painting advertisements?

Art is dead!

Long life to Cleverism!

Who is there to lament the decay of Art? Who is there that shall say the mess of pottage was not worth the birth-right? Only the religionists. Only the praters of Art for Art's sake.

Lo! we have broken another link that bound us to the beasts. Art was dependent upon Gods and Kings and Wars and Passion—on all things effete and obsolete.

We have no great artists. We have no great men. But, as a race we are more clever than any race the world has ever seen. The aristocracy of Art, like all the aristocracies, has had its day. The democracy of Cleverism has replaced it.

Man has realized at last that he has no immortal soul. Man has realized that the soul dies with the body; but that the mind of the race shall evolve through countless centuries into the image and likeness of the great Unnamed!

The Art of today is blended with all propaganda working towards this end. Art today is wedded with Work, with Commercialism, with Rationalism, for the regeneration of the world.

Art is no longer a priceless thing, an indulgence, a luxury. It is no longer pursued only by the favoured few, in schools, in cloisters, or under the patronage of princes. Art has evolved into Cleverism. It is the possession of the poor. It is to be found on the calendars that tradesmen present gratis to their customers; it is given away with a pound of tea; or exchanged for an accumulation of soap-wrappers.

Art was comprised of the noblest efforts of an aristocracy of great men. It is dead. Cleverdom is comprised of the noblest efforts of a democracy that joins hands across the world. It will live forever.

Bound up as it is with the mundane things, the hum-drum and the hey-day of life, it is slowly drawing humanity out of the mire; and shall eventually lead them across the psychic bridge to the Next Beyond, where transfigured man shall look back at his last stage of evolution, as he does now, with disgust and contempt.

Man shall some day be surpassed!

The Price of Peace

"Even if there were no other causes of war, the great historic and romantic tradition would suffice to kindle it. No generation likes to die without seeing this famous thing—war—with its own eyes. Every generation must have its war, and so the latest date for 'the next war' is fixed by the life of the generation now being born."

                                                            —ISRAEL ZANGWILL

Oh, the splendours of war! Oh, the glamour, the banners, the tramp of marching men, the flashing bayonets, those erect heads, those flushed cheeks, those eyes burning with the fire of a great resolve, the comradeship, the irresponsible gaiety, the clinging grip of friendly hands ... the goodbyes ... the first glimpse of the sea, the embarkation, the voyage, the mere fascination of shipboard, the immensity of sea and sky, the sudden glistening of cliffs in the sun—land!—a harbour bristling with life, long marches across a countryside filled with the singing of birds never heard before, the fever of nearing the front, reaching it, being thrown into the breach—saviours of one's country, of the world's liberty—and then, the pals, the spirit of men under fire, the good nature, the humour, the heroisms, the surging of youthful blood, the grim hardening of fibre when the circle of defeat closes in, the ennobling belief that perhaps this battle, this tiny phase of a battle, this scrap of a wrecked trench, held at all costs, may mean the stemming of a vast tide; that these few men standing about you—and you!—always you with them, bleeding and faint and with the harps of eternity in your ears, you with them till the last shot, till the last glimmer of forlorn hope!—you and these men may be saving the day!—an everlasting day, perhaps, that may live in history forever and forever! ... oh, that ever present sense of making history, that glow of individual fealty to a common cause, a glorious cause, always—as long as wars last—an invincible cause! ... and, oh, when it comes, when it comes, after dragging months of weariness, the quick scent of victory ... the throbbing breath of it in the very air, the sky lit with gorgeous fires, the never to be forgotten sight of the scampering foe, the advance, the advance! ... oh, the intoxication of it ... Victory! ... oh, the red headlines at home!

And, at last, after how long, the homecoming ... oh, the yearning for home, the breathless eternity of those last few miles, few minutes, seconds ... that sudden lump in your throat ... and then, cheers, cheers, crowds, turmoil, jostling, kisses, tears, gripped hands ... one's own folks breaking through the crush to clasp you, to burst into quiet sobbing over you and your empty sleeve ... your soul's mate smiling bravely into your eyes ... that baby you've never seen ... oh, youth, youth, back from the wars!

Would you have peace? Then all this must be cut from the living hearts of men. Work for steadiest of hands, and finest of scalpels.

But, you say, war is not like that anymore. Your picture is false. War is a deadly, deadening thing this time, that sends men back exhausted, dulled, horror-stricken. You haven't painted half the picture.

True. There is much more. There are the horrors, and worse than the horrors, the misery, the dreariness, the waiting, the mud, the stench, the vermin, the discipline, the standing for hours up to your knees in water, hunger, days and nights without sleep, the mistakes, the injustices, the impatience, the weariness, the homesickness ... I know, I know.

But that isn't what lasts. What lasts is the big persisting fact that you were there, that you were in it, that you struck a blow, that you killed a man in hot blood for a glorious cause ... for liberty! ... eternal echo of a magic word!

The thing that lasts, that spreads, takes root, lives, that passes down the ages in the proud hearts that have learned it on the knees of the veterans— what lasts is the glamour, however obscured by the mud of interminable trenches, however stultified by the immensity of operations that makes the merest pawn of a man ... the glamour persists, the bright things, the poignant, the piquant things ... the splendour, the splendour!

They have sent us glimpses of it in their letters home. They bring it back with them. And with every anniversary of those great days, with every slightest shock of circumstance there is struck from the deeply inscribed stone of their memory a glow of sparks ... warm recollections of the days of the great adventure, the great crusade.

The generation now being born will grow up with all that, with the spectacle ever before their eyes of a world sacrificing its millions to crush forever a frantic wrong; the spectacle of a race immolating itself for posterity's sake, meeting death gloriously with a vision of a world made secure, made sane, free of future hazards, impregnable against fresh assaults from unhatched hordes of marauders and vandals whose spawn even now, perhaps, old Time has hidden in his flowing sleeve.

This spectacle and this vision you must remove from the memories of men. Otherwise it will flame like a firebrand, leaping from heart to heart, from generation to generation, engendering an impatience with injustice and tyranny and producing a race whose pride in their purged world will make them swift to fling wide the doors of the temple of Janus at the slightest defiance of the principles for which their fathers died.

The task is there. And those who would now thrust a resolute hand into the future to erase from Destiny's scroll the date of the next war, must first accomplish it. War's splendour-germ must be rooted out of the souls of men. Bury your bugles deep. Muffle your drums forever. Hide away your banners, your medals, your scars. Batter into the earth your monuments and your triumphal arches. Revile the memory of your great captains. Burn your songs of victory.

For that is the bitter price of perpetual peace!

Free Prose

The idea came to me probably two or three weeks ago.

A sort of defence of my method of writing, but really much more than that.

Today at the office I wrote—

"We do not write for this time—Homer and Shaw as much together in the brief objective span—subjective span just starting—thousands of years

"We do not write for posterity in the same sense as the older poets—so called finished works of art—not concerned with ending anything—only starting—not personal glory or a great name—names are nothing—but to contribute to the new movement."

Then tonight in Robert Nichols' preface to *Fantastica* (which Will Staples told me about at the club yesterday) I find this—

"Undirected mythic thinking is just as important to the future of man as directed thinking, indeed that this form of thinking sometimes outstrips the directed form and explores and leads on to regions which the directed afterward makes its own." He cites as examples the apprehension of the kinship of man with Nature preceding Darwin, and the idea of the brotherhood of man the ethnological discovery of root races.

And also—

"Nothing is beautiful in itself: it is only so in relation to the senses, and these senses are not equally developed and trained in all individuals. Beauty is not something inherent in the object, but it is a name for the subjective state of the person who apprehends the object."

And quoting Goethe again—

"The spectacle of life is always new because the spectators are always new."

No colour sense at one time—no sight at all—and no flight—these have been solved and new forms of beauty and action have been discovered—subjective sight will reveal new forms of beauty and action and lead to the conquest of unutterable planes of activity. Science going one way, with business or industrialism as a handmaid. Art going another way, with religion as a handmaid. Or perhaps the other way round.

(from) Notes for the Free Prose

6TH AUGUST 1925

W rote *Dayspring* in present tense because all is now. Not concerned, as were former writers of fiction, to present a picture of objective life, but to get at the subjective underground of it. It is a process of exploration, rather than of presentation. We explore continents, why not individuals, and why not into the unknown quarters of mind. The geography of the soul more important than the geography of the earth.

Must be fluid, because all is passing. We do not want to create complete, superb works. We realize that all work is but a step to something other. We expect greater men to come after.

But language itself, too, must be fluid, for we are trying to create a new language to apprehend the inner life, which previously has been metaphorical, and may have to be metaphorical still, but new metaphors familiar to a scientifically minded public.

The word "the" is not important. We do not want to point at things, we are trying to get inside the thing-in-itself. The word "was" is not important in a sentence. Nothing was. Everything is. But apart from that verbs are not important unless they add something to the picture or the interpretation. Everything is active, so why add verbs to say so. Use only those verbs which describe the action taking place.

I haven't carried the new style either in arrangement or in the coinage of words as far as I hope to carry it, not because I am afraid to do so—although perhaps it is better to let the public walk before it runs—but because I am myself learning to walk. I am trying to break away from the old style, and it won't come right by mere arbitrary conventions established, it must come naturally and spontaneously from the practice of working in a different way at a different aim.

So far my aims are not always in the forefront of my mind. I relapse into old ways of thinking and feeling, and hence use the old idiom. But when I am accustomed to feeling in the new way—unsolidified—the new idiom will develop.

See Virginia Woolf on American Fiction, in *Saturday Review*.

It will begin formless, because our knowledge of the interior world is formless, but it will develop into sharper lines and surer phraseology as we progress in apprehension of the spirit.

"His opinion," says Blake, "who does not see spiritual agency is not worth any man's reading."

Again, in *The Descriptive Catalogue*, Blake says—"The great and golden rule of art, as well as of life, is this: That the more distinct, sharp, and wiry the bounding line, the more perfect the work of art; and the less keen and sharp, the greater is the evidence of weak imitation, plagiarism, and bungling. Great inventors, in all ages, knew this: Protegenes and Apelles knew each other by this line. Raphael and Michael Angelo, and Albert Durer, are known by this and this alone. The want of this determinate and bounding form evidences the idea of want in the artist's mind, and the pretence of the plagiary in all its branches ... Leave out this line and you leave out life itself; all is chaos again, and the line of the Almighty must be drawn out upon it before man or beast can exist."

We are going back to the father (prodigal son) and we must relearn the immaterial language we once spoke. It is not less hard or definite or inevitable than the language we speak now. It is more of these things; but to find it we must begin formlessly and let it come in of itself. We must not employ ancient imagery and symbols. We must try to get away from symbols of the old order and create new ones of the new order. We must exhaust all symbols and arrive at the heart of the thing itself.

Nudes and Prudes

I

There lives in Toronto an artist, a native of France and a frequenter of Paris, who has not been long in Canada. I first met him in a downtown store whither he had come looking for a picture of a horse. After we had been introduced by the keeper of the store, he mentioned his quest. In musical broken English he said:

"I want a picture of a 'orse."

When asked what kind of a horse and for what purpose, he very pleasantly explained:

"Tonight I give lecture to Art Students' League, and I want to show that animal is beautiful because every part made for function, without ornament. In Paris I would show woman, but in Toronto I show a 'orse."

II

There is in Toronto an art gallery conducted by a number of gentlemen who presumably are trustees for the public in matters of art. Here are some items from the history of this gallery:

1. Two or three years ago the gallery invited to be hung on its walls an exhibition of paintings by members of the Societe Anonyme, an association of artists living in 22 different countries, including our own Lawren Harris. Miss Dreier, organizer of the exhibition, was present when the show was hung. When she returned to the gallery in the evening for the private opening she found that two paintings

had been removed from the walls. One was a nude by Archipenko, and the other a nude by Max Weber.

2. A reproduction of a nude by Giorgione (an old master) was more recently removed from the walls of the print room of the gallery, presumably upon the complaint of some interested party.

3. In the last exhibition of paintings by the Group of Seven there were two canvases by Edwin H. Holgate, the Montreal painter, each of which represented a nude female figure. They were the subject of complaint both in person and by correspondence for as long as a year after the show was taken down. At the annual meeting of the members of the gallery this spring a gentleman appeared for the sole purpose of protesting against the hanging of these nudes.

4. The jury appointed by the Ontario Society of Artists to judge its annual exhibition this spring had 800 pictures to consider. One of these was a canvas of two nudes against a landscape background. The picture was accepted, placed in the gallery for hanging and listed in the catalogue. Before the show could be actually hung a suggestion was made that this picture might offend the Board of Education, under whose auspices hundreds of school children attend the gallery each week. No complaint was laid against the picture, but rather than risk the possibility of complaint the curator of the gallery and the president of the O.S.A. persuaded the jury to withdraw the canvas, as though it had not been accepted. When approached by the Toronto newspapers, who had heard of their action, these two gentlemen sought to avoid publicity by saying that the picture was crowded out for lack of room. Instead of avoiding publicity the conflicting stories of the jury and others concerned only succeeded in getting the incident on the front pages of newspapers, none of which took the trouble to make an issue of Toronto puritanism. Their concern was only with a sensational item of news.

III

A few weeks after the foregoing incident an exhibition of paintings and drawings by John Russell was hung in the art galleries of the new College Street store of the T. Eaton Company Limited, Toronto, the head of which company is also the president of the Toronto Art Gallery.

Mr. Russell, a Canadian artist who has lived for a good many years in Paris, had contributed a nude to the Canadian National Exhibition a couple years earlier which had caused a furore in the Toronto press. The puritanical Toronto public flocked to see it.

Another nude (not the same one, as so many people seemed to think) was included by Mr. Russell in the canvases sent to the Eaton store. It was hung with two or three other canvases in a tiny room off one of the main galleries, behind a closed door which no one would think of opening unless attention was called to it. The newspapers, of course, quickly apprized the public of the existence of this closeted nude, and when asked by curious visitors the store management made signs in the direction of the closed and inconspicuous door.

Not a word of criticism appeared in the Toronto press regarding this bootlegging of the nude.

IV

Related to this attitude of Toronto toward the nude in art is its very similar reaction to sex in literature. This phase of our puritanism was ably commented upon by William Arthur Deacon in his survey of literature for the *Yearbook of the Arts in Canada*, 1928–1929. Since the publication of that volume two more incidents have come to light which are highly symptomatic of the treatment these matters receive at the hands of certain Toronto press. Knowing only too well, apparently, that a puritanical public delights in the discussion of those things which it considers illicit, the press of Toronto make a great show of frowning upon anything which smacks of pornography. This policy provides an excuse for reporters and critics to smell out the faintest aroma of irregularity, which they pursue with gusto. (It would be interesting, for example, to count the number of times the words "nude" and "naked" were used in a column of comment written with evident relish by the art critic of the Star at the time that Mr. Russell's nude was piling up big attendances at the C.N.E. art gallery.)

These Toronto critics are not satisfied to nose out and spice the pages of their newspapers with every possible allusion to sex which they can squeeze out of a book. They must needs drag the personality of the artist into the muck, as well, imputing motives without evidence in order to have a full-course orgy of offensiveness with which to regale their readers.

This happened conspicuously in the case of Mr. Morley Callaghan, a writer who has been fated to receive so much less than justice from the critics of his own country that he may well regard his work as beyond their capacities to appreciate.

In a review of his latest novel, *It's Never Over*, a Toronto critic publicly charged Mr. Callaghan with the deliberate policy of using sex themes in his novels in order to increase his sales. It was stated in a way that made it perhaps not quite libellous.

The same critic who thus maligned a fellow townsman and a former colleague on his own newspaper, recently interviewed a writer who had won a prize in a nation-wide novel contest. His first questions were thoroughly in character. Having had no chance to read the novel he began prying at once for sex interest, asking the author if he had "cut loose," and with other queries insinuating that his motive in writing the book might have been the second-hand enjoyment he would derive from describing the sex emotions and acts of his characters. These suggestions were framed in a way that made it possible for the offender to escape with a whole skin.

V

It is time that artists in Canada raised their voices publicly against this sort of thing. Mr. Deacon did so fearlessly a couple of years ago in regard to literature, and was promptly slapped on the wrist for doing so by a writer on the *Globe* who considers himself something of a champion of the arts.

But the painters here have not faced the issue. They had an opportunity to do so this spring when the newspapers were eager to get facts and opinions about the removal of my picture, *Figures in Landscape*, from the O.S.A. show. Possibly some of them might have spoken for publication if so many lies and conflicting opinions had not beclouded the matter as a public issue. These lies, which made it appear that the picture was crowded out of the show because it was not good enough aesthetically to compete with other pictures, prevented me from making a public statement at the time. Had I done so I could easily have been accused of peevishness. I should also most certainly have been accused of trying to get publicity for myself, for I was accused of that, in print, at the time, although I refused to talk to the army of reporters, with their noses on the trail of nudery, who besieged me at the time.

At this distance it is possible to submerge the specific case in the issue it involves.

VI

Nobody pretends, I imagine, that nude paintings or books which deal frankly with sex are dangerous to the morals of grown men and women. The concern of prudes, I take it, is entirely with the younger generation.

It may be further assumed that adults, whose concern with sex becomes more and more a question of cerebral excitement, induced by imaginings and suspicions, in proportion to their lack of interest, physically, in the natural and normal sex act itself—it may be assumed, I suggest, that adults grow to fear the effect on young people of what happens in their own minds when they see a nude picture or read a lewd book.

In any case, and whatever the reason, the questions of nudity and lewdity become "questions" only because of the young. Which means that prudery can be reduced to an attitude solely concerned with education.

VII

Our educational system is probably wrong at almost every conceivable point, but the one point at which it is perhaps most flagrantly wrong is where it touches on questions of art.

Boards of education, of course, do not think so. Education in art is in their eyes a trivial and unimportant subject. They think of art as a sort of recreation—something to be indulged in on Friday afternoons when children are fed up with a week's studies—a matter of no practical value, either as a contribution to the student's possible earning power in later years, or to his character as a future citizen. Not until art education is tightened into a commercial course in the technical schools or concentrates on the making of craftsmen in art schools is it taken seriously by boards and teachers. At once the emphasis is placed on technical proficiency—that is to say—on craft.

Yet, if art means anything at all besides mere craft—and if it does not there is no need for another word for it—it implies more than the ability to make things—pictures, sculpture or what not. It implies, surely, a development of the capacity to see.

Through ages of evolution our senses have learned to recognize certain signals, largely, in the case of humans, through the eyesight, whereby we escape danger and are attracted to what is good for us. These sense-signals are wholly practical and by themselves lead to no acquaintance with the conception of beauty. This is not the place to delve into the basis of aesthetics, but it can be briefly stated that the concept of beauty arises only when an individual is detached from the purely personal urgencies of his own desires and fears. Beauty, in other words, is the product of a view of things which transcends the personal and glimpses the universal. It is a hint of the wholeness of life—a unity to which the individual, concerned only with purely practical problems of self-preservation, is wholly blind.

This larger vision is the essential difference between the artist and the non-artist. Nowadays, of course, after centuries of art, even the non-artist possesses at least a rudimentary idea of this detached perception. The legacy of art through the ages has taught him a little how to see, so that now a sky is beautiful for him as well as a mere portent of the weather, and a woman is beautiful as well as being simply the object of animal desire.

The function of the craftsman is to make things. The function of the artist is to *see* things in new relationships, detached from the insignificant unity of his own puny affairs and desires, so that they take on the grandeur of symbols—symbols of movements, adjustments and laws that are universal, unattached to any particular time or place, and bearing a relation only to the boundless and yet unified Being which is the central mystery of life.

The "art" of the craftsman and the "art" of the artist are thus quite distinct, and frequently have nothing to do with each other. Most artists, it is true, become craftsmen in projecting the expression of what they have seen. But most craftsmen do not become artists. They sometimes become good copyists of nature, without sensing any deeper beauty than attracts the eye of the average tourist.

Yet our educational system completely confuses the two, labels as "Art" the productions of both, and hides its head in the sand when any attempt is made to differentiate between them.

VIII

We are now a long way from nudes and prudes, but we must go still further before returning to the particular point of our discussion.

A proper understanding of the real function of art is more necessary today that it has ever been. Now that the orthodox religions are losing their hold, especially on the imaginations of the younger generation, art is more significant than ever before as the only unifying experience that remains to us—the only experience that approximates to the religious in its ability to make us feel *at one* with the universe.

To many, of course, this at-one-ness with the universe is not important at all. Even those who complain the loudest about the chaotic condition of modern society do not seem to realize that rules and laws, by means of which they expect to terrorize the masses into decency, are of little effect unless they have behind them something more than dressed-up authority. People will not dwell together in unity unless they can experience the unity. Our modern emphasis on the rights of the individual in relation both to God and to man has destroyed that unity which was once perceived, and which gave man a humble but happy place in nature.

The arrogance of the individual is the source of all our social chaos, and since religion in its orthodox and systematized forms has lost its power to curb that arrogance (has indeed contributed to it), the power of art is alone left in the world as a unifying influence, and from it somehow will surely come the next religion, for the prophets of all religions have themselves been artists essentially, seeing new relationships between man and the universe, new aspects of the unity of Being which alone has the power to touch men on finer issues.

Art, then, serving as the inspiration to all kinds of positive conduct (in contrast to the negative spur induced by rules and laws), and considered as a unifying force in modern life, can be seen as an important practical measure, and one which even boards of education might regard, without loss of dignity, as possibly their chiefest care.

IX

Art education, as at present constituted, is simply a tinkering with the child's natural wonder. Any educational system can only succeed in distorting the unity into which a child confidently emerges. The best that any system can do is not to distort it too much. Hence it is of the utmost importance that education in general, and art education in particular, should not be undertaken lightly by Gradgrinds who put faith only in facts, or, on the other hand, by theorists who are likely to warp young minds into twisted, narrow or extreme habits of seeing and doing.

Decisions as to what is to be withheld from a child are fully as important, if not more important, than decisions as to what he should be told or shown. One needs not to have studied modern psychology very deeply to realize that suppressions and inhibitions are dangerous, if not definitely pernicious.

Before either Freud or Dr. Watson were heard of, it was a matter of mere common sense to observe that the over-restrained child usually broke into extravagancies later in life.

To withhold knowledge of the human form and its functions, and to discourage appreciation of its beauty at an early age, is to bring a child up with a sneaking curiosity in respect to that unity which of all unities is perhaps the most mysterious and the most important for men and women. It is to implant in his mind the feeling that natural admiration for bodily beauty is sheer animalism, and something to be ashamed of.

Appreciation of the beauties of the nude figure is not altogether due to the impulses of sex, and even if it were—from the standpoint of a society which aims at continence and decency—surely it is better to shape such impulses openly into channels of delicacy and open-eyed admiration, than to let them smirkingly fester in secretive foulness of mind.

The tendency today is to tell children in a clean, straightforward, natural way about the functions of sex, so that they do not get their knowledge of it, half-guessed, from the filth they hear whispered in corners. And art is one method of acquainting children with the organs and functions of the body in an atmosphere of candour and beauty.

There is nothing filthy about the mystery of fatherhood and motherhood. He who says so blasphemes not merely against the special God he has been brought up to worship, but against any conceivable scheme of the unity of life that it is possible for men to hold. The vileness associated with sex is purely a man-made matter, and a product of the system of taboos surrounding an act of union which is probably the closest clue we have to the total unity of life.

The division we call sex, which is to be found in all organisms, and is perhaps the principle on which all forms of life are founded—in short, the principle of issuance—may very well be the primary division of Being, the first mysterious step taken by the primal unity toward multiplicity. As such, it is as fundamental as hunger, and in surrendering ourselves to its age-old attraction we may be nearer to the essential life-unity than we are apart and separate.

That, however, is a metaphysical speculation that has little bearing on normal conduct in society as at present constituted. It is merely a suggestion of the tremendous significance of sex, and of the possibility of discovering, if we approached it with open eyes, clean mouths and reverent minds, some deeper hint of that wholeness which, if we could grasp it entire, would make us all one.

When We Awake!

Perhaps it has not occurred to many people that the artist in Canada is more difficultly placed than artists have ever been before in any country. My original conception, in planning this book, was that it should deal as much with the handicaps and complications which beset artists in Canada as it does with their achievements. As editor I have attempted to provide contributions that discuss what might be called the soil of our art, as well as others which chronicle its blossoming. And as contributor—in this general introduction—my hope is to sketch a composite picture of the background against which all artists in Canada work, thus unifying the more intensive impressions of special observers in the various fields covered by this volume.

To make clear the claim contained in the first sentence it is necessary that the function of the artist should be stated as simply as possible. (It will be understood that when I speak of the artist, throughout this introduction, I mean to include and typify artists using any conceivable channel of expression; in other words, I am dealing with a certain kind of man and not with certain categories of craftsmen.)

The artist—to put the matter as inelaborately as possible, and, at the same time, to take the highest view—is *a person whose experiences crystallize into unified wholes that can be embodied in some medium, as contrasted with persons whose experiences seem fragmentary, unrelated and chaotic.*

The artist is not, I believe, distinguished from the layman either in the nature of his experiences or in the quality of his emotional reaction to them. The quantity or character of a man's experiences apparently have little to do with art, otherwise a man who has actually committed a murder might be expected to write a better tragedy than *Macbeth*, whose author, we may suppose, was never guilty of taking another's life. The quality or intensity of a man's emotional reactions can have little to do with art either, otherwise we might be led to the conclusion that the most hysterical people should make the greatest artists.

No; the faculty that differentiates the artist from the man in the street is what Coventry Patmore, I think, called "unitive apprehension." It is simply the faculty of seeing things *together* and *related* which normal people feel are all "at sixes and sevens."

When the artist is able thus to unify a certain experience, which is his special faculty, he proceeds to the extrication of it as a whole and the placing of it on paper or canvas or in wood or stone or what not, which is his special function. Faculty and function are not always equal, of course. Some artists are more adept at "unitive apprehension" than they are dexterous in the function of extrication and reproduction. Others possess great fluency in the embodiment of their experiences, but the faculty of relating and concentrating those experiences into wholes that have a new structure and life of their own is perhaps deficient, and hence their experiences do not count for much; they are little removed from the chaotic or sentimental apprehension of the general run of people, no matter how cleverly they manipulate the medium of their art.

Now, the efficacy of art—its power to produce effects—as distinct from the faculties and functions of artists, consists in the concentration of experience into deeper and simpler and more universal unifications, always approaching the total unity of life and conveying intimations of that eternal unity which has probably never been completely revealed to any single individual.

Some writers on Aesthetics prefer to speak of this efficacy of art as an *expansion* of experience, but whether we proceed outward or inward in our imagery the efficacy of art and the faculty of artists relies on this ability to see unity in multiplicity. It is the root of the "design" sense in the plastic arts and of the "metaphorical" sense in the arts of literature.

The true poet does not load his lines with metaphors merely for the sake of ornament, but because he has seen some hitherto hidden relationship between a man and a tree, or between the wind and a wolf. And the true artist does not twist and elongate his figures to look like storm-bent tree-trunks, as Michelangelo did, or make them soar like flames as El Greco did, merely to establish an individual style, but because he has sensed something of the universal rhythms which flow through every manifestation of nature.

And when I say that the artist in Canada is more difficultly placed than usual I mean precisely that it is more difficult for him than for artists elsewhere or in past times to concentrate his experiences into unities and universalities, and extricate them as newly-minted wholes bearing the fresh imprint of his own personality and his own conditions. This difficulty, unfortunately, is by no means a single one. It is rather a very multiple and complicated handicap, so involved, in fact, that few artists in Canada, probably, are aware of the extent of its ramifications.

II

Consider the difficulties of producing a unified art or literature, arising from individual unifications by artists attuned to our soil and conditions, when the background against which our artists must work is split up into the following incongruous and disassociated elements

- a country that is not unified geographically,
- a people that is not unified racially,
- a history that centres about a few picturesque personalities and events, failing to unify for us our past as a people,
- a population too small to provide an adequate audience for artists,
- a general conception of art that lacks any hint of national consciousness, but clings instead to old notions of connoisseurship borrowed from feudal times and countries.
- a disruption of the settling process, which might in time have unified some aspects of Canadian life, by the mechanization of civilisation

all over the world.

• a destruction of ethical-philosophic-religious stability by the encroaching scepticism of a science-ridden age.

Even geographically we are not unified. Conditions at our seacoasts vary greatly from conditions surrounding the great inland lakes. Life on the prairies and in the Rockies has little in common. In the north we border the Arctic and a scattered, illiterate population of Esquimaux. In the south we lay alongside a populous, wealthy, sophisticated republic. Variations of temperature produce marked differences in the flora and fauna of various portions of the country, and produce varying habits of occupation, recreation and even of clothing, among the human inhabitants. In short, an art or a literature that could be called indigenous to one portion of the Dominion would inevitably contain elements as alien to other portions as the art and literature of foreign countries.

Racially we are split "forty ways," to use a native colloquialism. Old European antagonisms still seethe in the blood of Canadian sons and daughters of Frenchmen, Englishmen, Scotsmen and Irishmen. To these have been added the confusing strains of middle-European blood and thought. Back of all this is the Indian, supplying occasional motifs for our art and subtly tincturing the national admixture in ways that we mostly ignore. And in front of us is the certainty of continuous and steadily increasing influences of all kinds—by actual contacts, intermarriage and uninterrupted communication—bearing on us from our neighbours in the United States.

Historically we have no past as a people. There is a history of costumed dare-devils who found perilous ways across the continent. There is a chronicle of what the French and English did to the Indians and to each other. These—the French, the English and the Indians—from to-day's standpoint, were all foreigners. The settlers from Scotland and England and France, they were all foreigners, too, until the second or third generation. Until a year or two ago we were all foreigners to each other in a land that we mutually called "ours." And even yet, particularly between the French-speaking and the English-speaking sections, this attitude still persists. We are *not yet a* people!

And in common with the politicians who think there are not enough of us yet to make a nation, the artists feel that there are not enough of us to make an audience. It is not merely that an artist must live and *can* live in New York or London, where markets exist for his work. An artist does not live by bread alone; he lives by understanding and sympathy and encouragement, even though he starves or clerks in a store for a material living. Those who can understand and encourage artists are few enough in any population—even among a hundred millions—but in nine millions they are very few indeed, and in Canada widely scattered. The artist, seeking the living sustenance of *togetherness* with an audience, loses heart here, lacks incentive and impetus, and either hurries to Europe or the States, or turns sour and cynical in the shop or the counting-house where he is forced to work.

And if the audience in Canada is quantitatively negligible it is even less stimulating to the artist from the qualitative standpoint, unless he still happens to be a "foreigner" in spirit, a purveyor of old-country wares which appeal to his fellow-foreigners, not yet awake to the fact that this country which we all call ours *is* ours, and not a colony, a temporary settlement, a place to make fortunes with which to scurry back to "the dear homeland." This is our homeland, and some of us can see it so with *our* eyes and not with the eyes we brought across the Atlantic, still hazy with Scottish mists and rose-tinted by English blossoms.

How shall the artist fare when the audience sees its country and its country's art through an old glamour—the product of centuries of blood, and flags, and creeping ivy, and the bells of churches in the fields—a glamour which is not here! Our own glamour is what the artist here is trying to show us, but at present we cannot see it.

When we can forget the old countries—when we really awake and *see* this country as ours instead of merely calling it ours—when we no longer regard ourselves as exiles and everybody else as foreigners—then, perhaps, we shall be able to "sing the Lord's song in a strange land," because it will be no longer strange.

III

That rapprochement between audience, critic and artist which is necessary to the establishment of an art, native or otherwise, has thus been very difficult, if not impossible, in Canada, up to the present time. The critic plays a more important part in such a consummation than many people realize. A single historic instance is perhaps sufficient to make this clear. Consider, for example, how long England would have delayed recognition of both Ibsen and Wagner had it not been for the pugnacious pen of Bernard Shaw.

Our critics, on the whole, have been as blind as the audience and many of the artists in Canada to the fact that we are situated in a country very different from any countries across the Atlantic—different not merely in physical conformation, rhythm, atmosphere, and so on, which are looked upon as subject-considerations that interest only the painters (although actually they have intangible influences on our whole national mood), but different also in the most practical aspects, in the way in which we make a living here, re-create ourselves, govern each other, provide for our unfortunates; to say nothing of language, manners, diet and the daily programme of our meals. Let us also say little of any possible differences in mental and emotional characteristics, bred of our sojourn here, which perhaps lead to ethical, philosophic and religious idiosyncrasies; for these are more intangible and would require too elaborate analysis for the present purpose.

All these the critic is as much inclined to ignore as the public. He defends his blindness by the assertion that the standards whereby art must be judged are universal. (I have myself taken this position and consequently know how common it is and how easy it is to adopt it.) The position would be an excellent one if anyone would really stick to it, but what actually happens is that these so-called "universal" standards we talk about nearly always turn out to be the art-shibboleths of two or three centuries of European culture. In many cases this narrow range of standards is even more curtailed, comprising only standards, and very low ones at that, which were prevalent in northern European countries during the nineteenth century alone. To readers of Spengler, Croce, Faure—if of no earlier writers on aesthetics—the gulfs fixed between postrenaissance art in northern Europe ("Faustian" art) and the art of Greece, and between the arts of Greece and China, for example, are fairly obvious, even when little understood.

The Canadian critic, as a rule, is not only unfamiliar with the art of Greece and China (the little he knows about an art as recent and accessible as that of Russia is usually only sufficient to make him detest it), he seems to be also unfamiliar with the broad historical fact that the aims of artists in certain countries and in certain ages have differed very greatly and that to judge the art of one by the standards of another is to ignore those "universal" standards he often postulates but rarely knows how to apply.

Perhaps the most comprehensive criterion of what constitutes art in any country or time is that it should crystallize into harmonious and unified wholes the experiences of people living at a certain time and in certain conditions. When it does this it inevitably *feels* Chinese, or Egyptian, or early Italian. But if the critics in a given country—in Canada, for example—possess only fragmentary, unrelated and chaotic impressions of their own country and their own time (and naturally so, lacking artists to unify these impressions for them), it stands to reason that what little art we possess that does tend to unify and portray a typically Canadian kind of thing—a thing found only in Canada—will be unrecognizable to them. It will have something of a new kind of unity which is totally unfamiliar to them.

That this lack of rapprochement between artists and critics occurs quite often, and particularly in new countries, is borne out by the fact that both Whitman and Edgar Allen Poe had to be recognized in Europe before the critics of the United States could accept them. The critics of another country can often sense the native unification in a foreign work of art more keenly than in their own, because, being unfamiliar with all the smaller complications which the local critic is aware of, they find in the simplified whole presented by the artist a coherent experience unlike that portrayed by artists among other peoples or in other times. This has in fact occurred in respect to what little art we have so far produced in Canada. In England, France and the United States the work of a few of our painters and writers (Morley Callaghan is the most recent example) is much more generally recognized than is the case here—recognized, that is to say, as embodying something peculiar to this country.

I have permitted myself this parenthetical discussion on the state of our criticism because it is really one of the major handicaps under which our artists labour. I would have given it a special place in the list of complexities that perplex the artist in Canada if it were not so inextricably bound up with the lacks and deficiencies that are symptomatic of the Canadian audience as a whole. Special stress is here laid upon it because I believe with St. John Ervine that "it is the business of critics not only to judge the work of an author, but to create an audience for him; and we enable authors to live and to grow by making more and more people capable of appreciating him. The better we are, the better the authors will be."

Expand this to include workers in all the arts and it becomes obvious that critics have a great *creative* duty to perform, besides the pettier business of pulling things to pieces. To criticize Morley Callaghan for writing about people that one would not think of asking to dinner, or Lawren Harris because his pictures are not likely to be conducive to immigration, is to mistake the highest function of criticism, which is to clarify for the public the artist's aims and show to what extent he has succeeded in realizing them.

In the face of those critics who prate so much of universal standards I assert with all the force of my convictions that the aim *of* artists in Canada to-day *should not be the same* as those of artists in England in the nineteenth century or in China a few thousand years before Christ. Their aims being different, their art should be different also.

IV

Brought back, then, to the aims, the tasks, and the difficulties of artists in Canada, there remains to be considered a fresh set of handicaps. So far we have been discussing our background here more or less historically. The lacks and complications we have discussed were perhaps more prominent and operative twenty years ago than they are to-day. And they are, besides, peculiar to this Dominion. I must now speak of disruptions which further hinder possible unifications by Canadian artists, but which are recent and world-wide in scope, affecting this country in common with many others. I refer to the mechanization of civilisation and the almost superstitious acceptance of scientific formulae as constituting a true account of the universe in which we live.

The first is the more easily disposed of. Everybody, by this time, is at least chaotically aware of what mechanization is doing for us and doing to us, but there are few, probably, who relate all these things and become conscious of them—not as a broadcasting aeroplane here, a globe-circling zeppelin there, a talking movie elsewhere, and television in the immediate distance—but as a unified and definitely new kind of civilisation, all of a piece, that our children are growing up into, half oblivious of its wonder.

Are there many who realize, for example (especially the enthusiasts for universal standards), that books like those of Henry James, George Meredith and Joseph Conrad simply cannot be written by a man who has just breakfasted with an electric toaster at his elbow and whose morning meditation in the garden has been disturbed by ukulele-music trickling out of the sky? Those of us who are forty or more have passed out of an old civilisation into a new one in half a lifetime—and *that has never happened before!* Every day, with the tremendously widened and intensified means of communication—by newspapers, movies, radio, etc.—new ideas are given so much publicity that we become accustomed to them and accept in a twelvemonth what in mediaeval times would have taken at least a century to become absorbed.

Moreover, the new civilisation into which we have stepped so hurriedly differs in a greater degree from the former one than has ever been the case before. The people who went to see Shakespeare's comedies differed very little from the people who went to see Aristophanes' comedies, either in their way of thinking or in their mode of living. The spread between the matter and manner of plays presented in ancient Greece and Elizabethan England is slight compared with the difference between what we saw when we used to go to Drury Lane to see Henry Irving and what we see now at a movie.

Yet, though we realize this, there persists a curious reservation in a great many minds. So long as these very rapid changes depend on a mechanical invention or improvement of some kind we are likely to accept them with only a slight degree of disturbance and irritation. We took to the new dramatic form of the movie like ducks to water. We have welcomed new architectural forms like the grain elevator and the skyscraper. But in the arts where form is divorced from mechanics— notably in literature and painting—we permit ourselves to be greatly disturbed by ingenuity, originality, and the invention of new contrivances, new moods, new modes. We can tolerate a machine being new, up-to-date, and ingenious; but the same qualities in a human being are intolerable. So long as imagination and inventiveness confine themselves to mechanical, scientific and commercial channels we approve and applaud; but let the same forces loose in the theatre, the novel, and in the art gallery, and we boo and hiss and write indignant letters to the newspapers. The artist is the last person on earth who is granted the right to originality.

The artist, unfortunately, is among the first to be affected by such changes as have taken place in the past few years. He is at once more sensitive to a pressure that makes life faster and noisier, and, on the other hand, his faculty of unification enables him to grasp more quickly than the lay mind the potentialities and possible culminations of a trend which is not yet recognized by many as a broad stream, gathering terrific impetus, and carrying us far from what we have always been pleased to call "human" moorings.

Mechanization, and the widespread obsession with it, in recent years, has affected art in at least two different ways. By compressing and speeding up our lives we are made less responsive to natural phenomena which bear the secrets of ultimate unity in their forms, rhythms and relationships. We are made more responsive to the forms, rhythms and relationships of artificial and mechanical reproductions of natural phenomena and so-called "improvements" on natural living conditions. This, in turn, produces a concern with, and an admiration for, the exactness and efficiency of machines, leading to more mathematical considerations in art and more geometrical forms. It is more than a coincidence that the modern revival of an overwhelming interest in "form" in painting (and a type of form based on cones, cylinders and circles), coupled with the stenographic accuracy sought by modern fiction writers, occurs at a time when the exact relationships of such forms and their accurate timing in all kinds of mechanism has become the most common concern of the age.

The artist in Canada, as elsewhere, is a sensitive receiving-station on which these concerns with mechanization impinge. His scene and his neighbours—the subjects of his art—are affected by them. They must be assimilated into the unifications of experience which he attempts.

Thus, before his country and his people could get themselves shaken down into some sort of homogeneous whole, the artist in Canada is confronted with these new disruptions which still further complicate his task.

Added to his local situation are the disturbing and influencing experiments conducted by fellow-artists in Europe who, having a homogeneous scene to deal with in their older-established countries, were quicker to react to mechanistic influences and motifs as constituting material or suggesting methods from which new art-forms might arise. These experiments have been variously labelled "modern" and "primitive." It seems to give the critics of the movement considerable cause for merriment in that such a supposed confusion should exist. Actually, however, it is most natural that a genuine "modern" to-day should react "primitively" to his surroundings. In the first place, it is a sign, in any age, of a freshness and honesty of outlook, uninfluenced by the technical traditions of his forerunners. And, in the second place, a certain kind of "primitiveness" is the most appropriate possible reaction to our particular time, for we are, in the strictest sense primitives, the first men of a new civilisation whose implications are incalculable.

These modern importations from Europe sometimes assist an artist here by suggesting a method of unifying mechanical with natural phenomena which, due to other preoccupations, he might arrive at very late. On the other hand, they often exert a bad influence, by suggesting merely technical innovations very easily imitated. No one can quarrel with an artist for learning from others how to see and seize upon reality, provided his unification of that reality and his interpretation of the experience he gets from it is expressed in his own terms.

The extent to which an artist in Canada should allow modern mechanization to disturb his as yet undigested knowledge of the natural phenomena of his country is a question that will be examined in a moment.

V

Before returning for a final estimate of the Canadian artist's difficulties and prerogatives there remains to be considered another world-wide movement which affects artists everywhere. I have referred to it as "the encroaching scepticism of a science-ridden age."

We have been accustomed to thinking that the terms scientist and agnostic are practically synonymous, but actually the scientist has been more superstitious than most of us. He has believed in a kind of reality that could be measured, bottled up, labelled and explained away, whereas most of us have known all along that the only reality is inside of us, and that to think of splitting it up is as futile as Shylock's notion of taking a pound of Antonio's flesh.

The scientist has now come round to our opinion. The whole structure of scientific thought has been destroyed by what is called the Fitzgerald "contraction"—which means simply that no measurements that man can devise can be relied on to measure anything with perfect accuracy. The deviation from perfect accuracy is so small that for ordinary terrestrial measurements the difference is negligible; yet this infinitesimal *inequality* has wrecked the former structure of science. On it has been built the whole new theory of relativity, the gist of which, from the layman's viewpoint, is that no *absolute* picture or knowledge of the universe can ever be attained by man. Such a picture will always be warped out of shape by the instruments that measure it. And man is one of the instruments! In short, the complete picture of the universe *will always be different and unequal for every human being!*

We face a universe whose inequalities can never be completely harmonized (scientifically) for and by any one individual. The dream of science, that it might some day reduce all phenomena and all laws to a simple and understandable manifestation of one original first cause, is shattered. Inequality, and its corollary, the unpredictability of events, are seen to be the essential pattern of the world *as viewed through the eyes of man.*

The conception of a universe continuously imperfect to human eyes, and full of inequalities, has not been accepted either suddenly or generally. It is a matter of slow growth and mysterious contagion. It is more like a mood that spreads—as through an audience—by veiled hints and cryptic allusions that affect the emotions deeply just because they are not clear to the intellect.

In this mood we are all now swimming. We may be able to "look through" the imperfections and inequalities of existence, and thus, for ourselves, are not disturbed by this newest destruction of idealism; but we cannot insulate ourselves against the electric current of a huge world-mood which rattles everything we touch.

The impossibility of harmonizing life's inequalities appears like a warrant authorizing eccentricity. Art therefore becomes aristocratic, in the sense that the artist no longer cares about the audience. He is concerned chiefly to pursue his own particular eccentricities and to ring the changes on the particular aspects of inequality to which his nature especially responds. Art consequently becomes devoid of "associational" values, lacks human interest, and, in the final extreme, communicates nothing except to the few who happen to be "conditioned" by the same kind of inequalities as the artist himself.

Artists of this type abound in Europe, but only a few names are familiar to us here—Mondrian, Kandinsky, Man Ray, Epstein, Joyce, Gertrude Stein, T. S. Eliot, and a few others. The pages of *Transition*, published in Paris in English, continually introduce new recruits, including many Americans, who are joining this group of what might be called "unintelligibles."

Lower in the scale, from the European standpoint—for the extreme of unintelligibility seems now to be the highest criterion of present-day art over there—is another group whose activities can only be described as "clinical." Their obsession with the diseased and the abnormal extends to people in the last stages of some malignant illness. The characters in their books are people who ought to be under observation in psychiatric institutions or receiving proper care in hospitals. And modern architects, instead of designing houses, are producing buildings that look like small hospitals to put all these sick people in.

To dismiss this trend in a paragraph, when it really requires a volume to itself, is not fair to the practitioners of this kind of art, many of whom are thoroughly sincere and hardly less ecstatically devoted to their notions of art than the "unintelligibles." But already this survey is becoming formidably long.

Certain tendencies in Canadian literature, painting, sculpture and architecture, however, are not easily understood without a side-glance at these European manifestations of the world-mood of the moment. Our artists cannot, even if they would, remain entirely unaffected by the clinical, scientific, aristocratic and "unintelligible" tendencies so rife abroad.

And this brings us to our final consideration of the extent to which an artist in Canada—or anywhere else, for that matter—should keep the pores of his temperament open to the heat and cold of waxing and waning moods throughout the world.

VI

In that remarkable passage which I have placed at the beginning of this book, Whitman says that the artist (he uses the word "poet" in much the same sense that I use the word artist), must "flood himself with the immediate age as with vast oceanic tides". In another place he clarifies and extends the meaning of this passage by saying that the poet (the artist) *"places himself where the future becomes present."*

This supplies the answer to the question asked above. It suggests that the artist should be aware of present tendencies, but not immersed in them to the extent of destroying his backward and forward perspective. Art and literature on the grand scale is never narrowly contemporary. It gathers its energies from the heroic exemplars of a past time and leaps forward at such a pace and with such herculean stride that it over-shoots the present, and to succeeding futures ever seems to recede, inevitably ahead of oncoming generations. Its essential grandeur is in this tremendous arch from past to future which swings high over the dwarfed concerns of the "present" of each generation that catches up to it.

Here we see another type of unification that has to do with time, and it is this particular unification which is most endangered by present tendencies. Artists almost everywhere have cut off the past, impatient with its superstitions, its dogmas, its antiquarianism. And having no faith, no ideals, no hopes, or even wishes (all these are *sentimental*), they cut off the future also. Like sick people in hospital, doomed to die, they deliberately prevent themselves from thinking of the great sunlit spaces outside and the expanding futures of individuals luckier than themselves.

Concerned only with the immediate sicknesses and eccentricities of the age they live in, they cannot see the colossal proportions of the race and its life, like a giant tree going down into the deep past and branching up into future infinity. They jump feverishly from leaf to leaf of one tiny branch of the towering tree, solicitous about a tiny touch of blight or the infinitesimal ravages of some short-lived insect. Devastation on this microscopic scale is sufficient to unnerve them, driving them to satire or cynicism, all forgetful of the great surrounding downshine of the sun and the upward-aspiring sap within. What they see of life is fragmentary, chaotic, unrelated, and if we apply to them our general test of the artist's faculty, we find that such unifications as they are able to make are only fragments, little bits of life which they break off or isolate in order to study them, as in a clinic, as in a vacuum, as specimens, rather than as manifestations of a great unified realm of being whose every part depends upon or gives birth to every other part, in an endless and subtly interrelated "becomingness".

To recognize this *unity of being* is obviously akin to the experiences which in the past have always been called religious. And perhaps the simplest way of describing the highest faculty of the artist is to say that it is essentially a religious sense—a sense of the mystery of the whole of life. And whether he manufactures a god who sits outside of this whole and guides it—either jealously as in the old testament interpretation, or lovingly as in the new testament interpretation—or whether he feels a sufficient godliness in the virility and variety and majesty of the whole to want no other god but this immense, pulsating being itself—or *whatever* other *doctrinal* view he takes, so long as he apprehends and is exalted by the *wholeness* and the *oneness* of life, he possesses the first qualification of a great artist.

"The altitude of literature and poetry," said Whitman, "has always been religion—and always will be ... the religious tone, the consciousness of mystery, the recognition of the future, of the unknown, of Deity over and under all, and of the divine purpose, are never absent, but indirectly give tone to all."

Is there, in Canada, any of this consciousness of unity to counteract the distracting influences from without and the many divisions within? Perhaps there is a little. But we are not really awake. We are not sensible of national unity and we are not sensible of universal unity. Yet there are signs that both may perhaps soon blossom into being. These signs, so far, are deducible only from the occasional work of isolated individuals. But the opportunities to build an art here and an audience that may be stirred by it are as great as have ever existed in any nation, if not greater.

There is a spirit here, a response to the new, the natural, the open, the massive—as contrasted with the old, artificial, enclosed littlenesses of Europe—that should eventually, when we rely on it less timidly, become actively creative. And this creativeness, recognized as our own, and proceeding from the awakened consciousness of a new people with a new future, will itself become a quickening power, jogging laggards out of their dose in the bosom of dying orthodoxies, or counteracting the narcotic effects of scepticism, so that religion—and hence art—becomes vital and fresh; an hourly response to life's exultations!

Prophets Wanted

"It is the heaviest stone that Melancholy can throw at a man," wrote Sir Thomas Browne, "to tell him he is at the end of his nature; or that there is no further state to come, into which this seems progressionall."

Such a statement might almost be taken as a contemporary diagnosis of the temper of the present day. Modern scepticism, with a Canute-like gesture, says to mankind—"Thus far, and no farther". Modern pessimists are feverishly scribbling "Finis" all over the latest page of history; while the "new" Humanists, with more practical minds, are engaged in building a palatial terminus (after Greek models) in which civilisation may conveniently come to a full stop.

The "new" Humanists have marked out a definite and restricted sphere for man, cut off on the one side from the natural world, and on the other, from the supernatural. They would set limits to his nature, believing that man cannot improve himself progressively, but only repressively. The best he can do is to discipline himself, and thus, by curbing his passions, his desires, his hopes, and his imagination, he may make the three-score-years' journey with a minimum of discomfort.

Although bolstered up with erudite references to the philosophers and poets of the past, the "law of measure," so ambiguously propounded by present-day Humanists, turns out to be nothing more than the simple doctrine of compromise, which is conveyed to every schoolboy in terms of a "happy medium".

It is mistaken for a contribution of considerable importance to modern thought because it has never before been propounded so diligently and on so grand a scale by persons who have the courage of very timid convictions.

Pertinacity of exposition—in an age accustomed to advertising—easily obscures, it seems, the essential faintheartedness of this "new" gospel, which seeks to combat the negativeness of a sceptical and pessimistic age by more far-reaching denials than those that have brought us to the present pass.

A group of denial-mongers leading humanity out of the wilderness of denialism is perhaps the most pathetic symptom of our contemporary disease.

Western man is afflicted with the accumulated results of spiritual malnutrition. It is our lacks, and not our excesses, that have made us an invalid generation. The spiritual and moral emptiness that rumbles vacantly in most attempts at expression to-day is brought about by four principal lacks:

- lack of authority.
- lack of centrality.
- lack of standards.
- lack of dignity.

Such excesses as we have managed to perpetrate in recent years can be traced to the complete disbelief in the effectiveness of any imposed autocratic order, whether of gods or men. Any autocracy—anything "strong-in-itself"—has aroused our suspicions, our scepticism and our impatience. Those things only are certain, those things only are good, that can be evolved individually and demonstrated as reasonable to a pragmatical intelligence. In a word, all forms of outer compulsion are galling to the modern mind.

This would not be so bad if a compensating trust in some inner compulsion—other than the promptings of the mite-like, contemporary, individual self and its "ishness"—were present to supersede our former reliance on outer authority. But the most conspicuous of our lacks, and easily the most damaging, is the loss of centrality. All our other impoverishments are derivable from this.

It is natural that we should have seen the absurdity of thinking that the inner could be controlled by the outer; but it is unnatural—unorganic, indeed, and we are nothing if not organisms—to ignore and even deny the prime power of inwardness to affect outwardness in every manifestation of life.

The essential inward oneness of the whole phenomenal world, which is sensed as a part of the commonplace experience of the humblest and least-endowed child, while at the same time forming the core of all transcendental philosophies and religions, is brushed aside as a metaphysical abstraction produced by the "pattern" of the mind. In its stead we enthrone a behavioristic rationalization of experience that is at once sterile and superstitious—superstitious, that is to say, in accepting the dead letter of mechanistic explanation for the living mystery of phenomenal action and interaction.

We live, as Henry Adams perceived, in a "multiverse", having lost all sense of a universe and the centrality which the conception of "turning-into-one" implies.

Discarding, as we do, the outer impositions of dogma and the inner compulsions of spirit, it is not surprising that we lack standards. And it is not surprising, either, that the "new" Humanists, who talk incessantly of standards deducible from an application of the "law of measure", are utterly unable to discover any.

Their catchwords—"moderation", "decorum", and so on—are actually negations of standards, whether considered as *measurements* (in which case they amount to marking a spot halfway between two necessary evils), or whether considered as *banners* to which bewildered humanity can rally.

In neither case do they *stand*—as standards obviously should— rooted in the real; but are simply signposts erected in abstraction, pointing nowhere, but rather warning the wayfarer not to stir from a safe and selfish middle ground.

Possessing no allegiances; adrift in a dead sea of "conditionings" and "complexes" and relativistic "events"; lacking standards that refer either to the real or to the ideal, the natural or the supernatural; it is only logical that this new brain-blown Homunculus—modern western man—should lack dignity; for, like Goethe's bottled pigmy, he is fragile, coddles himself against the gusts of experience, and does everything "modestly, lest that the glass I shatter".

What we know of human dignity, grandeur, and the "sense of glory", has not sprung from the cold recluses, but from men who felt at once their kinship with the animals and the angels, "ready to be anything, in the ecstacy of being ever".

It appears to be believed that dignity can be regained, together with lost authority and forgotten centrality, by a laboriously evolved dialectic that will hedge men about with prejudices and predilections—a system of "liking and disliking the right things."

It should be obvious—although seemingly it is not—that such an aim abandons the quest of centrality and concerns itself wholly with the circumference of experience.

Not the least tragic of the many confusions of thought into which the "new" Humanists have fallen, in their attempt to straddle all possible fences, is this inability to "measure" their own fundamental position. They imagine themselves as being close to a spiritual centre (Mr. Babbitt, particularly, thanking his stars that he is not "spiritually indolent", as other men are), whereas anyone possessing the faintest gleam of what Coventry Patmore called "unitive apprehension" can see distinctly the frigid pole where they really stand, at the furthest possible remove from any conceivable "core" of life.

Mr. Babbitt actually conceives the "universal centre" as a sort of pole that can be stuck up wherever one chooses, after the manner of Moses' rod, as an efficacious means of warding off the modern pestilence.

"Practically," he says, "the assertion of a universal centre means the setting up of some pattern or model for imitation ... Humanism, however, differs from religion in putting at the basis of the pattern it sets up, not man's divinity, but the something in his nature that sets him apart simply as man from other animals and that Cicero defines as a 'sense of order and decorum and measure in deeds and words' ... it (Humanism) holds that the world would have been a better place if more persons had made sure that they were human before setting out to be superhuman."

This, of course, is the worst possible example of putting the human cart before the universal horse, a practice which characterizes all "new" Humanistic thought. These Humanists talk grandly of a "universal centre", of "energy of soul", of "higher will" and of "higher immediacy"; yet they are concerned only with controlling the manifestations of a higher-universal-central-will-energy as it appears in man.

That they have merely derived their notions of centrality and soul-energy from ancient philosophers, and have never *experienced* the "higher immediacy" of which they prate, is obvious from their persistent suggestions that it should be and can be controlled. It seems superfluous to point out that if "higher" means anything in the vocabulary of these "measurers", it must mean *higher than lower*, and, if so, a higher will must control a lower will, and not the other way round.

The curious "belief" of the modern Humanists in this higher will is worth studying. Babbitt says "the higher will must simply be accepted as a mystery that may be studied in its practical effects, but that, in its ultimate nature, is incapable of formulation." He goes on to say that "the person who declines to turn the higher will to account until he is sure he has grasped its ultimate nature is very much on a level with the man who should refuse to make practical use of electrical energy until he is certain he has an impeccable theory of electricity."

These two quotations betray the reactionary character of Humanistic thought at its innermost centre. Here is an admission that no attempt should be made to "study" the higher will in its ultimate nature. All we should do is to switch it on and off like electricity. It is something that fortunately exists merely to be "turned to account".

If this is not a mechanistic notion, I should like to be shown one. But it is not merely mechanistic. It is an attitude which says, in effect: Great men in the past have studied or apprehended something of the ultimate nature of the higher will—just as physicists and mechanicians have learned something of the nature of electricity—but we shall not attempt to carry on their work any further; we shall simply press the buttons—adopt the "values" or "standards"—which they have made available for us.

Humanism, in other words, is a species of spiritual cowardice. Although fully appreciating that the "wisdom of the ages" was wrested from reality by men who had the courage and energy to grapple with the higher will—as Jacob did with the angel—refusing to give up the struggle until some glimpse of the ultimate secret had been revealed to them, Humanism is content to accept the rewards of their wrestling and turn them to account in a passive and repressive pattern of conduct that is favourable to comfort.

"The real humanist consents," says Babbitt, "like Aristotle, to limit his desires only in so far as this limitation can be shown to make for his own happiness." And in another place: "The humanist does not carry the exercise of this will beyond a subduing of his desires to the law of measure; but it may be carried much further until it amounts to a turning away from the desires of the natural man altogether—the 'dying to the world' of the Christian".

There is no lack of admission in "new" Humanist writings, if you search for it, that there have been men who have pressed further than they—the Humanists—intend to go. Babbitt confesses that "religion is in its purity the very height of man", and quotes, as an example of its purest and most "authentic" utterance, the words of Thomas à Kempis: "Know for certain that thou must lead a dying life; and the more a man dies to himself the more he begins to live in God."

A "new" Humanist can quote this appreciately, because he has determined to ignore its positive side and accept only the negative side, which fits in with his preconceived repressive pattern of conduct. He is not willing to "die to himself", or to "die into life", as Keats describes the process in *Hyperion*. He denies or ignores or explains away or declares "incapable of formulation" the God or the "life" which Keats and à Kempis postulate as the state in which a man lives when he has died to himself.

The "new" Humanist, in short, clings to the negative while denying the positive of which it is merely the obverse. He accepts the circumference while disregarding the centrality which holds it in position.

These quibblers must be opposed. Their wobbling dialectic, bolstered with quotations from writers whose mental and spiritual implications they either ignore or misrepresent (by selecting for emphasis only the negative aspects of their thought), must be resisted by poets and prophets who are capable of emphasizing the positive pole of reality.

It is the poet-prophet type alone who can re-create sublimity for us by recovering the sense of centrality that modern life has obscured. It is precisely because we have been concerned with "practical effects" and with "turning to account" the higher will, instead of "dying" into it, that we have lost the faculty of apprehending a "universal centre", whose immediacy, experienced in our lives, would create the values that we miss.

Only the poet, detached from practicality, can regain this experience and communicate it to a sceptical world. The difference, as Aristotle pointed out, between the historian or realistic writer, and the poet, is "that one tells what happened and the other *what might happen*".

The poet is able to reveal universal truths, instead of mere "particulars of sense", because, as one commentator observes, he can "create new happenings in the texture of which the pattern of life is plainer than in any 'particular' experience".

Instead of rationalizing from particulars on the circumference of life, he creates from a centrality—an inner apprehension of universal relationships converging in an ultimate unity. The poet, in short, puts the universal horse ahead of the human cart.

Emerson—himself something of the "whole man, the reconciler, the poet-priest" whose advent he eagerly awaited—was quite clear as to the circumferential character of facts and the centrality of spirit.

"There seems to be a necessity in spirit", he says, "to manifest itself in material forms; and day and night, river and storm, beast and bird, acid and alkali, pre-exist in necessary Ideas in the mind of God, and are what they are by virtue of preceding affections in the world of spirit. *A fact is the end or last issue of spirit.*"

Prophets are wanted to-day to re-assert and demonstrate this priority of spirit, showing us, as Herbert Read deduces from earlier poets, that "the true life" is lived "only by those who see beyond the futility of what is, to the glory of what might be."

This emphasis, from Aristotle to Read, on the sublimity of what might happen as compared with the tawdriness of what does happen—a doctrine which postulates spirit as a perfection existing eternally *ahead* of man, in the future as in the past—is exactly the doctrine that is necessary to-day to combat both the comfort-seeking Humanists and the prosperity-seeking mechanistic humanitarians.

To mechanize man into physical comfort and to repress him into mental comfort will not satisfy the essential craving of the human spirit, which is for spiritual comfort. Men are not *persuaded* into spiritual comfort. They cannot be mechanized or dogmatized or "Humanized" in that direction. "An accepted certainty", as Middleton Murry says, "is not a certainty ... man cannot accept certainties; he must *discover* them."

It is not persuaders that we need, but poets and prophets of our own time who will rediscover the sublimity of the possible as an antidote to the triviality of the actual.

And we want not merely poets and prophets who will transport us with the wonder of what might be; we want also critics who will view literature as the poet views nature, critics who will hold up, as Poe suggested, not merely the good, nor even the best that has been achieved, but the best that *can* be achieved.

Both poets and critics must be *ahead of attainment.* The new wonder, which recurs constantly in human history, arises when men realize, after a period of depression, that man has not reached the end of his nature, and that there are, indeed, no *ends.*

The human race is always changing, and its values with it — and perfection is perhaps reconstituted each moment as the sum total of constantly evolving relationships—so that the race may not be perfectible in the old sense, but it can *go on*, continually creating new and possibly grander consummations than have been attained in the past. These consummations may not find expression through single individuals or in single works of art. They may conceivably be attained by and for the race as a whole. And above all, they need not be—indeed, cannot be—*end* consummations.

"Instead of a will to this or that posited and ideal end", says Middleton Murry, "there is a will to pure self-emergence. We learn to wait upon the unknown that we are; we are dedicated to whatever of creative newness may emerge through us."

There are a few writers, and Murry is among them, with a thinker as unlike as Whitehead touching shoulders with him, who, in unpoetic fashion, are prophesying the coming gospel of creative newness. We need poets who will be at once less involved and more stimulating than the metaphysicians, to create wonder for this new conception—the idea of a spiritual centrality continually emerging in new consummations toward the circumference that is rounded and temporarily ended in the consciousness of each individual man.

Those who admit the existence of some sort of universal centrality, but have made up their minds not to seek it or understand it or dedicate themselves to it, are among the first and harshest of the critics of such a conception. They dub it pantheistic and "indefinite". Yet when the religionist asks them to "die" into it, to see whether or not it is indefinite, they say: We admit that religion is the height of man, but we are content with the lowlands.

Or when a "philosopher of flux", as they call Whitehead, attempts to make the conception more definite by scientific rationalization, they will have none of him either.

Their own kind of indefiniteness concerning the higher will, with its "incapacity of formulation", suits them perfectly, for it makes no calls on them. And their own kind of definiteness, which limits man's conduct and destiny to a tiny circle of prescribed "human" activity, suits them perfectly, also, for it comfortably shuts out the necessity of "dying into life —the turbulent, new, creative, emergent life of the spirit.

In England, Wyndham Lewis is much more candid in his objection to the "organic" philosophy of creative newness. "By this proposed transfer", he says, "from the beautiful objective, material world of common sense, over to the organic world of chronological mentalism, you lose not only the clearness of outline, the static beauty, of the things you commonly apprehend; you lose also the clearness of outline of your own individuality which apprehends them."

This, of course, has always been the objection to "high religion", as Mr. Lippmann calls the earlier and more emotional manifestations of the doctrine of creative newness. The individual is determined not to die into life—determined not to lose his soul to save it—determined not to be "born again".

Wyndham Lewis and the "new" Humanists, and many another crier in the wilderness of pessimism, all bewailing what men have lost, are yet afraid of losing something more. They cling to the hard outline and the comfortable concreteness of their world. They are cloistered and unadventurous, despite all their criticism of other philosophies as an "evasion of life".

The man who wants rules and standards in a measurable and clear-cut universe is himself the person who is trying to escape from life, in which, as Middleton Murry declares, crisis is continual.

These reactionaries are aware that if mankind comes to regard life as emerging constantly from a spiritual centrality, the race will soon be utterly changed. And they dislike the discomfort of change. They dread the new coming of poets and prophets who will dream of what might be, and will urge humanity, in le Gallienne's phrase, "to stretch the octave between dream and deed."

Like Joseph's brethren they point the finger of scorn and cry: Behold, this dreamer cometh.

But they cannot, with all their stubborn Canuteness, hold back the tide of eternal novelty.

Far from being at the end of his nature, man is at this moment emerging into a new consciousness of universality and unity. He is taking the first blundering steps toward a new conception of the old dogma-disguised truths at the core of life.

High above littered controversy and heaped polemics there can still be seen, except by these blinded ones who lead the blind, the "prophetic soul of the wide world, dreaming on things to come.

Textual Chronology and Editorial Procedures

The prose works in this edition are divided into three sections: Short Fiction, *The Wrong World*, and Essays and Polemics. The texts that comprise the first and third sections are subsequently arranged according to the chronology of the period depicted. As few of the pieces in this collection have been previously published, it was decided that the edition would not distinguish between published and previously unpublished works. In any event, the unpublished works are as strong as—and in many ways, more interesting than—the published work. Chronology poses its own problems: Brooker produced or typeset many of the eight short stories in this collection during the same period while living in Toronto at the same address while using the same typewriter. As he rarely dated his work, it is not possible to determine or infer the exact order of composition for some of the fiction. Instead, the chronology of the events depicted in the stories was chosen to organize the texts in this edition. In contrast to the fiction, Brooker left enough evidence to construct a more precise chronology of the eight non-fiction works, which were produced over a longer period of time—a quarter of a century. These texts all include direct references and responses to historical events and publications, corroborating the composition chronology. In the particular non-fiction texts included in this edition, by a convenient coincidence, the chronology of composition is the same as the period represented or discussed in the work. As a result of Brooker's interest in current affairs, the worlds depicted in the first and third sections of the book share a similar, linear march through time, both starting in the prairies at the turn of the century, and ending up in Toronto before the Second World War.

The seventeen titles included in this edition were selected from Brooker's archival collections, which include nearly one hundred unpublished works of short fiction and non-fiction, alongside thousands of pages of writing in various genres and formats ranging from utterly experimental to entirely banal. The selections were chosen based on a combination of the available evidence of completion (manuscript versus printed format, multiple drafts, submission for publication, or publication) and the more subjective literary merit of the work. As a result, numerous dimensions to Brooker's complex oeuvre—his children's stories, his experimental fictional autobiographies, and his numerous hard-boiled detective stories—are not included or represented in this edition.

In general, the latest version of a given work was chosen as the copy-text. Manuscripts for the unpublished material come from two sources: the Bertram Brooker collection in the Elizabeth Dafoe Library of University of Manitoba and the personal archives of the Bertram Brooker estate. For the stories "Head Waitress" and "Bad Order", and the essays "The Spread of Negativism", "The Decay of Art", "The Price of Peace", and "Free Prose" there exists only one extant manuscript each. The stories "Like Old Jehovah", "The Gilliland House", "A Glass of Catawba", and *The Wrong World* have two versions each: an original typeset manuscript and a carbon copy with either handset or typeset emendations. For instances where the variant archival versions follow a clear chronological pattern of editing, the choice of copy-text was uncomplicated. In contrast, Brooker appears to have produced multiple versions of "Youth's Manuscript" and "To All the Nations ....!" Of the former, three editions exist—identifiable by the physical markers on the cover pages as "26 Pages", "Three Boxes", and "Unmarked". Dates and a precise chronology are not available, but the pattern of textual deletions suggests that "26 Pages" is the oldest version, edited down to the "Three Boxes" version, which, in turn, was edited down to the "Unmarked" edition. While it remains possible that the sequence goes the other way, and that the additional passages were inserted with each new version—the strength of the final draft and the relative weakness of the deleted parts suggest my chronology. Furthermore, a handwritten note on "26 Pages" reads "Not revised", suggesting that it is, indeed, the first draft. In the case of "To All the Nations ....!" multiple versions of the manuscript versions are extant but parts of all have been lost. As a result, there are overlapping sections of the texts without a clear indication of chronology or finality. In other words, with the chronology confounded and significant portions of the variants missing, a stemma of versions is impossible to establish at this point in time. In this case, the two typeset versions were combined and chosen as copy-text and a transcription provided of the other pages. Without a clear indication of chronology, however, and despite the dangers and limitations of such an approach, it should be made clear that the copy-text ultimately was selected based on the principle of coherence and readability. All variants are, of course, recorded in the textual notes.

Things are only slightly more complicated with the previously published works. The excerpt from *The Tangled Miracle*, for instance, is based on the author's proof in the University of Manitoba archives, which was unchanged and unedited in the final book form (confirmed by the published copy in the Thomas Fisher Rare Books Library at the University of Toronto). Similarly, no variant texts exist in the archives for "When We Awake!" However, in the case of "Mrs. Hungerford's Milk", the story exists in two published forms, once in his lifetime, and once posthumously, as well as one unpublished manuscript form. Given that the text was published by the Toronto-based *Canadian Forum*, edited by his friend and fellow mystic Barker Fairley, there seems no reason to suggest that the first published version is unreliable in any way. As such, the first published version of the story functions as the copy-text here. Similarly, "Prophets Wanted" was published but once, and has only one archived manuscript, therefore the published version was chosen as copy-text.

Finally, things are at their most complicated for this edition with Brooker's essay "Nudes and Prudes". The article was first published in 1931 by Brooker's close friend William Arthur Deacon (whom he praises in the article itself) in a collection of essays called *Open House*. The article was reprinted in Douglas Fetherling's *Documents in Canadian Art* (1987), and more recently appeared online on arthistoryarchive.com (edited by Charles Moffat, and with an introduction by David Helwig). The complication comes from the fact that, while Fetherling used the *Open House* version, Charles Moffat chose an archived manuscript version as copy-text instead. The differences between the two versions are substantial as the published version excised the names of individuals and galleries responsible for censorship in Toronto. This information was subsequently restored by Moffat based on the manuscript version of the article in the University of Manitoba archives. The problematic information was likely removed for political and social expedience, even though the *Open House* version was published by a sympathetic friend. In his letter on 17 April 1931, Deacon writes Brooker to say, "if you and I are to stand together on this issue [censorship]—why we had better stand as close as possible." Still, the impetus for censoring the anti-censorship article seems to come from the editor: "Is it necessary to hit Gus so cruelly, and him an old man? Perhaps we'll never get anywhere if we stop for things like that. I hate to hit an old man; but he does do a lot of harm. About libel?? Will he??"

Despite the fact that Brooker was at least nominally involved in the editorial process, and that this was the only version published in his lifetime, because of the historical significance of the excised material, and further because the social sensitivity that once merited consideration no longer exists, the archival manuscript version will serve as the copy-text here. The online version differs only subtly, mostly as a result of typos, from the archival version.

This accounts for all cases of substantive differences, that is, the actual wording, among the variant texts. Given that Brooker occasionally deployed neologisms or deliberate errors, and was decidedly ambiguous on his preference of national orthography, most instances of the so-called accidentals, that is spelling, punctuation, paragraphing, and capitalization, are left unchanged. In a few instances, typographical errors, spelling inconsistencies, and the handful of distinctly Canadian spellings that we have finally embraced both broadly and coherently have been corrected—all of which are listed in the textual notes.

Explanatory Notes

The explanatory notes provide additional information to the numerous cultural and geographic allusions characteristic of Brooker's writing. The kinds of things that have been annotated include: brief biographical information for authors named or discussed; citations for books, poems, stories, and songs named or discussed where available; citations for hidden or subtle allusions to other works or public figures where they were available; significant connections to other Brooker texts and/or details of Brooker's biography; and geographic or other references that were deemed to be of significant scholarly or general interest.

Common sources that were consulted in the preparation of the Explanatory Notes include: the King James Version for all biblical quotations and allusions, the *Canadian Encyclopaedia* for references to Canadians, Canadian institutions (such as banks and parks), and Canadian places, the *Encyclopaedia Britannica* for references to Britons, British institutions, and British places, the *Oxford English Dictionary* for etymologies and definitions, and *The Riverside Shakespeare* for all Shakespearean quotations and allusions. For Brooker's common and complex references to music, I referred to *The Golden Encyclopaedia of Music* (Lloyd 1968), *The Billboard Encyclopaedia of Classical Music* (Sadie 2004) and David A. Jasen's *Tin Pan Alley: An Encyclopaedia of the Golden Age of American Song*. I also consulted the electronic databases Early Canadiana Online, *Toronto Star*'s Pages of the Past, and the *Globe and Mail* (Canada's Heritage from 1844 to 2002) to gain insight and background on some of Brooker's more obscure allusions to particular aspects of Canadian life, such as the business of alcohol in "A Glass of Catawba" or the saga of censorship in Toronto during the 1920s.

Like Old Jehovah

5.22 *Just the way ... the sky once:* Ezekiel 1.28: "As the appearance of the bow that is in the cloud in the day of rain, so was the appearance of the brightness round about. This was the appearance of the likeness of the glory of the LORD."

6.6 *Old Jehovah ... out of there:* Genesis 3.7: "And the eyes of them both were opened, and they knew that they were naked; and they sewed fig leaves together, and made themselves aprons."

The Gilliland House

7.1 *Zenith:* It remains unclear upon which small city Brooker based his fictional town of Zenith, Manitoba. One likely candidate is Neepawa, where Brooker lived from 1912 to 1914. Correspondent to details in the story, the Whitemud River runs through Neepawa, and the town is near Riding Mountain. The community is approximately 80 kilometres east of Riding Mountain, however, too far for the kind of visibility Brooker describes later in the story. There are, of course, many small and remote communities that potentially match the loose physical descriptions of Zenith, most notably Wasagaming (formerly Clear Water) through which the Whitemud river also runs, on the edge of the present Riding Mountain National Park.

7.20 *Riding Mountains:* The Riding Mountain region was incorporated as Manitoba's first National Park on 26 July 1933, and was *officially* named Riding Mountain National Park. At the centre of the park is the cabin made famous by Canadian author Archie Belaney (aka Grey Owl) in the 1930s. Despite Brooker's use of the plural, there is only one Riding Mountain, surrounded by prairie flatlands.

11.25 *Wilbur Malone:* Wilbur Malone, almost certainly modelled after the Canadian Confederation-era poet Wilson MacDonald, was a recurring character in Brooker's short fiction. See, for instance, "The Poet's Birthday" included in the "Texts" section on the Canadian Literature Collection website.

12.3 *Indian school:* The First Nations communities in the Riding Mountain area have changed dramatically in the past two hundred years—originally, the area was inhabited by Cree. After the demise of the bison, however, they left the area. Ojibway groups moved into the territory and inhabited the area in Brooker's time and to this day.

12.8 *White Mud River*: The river, properly named the Whitemud, forms in the foothills of Riding Mountain National Park.

13.11 *Brandon*: The city of Brandon, Manitoba, is 215 kilometres west of Winnipeg.

Bad Order

21.7 M.M.B.: The acronym refers to a fictional railway operator.

21.20 U.P.: The acronym refers to the real American railroad operator Union Pacific, a rival to the fictional M.M.B..

24.15 C.G.: It is unclear what the acronym specifically refers to, but it clearly refers to collecting final earnings after being fired.

25.23 B & B: The acronym refers to the "Bridge and Building division" used by railway operators to build and maintain bridges, buildings, culverts and other structures.

Mrs. Hungerford's Milk

28.18 quoit: A flat disc of stone or metal thrown for exercise.

32.2 *chasing around with that Lambert fellow*: Lambert Chace was the name of the detective in Brooker's photoplays.

A Glass of Catawba

36.21 *Bernard*: Bernard Bradley was one of Brooker's pseudonyms, associated primarily with his youth. See note 4 in introduction and his "Diary of Bernard Bradley" (1905) in the University of Manitoba Special Collections.

37.14 *Edmonton real estate deal*: Edmonton land speculation reappears in Brooker's first novel *Think of the Earth*. The capitalist Clem Anderson moves to the Alberta capital to "clean up" in the boom town. The exploitative manipulation of Anderson's land dealings set up the central murder in the novel.

37.31 *Maurice Hewlett … The Forest Lovers*: Maurice Henry Hewlett (1861–1923), British author of *The Forest Lovers: A Romance* (Macmillan 1909). Hewlett appears in Brooker's early play "The Measure of Gordon Craig", in a dramatized debate between George Bernard Shaw, G. K. Chesterton, Maurice Hewlett and Brooker himself.

38.7 *Souris:* Souris, Manitoba, lies 47 kilometres to the south of Brandon.

38.26 *for the Ottawa:* The Bank of Ottawa, established in 1874, was purchased in 1919 by The Bank of Nova Scotia.

38.28 *at the Commerce:* The Imperial Bank of Commerce, established in 1875, merged with the Canadian Bank of Commerce in 1961 to form the present Canadian Imperial Bank of Commerce (CIBC).

39.1 *At Flores … of the Armada:* The opening lines to "The Revenge: A Ballad of the Fleet" (1878) by Sir Alfred Lord Tennyson (1809–1892), British poet.

41.1 *the Ladies' Aid:* The Ladies' Aid in Winnipeg was established on 5 August 1886 by the First Lutheran Church of Manitoba, although informal women's charity associations using similar names appeared around the province even earlier. In various communities, the Ladies' Aid used variant names such as Hospital Ladies Auxiliary or Lady Hospital Aid. These groups were dedicated to supporting the church by helping the needy, often by raising funds for local hospitals.

41.16 *Catawba?:* Port made of the Catawba grape from Pelee Island, Ontario. Based on a survey of advertisements in the period prior to the First World War and prohibition, J. S. Hamilton & Co, of Brantford, Ontario, was the most prominent company to produce wines and ports from the grape.

42.24 *Portage and Main:* The most prominent intersection in the business district of downtown Winnipeg.

45.1 *Leonard Crane:* Character in "The Man Who Knew Too Much" (1922, see Chapter 6) by G. K. Chesterton (1874–1936), British writer. See "The Spread of Negativism" for more of Brooker's response to Chesterton.

45.1 *Chopin:* Fryderyk Franciszek Chopin (1810–1849), Polish composer.

45.6 *Steinway … Raveldebussycyrilscottplayedherelastyear:* Steinway was and remains a manufacturer of high-quality pianos used by many prominent musicians and composers; Maurice Ravel (1875–1937), French composer; Claude deBussy (1862–1918), French composer; and Cyril Scott (1879–1970), British composer, poet, and mystic. Scott, often touted as "the father of modern British music", toured Canada and the United States in 1920. When he played at Massey Hall in Toronto on 21 January 1920, he allowed his name to be used in advertisements: for instance, an advertisement in the *Globe* on the day of the performance reads in part: "Scott's favourite instrument for both concert and private use is the Steinway Piano" (Steinway & Sons).

Head Waitress

46.21 *Lake Rosseau*: Lake Rosseau is located in the Muskoka lakes region of Ontario, approximately 225 kilometres north of Toronto.

46.22 *Hekla*: Hecla Island lies in the middle of Lake Manitoba, approximately 85 kilometres north of Gimli.

47.15 *Port Carling*: Port Carling, Ontario, is located at the south end of Lake Rosseau, approximately 210 kilometres north of Toronto.

51.15 *Seaton's dress department*: The store is modelled after the premier Toronto location of the T. Eaton Co. Limited chain of department stores at the very prominent downtown intersection of Yonge and Queen streets. The company, once Canada's dominant retailer, folded in 1999.

51.18 *Jackson's Point*: Jackson's Point, Ontario, is 88 kilometres north of Toronto on Lake Simcoe.

52.12 *Einar Jonsson*: Einar Jónsson (1874–1954), Icelandic sculptor. His sculpture of Jón Sigursson, politician and expert on the Icelandic sagas, was purchased by Manitoba's Icelandic community in 1917 and placed on display in the Manitoba Legislative Buildings in Winnipeg.

54.4 *the viaduct over the Don*: The Prince Edward Viaduct System spans the Don River Valley in Toronto and was completed in 1917. The Danforth district lies on the eastern side of the valley.

56.8 *Tabarin*: The name alludes to the Le Treteau de Tabarin, the most famous cabaret in Paris at the turn of the century.

57.2 *the Tech*: Central Technical School where many of Brooker's colleagues and fellow artists worked and taught art and art history classes.

57.6 *the Grange*: The Grange was the name of the original house in which the

Toronto Art Gallery was built. The gallery was later renamed the Art Gallery of Ontario in 1966.

Youth's Manuscript

62.14 *Alas that youth's sweet-scented manuscript should close*: Misquotation of the *Rubáiyát of Omar Khayyám*: a collection of Persian rubáiyát or quatrains by Omar Khayyám (1048–1122), Persian poet and mathematician, popularly translated into English by Edward Fitzgerald (1809–1883). The 72nd verse reads: "Alas, that Spring should vanish with the Rose! / That Youth's sweet-scented Manuscript should close!" (1896: 186). Brooker's diary notes that he received as a gift a "swell edition" of the text on 15 February 1911.

63.22 *Liebestraum*: Song written by Franz Liszt (1811–1886), Hungarian composer. His extremely popular *Liebesträume* was a series of three piano solos first performed in 1850. The most famous of the three, and the one most likely to have been played at the Canadian party, was his *Liebestraum No. 3 in A-Flat*. The name translates as "a dream of love" or "dreams of love."

64.19 *Go pretty rose ... would dare*: Song No. 8 written by Frederick Woodman Root (1846–1916), American musician, for his *Miss Doremifasolasini's American Opera* (1894).

64.29 "*Down by the old mill stream*": Song written by Tell Taylor (1876–1937), American songwriter, c. 1910.

65.2 "*Moonlight and Roses*": Song written c. 1925 by Ben Black (1889–1950), English composer, Edwin Lemare (1865–1934), English composer, and Neil Morét, pseudonym of Charles N. Daniels (1878–1943), American composer.

65.7 *Kubelik and Ysaÿe*: Jan Kubelik (1880–1940), Czech composer and violinist. Eugene Ysaÿe (1858–1931), Belgian composer.

69.19 *St. Mike's*: St. Michael's Hospital in downtown Toronto was opened in 1892.

72.21 *the Parkdale ravine*: Parkdale is a neighbourhood in downtown Toronto, just north of the Canadian National Exhibition fairgrounds.

(from) The Tangled Miracle

74 Brooker's second published novel, also in the year 1936, depicts the

adventures of "psychic" detective Mortimer Hood and his assistant Rhoda. In the scenario excerpted here, Hood has been hired by a cult of ascensionism (Christian believers who claim that the physical body of Jesus Christ ascended to heaven) to prove that the leader of their cult also ascended upon her death—essentially, to prove that a miracle has occurred. Hood is reputed for debunking the mystical claims of occultist groups, and thus it is thought that his word would satisfy even the sceptics. In this scene, however, the sceptic demonstrates his familiarity and affinity for certain mystical ideas and philosophers. The people gathered are members of the cult, hoping the detective will help to legitimize their movement and miracle. For his part, like Hood, Brooker was emphatically mystical but very sceptical of institutional religions and occultism.

74.16 *the old trick movies*: Brooker operated a movie theatre with his brother prior to the First World War. He left the business 23 years before *The Tangled Miracle* was published.

75.9 *fourth dimension*: The fourth dimension was a source of fascination for avant-garde artists such as Claude Bragdon, Umberto Boccioni and Marcel Duchamp. Joyce Zemans notes that Brooker wrote an essay on the fourth dimension, and exhibited a "4 Dimensional Cube" in his 1929 OSA exhibition (Zemans 1989: 29). In a letter to an unknown advertising client, Brooker also suggests basing an ad-design on the "ultra-cubist" pattern ("Pattern"). The character Hood's interest in such phenomena, like two mystical thinkers who deeply influenced him (and Brooker), John Middleton Murry and Richard Maurice Bucke, was "purely scientific", a claim supported in the novel by repeated connections between the fictional detective and Albert Einstein. Hood is even described as looking like the scientist: we first meet him with his "grey hair standing on end—'like Einstein's', Rhoda thought" (4).

77.9 *Flatland*: Though the exercise might have been common to other sources, Brooker's use of the proper title suggests that he has borrowed the anecdote from E. A. Abbott's *Flatland* (1884). In his popular science-fiction novel, Abbott proposes a two-dimensional world in which a three-dimensional character suddenly appears.

78.12 *Fechner, Zollner, Morosoff, Ouspensky, Hinton, Bragdon, and others*: Gustav Theodor Fechner (1801–1887), German experimental psychologist; Johann

Karl Friedrich Zöllner (1834–1882), German astrophysicist and illusionist; Nicholas Morosoff (1899–1994), Russian avant-garde painter; Peter D. Ouspensky (1878–1947), Russian philosopher and mystic; Charles Howard Hinton (1853–1907), British mathematician; and Claude Fayette Bragdon (1866–1946), American architect and mystic. This list corresponds to Brooker's favoured mystical thinkers.

78.22 *Plato's cave*: From *The Republic*, book 7, by Plato (C. 428 BC–C. 348 BC), Greek philosopher.

The Wrong World

83.2 *Gawthorpe's*: The name Gawthorpe also appears in *Think of the Earth* with the character Dick Gawthorpe, editor and owner of *The Monitor*, the newspaper of the fictitious town Poplar Plains. Notably, the character hails from Brantford, Ontario, original home of the Toronto-based mystical painter Lawren Harris. Gawthorpe remembers a "fellow" from his home who used to talk for hours on spiritual themes without ever going to church, much like the non-Christian Theosophist Harris.

84.13 *George Pethick*: The character Pethick is undoubtedly based upon Brooker's childhood friend, George Calver. Brooker wrote Calver in 1921, enquiring about his performance at "The Hip" many years previous in which he played a "Will-o-the-Wisp". Calver's letterhead includes reviews of his performances, many of which highlight his imitation of animals. *The Evening News*, for instance, wrote, "George Calver is a man with a voice that might be called almost acrobatic, to so many uses does he put it. He appears singing a ballad in a mezzo-soprano voice, does an imitation of Harry Lauder's rooster imitating Lauder's 'Stop your tickling, Jock,' one of the funniest imitations I ever heard on the stage." Brooker's red notebook (box 1, folder 16) notes that he saw Calver at the Hippodrome and sleeping "at George's boarding house" on 16 December 1910. George Calver also joined him for dinner at Coulthards on 25 December. In the notes for "Shorts about Bernard" George Calver and Tom Coulthard are mentioned by name as characters to be used in the book.

84.21 *'The Martyr of Antioch.'*: Song written by Sir Arthur Seymour Sullivan (1842–1900), British composer most famous for his operatic collaborations with W. S. Gilbert.

85.8 *thirty-four years*: Brooker was 38 years old when writing *The Wrong World*.

85.13 *He had left Croydon … sailed for Canada*: This biography is shared by the protagonist of *Think of the Earth*, Geoffrey Tavistock. Brooker was also born in Croydon, England (then just outside of London, and now amalgamated into the city), but never travelled to South Africa: he came directly to Canada with his parents in 1905.

85.17 *his inheritance was not large*: Tavistock's large inheritance provides a crucial plot twist in *Think of the Earth*.

85.28 *Peace River*: Northern region of British Columbia and Alberta defined by its proximity to the Peace River.

85.32 *the Icelanders*: References to Icelandic-Canadians and their communities in northern Manitoba recur throughout Brooker's prose. In *Think of the Earth*, for instance, Icelandic-Canadian "Old Dan" Eggerston rents canoes and paddle-boats by the lake shore (71). In *Mr. Windle*, Katrin and Asta Petursson teach Augustus Windle Icelandic-Canadian folk-songs from their youth (200). According to John Matthiasson, the Icelandic-Canadian communities Brooker wrote about were settled in 1875 as part of a special Icelandic reservation set aside by the Canadian government (1132). "New Iceland" was officially created by a federal order-in-council and allowed a separate school system, legal system and language. Reflecting their exceptionally high literacy-rate, the community had its own newspaper, *Framfari*, and produced numerous note-worthy poets and writers, including Laura Goodman Salverson and Vilhjalmur Stefansson. Natural disasters and other hardships and complications saw the special territory incorporated into the province of Manitoba in 1881, though it has kept its distinctly Icelandic cultural connections to the present day.

86.4 *Minaki*: Minaki, Ontario, lies 50 kilometres north of Kenora, Ontario, or 250 kilometres east of Winnipeg, Manitoba.

87.3 *like Chatterton*: Thomas Chatterton (1752–1770), English poet. Chatterton's tragic suicide at the age of 17 concluded his short but famous career as a poet. Many noteworthy Romantic authors offered tribute to his life and talent: Keats dedicated *Endymion* (1818) to him, and Coleridge eulogized him in *Monody on the Death of Chatterton* (1790).

87.31 Gustave Flaubert (1821–1880), French novelist. Brooker is referring to the oft-repeated anecdote that Flaubert in his ardent quest for "le mot juste" would read his work aloud—including his novels—hoping to expose by the method every and all weakness.

88.19 *Henry Adams*: Henry Adams (1838–1918), American historian, journalist, novelist and memoirist. Adams was both the great-grandson and grandson of American presidents. Concordant with Densham in *The Wrong World*, Brooker was heavily influenced by Adams's writing, especially *The Education of Henry Adams* (1907). In a diary entry, Brooker noted his own experience reading Adams's text: "I know of no book I have yet read that is calculated to change my whole mental life, as I feel sure this will do" (10 March 1920). He also refers to and discusses Adams in "A Plan of Life" (1924), "Prophets Wanted" (1931), and "Opening" (1951).

88.26 *Thought then appears ... physical action*: Henry Adams's *The Degradation of Democratic Dogma* (Adams 1919: 243).

89.16 Archimedes (287–212 BCE), Greek mathematician and philosopher.

89.19 Arthur Machen (1863–1947), Welsh novelist and mystic.

95.18 Blaise Pascal (1623–1662), French mathematician and philosopher. Brooker's reference is to the 409th fragment of Pascal's book *Pensées* (1658). See Peter Kreeft's *Christianity for Modern Pagans* (59–61) for a discussion of this fragment.

97.17 *Empress Eugénie*: Eugénie de Montijo (1826–1920) was the last Empress of France. The Empress took refuge in England in 1870 after the fall of France during the Franco-Prussian war.

97.19 *Farnborough*: Farnborough, Hampshire, is located approximately 61 kilometres south-west of London.

102.23 *Rachmaninoff's*: Sergei Vasilievich Rachmaninoff (1873–1943), Russian composer.

102.27 *God keep us ... father protect you*: Opening line of "To the Children" from 15 Songs, Opus 26 No.7 (1906). Lyrics first appeared in the poem "K Detjam" (1856) by Aleksey Stepanovich Khomyakov (1804–1860), Russian poet.

103.16 *Borodine*: Alexander Borodin (1834–1887), Russian composer.

110.8 *"Hic Jacet!"*: Latin epitaph that translates as "Here lies" or "Here is buried."

114.11 *De Quincey's … was upon me*: Thomas De Quincey (1785–1859), English novelist. The passage comes from *Confessions of an English Opium-Eater and Other Writings* (77).

115.26 *The fault is not in our stars, but in ourselves, that we are underlings*: Misquotation of Cassius's line in Shakespeare's *Julius Caesar* (1599), Act I, Scene II: "The fault, dear Brutus, is not in our stars, / But in ourselves, that we are underlings."

116.15 *the lost drama of Thomas Kyd*: Thomas Kyd (1558–1594), English dramatist. Disputed evidence put forth by anti-Stratfordians (those who question the legitimacy of William Shakespeare's authorship of the plays attributed to him) suggests that Kyd produced a version of *Hamlet* decades prior to Shakespeare. Stratfordians (those who accept Shakespeare's authorship) counter that the evidence merely demonstrates that Shakespeare produced *Hamlet* (c. 1599) earlier than conventionally thought. The texts of all but one of Kyd's plays, *The Spanish Tragedy* (c. 1589), have been lost.

116.15 *even in the Bible*: Perhaps a reference to Job 41:1–34 on the Leviathan. This section of the King James version also contains the enigmatic phrase "he laugheth at the shaking of a spear."

116.19 *sicklied it o'er with the pale cast of thought*: Misquotation of Shakespeare's *Hamlet*, Act III, Scene I: "And thus the native hue of resolution / Is sicklied o'er with the pale cast of thought."

121.20 *I sit now, alone … in the soul*: Francis Thompson (1859–1907), English poet. The passage is from "Nature's Immortality" (Thompson 1913: 81).

122.20 *Thought appears in Nature as an arrested, a degraded physical action*: Henry Adams's *The Degradation of Democratic Dogma* (1919: 243).

124.9 *that was before the elements and owes no homage unto the Sun*: Sir Thomas Browne (1605–1682), English essayist and philosopher. Browne was particularly influential on modernist mystics, including H. P. Blavatsky and Jorge Luis Borges. The passage is a misquotation of *Religio Medici, Hydriotaphia, and the Garden of Cyrus* (1642). The original passage reads, "Whilst I study to find how I am a microcosm, or little world, I find myself something more than the great. There is surely a piece of divinity in us; something that was before the elements, and owes no homage unto the sun. Nature tells me, I am the image of God, as well as Scripture" (Browne 1642: 79).

124.12 *O Titan Nature! ... great for you*: Misquotation of Francis Thompson's "Nature's Immortality". The original passage reads, "O Titan Nature! a petty race, which has dwarfed its spirit in dwellings, and bounded it in selfish shallows of art, may find you too vast, may shrink from you into its earths: but though you be a very large thing, and my heart a very little thing, yet Titan as you are, my heart is too great for you" (Thompson 1913: 81).

126.21 *Micawber-like*: Wilkins Micawber was a fictional character in *David Copperfield* (1850) by Charles Dickens (1812–1870), British novelist. Though the name has become synonymous with one who lives in unfulfilled hope, Brooker seems to be utilizing the characteristic shabbiness and poverty of Dickens' character.

130.20 *One little hour ... sweetheart, and I*: Song unidentified, but reminiscent of J. C. Manning's "Elegy on the Death of a Little Child" (1877).

131.30 *a chap named Dichmont*: William Dichmont (1882–1943), Canadian composer and pianist. Winnipeg's Dichmont was primarily known for his populist musical *Miss Pepple (of New York)* (1909). He was widely regarded as one of the most successful Canadian songwriters of his period, and certainly well-known to Brooker who worked as music critic for all three Winnipeg newspapers.

139.1 *I have no words ... thoughts have wings*: Lyrics by Frances M. Gostling (–1935), British songwriter, from his song "Thoughts Have Wings" (1917).

146.18 *Penge*: Penge is a suburb to the south-east of London, near The Crystal Palace exhibition hall.

147.8 *Addiscombe Bridge, the ... down George Street*: Brooker refers to Addiscombe Bridge and George Street, both in Croydon, England, extensively in his fictionalized autobiography *A Candle in Sunshine*.

To All the Nations ....!

153.1 *Bernard Shaw ... exceedingly clever man"*: George Bernard Shaw (1856–1950), Irish dramatist. The passage is from *The Socialism of Shaw* (1926: 53–54).

153.7 *"Robinson Crusoe"*: *The Life and Strange Surprising Adventures of Robinson Crusoe, of York, Mariner: Who lived Eight and Twenty Years all alone in an un-inhabited Island on the Coast of America, near the Mouth of the Great River of Oroonoque; Having been cast on Shore by Shipwreck, where in all the Men perished but Himself. With An Account how he was at last as strangely deliver'd by Pyrates*, a novel by Daniel Defoe (c. 1659–1731), English writer, published in 1719.

153.22 *Jacob wrestling with the angel until the daybreak*: Genesis 32:24–32.

154.3 *Like Carlyle*: Thomas Carlyle (1795–1881), Scottish essayist.

154.4 *James Lane Allen's ... to have lost it.*": James Lane Allen (1849–1925), American novelist. The passage is a misquotation of *The Mettle and the Pasture*. The original passage reads, "To have one chance in life, in eternity, for a white name, and to lose it!" (Allen 1903: 404).

154.15 *Like Dives in Hades*: Luke 16:19–31; a parable by Jesus of a wealthy man and his experiences in Hades.

155.28 *The Underfolk!*: Though the term "underfolk" has come into prominence in contemporary science fiction and fantasy texts, it appears to have been a neologism coined for this essay. Most certainly, it was intended to function as antonym to Nietzsche's *Übermensch* or "over man"—often translated as "superman."

The Spread of Negativism

The essay appears to have been intended for a novella entitled "The Moving Finger" (a phrase borrowed from the *Rubáiyát of Omar Khayyám* [1896: 52]), notes for which appear in the University of Manitoba Special Collections, Box 8 folder 4.

157.15 *Dreadnoughts*: The name of the first British battleship, built in 1906, of a class superior to all that preceded it.

157.24 *Nobody can be ... actually fighting most*: Chesterton's *Heretics* (1906: 36–7).

158.13 *A thousand goals ... hath no goal yet*: Nietzsche's *Thus Spake Zarathustra* (1891: 38).

158.30 *pads and rats and hobble skirts*: While "pads and rats" refer to generally garish or ragged clothing, respectively, hobble skirts were a short-lived fashion of women's dress designed such that they severely impeded a wearer's stride.

158.32 *Miss Cicely Hamilton*: Cicely Hamilton (1872–1952), English dramatist and feminist.

159.8 *Thou shalt love thy neighbour as thyself*: Matthew 19:19.

159.10 *that Huxley*: Thomas Henry Huxley (1825–1895), British biologist. Huxley was a prominent defender of Darwin's theory of evolution.

159.12 *Herbert Spencer*: Herbert Spencer (1820–1903), British philosopher. Spencer founded and advocated the idea now known as Social Darwinism; that is, that the notion of "the survival of the fittest" (1864–1867: 444) in the natural world also applied to human societies.

159.15 *Comte's "Positivism"*: Auguste Comte (1798–1857), French philosopher. Brooker is referring to Comte's seminal text *The Positive Philosophy* (London: John Chapman, 1853).

159.22 *The Muck Rake*: Muckraker: "A person or thing which seeks out and publicizes evidence of corruption and scandal, esp. among powerful or well-known people or institutions; a prurient inquirer into private morals. Also (*rare*): a pornographer" (OED).

159.26 *"The Jungle"*: Upton Sinclair (1878–1968), American novelist, *The Jungle* (New York: Grosset & Dunlap, 1906).

159.27 *after Zola*: Émile Zola (1840–1902), French novelist. Texts referred to, respectively, include *La Débâcle* (Paris: Bibliothèque Charpentier, 1892) and *L'Assommoir* (Paris: Bibliothèque Charpentier, 1877).

159.28 *Tom Lawson's "Frenzied Finance"*: Thomas W. Lawson, *Frenzied Finance* (New York: Ridgway-Thayer, 1905).

159.29 *Whitaker Wright frauds*: In an extremely public trial, Whitaker Wright was convicted of fraud for his service as Managing Director of the London and Globe Financial Corporation following its bankruptcy. The case against Wright was famously prompted by evidence presented in the trial of Oscar Wilde two years earlier. For more on this topic, see Owen R. Covick and Beverley Vickers, *The Trials of Whitaker Wright* (2003).

160.2 *"Back-Worlds-Men" ... "The Much-too-many."*: Nietzsche, *Thus Spake Zarathustra*: "Back-Worlds-Men" (1891: 16); "Despisers of Body" (19); "Tarantulae" (65); and "The Much-too-many" (30).

160.10 *Ibsen is also ... and Mr. Bart Kennedy*: Henrik Johan Ibsen (1828–1906), Norwegian playwright. Maxim Gorky, pseudonym of Aleksei Maksimovich Peshkov (1868–1936), Russian novelist. John Galsworthy (1867–1933), English novelist and Nobel Laureate in 1932. Maurice Hewlett (1861–1923), English novelist. Robert Peel Glanville Blatchford (1851–1943), English journalist and founder of *The Clarion*. Bart Kennedy (1861–1930), American popular novelist.

160.23 *"The Eye-Opener"*: The *Calgary Eye Opener* published from January 1902 to December 1922.

161.23 *Dickens or Scott or Thomas a Kempis or the author of "Black-eyed Susan."*: Charles Dickens (1812–1870), English novelist. Probably Walter Scott (1771–1832), Scottish novelist. Thomas à Kempis (1380–1471), German monk and author. "Black-eyed Susan" is a song by John Gay (1685–1732), English poet.

161.30 *John Foster Fraser*: John Foster Fraser (1868–1936), British parliamentarian.

162.17 *Mr. Shaw had accepted ... Wells' "New Republican,"*: George Bernard Shaw, *Man and Superman: A Comedy and a Philosophy* (New York: Bretannos, 1903); Percy Bysshe Shelley (1792–1822), British poet, *Prometheus Unbound, A Lyrical Drama in Four Acts, With Other Poems*. (London: C. and J. Ollier, 1820); Ralph Waldo Emerson (1803–1882), American author, "The Over-soul", *Essays: First Series* (New York: Hurst & Co., 1841); Richard Wagner (1813–1883), German composer, *Siegfried* (1876); H. G. Wells (1866–1946), British author, *Mankind in the Making* (London: Chapman & Hall Ltd., 1903). Brooker (and Shaw) is referring to the first chapter, titled "The New Republic".

162.30 *What is great in man ... him to destruction*: Nietzsche, *Thus Spake Zarathustra* (1891: 5).

163.18 *Maeterlinck, in "Wisdom and Destiny" ... offer our life."*: Maurice Polydore Marie Bernard Maeterlinck (1862–1949), Belgian poet. The passage is from *La Sagesse et la destinée* (1898: 64).

163.29 *Mr. Holbrook Jackson*: George Holbrook Jackson (1874–1948), British journalist.

163.31 *Prof. Max Muller ... Science of Thought*: Friedrich Max Müller (1823–1900), German philologist. Brooker is referring to *The Science of Thought* (London: Longmans, Green & Co., 1887).

164.8 *subtract the values of good and evil*: Given the diversity of his career, Brooker remained surprisingly consistent in his embrace of this principle. His use of characters to express faith in this fundamental concept stretches throughout his career, from William Gordon's arguments against moral judgements (1911) to Tavistock's belief that there is no division between good and evil (1936) to Barabbas' ultimate realization of the same (1949). Brooker's resistance to this primary division helps to explain his perpetual resistance to codified, institutionalized, moral cosmologies—especially to the Theosophical Society. He writes, "My gospel, if you can call it that, is simply that Opposites do not exist." ("Mankindness" in "Son of My Son" written in 1948: 2).

165.10 *Ecclesiasticism and Constitutionalism ... the next reaction*: George Bernard Shaw, *The Perfect Wagnerite: A Commentary on the Niblung's Ring* (1898: 43).

165.27 *My acceptance of ... loving it more*: Chesterton, *Orthodoxy* (1908: 78).

167.7 *We know that ... they always live ...*: Maurice Maeterlinck, *Le Trésor des Humbles* (1896: xiii).

The Decay of Art

168.3 *Botticelli or Brangyn, with Pre-Raphaelitism or Post-Impressionalism, with Symbolism or Realism*: Botticelli, Sandro (1445–1510), or Alessandro di Mariano Filipepi, Italian painter. Brangyn: allusion unclear, but possibly a reference to Frank Brangwyn (1867–1956), Belgian/Welsh early modern artist influenced by William Morris. Brooker's "Pre-Raphaelitism" refers to the Pre-Raphaelite Brotherhood, a reformist movement in British visual arts, founded in 1848 by John Everett Millais, Dante Gabriel Rossetti, and William Holman Hunt. The term has been widely used to describe those influenced by the Pre-Raphaelites, including those associated with the Arts and Crafts movement at the end of the nineteenth century. Brooker's "Post-Impressionalism" refers to the Post-impressionist painters, such as Cézanne and Van Gogh, of the early twentieth century. Symbolism essentially means the practice of representing things by symbols. As such, Brooker's target here is wide, but most likely refers to those literary artists influenced by the French Symbolistes, including T. S. Eliot and

James Joyce. Realism, on the other hand, refers to art that avoids symbolic representation in the hopes of replicating the conditions of the world as they actually are. Social realism was particularly influential on the Canadian modernist novel, thus making Brooker's dismissal all the more significant.

169.27 *race of Gradgrinds*: An allusion to Charles Dickens' fact-focussed character, the teacher Mr. Thomas Gradgrind, in *Hard Times* (New York: Harper, 1854).

170.3 *Hassal painting advertisements*: John Hassal (1868–1948), English illustrator. Hassal spent two years in Manitoba working on a farm.

The Price of Peace

172.6 *Israel Zangwill*: Israel Zangwill (1864–1926), British Zionist activist.

Free Prose

175.12 *Robert Nichols' preface to Fantastica ... makes its own*: Robert Nichols (1893–1944), English playwright and poet. Misquotation of *Fantastica: Being the Smile of the Sphinx and other Tales of Imagination* (1923: 24–25). The original passage reads: "For I believe—and in this belief, I hazard, many poets consciously or unconsciously share—that *'undirected' 'mythic' thinking is just as important to the future of man as 'directed' thinking*, indeed that this form of thinking sometimes outstrips the 'directed' form and explores and leads on to regions which the 'directed' afterward makes its own."

175.21 *Nothing is beautiful ... apprehends the object*: (Nichols 1923: 9).

176.1 *The spectacle of life is always new because the spectators are always new*: Citation is an oft-quoted passage from T. H. Huxley's 1869 translation of Goethe's 1780s aphorisms on nature, published in *Nature* (Huxley 1869: 1: 9). Huxley's actual translation reads "The spectacle of nature is always new, for she is always renewing the spectators."

(from) Notes for the Free Prose

177.2 *Wrote Dayspring*: Reference unknown, but potentially a reference to Brooker's fictionalized autobiography *A Candle in Sunshine*.

177.6 *why not into the unknown quarters of mind*: In 1927, Brooker's play "Within" is staged entirely within the mind of his protagonist. The play was directed by Herman Voaden in Toronto in 1935.

178.8 See *Virginia Woolf on American Fiction*: Virginia Woolf (1882–1941), British author, "American Fiction", *Saturday Review of Literature* (2:1, 1925).

178.12 *His opinion," says … any man's reading*: William Blake (1757–1827), British poet and painter, "The Ancient Britons" (1809: 544).

178.14 *The great and golden … beast can exist*: Blake, "The Descriptive Catalogue" (1946: 530).

Nudes and Prudes

179.12 *There is in Toronto an art gallery*: The Art Gallery of Toronto was founded in 1919 and renamed the Art Gallery of Ontario in 1966.

179.16 *Societe Anonyme*: Properly, Société Anonyme. The avant-garde collective was based in New York and, later, New Haven, Connecticut, and lasted from 1920 to 1950. See Ramsay Cook's "Nothing Less Than the Theory of a New Religion" for more information on the group's important Toronto exhibition.

179.17 *our own Lawren Harris*: Lawren Harris (1885–1970), Toronto poet and painter, most famous for being the founder and leader of the Group of Seven.

179.19 *Miss Dreier*: Katherine Dreier (1877–1952), artist and founder of the Société Anonyme with Man Ray and Marcel Duchamp.

180.3 *a nude by Giorgione*: Giorgione, or Giorgio Barbarelli da Castelfranco, (1477–1510), Italian Renaissance painter. An exhibition of "The Works of Old Masters" ran at the Art Gallery of Toronto in May 1928.

180.7 *two canvases by Edwin H. Holgate*: Edwin H. Holgate (1892–1977), Canadian painter and later member of the Group of Seven.

181.2 *John Russell*: John W. Russell, R.A., Canadian painter who lived primarily in Paris.

181.2 *the new College Street store of the T. Eaton Company Limited*: The exhibition space of the Eaton's Department store at College was designed by Jacques Carlu (1890–1976), French architect. The building was later renamed College Park in 1977.

181.3 *the head of which company is also the president of the Toronto Art Gallery*: Augustus Bridle (1868–1952), prominent Toronto art critic and administrator. Reviews of exhibitions frequently included such anti-modernist comments as this, in praise of an O.S.A. exhibition of little pictures: "Very little futurism is shown here. The little picture has small space for freak expression" ("Pictures of Three Nations", 2 November 1928: 21).

181.7 *a furore in the Toronto press*: On 10 September 1927, the *Globe* ran a house editorial denouncing the display of two nudes at the summer exhibition at the Art Gallery of the Canadian National Exhibition from August through September, citing "the feelings of revulsion" that "thousands" experienced upon seeing the nudes (14). The paintings were John Russell's *A Modern Fantasy* and George Drinkwater's *Paolo and Francesca*. Letters fill the subsequent issues of the newspaper, the majority of which challenge the newspaper's denunciation. Similar stories and letters ran in the *Toronto Daily Star* from 27 August 1927 (22), making the front page on 3 September 1927 with the article "Box Office Rush at 'Ex' Art Gallery Not Due to Nude Art, Says Official." The debate resolved in gallery officials rejecting calls to censor nudes from their gallery walls (see "Art's Art in Gallery; Nudes Are Fine", *Toronto Daily Star* 14 September 1927: 2). Ironically, on 3 May 1927, *The Star* celebrated a John Russell nude that was given the "highest honor that can come to any painter" for being hung in the Spring Salon at the Société des Artistes Française in Paris. The newspaper declared: "It is Mr. Russell's masterpiece" ("Artist Honored at Paris": 9).

181.21 *commented upon by William Arthur Deacon*: William Arthur Deacon (1890–1977), Canadian literary critic, "Literature in Canada—In Its Centenary Year," *Yearbook of the Arts 1928–1929*. The collection of essays and art was edited by Bertram Brooker.

182.11 *Mr. Morley Callaghan*: Morley Callaghan (1903–2000), acclaimed Toronto novelist and short-story writer.

182.15 *In a review of his latest novel, It's Never Over,*: On 8 March 1930, the *Toronto Daily Star* published an unsigned article entitled "Writer's Third Book Contains High Art: Passages of Callaghan's New Novel Have Great Charm" that claimed that Callaghan's novel "will be criticized as a deliberate attempt to create a best seller through the medium of sex interest…. At times the sex theme is stressed strongly."

187.1 *Freud or Dr. Watson*: Sigmund Freud (1856–1939), Austrian psychologist and pioneer of psychoanalysis, and John B. Watson (1878–1958), American psychologist and pioneer of behaviourism.

When We Awake!

190.2 *Macbeth*: William Shakespeare, *Macbeth* (1608).

190.8 *Coventry Patmore, I think, called "unitive apprehension."*: Coventry Patmore (1823–1896), English poet. An allusion to Patmore's discussion, in *Religio Poetae*, etc., of the particular awakened consciousness of a genius that he describes as "unitive apprehension" (1907: 65).

191.6 *as Michelangelo did*: Michelangelo di Lodovico Buonarroti Simoni (1475–1564), Italian Renaissance painter, sculptor, and poet.

191.7 *as El Greco did*: El Greco (1541–1614), Spanish Renaissance painter, sculptor, and architect. Brooker delivered a free public lecture on El Greco at the Toronto Art Gallery on 28 February 1930.

195.7 *Spengler, Croce, Faure*: Oswald Spengler (1880–1936), German historian and philosopher. Benedetto Croce (1866–1952), Italian philosopher. Likely Sébastien Faure (1858–1942), French philosopher. These authors represent a diverse range of nineteenth century European thought including mathematical historicism, idealism, and anarchism, respectively.

196.1 *Whitman and Edgar Allen Poe*:　Walt Whitman (1819–1892), American mystical poet. Edgar Allen Poe (1809–1849), American gothic author.

196.19 *John Ervine*: St. John Greer Ervine (1883–1971), Irish playwright and critic.

197.20 *and television in the immediate distance*: The history of television dates back to 1884, only really taking shape with John Baird's 1925 advancements of the technology. In 1928, Baird conducted the first transcontinental television broadcast between London and New York. The technology was not widely or commercially available until the late 1930s.

197.25 *Henry James, George Meredith and Joseph Conrad:* Henry James (1843–1916), American/British novelist. George Meredith (1828–1909), British novelist. Joseph Conrad, originally Józef Teodor Konrad Korzeniowski, (1857–1924), Polish/British novelist.

198.10 *Aristophanes' comedies:* Aristophanes (456–386 BC), Greek playwright.

198.12 *and Elizabethan England:* Elizabethan England: reference is to the Elizabethan era in England, associated with the reign of Queen Elizabeth I (1558–1603).

198.14 *Drury Lane to see Henry Irving:* Drury Lane is a street in London, and also used to refer to Theatre Royal, Drury Lane. Henry Irving (1838–1905), British actor.

201.5 *as futile as Shylock's notion of taking a pound of Antonio's flesh:* Shakespeare, *The Merchant of Venice* (Act IV, Scene I). In the scene, Antonio cannot repay money owed to Shylock, who attempts to use the courts to exact his revenge, saying: "The pound of flesh which I demand of him / Is dearly bought, 'tis mine, and I will have it" (lines 99–100).

201.9 *the Fitzgerald "contraction":* The FitzGerald Contraction (also called the Lorentz-FitzGerald contraction, also called the Length Contraction) was a special theory proposed by H. A. Lorentz and G. F. FitzGerald to account for the findings of a previous experiment by Michelson-Morley in 1881. The theory proposed a contraction in length when an object reached the speed of light. It is considered in physics a major step en route to the Theory of Relativity (see Bork 1966 for more details).

202.16 *Mondrian, Kandinsky, Man Ray, Epstein, Joyce, Gertrude Stein, T. S. Eliot:* Piet Mondrian (1872–1944), Dutch painter. Wassily Kandinsky (1866–1944), Russian painter and philosopher. Man Ray (1890–1976), originally Emmanuel Radnitzky, American artist. Jacob Epstein (1880–1959), American/British sculptor. James Joyce (1882–1941), Irish author. Gertrude Stein (1874–1946), American author. T. S. Eliot (1888–1965), American/British poet and critic.

202.17 *The pages of Transition:* Founded by Eugene Jolas in 1927, the literary magazine *transition* became a focal point for avant-garde activity in Paris until

1938 when it published its twenty-seventh and final issue. Morley Callaghan's short fiction appeared in the journal alongside selections of Joyce's *Finnegans Wake* (then titled, simply, "Work in Progress").

202.23 *another group whose activities can only be described as "clinical.":* Brooker is alluding to the Surrealists, whose work was directly inspired by Sigmund Freud's interest in madness and neuroses. The Surrealists, especially André Breton, argued that dream imagery was inspired by the liberated imagination and suggested a truly revolutionary aesthetic.

203.15 *flood himself with ... future becomes present:* Walt Whitman, Preface to *Leaves of Grass* (1855: 23, 13).

205.5 *The altitude of literature ... tone to all:* Walt Whitman, "Democratic Vistas" (1871: 985).

Prophet's Wanted

206.1 *"It is the heaviest stone ... seems progressionall.":* The passage is a misquotation of *Religio Medici, Hydriotaphia, and the Garden of Cyrus* (1642). The original passage reads, "It is the heaviest stone that melancholy can throw at man, to tell him he is at the end of his nature; or that there is no further state to come, unto which this seems progressional, and otherwise made in vain" (125).

206.19 Irving Babbitt (1865–1933), American literary and cultural critic. The phrase "*law of measure*" was a common term used by Babbitt, as in the "Original Introduction" to *Rousseau and Romanticism* (see page lxxix).

208.17 *"multiverse":* Henry Adams, *The Education of Henry Adams* (370).

209.6 *"modestly, lest that the glass I shatter":* Johann Wolfgang von Goethe (1749–1832), German poet and playwright, *Faust* (166).

209.10 *"ready to be anything, in the ecstacy of being ever":* Browne, *Religio Medici, Hydriotaphia, and the Garden of Cyrus* (133).

209.23 *"spiritually indolent":* Irving Babbitt, *Democracy and Leadership* (25).

209.25 *"unitive apprehension":* Coventry Patmore, *Religio Poetae, etc.* (65).

209.28 *"universal centre":* Babbitt, *Democracy and Leadership* (222).

209.31 "*Practically the assertion of a universal centre ...*": Babbitt, "Humanism: An Essay at Definition" (197).

210.20 "*the higher will must simply be accepted*": ibid (202).

210.22 "*the person who declines to turn*": ibid (203).

211.14 "*The real humanist consents*": ibid (207).

211.16 "*The humanist does not carry*": ibid (206).

211.23 "*religion is in its purity*": ibid (206).

211.25 "*Know for certain*": Thomas à Kempis, *The Imitation of Christ* (108).

211.31 "*die into life*": John Keats (1795–1821), British poet, *Hyperion* (3.130). Brooker's novel *Think of the Earth* makes extended reference and use of *Hyperion*.

212.19 "*one tells what happened and the other what might happen*": Aristotle, *The Poetics* (35).

212.22 "*he can create new happenings, in the texture*": W. H. Fyfe and W. R. Roberts, Introduction (xiii).

212.29 "*whole man, the reconciler*": Norman Foerster, "Emerson on the Organic Principle in Art" (208).

212.32 "*There seems to be a necessity in spirit*": quoted in Foerster's "Emerson" (196).

213.6 *Herbert Read*: Herbert Read (1893–1968), English anarchist and avant-garde poet.

213.19 "*An accepted certainty*": John Middleton Murry, *Defending Romanticism* (143).

214.9 "*Instead of a will to this or that posited end*": Murry, *God* (268).

214.28 "*philosopher of flux*": A common description of philosophers associated with Henri Bergson as used by Wyndham Lewis in his essay "The Revolutionary Simpleton" (see 105).

215.5 *Wyndham Lewis*: Percy Wyndham Lewis (1882–1957), Canadian-born British avant-garde author and painter. Lewis was the founder and leader of the Vorticist movement, England's answer to Italian Futurism.

215.6　"*By this proposed transfer*": ibid (145).

215.13　*Mr. Lippmann*: Walter Lippmann (1889–1974), American journalist, *A Preface to Morals* (230).

215.29　*in le Gallienne's phrase*: Richard le Gallienne (1866–1947), British poet and journalist, "The Decadent to His Soul" (72).

215.31　*Behold, this dream cometh.*: Genesis 37:19.

216.8　"*prophetic soul of the wide world*: Shakespeare, Sonnet 107 (1609).

Textual Emendations
and Revisions

The textual notes for each work consist of a list of all texts collated for the poem, with an asterisk marking the copy-text, and a list of variants and emendations. The list of texts is divided into numbered typescripts, which are signalled by the source codes MS1, MS2, etc. The list of variants and emendations includes all substantives and accidentals. Brooker's inconsistent use of British, American, and Canadian spellings, for instance, which might provide some clues of their intended audience, are all listed. All changes and corrections of accidentals to the copy-text by the editor are also included and signalled by the source code *ed*. Brooker's revisions within a particular manuscript, often done by hand, are signalled by the formula — *changed to* —. The symbols <> are used to indicate material that has been deleted in the variant, and a slash (/) is used to mark a paragraph break. The reference format for each entry under each respective textual header is "page.line number"; so that the first line of text in "Like Old Jehovah" would be referenced as 1.1. A minimal selection of the text in question is included in italics.

Abbreviations
UM University of Manitoba, Elizabeth Defoe Library, Special Collections
BB Bertram Brooker Estate
ed. Corrections and alterations by the Editor to the Copy-Text

Like Old Jehovah
1. UM, box 7, folder 2 (MS)*; 2. BB, folder 2 (MS1)
MS is a revised draft. MS1 has one hand-script revision.

5.13: decides] decided *changed to* decides MS1

The Gilliland House

1. UM, box 7, folder 2 (MS)*; 2. UM, box 7, folder 2 (MS1). MS is a revised draft. MS1 has hand-script markings on title page, "Saturday Night / Scribners."

7.10: somewhere] somewheres MS1

7.23: best lumber] best selected lumber MS1

16.28: town] twon *changed to* town MS1

17.3: listen] listened *changed to* listen MS1

Bad Order

1. UM, Box 7, folder 3 (MS)*.

22.14: behaviour] *ed.*; behavior MS

22.14: system] *ed.*; sytem MS

22.16: employees] *ed.*; employes MS

25.6: honour] *ed.*; honor MS

Mrs. Hungerford's Milk

1. *Canadian Forum* January 1936 (MS)*; 2. *Voices of Discord* (MS1); 3. UM, box 7, folder 2 (MS2).

28.3: plodded side by side into the stable] plodded into the stable MS1

28.5: manure] manure, MS1

28.7: with the oats.] *paragraph break added* MS1

28.23: all right] allright MS1

29.1: the hell, his brother] the hell!—his brother MS1

29.3: rainwater] rain-water MS1

29.6: bending down washing] bending over, washing, MS1

29.11: His huge middle] His middle MS1

29.29: 2.40] 2:40 MS1

30.7: Hettie laughing.] Hettie, MS1

30.18: And, anyway] And anyway MS1

30.21: Joe put the comb down .... trying to rook him."] Joe put the comb down with a whack. "No *chance!* Said I'd asked him five bucks and five bucks was all I'd get—looking at me all the time like I was trying to rook him." MS1

30.27: He had got it off his mind] It was off his mind. MS1

31.11: milk-pail] milkpail MS1

31.13: him,] him MS1

31.32: going anywhere] going anywheres MS1

32.4: deliver that milk at] take that milk over at MS1

32.7: paper boy] paperboy MS1

32.12: *her*] her MS1

32.12: evenin'] evening MS1

32.13: glared into her] glared at her MS1

32.14: brow] brow *changed to* forehead MS2

32: 15: goin' to spoil *somebody's* evenin' if that milk ain't delivered this] going to spoil *somebody's* evening if that milk ain't took over this MS1

32.17: wantin'] wanting MS1

32.18: wantin' it or not That's *their* business. It's *our* business to get it over there right smart after milkin'] wanting it or not. She's supposed to get it over there right smart after milking MS1

32.24: bawlin' and get her eyes all red and spoil her evenin'] bawling and get her

eyes all red and spoil her evening MS1

32.27: watery eyes] colourless eyes MS1

32.28: strong—invincible! His voice, coming out of his great chest, roared in his ears like a torrent.] His anger made him feel strong. His voice, coming out of his great chest, roared in his ears. MS1

32.29: goin' to have them Hungerfords kept waitin' for their milk," he shouted. "You talk to *me* about runnin' my business, but where would I be if Dave

Hungerford quit gettin' me to do his haulin'] going to have them Hungerfords kept waiting for their milk," he shouted. "You talk to *me* about running my business, but where would I be if Dave Hungerford quit getting me to do his hauling MSI

33.1: not late *night after night*] AE: not—*night after night!* MSI

33.12: all right] allright MSI

33.14: were like] had got like MSI

33.15: They'd left him alone a lot lately.] *not in* MSI

33.31: little-girl] little girl MSI

34.7: cute] nice MSI

34.11: wainscotting] wainscoting MSI

34.17: all right. I don't want any monkey] allright. No monkey MSI

34.25: sort of sneaking] of sneaking MSI

35.3: stick-in-the-mud, don't you? Eh?" / "No, we don't, dad," said Myrtle softly. / "You're going] stick-in-the-mud—eh?" / "You're going MSI

A Glass of Catawba

1. UM, box 7, folder 2 (MS)*; 2. BB, folder 2 (MSI). MSI was inscribed with Brooker's Toronto address "107 Glenview Avenue", which means that it was produced after February 1926 when the family moved there.

37.5: parlours] parlors MSI

37.22: turkeys] turkeys turkeys *changed to* turkeys MSI

39.4: Grenvilles] Grenville's *changed to* Grenvilles MSI

Head Waitress

1. UM, box 7, folder 4 (MS)*.
55.19: "It's dead."] *ed.; open quotation mark added* MS

Youth's Manuscript

1. UM, box 7, folder 4 (MS)*; 2. UM, box 7, folder 4 (MS1); 3. UM, box 7, folder 4 (MS2). MS2 has the inscription "26 Pages", while MS1 has the inscription "Three Boxes", MS, in contrast, has no inscription.

58.1: Chapter I MS2

58.3: luxurious new car quietly to the curb under the chestnut trees.] new Cadillac quietly to the curb under the yellowing chestnut MS2

58.10: startled them. ... "What?] They had been out to see Mr. Kimber's chrysanthemums. He was the president of their firm and it was an event for Edna to go out there with D.J. He had wanted to stay all evening, but she wanted to be home in time for Mr. Kolessa's party. If the girls at the office knew she had come home to her boarding house crowd instead of staying out there with wealthy people like the Kimbers and their friends, they would have thought her crazy. But she never told the girls anything. In the office they called her "the clam." *additional text inserted at ellipsis* MS1

58.11: demanded, glaring around with his stern Sunday School Super-intendent's manner.] demanded. His dislike of the neighbourhood and his impatience with her for staying in such a place embittered his tone. MS1

58.14: night."] night, falling on the roof of Cooper's garage next door." MS2

58.17: colour] *ed.*; color MS, MS1, MS2

58.22: He ... party] Mrs. Kimber had been very nice to her and for the first time D.J. had dropped her married name and called her Edna in front of any of the higher-ups. He had wanted to stay all evening, but it was a drive of nearly sixty miles, and she wanted to be home for Mr. Kolessa's party *no paragraph break follows* MS2

59.6: birthdays;] birthdays, MS2

59.7: tomorrow] Monday MS2

59.7: It had slipped out because she wanted D.J. to see how important it was for her to get back early.] *sentence moved to after dialogue* MS1, MS2; *additional text follows* She could have bitten off her tongue, for he had pounced on it at once, and all the way home he had been pressing her to have dinner with him tomorrow at Gleneagle Inn, promising her a birthday present she could wear for the rest of her life. MS1, MS2

59.18: his ring.] *additional text* Lately she had wavered a little in her thoughts about him, but tonight she had felt a freezing sensation numbing her heart as he talked and talked about their future. MS2

59.21: on one of the smaller] on the weakest of the MS1, MS2

59.22: women's publications.] *additional text* She had taught herself, and her work was still crude. Often it had to be licked into shape by one of the senior artists. Sometimes she wondered why they kept her on. *paragraph break follows* MS2

59.22: He] D.J. MS1, MS2

59.24: years without speaking] *additional text* In the building he never did any kidding, like some of the managers. MS2

59.28: He was well over fifty.] *not in* MS2

59.29: Toward the end .... about his health.] Toward the end of the summer he had told her that his doctor had advised him to give up gold. Perhaps some of his solemnity was due to worrying about his health, although he looked well enough, rather ruddy and a trifle stout. A fiftyish waistline, she figured. A chestnut whacked on the hood of the car and bounced off. Edna withdrew her hand.

"I'd better be off," she said. "I wouldn't like to see your lovely new car all dinted up."

"It's early," said D.J., leaning toward her. "The party will hardly be started. Sit here a minute."

"Oh, yes," Edna broke in. "It will have started at five o'clock. People come and go all evening. Mostly musicians. Do you know George Copp?"

"In the wool business?"

"Yes."

"Slightly. But he's not a musician, is he?"

"He used to be a baritone in one of the big churches. Took lessons from Mr. Kolessa in the old days. Thinks the world of him. When the old boy reached eighty, George Copp drummed up nine of his friends, with himself making ten, to contribute something every month to Mr. Kolessa's supprt. On his birthday Mr. Copp always turns up with a cheque and a case of Scotch, and some of the others come around to have a drink with him."

"So you'll be up to all hours, drinking, I suppose," said D.J., severely. MS2

60.5: solemnly] greedily, MS2

60.6: birthday as a single woman.] *additional text* And about time, too."

"What do you mean, about time?" said Edna, a forced smile banishing resentment from her face. / "Well, you don't get younger every year, you know, Edna."

"How old do you think I am?" she asked. "Guess."

"I don't have to guess. I know how old you are. It surprised me."

"How do you know?"

"Your group insurance card at the office gives the date of your birth."

Edna let out a long-held breath. "So you know how old I am."

"Yes. Everybody thinks you're in your early thirties, at most. I did myself. Blondes always look younger. But tomorrow, my dear —" D.J. stopped and indulged a queer shrug of satisfaction.

"Tomorrow I shall be forty." MS2

60.9: Scarcely anyone ever guessed her age.] It was no wonder that scarcely anyone ever guessed her age. MS1, MS2

60.12: meekness in her manner.] *additional text* At times, when she wore a kerchief tied under her chin, she looked like a simple country saint. MS2

60.16: "But don't build too much on it—tomorrow night.] don't build too much on tomorrow night. Please don't. I like my independence too much. I may disappoint you again. I probably shall."

"Don't you put more value on security than on independence?" asked Mr. McConnell, in a tone he might use to members of the board.

"No, I don't. Not yet," said Edna simply.

"Wait until tomorrow," he insinuated, with a gloating smile. "Maybe you'll think differently."

"I know I shall hate to disappoint you. I shall feel terribly guilty. You've been so good to me, D.J."

"Don't call me D.J."

"Well, I just can't call you David Jonathan."

"No. Just David."

"If I called you David I'd think of the Jonathan. I'm sure I'll never be able to call you anything but D.J."

She had never thought of it before, but it became another mark against their possible marriage, their future, that she couldn't think of him without his office name, his initials, sticking to him like a label.

Whack!

"Another of those blessed chestnuts," he grumbled. MS2

60.19: She opened the door quickly and jumped out.] She spun the handle of the door quickly and jumped out. MS1; Edna spun the handle of the door quickly and jumped out. MS2

60.20: unpromising smile,] unpromising, almost mocking smile, MS2

60.21: Her teasing use of his two Christian names brought a vexed frown to his face.] He made a vexed face at her through the window as the car pulled away. MS1, MS2

60.23: While the glistening .... if she married him.] Standing on the curb, waving, while the glistening car swung around the crescent, she allowed her mind to imagine for a moment the luxury she would live in if she married him. MS1; Standing on the curb, waving, while the glistening Cadillac swung around the crescent, she allowed her mind to imagine for a moment the luxury she would live in if she married him. MS2

60.26: To be ordered about and fussed over at his age had grown unbearable.] not in MS1, MS2

60.29: Then he had shown ... for her own use.] Then he had shown her a wooded lot he intended to buy, overlooking a beautiful ravine at the north end of the city, and another time he had pointed out to her the little English car that he would buy for her own use. MS1

61.6: Chapter 2 MS2

61.8: men, red-faced and paunchy, shook his head gravely. "This will be his last, George," he said.] men, very red-faced and paunchy, was shaking his head gravely. "This will be his last, George," he was saying. MS1, MS2

61.12: George] George Copp MS1, MS2

61.14: to let her pass.] *additional text* "Thought you were never coming," he said. "The old boy's been asking for you." Turning to his companions, he made a tipsy little bow. "You remember Mrs. Colby, of course. Jack Whitfield. Lester Bowles." / She had only the faintest remembrance of them from previous years. They were elderly, and she took them to be among the ten friends who contributed annually to "the Kolessa fund." / "Go on in," said Copp, giving her shoulder a playful push. "And don't forget our duet." / In the dark hall she nearly collided with a young couple who were leaning against the wall with glasses in their hands. Their faces were almost touching as they tried to make their whispers heard over the buzz of voices in the parlor. / "What d'you say we get out of here," the girl was saying as Edna passed. MS2

61.19: of people] of gabbling people MS2

61.19: They were mostly students or teachers at the Academy of Music, and many of them shook her hand or nodded as she passed.] They were mostly students or teachers at the Academy of Music. MS1; They were mostly students or teachers at the Academy of Music. The organist of the church where she sang on Sundays reached behind somebody's back to squeeze her elbow and closed both eyes at her as she pressed sideways through a breach of huddled bodies. MS2

61.23: who sat,] who was sitting, MS1, MS2

61.25: uncanny transparency.] *paragraph break and additional text* He saw her at once and called out her name. His voice was cracked and petulant and he pouted at her for being so late. MS2

61.27: murmured] murmured, MS1

61.31: best I can look for."] *additional text*

"Where's George Copp? If George Copp keeps up this iniquitous practice of supplying me with Scotch—iniquitous!—"

"Inebrious!" George Copp called over somebody's shoulder as he pressed into the room.

"Listen, George," cried Mr. Kolessa raising a well-filled glass from the little table beside him. "If you keep this up I'll live another ten years. Ten years, without a doubt. Cheers, George."

While the old man sipped, Edna stood up beside him and smoothed down her skirt. He reeked of whisky and cigar smoke. She took a step away. "The fire is good. Makes it festive," she said.

"Yes," said Mr. Kolessa. "It isn't cold, but it's a bit damp."

Mr. Saunders [sic], the landlady, who was passing sandwiches, turned her head. "It's only downstairs is damp," she said, defensively. "But he doesn't want to climb the stairs any more, so --- "

"So!" Mr. Kolessa nodded, winking at Virginia Wilcox.

"Well, Virginia, how are you?" said Edna. Virginia was fiftyish and looking it at last. "So you came into town for the celebration."

"Couldn't miss it," said Miss Wilcox with her slight lisp.

Others were crowding around Edna to shake hands, mostly women. Some of them had begun taking lessons from Mr. Kolessa more than forty years before. Age showed itself in their dulled eyes and greying hair. Over their shoulders she glanced keenly at their old teacher. MS2

61.32: He had come to America] As a young man he had come out to America MS1, MS2

62.4: distinctly European.] *additional text* The whisky danced in his eyes, but Edna noticed that his speech was slower tonight, and he rarely raised his hands from his knees to gesticulate. MS2

62.4: Edna had never] She had never MS2

62.11: Looking around at her friends and thinking of how they were all ageing, she choked] Thinking of how they were all ageing, she swallowed quickly to choke MS1, MS2

62.18: stood in front of] was standing before her MS1

62.22: drink your health."] *paragraph break and additional text*
"It's in the cupboard on the right, Penelope. On the right. The tall bottle. Bristol Cream, it says on it. And bring a wine glass. Perhaps you'd better get it, George. She'll never get through that mob."

George Copp set down his glass and made his way to the room behind the parlor. It had once been the dining room, but a few years ago they had made it into a studio bed-sitting-room for Mr. Kolessa. George Copp knew his way around there. He spent an evening with "the old boy" almost every week.

"There, now, look at that," said Mr. Kolessa, when George returned with the sherry. "How long since you brought it?"

"Three or four weeks."

"Look at it. Hardly touched. A lovely wine. I keep it for special occasions. Pour Edna a glass, George, and then put the bottle down here beside the wall out of the way. Nobody will kick it over there. MS2

62.23: the glass awkwardly] the glass gingerly MS1, MS2

62.23: handed it to her.] *additional text* She was not used to balancing a drink. MS1, MS2

62.32: had never slackened] had never been tarnished MS1, MS2

62.33: a man whose counsel and advice and fatherly eagerness for everyone's welfare,] *not in* MS1

63.1: would] *would* MS1, MS2

63.4: around and lifted his glass.] around to face the old musician and lifted his glass. MS2

63.7: shoulders, there was a chorus of hushing] shoulders, there were cries of: "Drink to Daddy!" A young voice from the doorway shouted: "Speech!" A woman started to sing "Happy birthday to you," but immediately there was a chorus of hushing. MS2

63.9: arms] arms, but his legs would not hold him. MS2

63.10: moment his mouth opened, but only a hoarse cry] moment he balanced himself and a hoarse cry MS1, MS2

63.12: dabbed at his wet cheeks, and began nodding and smiling with the pleased air of a child who has said his piece.] brushed the tears from his cheeks, and began nodding and smiling with a childlike air of being pleased with himself after saying his piece. MS1

63.14: "Where's my drink, George?" he fussed, blinking tears from his eyes.] "Where's George?" he fussed, in a stronger voice, now that his ordeal was over. "Where's my drink, George?" MS1; "Where's George?" he fussed, in a stronger voice, now that his ordeal was over. "Where's my drink, George? I can't see very well." / "Here it is." Mr. Kolessa patted the hand that held out his drink so that he almost upset it. MS2

63.16: "Where's Virginia?"] *additional text* "and then the old man asked for Edna. She came and sank down on one knee beside his chair. / "How about your duet, now, you and George?" / "I'd like to hear Virginia play first, wouldn't you?" said Edna. / "Yes. Where's Virginia?" MS2

63.19: who had been standing near.] *not in* MS1, MS1

63.20: "Do you feel like playing, Virginia?"] "Do you feel like playing, Virgie?" MS1, MS1

63.24: he said, watching Virginia settle herself at the piano.] he said, as they made way for her to get to the piano. MS1; *additional text*
Now he was the music master again. "It was the first piece Virginia ever played in recital. How many years ago, Virginia? Won't tell? ach, these women and their ages!"

He turned on Edna who was still beside him. "I suppose you are not telling how old you are tomorrow."

"Ninety five," said Edna.

Mr. Kolessa swung his glance around the circle of faces. "Some of you younger ones may not know that this is my party only till midnight. After midnight it is Mrs. Colby's party. Her birthday is tomorrow. She never grows old. You don't look a day over eighty, Edna."

Impatient with the joke, he waved his hand at Virginia Wilcox.

"Everybody very quiet," he said," MS2

63.27: with her back to the fire, Edna clasped her hands in her lap, and when the piece was finished she returned from dreams of her first music lessons and joined in the applause.] with her back to the fire, Edna let her hands drift to her lap, one crossing the other, and when the piece was finished she returned from dreams of her first music lessons and joined in the applause. MS1; with her back to the fire, Edna let her hands drift to her lap, one crossing the other. With bent head she stared at her long polished nails, engrossed in the shape and shine of them, as though they did not belong to her body, but lay like two rows of lovely little pink shells against the dark stuff of her dress. The repetitive beat of the music sent her senses drifting into a dreamlike state where her mind and her body seemed to separate. / When Virginia finished the piece, Edna returned from far dreams and joined in the applause. MS2

64.2: It] Some knew that it MS1; Those who were watching felt that this had been her reward, like a blessing given, many times before. Some knew that it MS2

64.4: known a father.] known her own. MS2

64.6: George] George Copp MS1, MS2

64.8: the ends] the end MS1, MS2

64.17: "as in a "round" song] *additional text* Edna had the lead. It was an old-fashioned MS2

64.28: a few students] a few men MS2

64.29: the old mill stream."] *additional text*
George Copp carried his glass out through the hall to join them, and soon his voice was heard over them all, except when the tenor had a high note which he reached in a wailing falsetto.

While the room thinned of people, Edna sat down with Virginia and asked about her life in the small town where she was still teaching. Mr. Goodwin, the organist at Edna's church, came to their corner, dragging a chair, and presently they were joined by the young conductor of the Academy's student orchestra. The talk was about a new teacher, who was struggling to establish a class in their city.

Mr. Kolessa heard them and called out: "Where's Louis? He hasn't played tonight." MS2

64.31: find the young violinist] find Louis Kramer, a young violinist MS1

64.31: Someone went out .... be persuaded to play.] Someone went out to find Louis Kramer, a young violinist who lived in the house. He came promptly, but Mr. Kolessa could not persuade him to play. Louis shrugged and jerked his head in the direction of the kitchen where the raucous singers were repeating "Moonlight and Roses" for the third time. MS2

65.3: said Mr. Kolessa.] said Mr. Kolessa to Mrs. Saunders, who was going about the room with a tray, clearing up the glasses. MS2

65.6: where a remark about violinists launched Mr. Kolessa into a succession of anecdotes about] and a chance remark launched Mr. Kolessa into fond reminiscences of MS1, MS2

65.8: leaning heads] leaning hands, MS1

65.12: stool. When she stood up, smiling shyly,] stool, and when she stood up, smiling shyly, MS1, MS2

65.18: she held up her half-emptied sherry glass and] she found her half-emptied sherry glass on the mantelpiece and MS1

65.20: *Section break* MS1; Chapter 3 MS2

65.28: had been quite] had been quiet MS1

65.28: George Copp so] George Copp had grown so MS1, MS2

65.30: come in about midnight.] *additional text* The great names of composers and performers would have meant nothing to him, and certainly he would have been shocked by the behaviour of the noisier ones. MS2

65.32: them sat around] sat hunched around MS1, MS2

66.2: young.] young man. MS1, MS2

66.3: how she had experienced] how she had felt MS2

66.5: like a barrier] like a spiked barrier MS2

66.5: and all thought of D.J.] *additional text* How could she leave this house where people talked a language that exalted her and made her lonely life worth living? MS1, MS2

66.12: attacked her clothes] attacked the buttons and strings of her clothes MS1, MS2

66.18: her cheeks were flushed] her face was flushed MS1, MS2

66.19: a start] a little start MS2

66.26: She] Then she MS1, MS2

67.3: They had been young then,] Besides they had been young, MS2

67.5: Not that she was young, but perhaps] young. But perhaps MS2

67.16: "I cannot! I won't!"] "I cannot! I cannot!" MS1, MS2

67.20: Chapter 4 MS2

67.22: felt a little faint.] *additional text* Without warning her eyes would start swimming, as though she were looking down from a height. MS2

67.32: But she rarely saw him in the building,] But his office was two flights up. She rarely saw him in the building, MS2

68.16: but the doorman] but old Pendleton, the doorman, MS1, MS2

68.16: down the steps, pointing to the] the steps and pointed around the MS1, MS2

68.20: "An accident, d'you suppose?" Edna said.] Over the roar of the engine, Edna said: "I wonder who's ill?" MS2

68.23: Red-headed Stella] Stella Kochuk MS1, MS2

68.26: "Who's hurt?" said Janet,] "Who's hurt?" said Janet Hobbs, MS1; "Who is sick?" said Janet Hobbs, MS2

68.28: "They're taking McConnell to the hospital," said someone.] "McConnell," somebody called out. MS2

68.31: said the new French] said the new young French MS1, MS2

69.1: "Collapsed, beside his desk," said Paul.] "Collapsed, beside his desk," said Eugene. MS1; "Fell down beside his desk," said Eugene. "They think he's dead." / "Who thinks -- ?" demanded Edna, hoarsely. / "Joe Hersch was just in. Said there was no doctor there, but Mr. Sutton felt his heart and they think it's stopped. Joe was passing and they called him in. He saw Mr. McConnell on the floor. His face was sort of green and purple," Joe said. MS2

69.2: Janet and Paul jumped] Janet and Eugene jumped MS1, MS2

69.6: at Christmas.] *additional text* "The white gold setting was shaped into a dolphin. MS2

69.8: water, Paul,] water, Gene, MS1, MS2

69.9: muttered Edna, brushing tears from her cheeks.] muttered Edna, dabbing at the tears on her cheeks. MS1; muttered Edna through chattering teeth. MS2

69.11: Janet]. Janet Hobbs MS1, MS2

69.12: Tommy] Tommy Russell MS1, MS2

69.13: after the French boy.] scurried out after Eugene. MS1, MS2

69.15: "Kate Lawson is] "Kate Lawson's MS1; Kate Ainsworth's MS2

69.17: "What goes?"] "What's the news?" MS2

69.17: to the old janitor] to old Mr. Garvin MS1, MS2

69.19: "They've taken him to St. Mike's."] "He's gone," the old man called back. / "To the hospital?" / "No. He's gone. He's dead." / Edna shuddered violently. In his coffin! In his grave! In the awful earth! Stretched out for ever! MS2

69.20: Tommy] Tommy Russell MS1, MS2

69.20: Paul] Eugene MS1, MS2

69.26: Paul] Gene MS1, MS2

69.32: She allowed herself to be led.] *additional text* There were too many people around her. Staring people. Live people. MS2

70.1: Mrs. Lawson's couch.] Mrs. Ainsworth's couch. She wanted the live people shut out. The dead one lay in her mind, stretched out. Her body, too, was stretched out, hardly alive. Both stretched out, she thought, but not together, never together! / A sudden warm wave of relief smoothed the tension all through her body. It calmed her so quickly that she wondered if it could be the whisky. MS2

70.7: Janet] Janet Hobbs MS1, MS2

70.11: her mouth in jerks] her mouth jerkily MS1, MS2

70.17: "I thought you were."] *additional text* "No." MS1, MS2

70.19: "He—he told *you*?" faltered Edna.] *additional text* "Yes." MS1, MS2

70.25: Kate Lawson's] Kate Ainsworth's MS2

70.30: that this was her birthday.] *additional text* She knew herself for an isolated little person. A frozen heart, she thought. What had ever made her think that she might marry D.J.? Or anyone? MS2

70.33: Janet's masculine] Janet's large masculine MS2

70.33: like a man's sideburns] like a man's wideburns MS2

71.6: asked Janet, incredulously.] asked Janet, her brows puckering incredulously. MS1, MS2

71.10: God you know why, Edna.] *additional text* You must know. MS1, MS2

71.17: "He told me he was sick to death of a fourteen-room house.]"He never said a word against them, but he told me he was sick to death of a fourteen-room house. MS1, MS2

71.21: said Janet.] said Janet, pursing up the corners of her mouth. MS1, MS2

71.22: clasped] hooked MS1, MS2

71.22: Her shivering had ceased.] *not in* MS2

71.24: a hurt feeling of repugnance ... Janet crushed] a hurt feeling of repugnance. There was no more to say. How glad she felt. No more to say, or think, or worry about --- no dinner with him tonight, no arguing, no decision to make, no need to feel sorry for him any more. / She breathed out loud toward the ceiling a sort of prayer. "I hope where he's gone there'll be a garden—with a fountain in it." Janet crushed MS2

71.26: know," said Jane] *additional text* Do you suppose he'll live? she said aloud. / "I don't know," shrugged Janet. "He had a slight heart attack a few months ago, you know." MS1

71.29: Mrs. Lawson's] Mrs. Ainsworth's MS2

71.29: spotless ashtray ... Let's go out] *paragraph break* spotless ashtray. / "This would be a good night to get tight," she said. "Let's go out and get high. Surely you'll take a drink tonight." MS2

72.4: "You're the limit," said Janet, getting up and brushing down her hips.] "You little clam!" / Janet got up and brushed down her hips. MS2

72.9: "I don't feel like it.] "I don't feel like it—like talking, or anything. I feel sort of blank." MS1; "I don't feel like it—like talking, or anything. I feel sort of blank—empty." MS2

72.10: mirror she hated to face people in a crowded bus.] mirror she felt she could not face people in a crowded bus. MS2

72.16: eager expectation of freedom stirring in her.] *additional text* There was nothing now to decide, no one to face. Freedom! What sort of freedom was she expecting? Only to go her way alone, to become again the little isolated person she had been before she met D.J. MS2

72.17: She expected very … had met D.J.] *not in* MS2

72.20: "At my age some women would feel lonely," she thought.] "Am I lonely? Am I going to feel lonely, now?" MS1, MS2

72.26: see no more of him.] *additional text* "She tried to forget him, tried to think back over her forty years." MS1; *additional text* "But now—she tried to forget D.J. She tried to think back over the forty years. MS2

72.27: It was a struggle … candles, kisses!] Not in MS1

73.3: close," echoed in her mind.]close," she repeated to herself, as her mind filled with childhood memories of happy country faces, birthday cakes, candles, kisses— MS1, MS2

73.5: She should have gone with Janet.] After all, perhaps she should have gone with Janet, to celebrate her birthday. But she had never been in a bar in her life. MS1; After all, perhaps she should have gone with Janet, to celebrate her birthday. But she had never been in a bar in her life. She had never tasted whisky. MS2

73.6: A yearning for the treats of bygone birthdays.] Just something for her birthday. MS1, MS2

73.12: "Give me a chocolate soda," said Edna.] "I don't know," said Edna, feeling suddenly confused. "Give me a chocolate soda." MS1; "Oh, I don't know," said Edna, feeling suddenly confused. "Give me a chocolate soda." MS2

From *The Tangled Miracle*

1. UM, box 4, folder 3 (MS)*.

    MS is a perfect-bound author's proof supplied by the publisher. There are no markings on the text.

74.1: Chapter break precedes text. MS

The Wrong World

1. UM, box 7, folder 1 (MS)*; 2. BB, folder *The Wrong World* (MS1); 3. UM, box 7, folder 1 (MS2); 4. *Think of the Earth* (MS3). MS is a revised typescript of MS1. Given the evidence of repeated typos between MS and MS1, Brooker most likely corrected only individual pages. MS1 is a photocopy of a typescript not in the archives. It is possible that MS is the missing MS1 with the corrected pages. MS2 is one page of a missing variant edition. MS3 is the 2000 Brown Bear edition of *Think of the Earth*.

84.11: Milónoffs] Milonoffs MS1

84.12: Milónoffs] Milonoffs MS1

84.23: artist!] artist. MS1

85.13: Croydon] Croydan MS1

86.5: labouring] *ed.*; laboring MS, MS1

86.23: which, as it stood .... got out of his way for ever.] *alternate text*
   ... which, as it stood, seemed to satisfy them both.
   After the honeymoon Densham found that he could not get on with the Icelandic novel. The ever-recurring doubt that he had sufficient concentration for literary work took hold of him again. He went into partnership with a bond-broker, and decided that perhaps he would scribble a little in a dilettantish sort of way in his spare time. Perhaps that would satisfy his perpetual craving to achieve something with his pen. Instead it aggravated him. His wife found him moody, absorbed in a never-ending succession of ambitious projects, none of which he ever completed. His periods of passionate enthusiasm, when some new theme seethed in his brain, were scarcely less devastating than the spells of dejection which followed his failure to consummate—one after another—his elaborate plans.
   It could scarcely have been said that they were happy; and yet, although constantly and openly grieved over what he termed her "low blood pressure," Densham secretly realized that had she been more emotional their life together would have been almost unbearable; while she, wounded to the quick by his contempt for her intelligence and his complete indifference to her during solid weeks of frenzied composition, found some solace in the impetuous fits

of tenderness which seized him in black hours of failure, when he would hold her close, murmuring that she alone would have borne his tantrums, that she alone "believed" in him, and that some day he would requite her for her. MS2

86.23: had "spoiled"] "spoiled" *changed to* had "spoiled" MS1

87.1: had pampered] pampered *changed to* had pampered MS1

87.29: face downward in] face in *changed to* face downward in MS1

89.24: "Nine out of] Nine out of *changed to* "Nine out of MS1

89.33: Ecstasy] *ed.*; Ecstasty MS, MS1

91.5: futures. How] *ed.*; futures, How MS, MS1

91.29: "I'm inclined] *ed.*; *open quotation added* MS, MS1

92.5: Gawthorpe sat forward]*ed.*; "Gawthorpe sat forward MS, MS1

92.17: suddenly] suddently MS1

92.24: His voice] His voice voice MS1

92.25: impulse of pagan] *ed.*; impulse of pagen MS, MS1

94.25 His greenish eyes ... except a deposed king] this section of MS reappears only slightly altered on page 125 of MS3:

The lines across Gawthorpe's broad forehead deepened and drew together, but before he could even shake his head Tavistock swung himself around and spoke in a great hurry.

'Pascal was a doleful philosopher—but there's one thought of his—I was just recalling it—about the man who has lost an eye. There is something about man's present state, Pascal said, that makes us all miserable. We are always wishing for some happier condition. We long for an ideal state—a Utopia—a paradise. You've known plenty of people who feel that way, haven't you?'

Gawthorpe nodded.

'Pascal,' Tavistock went on, less hurriedly, 'has an interesting explanation of it. At least, it has always seemed so to me. He says that we must once have known a happier state—and lost it—or we shouldn't long for it. A man who has two eyes, he says, doesn't long for a third. But a man who has possessed two, mourns the loss of one, if an accident happens to him. It sounds plausible, don't you think? It fits in, doesn't it, with the myth—or whatever you like to call it—of man's lost innocence?'

Gawthorpe leaned forward and looked sideways at the floor. He felt that Tavistock did not expect him even to nod. MS3

95.25: Milónoff] Milonoff MS1

95.28: Milónoff] Milonoff MS1

97.10: Milónoff] Milonoff MS1

97.17: Eugénie] Eugenie MS1

98.19: indistinctly. He] *ed.*; indistinctly, He MS

99.2: No, it] *ed.*; No, It MS

99.13: cushions] *ed.*; cusions MS

99.15: which opened] which <wa> opened MS1

99.22: speak. At] *ed.*; speak, At MS1

100.17: 'born to unusual conquests?'] born to unusual conquests? *changed to* 'born to unusual conquests?' MS1

100.27: "You] You *changed to* "You MS1

101.8: singing] sininging *changed to* singing MS1

102.31: monotone] *ed.*; monontone MS, MS1

105.1: Pethick] Pethic *changed to* Pethick MS1 *in all instances of name up to page* 115

105.16: displayed] displaed *changed to* displayed MS1

106.1: 'war-paint'."] *ed.*; 'war-paint'," MS, MS1

107.6: Whispers were] *ed.*; Whispers where MS, MS1

107.7: Peacock."] *ed.*; Peacock", MS, MS1

109.7: multi-coloured] multi-colored MS1

109.8: of snowy arMS] of snowy <ribbands> arms MS1

110.9: crumble] crumbe *changed to* crumble MS1

110.13 Pethick] Pethick *spelled as in* MS *for remainder of* MS1

111.22: absolutely. Why] *ed.*; absolutely, Why MS, MSI

118.18: From the back of the house] From the house *changed to* From the back of
the house MSI

113.3: The old footman] The<n>old footman MSI

115.18: which] whch *changed to* which MSI

115.22: seem] seem<ed> MSI

115.23: you know] you<n> know MSI

116.30: asked. "It] *ed.*; asked "It MS, MSI

117.9: "Why] *ed.*; *open quotation added* MS, MSI

118.9: was] were *changed to* were MSI

118.22: ever since,] ever since— MSI

119.27: Oh, yes, yes."] *ed.*; Oh, yes, yes," MS, MSI

119.31: hand and] hand <for> and MSI

123.3: quietus] quitus *changed to* quietus MSI

123.16: left to] led to MSI

126.30: room] *ed.*; rooms MS, MSI

127.20: assisted] *ed.*; asisted MS, MSI

127.23: "But I have] But have *changed to* But I have MSI

128.11: seemed] seemd *changed to* seemed MSI

129.7: aching, slowly] *ed.*; aching, Slowly MS, MSI

131.13: a woman's] a wonman's MSI

132.1: "No, sing] *ed.*; "No, Sing MS, MSI

134.20: swept noiselessly] *ed.*; swept noiselessy MS, MSI

136.11: Polinka."] Polinka. *changed to* Polinka." MSI

136.14: blooming in a jardinière] blooming jardiniere *changed to* blooming in a
jardiniere MSI

136.15: jardinière] *ed.*; jardiniere MS, MSI

136.18:   cherry-coloured] *ed.*; cherry-colored MS, MS1

137.20: Feódorovna!!] Feódorovna!. MS1

140.14: now?"] *ed.*; now? MS, MS1

140.28: "You may] *ed.*; *open quotation added* MS, MS1

140.31: tree which hung] *ed.*; tree whuch hung MS, MS1

141.2: "I must] *ed.*; *open quotation added* MS, MS1

145.1: train bound for] train for *changed to* train bound for MS1

145.10: he wanted now] he wanted <to> now MS1

146.26: Croydon, take a cab,] *ed.*; Croydon., take a cab, MS, MS1

147.24: Polinka appeared] *ed.*; Polinka appeard MS, MS1

148.2: of Mary.] *ed.*; of Mary'. MS, MS1

149.23: a look of amazed] a look amazed *changed to* a look of amazed MS1

To All the Nations ....!

1. UM, box 8, folder 3 (MS)*; 2. UM, box 8, folder 3 (MS1). MS1 is compiled from various incomplete hand-script editions. See note on page 208 for more. The follow is a reproduction of MS1, the various incomplete hand-script editions in their entirety:

154.27: And in the silence] And in the <silen> silence MS

154.29: labour] *ed.*; labor MS

[page 1]

To All the Nations—!
from
Bailly Bartholdy

Most excellent and most execrable majesties, most reverend and most irreverent fathers in God; my lords and gentlemen, if there be any such left on the earth; you,—poets, artists, scientists, logicians, who philander with forms and figures; you,—astronomers, who concern yourselves with far-off worlds; and you, religionists of a thousand sects, devotees of all sorts and conditions of invisible gods; you,—the butt of the scorn of centuries, heathens, Jews, negroes, and you yellow millions;—all peoples, all nations; swarming in pestilential myriads on the green shores o' the world; you,—coward men and ineffectual women, huddled together ~~in ludicrous communities~~ on this lonely ~~earth~~ clod of matter that men call earth,—Listen—!

~~I~~

I have risen up from among you to shout at you.

[labelled page 2]

In silence and in solitude channels of hate have been carved in ~~my breast; but the Time has come now to spill the vial of my wrath upon your heads. The Time for me to roar at you has come now~~ me.

I have waited in silence many years. I said to myself, the time is not yet; what I have to say must be said boldly, broadly; it must roll like thunder; it must roar like the sea. Only the measure of Homer, the vocabulary of Shakespeare, the passion of Dante, the ruthlessness of Ibsen,—all these must I have in some measure, before I lift up my voice to scourge the ~~world~~ nations. So I read diligently, I practised diligently. Many a time I thought all was ready, and sat down to write,—only to fail. But I have changed now. I feel now that so long as my heart is behind all this; yes, and my body and blood, if need be,—no man can fail to listen. Rough-hewn, this little book goes out to all the nations. Misshapen, ugly,

[labelled page 3]

crude,—like some rock wrenched from the heart of the world, I hurl it back at the world.

Poets, you will find no felicitous phrasing; O logicians, you will find no artful juxtaposition of meaningless terms; O idlers, you will find no amusement here. This is no idle book. I ask no idlers to trifle with it. A very stern and terrible little book it seems to me.

[labelled page 4]

~~II~~

~~II~~ I

~~Listen!~~

What is that low, vast, terrible, murmuring? —

~~Listen!~~

Those sighs issuing from thousands of throats? that calamitous ~~continuous~~ moaning that never ends, never abates, never ceases for a second? ~~those heart-stabbing groans that greet the rising cup of the sun; those ghastly whispers that attend its going down~~; that tumultuous torrent of tears? those sobs? those frenzied fists beating at breasts? those frightful shrieks? those cries in the dead of night? that awful monotone of moaning? that pandemonium of sorrow? that buzz of grief? that chaotic chorus of wailing?

~~Listen to it.~~ What is it?

Whose voices are those? ~~that utter throttled throats thronging to high heaven~~ Whose bodies are these, rocking to and fro, racked in torment? Whose eyes

[labelled page 2]

~~Listen.~~

~~It seems to rise from the earth. Is it true after all that Hell is in the center of the earth? Is it true after all that lost spirits somewhere beneath us in the bowels of the world shiver in torment? Is it true that this unutterable voice of melancholy issues from her home of fallen angels?~~

~~No.~~

~~NO!~~

~~Whose voices are these that wail through the night? whose bodies are these racked with torment? Whose lips are these that quiver? Whose eyes are these overflowing with tears? Whose heaving bosoms are there? What are is this multitude of sufferers?~~

~~The Underfolk!~~

~~H~~

~~Humanity is One.~~

~~Mankind is a Unit.~~

~~Human life is possibly more than a cypher.~~

[labelled page 5]

are these so red and wet and swollen with tears? ~~Whose blood is this on the ground, reeking to heaven? Whose~~ What is this on the ground here? Is it blood? ~~Is it?~~ Whose blood? ~~What is that heap there? Come closer? Is it A heap of Can they be bones? Are they human bones? Whose bones are they?~~ Who are these people walking ~~sitting~~ in blood? ~~and among heaps of bones?~~ What is this multitude that sit ~~laden, overwhelmed, annihilated with grief?~~ in darkness and in the shadow of death.

The Underfolk!

II

~~Humanity is One,—a Unit.~~
~~Or perhaps it were better to say,—a cipher.~~
~~Nevertheless, Mankind may be roughly divided into three classes~~
~~The Underfolk~~
~~The Middlefolk~~
~~The Upperfolk~~
~~Drawn from all three of these classes is another—hardly to be called a~~

[labelled page 6]

II

You labellers and classifiers of Humanity, I give you new labels for your three classes,—
The Underfolk
The Middlefolk
The Upperfolk
It is of the Underfolk that I would speak now.
Who am I?
I will tell you~~?~~.

III

I am the Champion of the Underfolk.

So long as there be any poverty left in the world and breath in me, I shall fight.

I shall fight hard.

The silence and the solitude of those past years, ~~have hardened me~~ 'the vile blows and buffets of the world,' have hardened me. Tears and the grim sulking of those 'weary with disasters,'—that part of my life is swallowed up in this,—this solid; satisfying rage, this consuming anger as of a ~~spite~~ fire, spouting heated, volcanic~~, rage~~ words to your everlasting heart.

I am a mountain,

[labelled page 7]

pouring forth the terrible lava of a soul on fire. I shall not cease till you remove me. This book is one eruption of that lava. Beware of it and me, and that awful urge—I know not what it is,—behind us both.

For I am not alone. Pervading my solitude there is a presence,—a terrible presence. If it be God, then God is indeed terrible,—the overflowing scourge is in his hands. If it be nought but the revival of ancestral hate, some relic of bestial fierceness, some cerebral rudiment of a once physical and material tooth and claw,—beware! I lie couchant in my lair, ready to spring out upon the earth, with the blazing wrath of a thousand centuries fanned to fiercer ferocity in this burning heart.

Beware of me, I say, and this awful urge behind me that drives me on,—'down the nights and down the days; down the arches of the years; down the labyrinthine ways of my own mind.'

[labelled page 8]

Shade of the Thompson, forgive me.

Till now, I have been unknown. Soon, the thrones and parliaments of the world shall ~~ring with my name~~ be troubled and trembling because of me. Destiny does not halt, and Destiny is behind me. Alone and unafraid by this inexorable wind of an unseen will.

~~I am the Champion of the Underfolk.~~

My life is not my own. It is His,—whoever He is,—who gave it me. I am careless of it save when He shapes its course, its culmination, and its end.

I am the Champion of the Underfolk, bent on the hurt of all who hurt them.

Read on.

IV

Believe me, you Upperfolk, I am not taking my lance,—nay, it is not a lance, but a bludgeon,—it shall not come down only upon your heads. As Shaw says,— 'there are no absolute scoundrels.'

[labelled page 9]

~~My hand is against every man's hand who oppresses the~~ poor ~~Underfolk, even though there be many such among the Underfolk themselves. At another time I shall call all the Underfolk to account,—that is not my business here. Whoever he be, I care not if he be the fifth George of England or some pig-headed cottager. I am against all such traitors to the race.~~

Do not misunderstand me when I tell you that I am the Champion of the Underfolk. Do not think that I love or admire or pity the Underfolk. I despise them. When I see a man clothed in rags I am ashamed of him; I feel as if it were my duty to kill him, hide him, get him and his reeking clothes under ground,— out of sight,—anywhere. A ragged and dirty child is to me like a hideous sore; a strumpet—a loathsome weed. I want to take all these ~~fif~~ filthy creatues as one would an accumulation of refuse and burn them,—burn them, and bury their ashes deep, deep, lest some

[labelled page 10]

faint stench of their dirty bodies be left even in them. O, I hate the Underfolk. Far is it from me to uphold them, sustain them,—in any way help to keep them above ground. I want them exterminated. I will not be silent until they are exterminated.

Thrones and parliaments of the world, I demand that every ~~starving~~ ill-fed, ill-clad ~~vicious~~, ill-used man, woman and child now living on this filthy world of ours, be killed,—done away with,—NOW; or —

What?

What is the alternative?

Give them death or life,—one or the other. Either add something to them or take them away,—take them entirely away. ~~This frightful sore of Poverty must not stain the~~ fair ~~face of the dirt-encumbered earth any longer~~ The Time has come to amputate Humanity. The Time has come for the word 'Poverty' ~~must~~ to be erased from our dictionaries, expelled from our languages, and forgotten by all the

[labelled page 11]

children of men. The time has come when every poverty-stricken being in the world is a shrieking shame; every beggar ~~shoves~~ casts the words 'civilization' and 'Christianity' in our teeth; every starving child is a monument to the insufferable laziness, cowardice, obstinacy, and treachery of the peoples of the twentieth century; every emaciated hand of every pariah slaps the face of Christ. The stench of the poor rises to high heaven and smells in the nostrils of the most high God.

Not one of these Underfolk must be left above ground; no, not one. You shall kill them or you shall so serve them that they are Underfolk no more. I demand that the world shall be lit from shore to shore and from sea to sea with colossal fires,—and on those fires shall be cast all the bodies or else all the habilaments of the poor,—so that men watching those ~~fires~~ spreading

[labelled page 12]

fires, leaping from hill to hill, cape to cape, ~~ocean to ocean~~ promontory to promontory, as Clytemnestra watched the beacons that signalled Agammemnon's home-coming, shall, with united voice, shout a great shout, echoing among the stars, ~~and jarring the gates of Paradise and of Dio~~, --

THE WORLD IS CLEAN!

V

That is what I demand,—A clean world. As Hercules set out single-handed to cleanse the Augean stables, so set I out to cleanse the world. There have been men before me who have demanded clean cities, clean states,—but I shall not rest, I shall not cease to conjure ways and means,—till that tremendous shout jars the gateways of the universe.

O, you,—who nightly, or perhaps only weekly now, pray with earnestness or indifference,—'Thy Kingdom

[labelled page 13]

come; Thy will be done on earth;—think you that His kingdom can ever come while ~~the houses you own,~~ there remains one homeless wretch in all this sorry world.

O, you,—who, when time-honored custom sanctions it, sit in state to administer the state's laws ~~that are boasted to be emanate from the will of the people,~~—are you ~~that~~ satisfied with these gutters that are called streets? with these hells that are called homes?—with these greasy, reeking, bestial objects that are called men and women?

~~You, Englanders, who seek to link the chains of Empire from Westminster to Westminster again,—are you proud of Whitechapel?~~

~~You, Germans, spending millions in instrumenst of war year after year, are you satisfied with every human instrument within your borders? I know you are not.~~

~~You, France,—you, Russia,~~

[labelled page 14]

~~Spain, Japan; and you, most inappropriately named, United States, have you no festering filth-holes?—Norway, China, Chile, Italy, have you no suicides, preferring death to life in such domains as yours? I know you have.~~

VI

Spare me your pleas of charity, your old-age-pensions, your minimum wages, your royal or far from royal commissions, your committees and departments and secretaries and all that insufferable foolery. I have no patience with these little sporadic measures,—your insularity,—your littleness.

This thing is not to be remedied by royal commissions or Salvation Armies, or Church Armies, or any kind of army, save the army of the united nations of the world. Think not that this ugly thing can be wiped out by edifying talk and

[labelled page 15]

endless discussion ~~by~~ in futile Ethical Societies, in Socialist conclaves, or in anarchist dens.

There must be and here shall be a gathering together of the peoples to remedy this evil. Nation must stand shoulder to shoulder with nation, and this people must grasp the hand of this people; and all barriers of national prejudice and jealousy must be broken down until this word 'poverty' be abolished. From every nation there must be chosen a number of men,—not cowards; not idiots; ~~not old-fashioned~~ none with hard heads or soft hearts,—but men; some from the Underfolk, some from the Middlefolk, some from the Upperfolk, of every nation and of every people. And you shall not except the Jew and the negro and the Turk. All men shall come together concerning this, for all men are vitally interested in this.

And these men must be

[labelled page 16]

set apart from the work of the world and the play of the world for a term of years. It is idle to say how long. But these men shall stay in serious and deliberate conference until the day comes when there remains no vestige or trace of what was once the Underfolk. Time and money must not be spared. The money that now is spent in charity must go into the coffers of this conference. And this conference shall be devoid of all nationality. These men must forget that they are Germans or Jews or Italians, they must remember that they are men. And when the time comes, when they have decided what it is to be done and how it is to be done, they shall send to every nation a command, and every nation shall send to its governors and its mayors a secondary command, and all that is to be done must be done speedily, yet

[labelled page 17]

without haste.

The Spread of Negativism

1. UM, box 8, folder 2 (MS)*.

159.16: "isms" of] *ed.*; "isms" od MS

160.13: honoured] *ed.*; honoured MS

160.17: Labour] *ed.*; Labor MS

160.26: dishonoured] *ed.*; dishonored MS

161.33: do more." He says] do more." <Three cheers for John Foster Fraser.> He says MS

162.1: Society] *ed.*; Socity MS

165.18: until it] *ed.*; untillit MS

The Decay of Art
1. UM, box 8, folder 2 (MS)*.

168.5: colours] *ed.*; colors MS

168.7: colour] *ed.*; color MS

170.24: favoured] *ed.*; favored MS

The Price of Peace
1. UM, box 8, folder 3 (MS)*. 2. UM, box 8, folder 3 (MS1).

172.13: harbour] *ed.*; harbor MS, MS1

174.22: would now thrust a resolute hand] would not thrust a hand *changed to* would now thrust a resolute hand MS2

Free Prose
1. UM, box 1, folder 16 (MS)*.
MS is dated 22 July 1925.

Notes for the *Free Prose*
1. UM, box 1, folder 16 (MS)*.
MS is dated 6 August 1925.

178.8: Virginia Woolf] *ed.*; Virginia Wolff MS

Nudes and Prudes
1. UM, box 8, folder 3 (MS1); 2. Open House (MS)*; 3. arthistoryarchive.com (MS2). MS is an archived version of MS1 prior to final editing for publication. MS1 is the published version from *Open House* (Deacon 1931). MS2 is an online version edited by Charles Moffat, available at http://www.arthistoryarchive. com/arthistory/canadian/Nudes-and-Prudes.html. MS2 utilizes MS1 as copy-

text. See note on page 208 for an explanation of why the published version was not chosen as copy-text.

179.2: I first met him in a downtown store whither he had come looking for a picture of a horse.] I met him one day in a downtown store. He had come looking for a picture of a horse. MS1

179.3: After we had been introduced by the keeper of the store, he mentioned his quest.] After a few minutes chat he was accosted by a clerk, who knew him, and he mentioned his quest. MS1

179.9: League, and I want to] League. I want to MS1

180.2: the other a nude by] the other a nute by MS2

181.2: hung in the art galleries of the new College Street store of the T. Eaton Company Limited, Toronto, the head of which company is also the president of the Toronto Art Gallery.] hung in the art galleries of a Toronto department store. MS1

181.6: had contributed a nude to the Canadian National Exhibition a couple years earlier which had caused a furore in the] had contributed to the Canadian National Exhibition, a couple of years earlier, a nude which had caused a furore in the MS1

181.10: sent to the Eaton store] sent to this store MS1

181.24: hands of certain Toronto press] certain Toronto newspapers make MS; hands of the Toronto press MS2

181.26: the press of Toronto] these papers MS1

182.8: They must needs] They need to MS2

182.13: work as beyond] work as beyong MS2

182.18: quite libellous] quite libel MS2

182.19: The same critic who thus maligned a fellow townsman and a former colleague on his own newspaper, recently interviewed] The same critic recently interviewed MS1

182.26: These suggestions were framed in a way that made it possible for the offender to escape with a whole skin.] Not in MS1

182.30: and was promptly slapped on the wrist for doing so by a writer on the *Globe* who considers himself something of a champion of the arts.] and was promptly slapped on the wrist by the *Globe* for doing so. MS1

182.31: a champion of the arts.] *paragraph break added* MS2

183.3: about the removal] about the removel MS2

183.11: at the time, although I refused to talk to the army of reporters, with their noses on the trail of nudery, who besieged me at the time.] at the time, although I had not uttered a word for publication. MS1

183.24: a lewd book.] *no paragraph break follows* MS1

184.12: — that is to say— on]— that is to say, on MS2

184.24: detached from the purely personal urgencies of his own desires and fears.] detached from his own puny affairs MS1; detached from the insignificant unity of his own puny affairs MS2

184.27: a unity] an unity MS2

185.5: is to *see* things] is to see things MS2

185.15: the eye of the average tourist.] the eye of tourists. MS1

185.21: returning to the particular point of our] returning to the theme of our MS1

185.28: this at-one-ness with] this 'at-one-ness' with MS1

186.3: individual in relation both to God and to man has] individual, in relation both to God and to man, has MS1

186.9: a unifying influence, and from it somehow] a unifying influence. From it somehow MS1

186.16: important practical measure] important socially-practical measure MS1

186.18: their chiefest care.] their primary concern. MS2

186.21: The best that any] The best way that any MS2

187.1: Watson were heard] Watson was heard MS1

187.4: to discourage appreciation] to discourage appreciatio MS2

187.6: a sneaking curiosity] a sneaking curiousity MS2

187.19: of candour and] of candor and MS1

187.27: The division] "The devision MS2

188.4: reverent minds, some deeper hint of that wholeness which, if we could grasp it entire, would make us all one.] reverent minds, some deeper hint of that wholeness, guessed at and aspired to in the past as the ultimate secret, through knowledge of which we might all be one. MS1

When We Awake!
1. *Yearbook* (MS)*.
   MS is the published version of the article from *Yearbook of the Arts 1928–1929* (Brooker 1929).

Prophet's Wanted
1. UM, box 7, folder 3 (MS1); 2. *The Adelphi* (MS)*.
   MS1 is an archived version. MS is the published version from *The Adelphi* (Ed. John Middleton Murry, 2.3 (June 1931): 183–193).

207.14: to-day] today MS1

208.10: while at the same time forming] while, at the same time, forming MS1

208.28: *banners*] banners MS1

209.5: for, like Goethe's bottled pigmy, he] for like Goethe's bottled pigmy he MS1

211.13: favourable] conducive MS1

212.6: opposed.] opposed! MS1

213.2: pre-exist] preexist MS1

213.5: to-day] today MS1

213.7: what is, to] what is to MS1

213.12: to-day] today MS1

213.22: possible as] possible, as MS1

215.19: cling to the hard] cling, in spite of their lamentations, to the hard MS1

215.20: of their world.] of their world. They are possessive, despite all their talk of repressed desires. MS1

215.29: le Gallienne's phrase] corrected from le Galliene MS, MS1

Works Cited

Abbott, E. A. 1894. *Flatland: A Romance of Many Dimensions*. (1991). Princeton: Princeton Science Library.

Adams, Henry. 1919. *The Degradation of Democratic Dogma*. Macmillan: New York.

Allen, James Lane. 1903. *The Mettle and the Pasture*. Toronto: George N. Moray and Co.

Apollinaire, Guillaume. 1912. "The New Painting." In *Manifesto: a century of isms*. (2001). Ed. Mary Ann Caws. Lincoln: University of Nebraska Press, 120–123.

Aristotle. 1960. *Aristotle: The Poetics. "Longinus": On the Sublime. Demetrius: On Style*. Trans. W. H. Fyfe. Cambridge : Harvard University Press.

Arnason, David. 1989. "Reluctant Modernist." In *Provincial Essays*, ed. Jennifer Oille Sinclair. Volume 7. Toronto: Phacops Publishing Society, 77–88.

Babbitt, Irving. *Democracy and Leadership*. Houghton Mifflin Company, 1924. Page 25.

———— 1963. "Humanism: An Essay at Definition." *Modern Criticism: Theory and Practice*. Eds. Walter E. Sutton, Richard Jackson Foster. Odyssey Press. 195–208.

————1991. Original Introduction. *Rousseau and Romanticism*. Ed. Claes G. Ryn. New York: Transaction Publishers. lxix–lxxxiii.

Ball, Hugo. 1974. *Flight Out of Time*. New York: Viking.

Betts, Gregory. 2005. "The Destroyer: Modernism and Mystical Revolution in Bertram Brooker." Ph.D dissertation, York University.

Blake, William. 1809. "The Ancient Britons." In *The Complete Poetry and Prose of William Blake*. (1982). Berkeley: University of California Press, 544.

————. 1946. "The Descriptive Catalogue." In *The Portable Blake*, ed. Alfred Kazin. New York: Penguin Books, 530.

Bowers, Fredson. 1950 (August). "Current Theories of Copy-Text, with an Illustration from Dryden." *Modern Philology*, 48: 1: 12–20.

Bork, Alfred M. 1966. "The 'FitzGerald' Contraction." *Isis: The History of Science Society*, 57: 2: 199–207.

Breton, André. 1924. "Manifesto of Surrealism." In *Manifestoes of Surrealism*. 1969. Ann Arbour: University of Michigan Press.

Brooker, Bertram. *A Candle in Sunshine*. Bertram Brooker Estate. Box 2, folder 7.

———. "The Measure of Gordon Craig." University of Manitoba Special Collections. Box 2, folder 1.

———. Red notebook. University of Manitoba Special Collections. Box 1, folder 16.

———. "Shorts about Bernard." University of Manitoba Special Collections. Box 1, folder 16.

———."Years." University of Manitoba Special Collections. Box 1, folder 16.

———. 1905. "Diary." University of Manitoba Special Collections. Box 1, folder 16.

———. 1905. "Diary of Bernard Bradley." University of Manitoba Special Collections. Box 1, folder 16.

———. 1913 (April). "The Censorship of Photoplays: Is Immorality Immoral?" *The Photoplay Author*. Published under pseudonym Bailly Bartholdy. University of Manitoba Special Collections. Box 8, folder 1.

———. 1926 (April 16) and 14 May 1927. "The Bread of Carefulness." University of Manitoba Special Collections. Box 7, folder 4.

———. 1926 (June). "Canada's Modern Arts Movement." *The Canadian Forum*, 6: 69: 276–279.

———. 1927. "Blake." Public lecture, with notes, given to Hart House Sketch Club. 1 November. University of Manitoba Special Collections. Box 10, folder 13.

———. 1928 (April 5). "Beauty's Place in Business: The Decade of the Artist is Now At Hand." *Printer's Ink*, 153: 1: 3–6, 178.

———. 1928. "The Modern Bug Will Get You If You Don't Watch Out." University of Manitoba Special Collections. Box 9, folder 12.

———, ed. 1929. *Yearbook of the Arts 1928–1929*. Toronto: Macmillan.

————. 1930 (July). "The Poetry of E. E. Cummings." *The Canadian Forum*, 10: 118: 370–371. Rpt. In *Sounds Assembling: The Poetry of Bertram Brooker*, ed. Birk Sproxton. Winnipeg: Turnstone Press, 1980. 68–71.

————. 1930 (27 September). "The Seven Arts: Architecture, Sculpture, Painting, Music, Poetry, Dancing, Drama." *The Winnipeg Evening Tribune*.

————. 1931 (January 8). "Business Man—1961 Model." *Printer's Ink*, 154: 2: 44–52.

————. 1931 (July–September). "Idolators of Brevity." *Seewanee Review*, 19: 263–268.

————. 1934, 1953. "The World and I—A Voyage of Self Exploration." University of Manitoba Special Collections. Box 6, folder 2.

————. 1936 (January). "Mrs. Hungerford's Milk." *The Canadian Forum*, 14: 160. Rpt. in *Voices of Discord*. Toronto: New Hogtown Press, 1979. 92–100.

————. 1936. "Art and Society: A General Introduction." *Yearbook of the Arts*. Toronto: Macmillan, xiii–xxviii.

————. 1938. "The Future of the Novel in Canada." *Association of Canadian Bookmen's Library Bulletin*. Rpt. in *Canadian Novelists and the Novel*, eds. Douglas Daymond and Leslie Monkman. Ottawa: Borealis Press. 150–153.

————. 1946 (2 December). "Bloodless Revolution." University of Manitoba Special Collections. Box 6, folder 6.

————. 1951. "Opening." University of Manitoba Special Collections. Box 6, folder 10.

————. 1953 (January 4). "Son of My Son." University of Manitoba Special Collections. Box 6, folder 1.

Brooker, Victor. 1970 (September 25). Interview with Robert Fulford. *This is Robert Fulford*. CBC, Winnipeg. University of Manitoba Special Collections.

————. 1972 (October 11). Letter to Dennis Reid. University of Manitoba Special Collections.

————. [1982?]. Interview. *For Art's Sake*. CBC. University of Manitoba Special Collections.

Browne, Sir Thomas. 1642. *Religio Medici, Hydriotaphia, and the Garden of Cyrus*. (1972). Oxford: Oxford University Press.

Bucke, Richard Maurice. 1969. *Cosmic Consciousness: A Study in the Evolution of the Human Mind*. New York: E. P. Dutton.

———. 1879. *Man's Moral Nature.* New York: G. Putman.

———. 1894 (May 18). "Cosmic Consciousness." Proceedings of the American Medico-Psychological Association Annual Meeting. Philadelphia.

Burtonshaw, Nell. 1973. Interview with Victor Brooker. Portage La Prairie. University of Manitoba Special Collections.

Chesterton, G. K. 1905. *Heretics.* 3rd ed. New York: John Lane, 36–37.

———. 1908. *Orthodoxy.* London: Bodley Head. Rpt. in Vancouver: Regent College, 2004. 78.

———. 1922. *The Man Who Knew Too Much, and Other Stories.* London: Cassell and Co. Ltd.

Clayton, Jay. 1991 (September). "Dickens and the Genealogy of Postmodernism." *Nineteenth-Century Literature,* 46: 2: 181–195.

Covick, Owen R. and Beverley Vickers. 2003 (July 15–18). "The Trials of Whitaker Wright." History of Economic Thought Society of Australia. 16th Conference. Melbourne.

Davis, Ann. 1992. *The Logic of Ecstasy: Canadian Mystical Painting 1920–40.* Toronto: University of Toronto Press.

Deacon, William Arthur. 1929. "Literature in Canada—In Its Centenary Year." In *Yearbook of the Arts 1928–1929.* Toronto: Macmillan, 21–36.

———, ed. 1931. *Open House.* Ottawa: The Graphic Press.

Defoe, Daniel. 1719. *The Life and Strange Surprising Adventures of Robinson Crusoe, of York, Mariner: Who lived Eight and Twenty Years all alone in an un-inhabited Island on the Coast of America, near the Mouth of the Great River of Oroonoque; Having been cast on Shore by Shipwreck, where in all the Men perished but Himself. With An Account how he was at last as strangely deliver'd by Pyrates.* Pater-Noster: W. Taylor.

De Quincey, Thomas. 1822. *Confessions of an English Opium-Eater and Other Writings.* (1985). New York: Oxford University Press, 77.

Evans, Blakemore G., ed. and J. J. M. Tobin, ed. 1974. *The Riverside Shakespeare.* Boston: Houghton Mifflin Company.

Foerster, Norman. 1926 (March) "Emerson on the Organic Principle in Art." PMLA. 41.1: 193–208.

Freshwater, Helen. 2003 (Winter). "The Allure of the Archive." *Poetics Today,* 24: 4: 729–758.

Fyfe, W. H. and W. R. Roberts. 1960. Introduction. *Aristotle: The Poetics. "Longinus": On the Sublime. Demetrius: On Style.* Cambridge: Harvard University Press. i–xiii.

Gallienne, Richard le. 2004. "The Decadent to His Soul." English Poems. 1892. Whitefish, M. T.: Kessinger Publishing. 71–74.

Goethe, Johann Wolfgang von. 1908. *Goethe's Faust Parts I & II*. Trans. Albert G. Latham. London: J. M. Dent and Sons.

Grace, Sherrill. 1989. "Figures in a Ground: The Fiction." In *Provincial Essays*, ed. Jennifer Oille Sinclair. Volume 7. Toronto: Phacops Publishing Society, 63–76.

———. 1989. *Regression and Apocalypse: Studies in North American Literary Expressionism*. Toronto: University of Toronto Press.

———. 1985 (Spring). "'The Living Soul of Man': Bertram Brooker and Expressionist Theatre." *Theatre History in Canada*, 1–22.

Harris, Lawren. 1929 (July 15). "Revelation of Art in Canada." *Canadian Theosophist*, 7: 5: 85–88.

———. 1924 (February). "The Greatest Book by a Canadian and Another." *The Canadian Bookman*, 5: 2: 38.

———. 2008. *In the Ward: His Urban Poetry and painting*, ed. Gregory Betts. Toronto: Exile Editions.

Hewlett, Maurice Henry. 1909. *The Forest Lovers: A Romance*. New York: Macmillan.

Houser, F. B. 1926. *A Canadian Art Movement*. Toronto: Macmillan.

Hughes, Kenneth J. 1979. Introduction. *Voices of Discord: Canadian Short Stories from the 1930s*. Ed. Donna Phillips. Toronto: New Hogtown.

Jasen, David A., ed. 2003. *Tin Pan Alley: An Encyclopaedia of the Golden Age of American Song*. Abingdon: Routledge.

Keats, John. 1996. "Hyperion: A Fragment" and "The Fall of Hyperion." *British Literature 1780–1830*. New York: Harcourt Brace. 1285–1295, 1314–1320.

Kempis, Thomas à. 2006. *The Imitation of Christ*. Trans. George F. Maine. New York: Read Books, 2006.

Kenner, Hugh. 1978. *Joyce's Voices*. Los Angeles: University of California Press.

Khayyám, Omar. 1896. *Rubáiyát: English, French, and German*, trans. Edward Fitzgerald and Nathan Haskell Dole. Boston: Joseph Knight Company.

Knapp, James A. 2003 (Winter). "Ocular Proof": Archival Revelations and Aesthetic Response." *Poetics Today*, 24: 4: 695–727.

Kreeft, Peter. 1993. *Christianity for Modern Pagans: Pascal's Pensées Edited, Outlined, and Explained*. San Francisco: Ignatius Press.

Lacombe, Michele. 1982 (Summer). "Theosophy and the Canadian Idealist

Tradition: A Preliminary Exploration." *Journal of Canadian Studies,* 17: 2: 100 118.

Laurence, Margaret. 1970. *A Bird in the House.* (1974). New Canadian Library. Toronto: McClelland and Stewart.

Lewis, Wyndham. 1994. "The Revolutionary Simpleton." *The Enemy: A Review of Art and Literature.* 1927. London: Taylor & Francis, 27–189.

Lippmann, Walter. 1982. *A Preface to Morals.* 1929. New Brunswick, NJ: Transaction Publishers.

Lloyd, Norman, ed. 1968. *The Golden Encyclopaedia of Music.* New York: Golden Press.

Maeterlinck, Maurice. 1898. *La Sagesse et la destinée* [*Wisdom and Destiny*]. (1908). Trans. Alfred Sutro. New York: Dodd, Mead.

———. 1896. *Le Trésor des Humbles* [*The Treasure of the Humble*]. (1901). Trans. Alfred Sutro. New York: Dodd, Mead. Rpt. Montana: Kessinger Publishing, 2005.

Marinetti, F. T. 1909. "The Founding and Manifesto of Futurism." In *Let's Murder the Moonshine: Selected Writings by F. T. Marinetti.* (1991). Los Angeles: Sun and Moon Press.

McKillop, A. B. 1999 (June). "Who Killed Canadian History? A View from the Trenches." *Canadian Historical Review,* 80: 2: 269–299.

Murry, John Middleton. *Defending Romanticism: selected criticism of John Middleton Murry.* Bristol: Bristol Press, 1989.

———. 1929. *God: Being An Introduction to the Science of Metabiology.* London: Cape, 1929.

Nichols, Robert. 1923. *Fantastica: Being the Smile of the Sphinx and other Tales of Imagination.* Rpt. Manchester, NH: Ayer, 1970. 24–25.

Nietzsche, Friedrich. 1891. *Thus Spake Zarathustra.* (1911). Trans. Thomas Common. New York: Dover Publications, 1999.

Patmore, Coventry. 1907. *Religio Poetae, etc.* London: G. Bell and Sons.

Philips, Donna, ed. 1979. *Voices of Discord.* Toronto: New Hogtown Press.

Plato. 360 BCE. *The Republic.* (1985). Trans. Richard W. Sterling and William C. Scott. New York; London: W. W. Norton and Company.

Pound, Ezra. 1968. "The Serious Artist." In *Literary Essays of Ezra Pound,* ed. T. S. Eliot. New York: New Directions, 41–57.

Reid, Dennis. 1985. *Atma Buddhi Manas: The Later Works of Lawren S. Harris*. Toronto: Art Gallery of Ontario.

——, ed. 1979. Introduction. *Bertram Brooker 1888–1955*. Canadian Artists Series: 1. Ottawa: National Gallery of Canada.

Sadie, Stanley, ed. 2004. *The Billboard Encyclopaedia of Classical Music*. New York: Billboard Books.

Shaw, George Bernard. 1898. *The Perfect Wagnerite: A Commentary on the Niblung's Ring*. London: Constable. Rpt. London: Kessinger, 2004.

——. 1926. *The Socialism of Shaw*, ed. James Fuchs. New York: Vanguard Press, 49–86.

Spencer, Herbert. 1864–1867. *Principles of Biology*. Volume 1. London: Williams & Norgate.

Sproxton, Birk. 1989. "'The Subjective Underground': The Stream of Consciousness." *Provincial Essays*, ed. Jennifer Oille Sinclair. Volume 7. Toronto: Phacops Publishing Society, 52–62.

——, ed. 1980. Introduction. *Sounds Assembling: The Poetry of Bertram Brooker*. Winnipeg: Turnstone.

Steinway & Sons. 1920 (January 21). Advertisement. *The Globe*, 2.

Stevenson, Lionel. 1926. *Appraisals of Canadian Literature*. (1977). Norwood: Norwood Editions.

Thompson, Francis. 1913. "Nature's Immortality." In *The Works of Francis Thompson*. London: Burns & Oates, 81.

Trehearne, Brian. 1989. *Aestheticism and the Canadian Modernists: Aspects of a Poetic Influence*. Montreal: McGill-Queen's University Press.

——. 2005. "A. J. M. Smith's Eclectic Surrealism." *The Canadian Modernists Meet*, ed. Dean Irvine. Ottawa: University of Ottawa Press, 119–138.

Tzara, Tristan. 1918. "Dada Manifesto." *Manifesto: A Century of isms*. (2001). Ed. Mary Ann Caws. Lincoln: University of Nebraska Press, 297–304.

Wagner, Anton. 1984. "Herman Voaden's Symphonic Expressionism." Dissertation. University of Toronto.

——. 1989. "'God Crucified Upside Down': The Search for Dramatic Form and Meaning." In *Provincial Essays*, ed. Jennifer Oille Sinclair. Volume 7. Toronto: Phacops Publishing Society, 38–51.

Whitman, Walt. 1855. Preface to *Leaves of Grass*. In *Complete Poetry and Prose*. (1982). Ed. Justin Kaplan. Library of America; Cambridge, 5–26.

————. 1871. "Democratic Vistas." In *Complete Poetry and Prose*. (1982). Ed. Justin Kaplan. Library of America; Cambridge, 929–994.

Williams, Glenn. 2000. "Translating Music in Visual Form: The Influence of Music in the Work of Bertram Brooker."RACAR, 27: 1/2: 111–122.

Willmott, Glenn, ed. 2000. Introduction. *Think of the Earth*. Toronto: Brown Bear Press.

————. 2002. *Unreal Country: Modernity in the Canadian Novel in English*. Montreal: McGill-Queen's University Press.

Zemans, Joyce. 1989. "First Fruits: The World and Spirit Paintings." In *Provincial Essays*, ed. Jennifer Oille Sinclair. Volume 7. Toronto: Phacops Publishing Society, 17–37.

————. 1973 (February–March). "The Art and Weltanshauung of Bertram Brooker." *Arts/Canada*, 176/177: 65–68.

www.ingramcontent.com/pod-product-compliance
Lightning Source LLC
Chambersburg PA
CBHW050129030726
47505CB00007B/2101